## "I THINK WE HAVE

Wiz looked at the set[...] front of him were twenty-one Emacs, all sitting cross legged on the floor of the Bull Pen. All of them had their quill pens out and poised expectantly.

**"backslash"** he proclaimed.

**"?"** responded the first Emac.

**"fractal_find exe,"** Wiz said. The Emac on the far left turned to the others and began to gabble at them. The other twenty Emacs bent to their tasks immediately.

The air above the Emacs began to thicken and take on a bluish tinge. It grew denser and bluer until a neon blue cloud hung over their heads.

"It's working!" Danny said.

The form began to pulse and Wiz realized he was getting a headache. "Do you guys feel all right?" Wiz asked.

"I feel fine," said a large Saint Bernard with Jerry's voice. To his left a six-foot-tall cockroach waved its feelers in agreement.

"Well, I don't," Wiz sang with two of his mouths, creating a bell-like harmony. Vaguely he realized they were standing not in the Bull Pen but under an enormous crystal canopy that shimmered with pastel highlights. And wasn't he supposed to have only two arms and one body segment?

As he watched, dog, cockroach and canopy all began to melt and run together. He felt his own body grow indistinct at the edges and begin to flow.

**"SIGTERM!!"** Wiz screamed.

The universe, canopy, cockroach and dog all froze in a half-melted state.

**"UNDO!"** he commanded. Instantly Wiz, Jerry and Danny were standing in the Bull Pen again.

"I think we have a problem here," Jerry said.

# RICK COOK

THE WIZARDRY CURSED

A Baen Books Original

Baen Publishing Enterprises
P.O. Box 1403
Riverdale, NY 10471

ISBN: 0-671-72049-X

Cover art by Gary Ruddell

First Printing, April 1991

Printed in the United States of America

Distributed by Simon & Schuster
1230 Avenue of the Americas
New York, NY 10020

For all the ones who helped:

Pete and Joan for their technical expertise, Paul for pulling me out of a hole I didn't realize I was in, Julie for her eagle eye, Doug and Cynthia for their reading, Jan for a line, Greg for keeping me up and running, and many, many others.

And most of all

For Pati. Because she puts up with it.

# One
## CONTRACT

*Beware of open-ended contracts. They are hell to support.*

**—Programmers' saying**

Torches flickered and smoked, casting fitful light through the cavern. Tosig Longbeard, King of the Dwarves—or at least the Mid-Northeastern Dwarves of the Southern Forest Range—shifted on his carved alabaster throne and eyed his visitors with distaste.

It was, he had to admit, a most unusual sight. Three Troll Kings in the same room and not fighting. The sight and stench would have been enough to gag a human; but dwarves have a somewhat different aesthetic and King Tosig's attitude owed more to the delegation's demands than their looks or smell. He drummed his fingers on the throne arm as he tried to figure a diplomatic way out of this mess.

The smaller troll in the center did the talking. He was unusually intelligent for a troll and their host had no doubt he was the one who had organized this meeting. *Pox rot him!* Tosig thought as he waited for him to run down.

"This is not a matter for me or my people," Tosig broke in at last. "If this new human wizard bothers you, then destroy him."

"We cannot," the troll king replied. "This magic is too strong." His face split into a snaggle-toothed grin. "But dwarves have powerful magic. Dwarves can kill this new wizard."

His two companions nodded and growled assent. King Tosig glowered back and felt a tiny burning sensation kindle somewhere up under his breastbone. At that moment he truly wanted to kill the new wizard who had brought him all this trouble.

At that moment the new wizard wouldn't have been at all adverse to being killed.

Like King Tosig's hall, the chamber was underground and dimly lit. But instead of rough stone, the walls were fine mosaics in subdued and tasteful patterns. There were no smoky torches here, only a diffuse radiance that seemed to emanate from everywhere in the room. And while the creature that faced the two humans across the table might be decidedly odd, by no stretch of the imagination could it be called either ugly or stinking.

But that did not mean the wizard was enjoying himself.

"Okay, look," William Irving Zumwalt said. "If the dryads mark their trees our woodcutters will leave them alone. But in return our people can cut other trees and use the forest without being harassed."

The being across the nacreous table cocked its head, as if listening to far-away voices. It was manlike, but then so is a gorilla if you stretch the term far enough. Parchment skin stretched over delicate bones. Fingers so long they were almost tentacles. Enormous dark eyes that slanted at the corners. Ears blood-pink and pointed. The thing was at once inhumanly beautiful and deeply disturbing.

The silence dragged on. Wiz shifted and fidgeted while the creature sat with its head to one side and its eyes focused on things far beyond its visitor. Elven magic could warp time to make centuries pass in a single night. But Wiz was finding that non-mortals didn't need magic to make a night drag on for centuries.

"It will be done," the creature said finally. "The trees will be marked."

"But when?"

The other lifted a delicate hand and waved it airily. "Soon," it fluted.

2

Wiz took a tighter rein on his temper. "Soon" to a non-mortal meant any time in the next geologic eon—if then.

"But precisely when? I can't go back to my people and tell them just 'soon.' We've got to be able to go into the forests to cut wood and gather food."

"You wish it done soon. I say it will be soon. That is enough."

"Fine, but we need . . ." Wiz was talking to empty air. The being had vanished, leaving Wiz and his companion alone in the gently glowing chamber. Slowly and inexorably the light was dying, a none-too-subtle hint that the meeting was over.

"Well, then . . ." Jerry Andrews put his palms on the opalescent table and heaved himself up from the low chair. He had lost weight in the year or so he had been in this world, but he still outweighed Wiz by nearly 100 pounds just as he overtopped him by a head.

"Next full moon," Wiz agreed and got up as well.

*I hope they will be here then,* he thought as he followed Jerry through the fading light of the corridor and out into the clear frosty air outside the hill. There was no door or other obvious exit. One step they were within the enchanted hill and the next step they were outside, with the forest looming up behind them and the gently glowing magic barrier that cordoned off this place in front of them.

Reflexively they both inhaled deeply. There was nothing wrong with the air inside, but the air outside seemed sweeter. *The smell of freedom,* Wiz decided. It was just a few more steps along the moonlit path and they were past the barrier and back in the forest that belonged to men.

"Mortals drive us from the forest," the troll king's voice echoed off the walls of the cavern. "We cannot hunt where we did."

*Meaning you can't hunt mortals,* King Tosig thought

3

sourly. *Well, what did you expect, you silly nit? You go around eating people, even mortals, and naturally they'll object.* The burning in his stomach was stronger and he knew he would be up all night, walking the floor and drinking ground chalk.

He understood the trolls' problem in a general way. For time out of mind trolls had roamed the marches of the human realms, devouring human travelers and occasionally daring to attack mortal farms and villages. Then three or four seasons ago a new magician had arisen among the humans. Brought from outside the World, or so the story went.

At first this alien wizard had only used his power in human quarrels. But before long his vastly more powerful magic had begun to spread among mortals. Suddenly the humans had respectable magical powers and the trolls, who had almost none, had lost a major item in their diet.

Tosig tugged his beard. This was a pretty problem indeed. So far there had been little contact between humans and dwarves and he would just as soon keep it that way. His realms were far from the lands of mortals and his people had not suffered from the humans' new magic. However he had heard stories and they were not the sort to encourage him to stir up trouble in that direction.

Well, maybe he wouldn't have to. The troll king had been talking for nearly a day-tenth and hadn't yet . . .

"I call debt-right!" the troll king thundered. "Blood for my people."

A stillness settled over the hall. All the dwarves present knew that the troll kings' claim was legitimate. Tosig sighed and inwardly cursed the day he had contracted a debt to a gang of trolls. But contract it he had, and now the troll had made a formal demand. Debts must be paid.

There were practical considerations as well. The

4

dwarves traded salt and iron to the trolls for hides, some forest products and the odd bit of booty. It was not a terribly profitable trade, but if the truth be known the Mid-Northeastern Dwarves of the Southern Forest Range were not a terribly wealthy tribe. They didn't need complications with the trolls just now.

*As if I didn't have enough problems!* Tosig thought as the pain in his stomach gnawed and the silence stretched on. *As if . . .* Suddenly he stopped short and thought furiously.

Ignoring the burning inside he nodded to his visitors.

"It pleases me to grant your request. The thing shall be done." He waved dismissal. "Now go."

"When?" the small troll demanded eagerly.

"Soon," Tosig said loftily. "Return to your forests." He repeated the dismissing gesture. The guards around the perimeter of the hall shifted and the trolls took the hint. Jostling and squabbling, they made their way out of the hall.

As soon as his unwelcome guests were gone, he motioned to his seneschal.

"Make sure they leave immediately," he said, rising from his throne. "And see that their rooms are fumigated. The last batch had lice."

The seneschal nodded and began to back away, but the dwarf king caught his sleeve and pulled him close.

"Send Glandurg to me in my chamber," he commanded in a low voice.

There was a flash of bewilderment on the seneschal's leathery face. Normally it was part of his job to keep Glandurg as far away from his royal relative as he could. But he nodded, sketched another bow and hurried to do his master's bidding.

Beyond the barrier, Bal-Simba was waiting. The enormous black wizard sat patiently on a rock

5

wrapped in a cloak against the evening chill. Beside him was Danny, the other member of the programming team. Huddled next to Danny was his wife June. Fortunately it was a large rock.

Bal-Simba was there because it was as close as he could get to the negotiations. Despite being the head of the Council of the North and as such the leader of nearly all the mortals in the World, the non-mortals would not treat with him. Wiz Zumwalt's new magic was stronger and to the non-mortals that made him the only mortal who mattered. They would tolerate Jerry, Wiz's cubicle mate from his days as a programmer in Cupertino, because Jerry was Wiz's right-hand man and also an expert with the new magic.

Danny was there because Wiz and Jerry were. Like Jerry, he had been magically brought to this world to help Wiz complete his magic compiler and like Jerry he had chosen to stay behind when most of the programmers went back. He had matured considerably in the year or so since he had come to the World, but there was still a lot of punk kid and hacker in Danny.

June was there because Danny was. If being a father and husband had matured Danny, being mother and wife apparently affected June not at all. She was still an almost feral presence; shy, silent and remote from everyone except Danny and their infant son. Even pregnancy and motherhood had not added a single pound to her painfully thin frame.

Sitting pressed up against Danny she reminded Wiz of a wild animal, unsure of her surroundings and ready to lash out at anyone who came too close. As she moved, Wiz saw that she had Ian with her, nursing under the cloak.

"Well, Sparrow?" Bal-Simba asked as they approached.

"They said they'd do it, but they won't say when. I

6

think we're supposed to meet again at the next full moon."

Bal-Simba nodded. He had hoped for something definite to tell the farmers, but he had not really expected much more.

Wiz sighed. "Lord, do you think we're making any progress at all?"

Bal-Simba sighed in return. "How am I to judge, Sparrow? I know as little of dealing with these creatures as you do. Less perhaps." He rubbed his massive forehead with a meaty hand. "Still, they continue to treat with us and that is no small thing. Nor is there any sign of war by non-mortals against mortals and that is a large thing indeed."

Wiz nodded. His new magic had upset the balance of this World and sent humans thrusting out past their ancient boundaries in a wave of settlement, destroying magical creatures as they went. The non-mortals had reacted and the World had teetered on the brink of a war of extermination against humans. With the aid of a team of shanghaied computer programmers, Wiz had been able to stem the tide and temporarily confine the humans within somewhat larger boundaries, blunting the threat and removing the danger of war.

But to keep the peace the humans needed some kind of treaty with the World's non-mortals, something that would set out rules for both groups. The negotiations had dragged on for months with many different beings. Apparently most of the non-mortals either couldn't conceive of the idea of a general policy or weren't interested in negotiating one with the humans. So arrangements had to be made a bit at a time with one group of non-mortals after another.

It would have tried the patience of a seasoned diplomat and Wiz was a long way from being any sort of diplomat. Worse, he was the only mortal the elves and others wanted to deal with and to him the meetings were a form of exquisite torture.

"Well, now what?"

Bal-Simba heaved his bulk up off the rock and picked up his wizard's staff. "That we shall know at the next full moon, Sparrow."

"You sent for me, Uncle?"

King Tosig looked up sourly at the young dwarf standing in the door of his study. His sister's niece's son was well-enough formed, with broad shoulders and powerful limbs. His beard was long and thick, as a dwarf's beard should be, and his craggy features bore a hint of the dwarf king's own.

The face was fine. It was what was behind it that was the problem.

Instead of digging, making, hoarding and other normal dwarfish pursuits, Glandurg's mind was forever on other things. Where the average dwarf is an intensely practical, rather unimaginative sort, Glandurg was a dreamer and a romantic.

The young dwarf knew that there was more to life than the tunnels and forges of his subterranean home. He just wasn't sure what. Being young, inexperienced and a romantic, he was convinced it was better than what was here.

Worse, he had gathered a group of young dwarves about him and converted them with his cockamamie chatter. They careened about the tunnels, refusing to listen to their elders and engaging in all sorts of un-dwarvish nonsense.

To Tosig, who was practical and unimaginative even for a dwarf, Glandurg and his friends were a constant source of trouble. If such a thing were possible Tosig would have suspected a taint of mortal blood in his ancestry.

The dwarf king forced his face into an unaccustomed smile and gestured at his visitor. "Come in, boy. And close the door behind you."

"Uncle, I really am sorry about the sewage tunnel," Glandurg began breathlessly. "But the survey showed . . ."

The dwarf king reddened at the thought of the stope flooded when that tunnel broke through, and his already perilous hold on his temper weakened. As if a dwarf had to rely on a survey to know where he was underground!

"Never mind that," he cut his near-nephew off. "I have another job for you and your friends."

"It's not another sewage tunnel, is it?" Glandurg began apprehensively. "Because if it is . . ."

"No, this is something else. Something more suited to your talents. Oh sit down, boy! Sit!" He shooed the young dwarf into a three-legged chair in front of his desk.

Apprehensive at this unprecedented honor, Glandurg sank into the chair, his eyes riveted on Tosig's face.

"Now then," said Tosig, composing his thoughts. "You know I had an embassy from the trolls this evening? "

Glandurg nodded eagerly. "Three mighty kings of the trolls—or so it is said." His face fell. "I was on guard duty on the peaks."

Tosig nodded. He did not mention he had given standing orders to keep Glandurg out of the throne room during audiences.

"The trolls came asking a great favor and for reasons of state I have decided to grant their request."

Glandurg leaned forward expectantly.

"The trolls are threatened by a new wizard who has arisen among the mortals. A wizard from beyond the World, bringing with him strange and powerful magic. Our allies the trolls suffer cruelly under his influence and they beg succor."

9

He fixed his young relative with an eagle stare. "You are to be their succor. I want you to gather a troop of hardy adventurers and kill the human wizard with the new magic."

Glandurg gulped. "You mean go Outside? Out into the World?"

"Well, you're not going to find him in our tunnels are you?" Tosig snapped.

"No, I mean, of course not, but . . ."

The dwarf king glared and the young dwarf trailed off. Glandurg was all for adventure and travel, in the abstract. But now that he was facing the possibility of leaving the tunnels where he had lived all his 184 years, he discovered he wasn't so sure he wanted to go.

"We'll need supplies," he said at last. "And gold."

Tosig's stomach flared again, but he nodded. "Anything you need. Within reason, boy! Within reason. Now, how soon can you leave?"

"I don't know. A week perhaps."

Tosig nodded. "A week if you must, then. Sooner if you can. Our allies depend on us in this and I am depending on you."

Glandurg's face glowed.

"Thank you, Uncle. I will strive to prove myself worthy." He bowed deeply and then whirled and raced out the door, slamming it behind him.

As the door reverberated behind his young relative, King Tosig allowed himself a tight little smile.

A debt was a debt and debts must be paid, even to trolls. *On the other hand,* he thought, *nowhere it is written what coin they must be paid in.* Clearly there must be an effort to crush this Sparrow, but if the effort failed and one of his blood relatives perished in the attempt, why, who could blame the king or his people? Even mortal magicians were not without defenses after all.

He shifted and the pain in his stomach came back, but not so bad this time. Maybe he wouldn't need the ground chalk after all.

10

"Dammit, they're stalling!" Danny said as the group picked its way along the trail in the moonlight. "They're just keeping us hanging."

"Why?" asked Jerry. "It doesn't get them anything."

"I dunno why," Danny said stubbornly, "but we're being stalled."

Wiz walked beside his fellows, too tired to join the argument. *Pointless, anyway,* he thought. *No matter what their motives are we've got to keep negotiating with them. It's the best we've got.*

Behind them Ian made a tentative whimper. June quickly hushed him.

"I thought you were going to leave her home," Wiz said in an undervoice as he jerked his head back at June.

"Well, I tried," Danny said defensively. "But she came anyway. You can't argue with her. It's like she doesn't hear."

"If you can't keep her at home maybe it would be better if you didn't come to these things."

"No way, man. This is where stuff is happening. Besides, she's not a problem. She just sits with me." Wiz saw the angry jut of his jaw and decided to try a different approach.

"Okay, but it can't be good for the baby to be out in this weather. And it will be even colder next full moon."

Danny's expression cleared as he thought about it. "Yeah. You're right. Maybe I should stay home."

Wiz nodded. The new Danny could be just as obnoxious as the know-it-all kid who had come to this world a little over a year ago, but at least you could reason with him.

*More or less,* Wiz reminded himself.

At the base of the enchanted hill Bal-Simba motioned the party to halt in a clearing. They clustered together while he began the chant to transport them back to the Capital on the Wizard's Way.

A quickly spoken spell, a flash of familiar darkness and they were standing on the flagstones of the Outer Court of the Wizard's Keep, just inside the main gates of the castle.

Wiz blinked at the brightness of the lantern-lit courtyard after the moonlit forest clearing.

"You know, this is still wrong," Jerry said as the guardsmen hurried to open the inner gate that separated the Outer Court from the Keep proper.

"Looks fine to me," Wiz said as his wife Moira came through the gate to meet him. The mellow glow of the lanterns caught the coppery highlights in her red hair and warmed the creamy tones of her freckled skin. She was easily the best thing Wiz had seen all day and he hugged her tight and kissed her soundly.

"No, think about it," Jerry persisted as Wiz and Moira broke the clinch. "We just teleported in here. But what about the velocity differences caused by the rotation of the planet? There should be a speed difference. And there's the energy gradient, and . . ."

Moira's green eyes gleamed with amusement. "Has he been like this all evening, love?"

"Just since we got back," Wiz told her.

"But . . ." Jerry interjected.

Wiz was in no mood for one of Jerry's attempts to apply the finer points of physics to this world. "It's magic, okay?"

"Yeah," Jerry persisted as they went through the inner gate, "but magic has rules."

"But that doesn't mean we understand them."

"Still . . ."

"Look, there are a lot weirder things about this place than some missing energy when we teleport. Let's leave it, all right?"

Jerry looked at him sympathetically.

"You're really beat, aren't you?"

12

Wiz sighed and put his arm around Moira's waist. "Yeah, but at least that's over for another month. Maybe we can concentrate on writing software for a while."

"Oh, a week at least," Jerry said. "Then we've got a couple of other loose ends to deal with."

Wiz thought about those "loose ends" and glared at his friend. "You had to remind me, didn't you?"

## Two
# DRAGON TROUBLE

The day was bright, the air was crisp and Judith Conally was off in a world full of dragons, elves and heroes.

*So Prince Leopold slays the dragon Ferocious before he meets the wood elves,* she thought as the trolley car jolted to a stop in front of the San Jose Public Library. *But then where does he meet Bronwyn Halfelven? It can't be in the troll's cave. That's too trite. And if he kills the dragon before he confronts Gorbash Fleshripper, why does Bronwyn agree to accompany him on the quest?*

She sighed and shifted on the hard fiberglass seat. Her fellow passengers ignored her. Their thoughts might not be as colorful as Judith's, but they were just as lost in them.

Externally, Judith was no different from the other passengers. Her clothing was more comfortable than stylish and while no one would have called her ugly, they wouldn't have called her beautiful either. Her long dark hair was lustrous, but it was caught back in a severe bun. Her figure was substantial rather than eye-catching, her jaw was square and her nose on the large side. She looked, well, ordinary.

Judith sighed again and rose with the rest of the passengers. Working out the details of a novel wasn't nearly as easy as she had thought. Maybe she could find a solution in the book on Celtic magic the library had gotten her through interlibrary loan. If not she would have to invent something that would be magically consistent with the universe she had created.

Problems, problems. She never knew being a successful fantasy author could be this difficult.

*Well, almost a successful fantasy author,* she admitted as she stepped down onto the trolley platform. The outline of her trilogy had caught the eye of an editor at

Nemesis Books. The sample chapters had passed muster and now the editor wanted to see the completed manuscript of the first novel.

The other passengers had stepped off the platform to cross the street in either direction, but Judith still stood there, trying to decide.

For a moment she concentrated on dragons. Not dragons as they were—quarrelsome, nasty-tempered beasts that stank of sulfur and snake—but dragons as she had first seen them. Mighty, ethereal creatures printed against the pale pink glow of clouds at earliest morning as they swooped around the tower of the Wizard's Keep.

She was bound by oath not to reveal what she had seen in that other world. As part of the small team of programmers who had taken Wiz Zumwalt's crude magic compiler and turned it into a piece of production software she had really experienced magic and dragons and the rest of it. She couldn't *directly* refer to her time in a world where magic worked and dragon riders were as common as 747s are here. But she could draw on what she had seen and done to make her novel come alive. And most of all she had the memories to sustain her as she struggled to write.

As always thinking about her time in another world refreshed her. Judith started to cross to the library, head high and still lost in thought.

*Can I do it in two trilogies?* she wondered as she stepped off the curb. *Or will I need to stretch it to three?*

If Judith was lost in thought, the truck driver was just plain lost. He had driven the semi all the way from Minneapolis to deliver a load of exhibits to the San Jose convention center next to the library. But he had gotten his directions mixed up and instead of arriving at the back of the center and the loading docks, he ended up in front of the building, on a street that wasn't supposed to have truck traffic. He certainly didn't know the neighborhood well enough to realize that people on the trolley platform in the center of the street were given to crossing no matter what the traffic light said.

The blare of the horn and the screech of air brakes brought Judith half out of her reverie. Instinctively she jumped back as the driver yanked the wheel desperately in an effort to avoid her.

Together it was almost enough. Instead of receiving an obliterating blow from the truck's front bumper, Judith Connally was only kissed by the left fender. But the kiss was near as deadly as a blow. Her purse flew out of her hands in a high arc, opening in mid-air and spilling wallet, tissues, keys and coins along the curbside. Limbs flailing, Judith spun away and slammed headfirst into the curb.

She did not move again.

A woman and a dragon waited for them when they entered the programmers' quarters in the Wizard's Keep.

Of the two the woman was slightly the larger and by far the more formidable. Shauna was broad-beamed with brown hair and an easy gap-toothed smile. She had an infant daughter of her own and she was more than happy to nurse Ian—and mother June and Danny as well.

"My Lords, Lady," she curtsied. "I have a cold supper waiting."

"Thanks," Wiz said, "but I'll just have something to drink." He drew a mug of ale from the small cask at the end of the table and plopped down on a bench along the wall. It was something past midnight, but all of them were too keyed up to sleep. A light meal and light conversation had become a ritual after meeting with the non-humans by the light of the full moon.

Shauna surveyed Wiz's thin frame disapprovingly. "You'll never put on any meat that way." Then she turned to June. "Here child, let me hold the baby and you get yourself something to eat."

Shauna, Moira and Danny were the only three people June would allow to hold Ian. Without protest June handed the baby to Shauna and went to heap her plate. Jerry, Danny and Bal-Simba joined her while Moira stayed with Shauna and Ian.

"It's a wonder you don't catch the ague, all of you. Out all night in the cold and damp consorting with uncanny beings. And taking the child to such doings, well . . ." Shauna peered under the blanket at the sleeping infant.

Ian awoke briefly, saw he was being made much of, accepted it as his due and drifted back to sleep.

Wiz took a pull on his mug and nearly lost it when the dragon rammed his head into his ribs.

"Well, what's your problem, Scales-For-Brains?" he said, reaching out to scratch the dragon behind its ears.

Shauna looked up from Ian. "Naming such a beast 'Lord,'" she said with a shake of her head.

"Not Lord," Wiz corrected as he dug his fingers into the scaly hide. "LRD." The dragon stretched his neck out luxuriously to expose a spot behind his right ear.

"LRD?"

"It's a TLA for Little Red Dragon," Jerry put in from where he was building a triple-decker sandwich.

"What is a TLA?"

"Three-letter acronym."

Shauna looked puzzled and Moira chuckled. "Never ask them for an explanation. You will only end up worse confused."

Shauna sniffed and turned her attention back to June and Ian. LRD reminded Wiz to keep scratching with a butt to the side that nearly knocked him off the bench.

As a two-foot hatchling, LRD had been as cute as a

17

kitten when he wandered into the programmers' makeshift workshop and decided he liked the company. Now, a little over a year later, LRD was something more than six feet from snout to tail-tip and massive in proportion. Compared to the 80- to 100-foot cavalry mounts in the aeries below the castle, LRD was still tiny. Compared to the scale of the rooms and passages in the castle, LRD was definitely on the large side and getting bigger every day.

He had given up trying to sleep on tables after a couple of them collapsed under his weight, but he still liked to nudge people to have his head scratched. Of course what had once been just a firm, insistent push was now enough to knock a grown man off his feet. He was also beginning to show flashes of typically dragonish temper—which is to say he could turn nasty in an instant—and occasionally he would burp a little tongue of flame. Almost everyone steered clear of him and the only place he was really welcome was the programmers' workrooms and their living quarters.

The dragon decided he had had enough head scratching and ambled over to see how Ian was doing. Shauna eyed him disapprovingly but he extended his neck and sniffed the sleeping infant, giving nurse and baby a good snort of dragon breath in the process. Ian opened his eyes and cooed at the scaly monster looking down at him.

For some inexplicable reason LRD had decided he liked Ian. He would curl up next to the baby's crib for hours, dozing or watching the infant with an unwinking golden stare. If Ian was distressed or uncomfortable, LRD became frantic. When he wasn't with Ian, the dragon divided his time between chasing the castle's cats and sunning himself on any convenient surface.

He seemed mildly approving of June, and he and

Shauna had arrived at an armed truce. Everyone else he ignored—unless he wanted his head scratched.

Wiz finished his ale and debated making himself a sandwich. He decided he wasn't hungry and putting food in his stomach would only dilute the soporific effect of the ale. He needed something to help him sleep after the hours spent under the magic hill.

Moira left June and Shauna and came over to sit by him.

"You're not eating?"

Wiz took a moment just to admire her. Moira was broad-hipped, deep-bosomed and had a pair of wonderful green eyes set in a wide freckled face under a mane of red hair. The hedge witch was the first person he had seen when he had been kidnapped into this world and he had thought she was breathtakingly beautiful then. They had been married nearly two years and she still took his breath away.

"I want to make sure I can sleep tonight," he said, slipping his arm around her waist. Then he leaned close and nuzzled her hair. "What's the matter, do you want your ears scratched too?"

Moira turned and gave him one of her patented 10,000-volt looks. "Perhaps we should discuss that back in our chambers, my Lord."

Wiz rose and pulled her up with him. "Maybe we should at that."

*Looks like the ale was wasted,* he thought as they made their goodbyes to the others and headed off to bed.

Once again torches lit a meeting of dwarves in an underground chamber. But this was a much smaller gathering in much less impressive surroundings than King Tosig's audience hall.

It was, in fact, a storeroom for hides. The torches were leftovers plundered from wall sconces elsewhere in the hold and the twelve dwarves sitting on the smelly bales or lounging against the rough-hewn walls had no more right to be there than the torches did.

*A minor detail*, Glandurg thought as the last of his followers slipped into the room and closed the storeroom door. Anyway, now that he was acting under his uncle's orders, not even old Samlig, the keeper of the storehouses, would dare to question them.

Still Glandurg couldn't help looking over his shoulder. Samlig was a crusty one and he'd just as soon not put his new legitimacy to the test.

Taking a deep breath, he drew himself up to his full three-foot-eight and faced his men.

"Comrades," he proclaimed, but softly. "At last we have a mission worthy of us."

"Not another sewage tunnel, is it?" asked a dwarf named Ragnar.

Glandurg dismissed the question with a lofty gesture. "This is a mission to the Outside World. Beyond the tunnels of the Hold."

A couple of the dwarves exchanged suspicious glances, wondering what kind of unpleasant and menial chore had been arranged for them now.

"I have just come from a secret audience with my uncle, the King," Glandurg told them. "He has entrusted us with an important mission."

"I thought the King said he'd cut your ears off if you came next nor nigh him," put in a dwarf named Gimli who was so young his beard barely touched his chest.

Glandurg glared at him and planted his hands on his hips. "Do you want to hear this or don't you?"

Gimli wilted under his leader's stare and Glandurg adopted his heroic pose again.

"As I was saying, a secret audience with the King. He has commanded us upon a vital mission for all of dwarfdom."

He paused for effect and the other dwarves leaned forward expectantly.

"We are to penetrate the world of mortals to its very heart and there find and slay a wizard from beyond our World! It is a dangerous, desperate quest and in his hour of need my uncle the King has turned to us as the staunchest, bravest among all his subjects." He surveyed his wide-eyed followers and saw they were satisfactorily impressed.

"This isn't another one of your stories?" one of the dwarves asked at last.

"Why don't you go to my uncle the King and put that question to him?"

That settled it. None of them would go anywhere near King Tosig, but the assurance with which Glandurg issued the challenge told them that for once their leader was not exaggerating. At least not much.

"How are we supposed to get there?" asked Thorfin, always the practical one. "That's two hundred leagues at least."

"We will ride," Glandurg said loftily. "It has been arranged."

"I don't know about horses," a dwarf named Snorri said dubiously. "I'm not much for them."

"We will not ride horses. We will fly."

"I thought you said we'd ride," said Ragnar. "Which will it be then?"

"You'll see soon enough," Glandurg told him with a superior smile. He was pleased that he had thought of the transportation problem and he was even more pleased with the solution he had worked out in the few hours since meeting with the king. But he didn't want to tip his hand. His companions might not be as happy with his cleverness as Glandurg was.

"What about supplies?" Ragnar asked.

"Our every need will be supplied from the hold's storehouses," Glandurg said. He smiled at the thought of old Samlig's face when he issued out the

21

carefully hoarded goods. "We shall have the weapons, the armor and the gold we need from my uncle the King's personal treasury."

He looked them over again. "This will not be easy. The alien wizard has mighty magic and his legions of mortal warriors are numberless and not to be despised. It will be a long, difficult adventure and danger awaits us at every turn."

The dwarves all nodded. Danger and adventure were fine with them.

"This will be to the death," he proclaimed. "Some of us—nay, all of us!—may not return."

He swept his gaze over his followers impressively.

"Now swear with me in blood!" Glandurg drew his knife and nicked himself on the wrist. He cut deeper than he meant to and winced slightly at the sudden pain. There was a lot more blood than he intended, but his sleeve reddened satisfactorily and the blood dripping off his wrist made a most impressive touch.

One by one the other dwarves cut themselves and mingled their blood with their leader's for the oath.

"To the wizard's death—or our own."

## Three
# OPERATION 500-POUND PARAKEET

*The problem with a kludge is eventually you're going to have to go back and do it right.*
—**Programmers' saying**

"You're sure this will work?" Wiz asked for the fourth time that morning amid the bustle of final preparations. He was wearing warm wool tunic and pants, a heavy travelling cloak and a very apprehensive look.

"If you can remember to do your part of it," Moira said a little sharply. Then she caught his expression and placed her hand on his arm.

"Do not worry, love," she said softly. "The spells are as simple and foolproof as we can make them. What was your phrase?—'Idiots-and-English-majors' simple.'"

Wiz didn't object to the characterization. In spite of the power his spell compiler gave him, he had absolutely no talent for this world's magic. It had taken Moira and Bal-Simba weeks to teach him what he would have to do today.

Wiz was much more warmly dressed than necessary for the Council chantry where he stood. But the clothing didn't entirely explain the sweat beading on his forehead.

He was standing in the middle of a circle traced in white powder on the flagged stone floor. Around him stood eight of the blue-robed wizards of the Mighty, each of them at one of the points of the compass. Late morning sunlight pouring in through the stained glass windows cast gaily colored patterns on the floor and the wizards, but beside each of them burned a pair of tall wax candles. Apprentices bustled around the edges of the room putting the finishing touches

23

on preparations and sometimes conferring in hushed low tones. On the dais at one end of the room, Arianne, Bal-Simba's second in command, was overseeing three Watchers hunched over their communications crystals. Next to the tall blonde woman stood a pudgy little man in the blue robe of the Mighty, his lips moving silently and his eyes focused far away as he maintained contact with other of his fellows at their assigned tasks.

"Are we prepared then?" asked Bal-Simba from his spot on the circle.

"Lord, the patrols are off the beach," Arianne told him, pushing back a stray lock of blonde hair.

"The other wizards are standing by," reported Malus, the wizard next to her.

"Operation 500-Pound Parakeet is ready to go," Jerry called from his place at the side of the room. Everyone looked to the sun stick which cast a shortening shadow on the marks on the opposite wall. The tip of the shadow was inexorably approaching one of the marks.

Danny and Jerry stepped into the circle to clap Wiz on the back and wish him well.

"I never did understand why you call this after a giant parrot," Moira said as they waited for the last minutes to pass.

"Parakeet," Danny corrected. "It's how you get rid of cats. You get a 500-pound parakeet and teach it to say 'here, kitty kitty kitty.' "

Moira started to frown and then laughed as she caught the joke.

"So you call this Operation 500-Pound Parakeet."

"*They* call it Operation 500-Pound Parakeet," Wiz said sourly. "I had nothing to do with the name."

"Hey man, it's gonna be easy," Danny told him lightly. "All you gotta do is zip back to the City of Night, off a demon who's waiting to toast you, and then call for the cavalry—us. We handle the rest." He made a palm-down gesture as if sweeping aside minor details. "Nooo problemo."

"It is indeed simple if you remember your spells and execute them correctly," Moira agreed.

"I rest my case," Wiz said sourly.

"Crave pardon?"

"Almost time," Bal-Simba called from his place at the head of the circle. "Make ready."

"I mean you just proved my point. Oh well, if we're going to do this thing, let's get on with it."

He kissed Moira long and hard.

"Okay," he said. "Places everyone."

Moira, Jerry and Danny stepped back and out of the circle, being careful not to scuff the chalked lines. The seven other wizards looked at Bal-Simba and he watched the sun stick as the shadow crept the last fraction of an inch along its track.

Then all the wizards raised their hands and began chanting. Wiz gripped his staff and tried to breathe slowly and evenly as the chant rose around him and the air seemed to fill with smoke. The sound became louder and louder, then began to fade as the air around him became thick and opaque.

There was a flash of darkness and suddenly the air was so cold it burned his lungs.

Wiz Zumwalt clung to his staff and pressed his eyes tightly shut as waves of dizziness washed over him. When he opened his eyes he found he was nose to nose with a wall of crudely dressed black basalt.

He turned and nearly fell when he stepped on a patch of ice in the wall's shadow. He scraped his palm as he caught himself against the rough wall. Then his vision cleared and the dizziness receded as he looked out over desolation.

Even at its height the City of Night had not been attractive. Its builders, the wizards of the Dark League, had cared much more for power than for beauty. Most of the city had been crudely built out of the volcanic stone of the southern continent with no regard to appearance or city planning.

But when the Dark League had ruled here at least there had been a kind of sinister vitality to the place. In its ruin and abandonment the city was simply ugly. The cobbled street fell away steeply and over the roofs of the close-huddled buildings Wiz could see the steel-gray harbor merging at the horizon into steel-gray sky. Behind him the volcano on whose flank the city stood curled a thin plume of smoke to the leaden sky. Even the snow that capped the mountain was dirty gray.

Studded here and there around the city were gaunt black towers, several of them with their tops blown off. A few yards ahead of Wiz the street was blocked by rubble where one of the buildings had collapsed. Many of the buildings between him and the harbor were ruined, roofless or in a couple of cases simply melted.

He reached inside his shirt and pulled out a tiny bit of blue crystal he wore on a thong around his neck. "I'm here," he said into the communications crystal. "Start Operation 500-Pound Parakeet."

Then he looked out over his handiwork again and shivered, not entirely from the cold.

Directly or indirectly, Wiz was responsible for most of the destruction. In his first great battle with the Dark League he had used his mixture of computer programming and magic to rout the League and destroyed a good part of the city in the process. In the second confrontation, he had been kidnapped to this place by the remnants of the League. For weeks the enemy wizards had hunted him through the freezing ruins of the City of Night while a tracking demon waited to destroy him if he used the least of his new magic.

He had been rescued after he had incited a magical

battle between the wizards and Bale-Zur, the invincible slaying demon who had once served them. The effect of so much magic unleashed had attracted the attention of the Council's Watchers and brought a patrol of dragons south over the City to his rescue.

However the battle had stirred up the slaying demon. Instead of staying in one place and killing whatever came to him, the Watchers reported Bale-Zur now roamed the City of Night ceaselessly looking for victims. Worse, it had begun to range beyond the City itself. If this kept up it was sure to use its powers to travel across the Freshened Sea to the lands of men.

Wiz knew he was safe enough, but he kept his back to the freezing wall anyway. The communications crystal used the old magic of the Mighty, not his new spell compiler that would activate the tracking demon. Even though it needed eight powerful wizards and a complicated ceremony, Bal-Simba had sent him along the Wizard's Way by conventional magic so he did not have to use his own spells.

Of all the mortals in the World only three were safe from Bale-Zur. The demon would not touch Wiz, Jerry and Danny because their full names—their true names—had never been spoken anywhere in the World. To Bale-Zur they were no more prey than a rock.

However Bale-Zur was only half the problem. The other half was the hunting demon the Dark League had created in their attempt to destroy Wiz. Unlike Bale-Zur it could not range much beyond the Southern Continent. However it was keyed to Wiz's special brand of magic and would attack and destroy anything that used it.

But spells built with the magic compiler were the only kind Wiz, Jerry and Danny knew. If they tried to make magic the demon would be on them instantly.

It presented a pretty problem. Wiz, Jerry and Danny were immune to Bale-Zur, but if they used

27

their magic they would be immediately attacked by the hunting demon. The hunting demon would not respond to conventional magic, but not even all of the Mighty together could hope to stand against Bale-Zur.

Until Bale-Zur was contained it was horribly risky for any mortal but Wiz or his friends to enter the City of Night and until the hunting demon was contained, they could not be safe here.

The demons weren't the only dangers in the City of Night. Remnants of the League's old magic remained and there were other monsters here as well. However none of those were the equal of a well-prepared magician—*well, probably not,* Wiz told himself—and most of them were not active by daylight in the open. *We don't think!*

Naturally they had backup. He was being closely watched by magical means, and several of the Mighty were poised to jump to his aid if he appeared to be in danger. There were two squadrons of dragon riders circling just off the beach. But he was still here alone and if anything went wrong he would be the first to know it.

*Well, now I know how a worm on a hook feels,* Wiz thought. He pulled his cloak tighter and set to work.

After hashing it over repeatedly, they had worked out a plan. It seemed like a good idea back at the Capital, but standing in the shattered city, Wiz was growing less fond of it by the minute.

He shifted his grip on his staff. The sooner they got this part of the operation over with the sooner he would be able to protect himself. *And the sooner I can use a spell to stay warm.*

He reached into his pouch, drew out four pieces of blue stone and set one at each point of the compass. Then he stood between them and began to scratch in the frozen dust with his staff.

Carefully he traced the figure in the dust as he had been taught. The old magic of this world depended for its success on precise execution. Everything had to be done just right and even the tiniest deviation from the rituals could mean disastrous changes in the outcome. The secret of the success of his magic compiler lay in the fact that it used extremely simple, reliable little spells that could be built up to produce complex, powerful effects with little or no talent on the part of the user.

With his new magic Wiz was easily the most powerful mortal magician in this world. But he was as natural a klutz as he was a computer programmer. Even this simple spell would tax him to the limit.

He finished the tracing and made especially sure the lines crossed to close the figure around him. The freezing wind whipped up little eddies of dust, but it did not erase the pentagram.

Finally he surveyed his handiwork one more time and reached back into his pouch. This time he pulled out a bit of forked, twisted root. Stepping to the edge of the circle, he lifted the root to his mouth and whispered to it the words Moira and Bal-Simba had spent so long pounding into his head. He leaned over and placed it outside the circle. Then he stepped back and waited.

He had barely reached the center when the root stirred in the dust. As he watched it seemed to untwist and swell until it became a tiny brown man shape, no longer than Wiz's thumb. It got to its knees and then to its feet and then shook itself once, as if to clear its head. It strode forward, placed its hands on its hips, threw back its head and began to shout.

Inside the circle Wiz heard nothing but the wind. He knew that the manikin was reciting a simple spell in the new magic. The spell didn't do much, but it should be enough to attract the demon. Wiz gripped his staff harder and forced himself not to hold his breath as he watched.

Suddenly with an earsplitting roar the demon arrived.

A clawed foot crushed the mandrake manikin to the dust. The burning red eyes searched right and left and the horned, scaled, fanged head swiveled on the snakelike neck as it scanned for more prey. It stopped when it saw Wiz standing perhaps twenty feet away, seemingly unprotected and reeking of traces of the new magic. Without warning and without seeming to gather itself it leapt at Wiz, jaws gaping and talons spread. Its bellows rang off the surrounding stone walls.

Perhaps five feet from the human, the demon bounced. It stopped dead in mid-air and with talons scrabbling for purchase it slid slowly down the invisible barrier that lay between it and its would-be prey.

Again and again, the thing hurled itself against the invisible barrier that separated it from its prey. In spite of himself Wiz flinched and shrank back from its fury.

It was wasted effort. The demon clawed impotently at the barrier and scrabbled frantically against it, but it could not come close to penetrating it.

Wiz raised his staff and spoke. "**demon debug begone exe!**" he proclaimed.

The demon renewed its desperate attack on the magical barrier and its screams rose to a crescendo. Then the spell took hold. The demon became translucent. Its roars faded to the merely deafening, down through the loud and then trailed away like a locomotive whistle disappearing in the distance. It became transparent, faded to a mere outline and then it was gone.

Wiz let out his breath in a great gasping sigh and sagged against his staff.

"Okay," he said into the communications crystal. "Phase one is accomplished. Come on through and let's get the rest of this thing over with."

There were two soft pops behind him and there were Jerry and Danny, looking disoriented and a little sick, but clutching their staffs gamely. They were burdened with packs and hung about with an assortment of pouches, crystals, strangely shaped bits of metal and other less identifiable things. In addition Danny carried a large leather sack that pulsated and moved as if the contents were alive.

The contents of the sack were to help them in their search. Everything else Danny and Jerry carried was for protection or defense. Looking them over, Wiz reflected there was probably enough magical firepower between the pair of them to defeat the Dark League ten times over. Far more than they would need for anything they were likely to meet here.

Which was fine with Wiz. He had not the slightest intention of giving anything in the City of Night an even break.

"You okay?" Wiz asked as his friends seemed to become aware of their surroundings.

"Yeah," Danny mumbled. Then he shook his head to clear it. "Boy, that's a weird feeling."

"It'll be a good feeling when we get out of here. And the sooner we start the search the sooner that will be."

Danny nodded and bent to open the leather bag.

Hundreds of things like dirty gossamer handkerchiefs half-flapped half-floated out of the sack and wafted off in all directions. Behind them came a half-dozen things of the same stuff about the size of a bath towel. Finally Danny reached in and pulled out a crystalline object about a foot high. The facets flashed in the pale light and the thing began buzzing weakly as it started receiving data from the searching units.

"It will take them a few minutes to get some kind of search pattern set up," Wiz said into the comm crystal. "There's not a lot we can do until then."

"Just be careful doing nothing," Moira's voice admonished them. "That place is not safe."

"No kidding," Wiz said, thinking of the close calls he had when he was a fugitive in the city.

"They're spreading out fast," Jerry said, craning his neck and shielding his eyes with his hands to try to follow the searchers' progress.

All the things in the sack were variants of the system of searching demons which had been one of Wiz's first projects with his new magic. The smaller searchers had almost no intelligence or volition. They were passive receptors which passed information back to the bath towel things for concentration and interpretation. They in turn passed the information back to the crystal object which did the final evaluation.

Unlike Wiz's original system, this one was tuned to look for only one object, the heart of Bale-Zur. The demons had been trained on similar demon hearts held in the vaults beneath the Capital. When they found a demon heart they would report back to the humans.

Danny poked at the rubble with his staff. "What does the heart of a demon look like anyway?"

"It's a cloudy sphere about as big as your head," Wiz told him. "Anyway, that's how it was described to me."

"Do not worry about identifying it," Moira's voice came inside their heads. "Your searching demons will know it when they see it."

"If it still exists, it should be somewhere in Toth-Set-Ra's old palace," Moira's voice told them. "That is," she paused for a second while she translated what the Watcher's crystal was showing her into their coordinate system, "almost straight behind you."

"I hope it is there," Wiz said. "It will make our job a lot easier."

He motioned toward the palace and all three of them gathered up their magical paraphernalia and set off.

## Four
# COMA

"Hi. Uh, I'd like to see Judith Conally."

The nurse looked up from her paperwork and flashed a professional smile. "Are you a relative?"

"No, I'm a friend."

"I'm sorry, but only relatives are allowed to visit patients in the neurological unit."

"She doesn't have any relatives out here. I'm her best friend. Can't I please see her?"

The nurse looked him over. He wasn't much more than twenty. A pale and soft youth with brown hair and a complexion that bore a trace of adolescent acne. He was wearing an old flight jacket with several felt-tip pens in the left sleeve pocket and a T-shirt with a picture of a warrior in a horned helmet air-brushed on it.

He had laid a three-ring notebook on the counter with a couple of library books on top.

A student, she decided. Harmless and very earnest.

The nurse glanced at the chart. The visiting rule wasn't rigidly enforced in the Neurological unit unless the doctor requested it and there was nothing on the chart about that. The patient hadn't had a visitor in a while.

She smiled again, a little less professionally. "I suppose it would be all right, but you'll have to be very quiet."

The searchers found the heart of the demon before Wiz and his friends reached the palace.

As they got close to the former seat of the Dark League's power the destruction got worse and the going got harder. In some places it was hard to tell the streets from the flattened houses and in a couple of instances it was easier to avoid the street and go over the remains of the buildings. Once they came to a place where the stone had melted into glassy slag with razor sharp edges everywhere. Another time seeping water in deep shadows had formed a waterfall of ice nearly ten feet tall.

They saw no signs of life, but once they heard something scrabbling over the rubble as if fleeing their approach.

"Boy, what a mess," Jerry panted as they pulled themselves to the top of the latest obstacle.

Wiz shaded his eyes and looked ahead, trying to find the easiest route. "I don't remember it being this bad. On the other hand, I stayed away from this part of town as much as I could."

Danny consulted the crystal device. "It's over that way, in that big black pile of rubble."

Jerry scanned the horizon. "*Which* big black pile of rubble?"

"That one," Wiz pointed. "Let's go."

Another fifteen minutes of hard travel brought them through the shattered black gates of the palace. The going was easier here because there had been just one building set in an extensive courtyard. None of the roof remained and everything had collapsed in on itself, but enough of the walls still stood that you could pick out the general outlines of the floor plan.

"This guy sure had lousy taste," Jerry said, eyeing the remains of a strangely twisted mosaic on a partly standing wall.

"I think some of it's kind of neat," Danny said as he looked over a doorway shaped like the gaping mouth of a monster. He reached out and stroked the door jamb admiringly.

The door growled and Danny jumped back, landing sprawled on the rubble.

"I told you not to touch stuff," Wiz said.

"Yeah." He consulted the locator to hide his embarrassment. "Uh, what we want is down this way."

Another couple of hundred yards and the trio came to an archway that was still mostly standing. Through it they saw five or six searchers hovering around like a patch of smog, pulsing weakly as they sensed their quarry.

"I guess it's down there," Danny said.

"Great," Wiz said, eyeing the remains of the room. "The debris is only about ten feet deep in there. I don't suppose you guys brought shovels?"

Jerry looked down at the equipment festooned about him. "No. We've got enough stuff here to flatten this place in an eyeblink, but we don't have anything that will let us move the rubble."

"I could send shovels to you," Moira's voice said in Wiz's ear.

Wiz considered. "Let's try it bare-handed first. Where's Bale-Zur?"

"The Watchers say it is down by the harbor."

"Moving this way?"

"Not yet. We will let you know."

"Well, come on," Wiz said to his companions. "Maybe the heart is close to the top."

"Maybe pigs will grow wings," Danny said, eyeing the rubble.

"Around this place you never know," Wiz said as he cast the first stone.


As he followed the nurse down the hall, Craig felt like the place was closing in on him. Everything was hushed, like sound didn't carry here. The lighting was all indirect and the colors were all neutral browns or dark greens. It was like your senses didn't work right.

He didn't like hospitals anyway. They reminded him of the time he had spent in corridors, rooms and visitors' lounges waiting for his mother to die. But even for a hospital this place was spooky. It was visiting hours, but most of the room doors were closed. Only once did he catch a glimpse of someone sitting at a bedside, a dark form outlined in the flickering glow of a TV screen.

The nurse stopped before one of the too-wide doors, gently pushed it open and then motioned him to follow her in.

At first he thought Judith was someone else. She was wizened and shrunken down into the immaculate white sheets of the hospital bed. They had cut her hair short and shaved part of one side of her head. There was a tube in her nose and another one running from her arm to a bottle of clear liquid hanging by the bed.

Craig looked dubiously at the nurse.

"Can she hear me?" he whispered.

"Perhaps," the nurse said gently. "Try talking to her. You don't have to whisper."

"Thank . . ." Craig started to whisper and caught himself. "Thank you."

"I'll be at the nurse's station."

As she went out the door the nurse felt a flash of pity. The young accident victims were about the worst, second only to the little kids who had nearly drowned. Maybe the visitor would do the patient good, but she doubted it. After six years on Neuro she had a feel for the patients and this one probably wasn't ever going to come out of it.


At first the programmers didn't have too much trouble digging through the rubble. The pieces were about the size of Wiz's head; small enough to handle easily and big enough to make obvious progress. The stone was freezing cold, but their sturdy gloves protected their hands and kept their fingers warm.

The heart wasn't under the first layer of rubble, or the next. By now the job was getting harder. They started to run into pieces that took two or all three of them to shift. More and more of the pieces were locked together like jackstraws and could only be moved in order. Soon all three of them were sweating in spite of the cold and panting from the effort.

"You know," Jerry said as they took a breather, "logically the heart should be all the way at the bottom of this pile."

Danny picked up a pebble and chucked it against the wall. It bounced off with a metallic clang. "It'll take us days to dig down that far, even with picks and shovels."

"Well, we can't bring anyone through to do our digging for us," Wiz said. "We're the only ones the demon won't harm."

Jerry rubbed his thumb where he had mashed it between two stones. "This seems to be an ideal job for magic. We could use a summoning spell and just call the heart to the surface."

"We could also summon Bale-Zur right on top of us. No thanks."

"So?" Danny interjected. "He won't hurt us."

Wiz thought of the huge black demon with the yard-wide mouth and glowing red eyes. "You *seriously* do not want to meet this guy. I still have nightmares about what he did to those Dark League wizards. Anyway, we can't conduct the next phase of the operation with him right on top of us."

"May I make a suggestion?" Moira's voice spoke in his ear.

"Sure darling, go ahead."

Danny started and then realized Wiz wasn't talking to him.

"Jerry is right. Could you use magic to do your digging?"

"Won't that attract Bale-Zur?"

There was muffled noise over the crystal as Moira conferred with other wizards.

"Perhaps, but it is imperative we complete this before nightfall. Unless you want to spend the night there."

Wiz remembered some of the things that inhabited the City of Night after dark and he shuddered again. "No thanks."

"Besides, should worse come to worst we can lay the demon elsewhere."

Wiz weighed that. "Okay. We'll give it a try." He turned to his companions. "Now does anyone have any good ideas for a digging spell?"

As the nurse left, Craig pulled a chair close to the bed, wincing at the slight scraping sound.

"Hi, Judith. Can you hear me?" Always Judith. She hated to be called Judy and she had pinned his ears back when he slipped the first time they met.

The figure in the bed did not respond. There was not a flicker from the eyelids and the rhythm of breathing continued uninterrupted.

Craig wanted to bolt. This was too much like his mother had been, before she'd wake up and start screaming for her shot. The only thing that kept him in the chair was knowing he'd have to pass the nurse and she'd know he couldn't take it. He had to stay for a few minutes anyway.

He felt like an idiot for coming. None of the others had, not since Judith was transferred out of ICU. So he'd said he would at the last gaming session and then he was committed.

"Everybody misses you on Friday nights," he said brightly.

"Bill and Sheri are taking your place in the campaign, but they're really not very good."

Still no response from the bed.

"We had a really good game last Friday. Joe was dungeon master and he set up a really nasty scenario. You had all these flocks of dragonlets in a crystal cave and they'd just swarm the party from all directions. But you had to be careful what spells you used because a lot of the crystals were Reflect Magic and you

38

could get the spell thrown right back in your face." His grin made him look even younger. "Boy, you should have seen it! Dragons diving on us everywhere. They'd make flame attacks and then swoop down with claws and tail, ssshhhewww." He imitated the motion with his hands.

Judith tossed restlessly and mumbled.

"Anyway we were up to our asses in dragons. Then Howard's mage figured out you could use the Reflect Magic crystals for bank shots and he started bouncing stuff off the walls and hitting the dragons from behind! Hey, did you say something?"

" . . . real dragons ugly," Judith mumbled. "Smell like snakes . . . ride over the castle."

She was talking! For an instant Craig thought about ringing for the nurse, but then he realized she probably wouldn't give a shit.

" . . . tie into the saddle . . ." Judith went on. " . . . takes years to learn to ride. No fun, anyway . . . better dragons imagine . . ."

"Yeah, dragons are neat all right."

"Real," Judith said very distinctly.

"Huh?"

"Real dragons. Saw them myself come over the Wizard's Keep first morning we were there. Real dragons . . ." She settled back and trailed off into incomprehensibility.

Craig hunched closer to the bed.

"Tell me more, Judith. What about the dragons?"

## Five
# UNSOUGHT PROPHECY

It was late in the afternoon when they got the digging spell working. The wan sun was sinking toward the horizon, throwing highlights off the sullen gray surface of the Freshened Sea and sending dark shadows creeping out across the ruins. The cold deepened with the growing twilight and all three programmer/magicians had wrapped their cloaks tightly around themselves to try to stay warm.

"I'm not sure I like this," Jerry said as they huddled together for a final review of their handiwork. "We really should run a couple more tests."

"We don't have time. Unless you want to stay here all night?"

Jerry looked around at the menacing ruins and pulled his cloak tighter. "No thanks. I just wish . . ."

"Oh come on, we've tested the thing to death," Danny said. "Let's get this over with. I'm freezing."

Mentally Wiz reviewed the spell one more time. It simply checked each loose piece within its radius of operation to see if it was the heart of the demon and if it wasn't, tossed it aside. When it reached the demon's heart, it would stop. It was straightforward enough and Wiz couldn't find any flaws. Besides he was as cold as Danny was.

"Okay," he said. "Let's do it."

All three of them stepped back from the pile of rubble and out the collapsed archway. When they were in position, Wiz called:

**"emac"**

A three-foot-high demon with enormous ears popped up before him. "**?**" it said.

Wiz pointed his staff at the rubble choking the room. **"kill exe!"** he commanded.

The Emac turned toward the spot and gabbled

soundlessly. Then it bowed and popped out of existence.

For a moment nothing happened.

"It takes a while for the effect to build up," Wiz explained unnecessarily.

"I just wish . . ." Jerry began. "I have this awful feeling we forgot something."

"It's working!" Danny shouted, pointing at the rubble. A single pebble detached itself from the pile and flew off in a flat arc. Then another pebble whipped off in another direction, and another and another.

As the three watched a head-sized chunk of material shook itself loose and lobbed away from the rubble. Then several more pebbles.

One of the pebbles flew over Wiz's head with an ugly singing whirr.

"Direction," Jerry said abstractedly. "Did we put anything in the spell to control which way the rubble would go when it left the pile?"

"No," Wiz said apprehensively, as another volley of material broke loose from the mound.

"*Then hit the dirt!*" Jerry shouted as a dozen big chunks of rubble came flying straight at them.

All three of them dropped and rolled behind the remains of the wall just as a half-dozen pieces of stone went through the spot where they had been standing, humming like angry bees. Then a torso-sized slab of black marble lofted over the wall and crashed into the frozen dust behind them.

Then all Hell broke loose.

The pile of rubble exploded outwards in all directions. The small stuff came off with the velocity of rifle bullets. The bigger pieces arced away like mortar shells. The three wizards pressed themselves against the base of the wall and tried to burrow into the dirt as debris landed all around them.

*I am not a target,* Wiz told himself as he tried to become one with the base of the wall. *This is not aimed at me.* He shifted slightly just as the remains of a large piece of furniture sailed over the ruined wall and crashed to earth a few feet from him. Abstractedly he realized there should be a simple command to shut the spell down, but it's hard to think when you're in the middle of an artillery barrage and impossible to talk when your mouth is full of dirt.

There were crashes and thuds and whizzes and occasionally a nasty *spang* as something hit the wall and ricocheted away. Once a big piece hit the top of the wall, knocking off chips and showering them down on the cowering trio. The dust grew so thick that Wiz couldn't see two feet in front of him—not that he was looking.

Then suddenly it was quiet.

No more crashes. No more earth-shaking thuds. Just a couple of zips from small stuff and then silence. Even the dust started to settle.

Wiz raised his head and looked around wonderingly. Then he realized Moira was screaming at him through the communications crystal.

"We're fine," he told her, looking at his companions. "The spell was just a little more effective than we thought."

"Oh man," Danny muttered. "Anyone got anything for shell shock?"

"It's the details," Jerry said to no one in particular. "It's always the details that get you in trouble."

Wiz made a feeble attempt to brush himself off and peered around the archway.

The remains of the arch were pocked and scarred with fresh blemishes, white against the polished black granite. But the room itself was as clean as if it had been excavated by a team of expert archaeologists and then scrubbed and vacuumed by a village of Japanese housewives. There, almost exactly in the center of the room, sitting on the newly exposed mosaics of the floor, was a cloudy gray sphere.

Wiz stepped through the archway and realized he was tracking dirt back onto the clean floor.

"Okay," he said into the communications crystal. "We have the thing located. If it's safe come on through."

Then he looked around and bit his lip.

Wiz didn't like *any* part of the operation, but this next step was his least favorite, even counting facing the golden demon. Moira was not immune to Bale-Zur, but she knew more about controlling a demon than any of the programmers. In addition to having more skill at natural magic, she had spent long sessions at Heart's Ease with Shiara the Silver learning all the former wizardess could tell her about such things. If their plan failed, Moira was their last line of defense.

"Sharp lookout everyone," he called over his shoulder. Danny and Jerry spread out, staffs ready, peering into the building gloom for any sign of trouble.

Two figures popped into existence on the polished floor, not just one.

"What the hell is she doing here?" Wiz demanded.

Moira frowned at the greeting and then she whirled. Standing behind her, not two paces away, was June.

"How did you get here?" Moira asked sharply. But June just smiled triumphantly and made a beeline for Danny.

"I thought you said she didn't have any magical ability," Wiz whispered to Moira as the couple hugged and June clung to Danny's arm.

"She does not—I think," Moira whispered back.

"Well then?"

Moira only shrugged.

"Let us get it over with," Moira said. With Danny, Wiz and Jerry forming a perimeter guard, she knelt by the heart of Bale-Zur and reached slowly out to it.

43

For a long time she stayed motionless, her hand hovering over the cloudy crystal sphere. At last she began to move her fingers slowly over the surface, caressing it without quite touching it. Her lips began to move as she started the chant she had been taught to bring the demon back under control.

With the point of her staff she marked a pentagram around the demon's heart. Then she stood up, backed off a step and raised her staff. Her voice rose to a wild cry as she gestured into the air. In spite of himself Wiz found his attention was drawn to his wife and her work.

The sphere pulsed and glowed with an inner light, casting a greenish-gray luminance around itself and Moira. It rocked back and forth as if seeking to break free of the imprisoning figure. Still Moira continued the eerie chant, bouncing the words off the ruined walls like bullets.

And then Bale-Zur was there.

Half-hopping, half-shambling, the huge demon moved into the circle of weird radiance. Its great horned head turned neither right nor left and its glowing eyes, red as the fires of Hell, stayed fixed on the hedge witch and the heart. For an awful moment Wiz thought the monster would reach out and grind Moira into a red smear, as he had done with a legion of wizards from the Dark League. Instead the demon approached her across its heart and sank down on its haunches to stare motionless at the woman and the sphere.

Moira continued her chant as if nothing had changed. She lowered her staff and pointed at the heart. Bale-Zur stayed motionless, great taloned hands resting on his misshapen horned knees. The hedge witch extended her staff and tapped the crystal sphere once, twice, three times. The demon leaned forward as if in special interest. Moira repeated the three taps and Bale-Zur cocked its head. Again the three taps and this time the demon seemed to shrink in on itself like a deflating balloon. Suddenly, noiselessly, it shrank and vanished without a trace. The glow faded and all that was left was a woman and a head-sized ball of some shiny black material.

Moira grounded her staff and sighed deeply. Then she sagged against it.

That broke the spell. Wiz rushed to her and put his arms about her shoulders. She leaned against him and he could feel her heart pounding even through the thick cloak she wore.

"Fine," she muttered. " 'M fine. Just hold me, will you?"

Danny, Jerry and June all gathered around them in the deepening gloom of evening. Moira took a deep breath and straightened in Wiz's arms.

"It is done," she said in a surprisingly strong voice.

Wiz looked at the globe, now cold and dark. "That's it then," he said. "Bale-Zur is gone."

"May we never see its like again," Moira said fervently.

"Oh, you will not, mortals," said a sweetly mocking voice behind them. "I see that in your future."

All four of them whirled. There, standing poised on the ruined wall, was an elf.

Like all her kind, she was tall and slender. The delicate points of her ears peeked through the long dark hair that curved around her face and fell loose down her back. Her oddly slanted eyes were as blue as Moira's were green. In spite of the cold she wore a shoulderless gown of fine pale pink stuff that rippled in the chill wind and set off her pale skin and dark hair. She was as alien as she was beautiful, utterly relaxed and as menacing as a tiger poised to spring.

June screamed and sank back against Danny. Moira stepped to the side and held her staff aloft as if to strike. Danny clutched June to him and Wiz and Jerry simply goggled.

"Uh, hi," Wiz said, completely nonplussed. "Lisella, isn't it?"

The elf maiden arched her beautifully formed brows and pursed her red lips in a mock pout.

"You have forgotten me already. I am disappointed, Sparrow."

"Ah, not exactly." *I never forget someone who's tried to kill me.* The elf looked amused at his discomfort.

"So," he said at last "what brings you here?"

Lisella smiled, bright and cold as the moon at midwinter. "Why, I came to renew our acquaintance, Sparrow, and to offer you a gift of prophecy. Shall I tell you your future?"

"Uh, no thanks."

"Ruin and loss," Lisella went on as if he had not spoken. "Your company shall meet your greatest enemy, one like you with powers as great as yours and allies greater than you can imagine." Her voice rang off the stones and the wind pulled at her skirt and hair. "At the crossroads of the worlds you and your companions shall meet him in a great battle. The mightiest among you shall die, each of your number shall suffer great loss and your enemy shall achieve his heart's desire."

She raised her arm and made a sweeping gesture that encompassed all of them. "That is your future, mortals. That is what lies ahead."

And then she was gone. The only sound was June's harsh sobbing echoing off the cold stone.

They looked at each other.

"Bitch!" Danny said fiercely as he clung to his wife. "Goddamn bitch."

"That's the one who was trying to kill you?" Jerry asked Wiz.

"Yeah. She kept trying to set up magical accidents."

"Why?"

"Who knows? I met her once at Duke Aelric's but by that time she'd been after me for months. I think it

46

was some sort of cat-and-mouse game between her and Aelric—with them as cats and me as the mouse. She'd try to kill me by accident and Aelric would help me escape by the skin of my teeth."

"Do you think she's after you again?"

Wiz looked apprehensively at the place on the wall where Lisella had stood. Then he shrugged. "Maybe."

Jerry followed his gaze. "It sounds like we're in for some real trouble."

"If she's right, maybe."

"Well, elves can foretell the future, can't they?"

"Foretelling and true speaking are two different things," Moira said firmly. "Elves can see truly but they are as false and tricksome as a piskhie maze. Clearly she means us no good and we had best ignore what she has said."

It would have been more convincing, Wiz thought, if her knuckles hadn't been white on her staff.

"Well anyway, I think we'd better wind up here and get back to the Capital," Jerry said. "Bal-Simba needs to know about this."

"I don't think he's going to like it much," Wiz predicted.

Wiz's prophecy, at least, was correct. The enormous black wizard heard them out and then led them back through their story time and again with sharp questions. At last he had no more questions and simply sat with his head sunk into his hamlike hands. The group of programmers sat clustered around the table, unsure what to do next but unwilling to depart without his leave.

"What do you think it means, Lord?" Wiz ventured at last.

"I wish I knew, Sparrow." He lapsed into silence again.

"There have been other elven prophecies to mortals," Moira said. "Or so the stories say."

"Not like this," Arianne said from her place behind Bal-Simba's chair. "Those stories speak of chance meetings and a prophecy given either as a reward or punishment."

"This was neither," Bal-Simba said. "She asked for nothing. More, she obviously sought you out at a time when you would all be together and away from the Capital and its protections."

"What should we do?"

"There is nothing we can do. The future may be open to elves, but to us it is closed and hidden. We can only live our lives as best we can and see what comes of all this."

"I wish I knew what her game was," Wiz said.

"I wish I knew why she wanted you dead," Moira replied.

"She hasn't tried to kill me since I was kidnapped to the City of Night. That's something anyway."

"True," Bal-Simba said. "It is something. I only wish I knew what."

# Six

# QUEST COMPANION

*Good help is so hard to find nowadays.*
                    **—Personnel manager's lament**

Craig paused at the foot of the stairs and went over
his spiel again. He wanted to get this just right, otherwise Panda would think he was crazy.

For two weeks he had visited Judith every night,
even missing two Friday gaming sessions in a row.
Slowly and patiently he had worked the story out of
her; where she had gone and what she had seen and
done.

It was unbelievable. It was fantastic. Except that it
made sense. When you put it together with other little
things over the last year, it *had* to be true!

The exultation grew until a lump rose in his throat
from sheer joy. *There were other worlds where magic
worked!* It wasn't all just game scenarios and science fiction. Those places really did exist and you could get
there from here! He shivered again at the wonder of
it all.

Only—now he needed help.

Out on the street the traffic rushed by unheeded.
Craig stared unseeing, while he went over his dilem-
ma one more time.

Somehow he had to find a way to open that door
into the other world. He wanted that more desperately than he had ever wanted anything in his life, even,
he realized with a guilty start, more than he had
wanted his mother to live. But he had to have a Quest
Companion, someone to help him push that door
open.

Who? He had spent most of the last three days
going over possibilities and the list was disappointing-
ly small. When you got right down to it, Craig

realized, he didn't have any close friends except maybe Judith.

The gamers were the only people he actually knew. But he really didn't like them much and most of them thought he was kind of strange. Besides, they couldn't help him. The thought of Joe or Howard as Quest Companions on a real quest was silly and the rest didn't know enough about computers.

There were the others, the ones he met in the shadowy neverland of bulletin boards in his secret identity as Skullslayer, the master hacker. But he knew as little about them as they did about him. It would be embarrassing to confide in someone and then have it turn out to be a pimply faced thirteen-year-old.

There was one whose real identity he did know. A year and a half ago Panda had taken the unusual and dangerous step of contacting him in person. He was such an outtasight hacker that he'd discovered Skullslayer's identity and found that he used to work as a part-time operator in the University computer center. Not only that, he knew that Craig's password and login were still active!

The stuff about the virus, that had been an accident. Mikey had explained it all to him the night he showed up at his apartment and wanted help to cover it up. At first he'd been scared that Mikey was going to turn him over to the FBI, but Mikey just sort of mentioned in passing that he knew a lot about Skullslayer and of course if he was picked up he'd have to make a deal to save his own skin. Just this one favor, Mikey had promised, and we'll be square.

Actually it was a thrill and kind of an honor to be involved in something as big as the Jesse James virus. So in a matter of ten minutes from his living room he had hopelessly muddled the trail that led from the out-of-control computer virus back to Panda.

They'd never met in person again, but they had become good friends over the BBSs. Mikey followed

Panda's exploits with admiration and more than a little awe. The guy was not only good, he was, well, *daring*. A dozen times or more Panda had boldly gone where no hacker had gone before, coming up with phone numbers and access codes to some of the most outrageous systems.

A woman with a bag of groceries in either arm came up the walk from the parking lot. She stepped off the sidewalk to pass well around Craig, eyeing him suspiciously as she did so.

*She's gonna call the cops on me.* Well, he couldn't delay any longer.

The name on the door was "Michael E. Baker," but Craig knew everyone called him Mikey—like in the cereal commercial.

"Panda? It's me. Skullslayer."

There was a muffled "just a minute" and the sound of a lock turning.

The door opened a crack and a blue eye peered out.

"You alone?"

"Yeah. Just me."

The door closed and then opened wide.

Mikey was shirtless and barefoot. He was several years older than Craig, but Craig was already beginning to bulge and Mikey was lean without being skinny. His blonde hair was cut surfer style and wire rimmed glasses hid mild blue eyes. While Craig looked like a computer nerd, nothing suggested Mikey Baker was one of the most accomplished hackers in Silicon Valley.

"Come on in." He turned his back on his guest and strode back into the apartment.

"Nice place," Craig said as he closed the door behind him. The living room was furnished in modern chrome-and-leather furniture. Brown leather that complemented the beige carpet and the darker brown drapes. One entire wall was taken up with an elaborate entertainment center, including a big-screen television that was playing soundlessly. It was fairly neat for a hacker pad. No printouts, no posters, no stacks of books and magazines, just the day's newspaper on the floor by the recliner and a couple of empty beer cans.

Mikey went back into the kitchenette and opened the refrigerator. "Want a beer?"

Craig plopped himself down on the leather and chrome sofa. "No thanks." Then he saw what was on television and his jaw dropped.

A luscious brunette was squatting before a man who was hung like a horse. The man's pants were down around his ankles and the woman was completely naked. The camera closed in tight on the man's crotch and the woman's mouth.

"X channel," Mikey said as he came back into the living room with a beer in his hand. "Satellite feed."

"Wow. I thought you couldn't get those here."

Mikey smiled. "They're up on the satellites if you know where to look."

Craig watched the action on the screen some more. "Wow."

"How'd you find me?"

Craig tore his eyes away from the television.

"The day you—uh—came over to my place. I got your license number." He shrugged. To any true system breaker the rest was obvious.

Mikey grunted. "Pretty cute. So what brings you here?"

Craig tore his eyes away again.

"You know Judith Conally?"

"No."

"Well, I game with her and . . ."

Mikey grinned. "Is she a good fuck?"

Craig colored. "I never . . . I mean, I don't know her that well."

Mikey's grin got even wider. "So if she's not a good fuck why play games with her?"

Craig stopped dead. That was the thing about Panda. He had a way of derailing your train of thought. And you could never be *quite* sure when he was kidding.

"Well, she's in the hospital, see? She had a real bad accident. I've been going to see her and sometimes she, like, talks, you know? Like she doesn't know what she's saying.

"Anyway," he hurried on, "she's been talking about this world where magic works and there are dragons and wizards and all that kind of shit."

Mikey popped the top of the beer. "So?"

"So I don't think it's just a story."

"Get real!" Mike took a hefty swig from the can and turned back toward the TV. A skinny blonde with a haystack hairdo and basketball breasts was being caressed from behind by a black man.

"No, listen man. She went someplace last year, her and a bunch of other people. They were recruited at an SCA war and they were gone for maybe six months. Everyone who went has been real secretive. It was right after Judith came back that she started trying to write fantasy.

"And," he concluded triumphantly, "they got paid in gold! I remember Judith bitching about how hard it was to get it changed into money."

Mike turned back to his visitor. "And you think they went to Middle Earth or something?" he said contemptuously.

"They sure as hell didn't go to Redmond, Washington. Microsoft doesn't pay its people in gold."

Mikey turned back to the television. "Bullshit."

"Wait, there's more. They were recruited to, like, program magic. Over there you can hack magic the way you can computers. Programmers are super-wizards in that world."

53

"And you believe her. This cunt's wacked out of her mind in the hospital and you still believe her."

"I'm telling you it all fits!" Craig said desperately. "It's *gotta* be true."

"It's still bullshit. And even if it's true, so what? What's that got to do with us?"

"Don't you see, we can go there too!"

Mikey set the beer down. "Why the fuck would we want to do that?"

Craig stopped with his mouth open. In all his planning, in all his imagining this meeting, that question never occurred to him. "Well," he said lamely, "it would be an adventure."

Mikey snorted.

"There's gotta be all kinds of treasure and stuff laying around. They paid all those people in *gold*, man! And we'd be wizards. Super-powerful wizards over there."

Mikey stared at the television and said nothing. On the screen the blonde was pistoning up and down on the black man. Her breasts were flapping like tethered balloons, but not a strand of her haystack hair was out of place.

"So what do you want me to do?"

"I, uh, need help figuring out how to make the stuff work. I need someone who's even better than I am and Panda's the *best*!"

Mikey accepted the compliment without comment. For a long time he sat and drank his beer, watching the screen and saying nothing while Craig fidgeted in silence.

Finally he tilted the bottle and drained the last drops. "I want to talk to your friend."

Craig hesitated. "She's kind of hard to talk to."

Mikey smiled a 1,000-watt smile. All of a sudden he looked about fifteen and utterly charming. "I think I can get through to her."

\* \* \*

54

"Hi, Sheila, we're here to see Judith."

The young black nurse stood up from the filing cabinet and turned around. "Hi, Craig. One of you will have to stay here. Rules say only one visitor at a time."

"Oh, come on Sheila, it would only be for a couple of minutes."

"Please," Mikey said, flashing one of his winning smiles. "We'll only be a few minutes and I really think it would do her good to see us both."

He looked so sincere, so innocent and so vulnerable that Sheila hesitated and then nodded. "Well, all right. But don't tire her out. And if the supervisor comes around, you snuck by me. Okay?"

"Did you catch the ass on that nurse?" Mikey asked in an undervoice as they headed for Judith's room.

Judith had a roommate now, an elderly Italian woman who lay spread-eagled beneath the sheets and breathed in great, wracking gasps. Otherwise everything was exactly as it had been on Craig's first visit.

"Hi, Judith," Craig said brightly. "This is Mikey. He's a friend."

There was no response from the bed. Mikey glared at Craig.

"It takes a little bit to get her talking," he whispered. Then he turned back to Judith.

"Mikey's interested in dragons, Judith. Dragons and wizards and magic. You know, the stuff you saw in the other place."

The woman's eyelids fluttered.

"You remember the dragons you saw. The ones you could ride on."

Judith's lips moved. Out of the corner of his eye Craig could see Mikey sitting impassively.

"You remember the flying dragons, don't you, Judith?" Craig went on with a tinge of desperation. The ones you rode?"

" . . . not ride," Judith mumbled. "Mad at me . . ."

Craig threw a triumphant look at Mikey, but Mikey's expression didn't change.

"Magic, Judith. You did magic there."

" . . . spell compiler . . . full of spaghetti code. Worked asses off to fix it." Her arms twitched restlessly against the soft restraints that tied them to the bed.

"The magic compiler, how did it work?"

"Weird language . . . hacked together." She drifted off into incomprehensibility.

"Have you got a copy of the code?" Mikey put in sharply.

Judith tossed and mumbled. ". . . secret. All secret . . ."

Mikey leaned closed to the bed.

"Have you got notes?" he demanded. "Where are your notes?"

" . . . notebook . . . projects."

"Where's the notebook, Judith?" Mikey persisted. "Where did you put it?"

Judith began to move her whole body against the bed.

"Hey, she's getting upset. I think we'd better leave her alone."

Mikey ignored him. "Tell me!" he hissed, grabbing Judith's hand and squeezing hard. Judith moaned and tried to pull away from his grip.

"Hey! You're hurting her."

Mikey squeezed harder, bearing down on each word. "Where. Are. Your. Notes?"

"Home," Judith gasped. "Desk." She was thrashing from side to side and breathing hard now.

Mikey released her hand. "That's fine, Judith," he said gently. "You did real good."

He turned to Craig. "You heard her. She's got stuff back at her apartment. Can you get in?"

"Well, yeah but . . ."

"Then come on." He stood up and headed for the door without another look at Judith. Craig followed more slowly. At the doorway he looked back. Judith was still moving restlessly, panting with hard, regular gasps.

It was almost like she was sobbing.

Judith's apartment was on the ground floor of a two-story complex in a quiet residential neighborhood. There were maybe fifty apartments grouped around a big central terrace and pool. They had obviously been built in the '60s, before San Jose land values went crazy, but they were well-maintained. Probably not a bargain, Craig thought as he led Mikey through the wrought iron gate into the court, but still the sort of place that was passed down from friend to friend.

The apartment was dark and the drapes were drawn. One of the nearby apartments had a television game show on, but no one was in the courtyard.

"There's a key in the planter by the door, under one of those phony rocks," Craig said. "She showed it to me when I stayed here."

Mikey gave him a knowing smile.

"Not like that! I just crashed on her couch a couple of nights." He didn't add that it had been while his mother had been in the hospital and he couldn't face going back to the house alone. Somehow that wasn't the sort of thing you told Mikey.

He groped around, picking up rocks from the planter.

"Shit. It's not here."

"May I help you?" a voice demanded sharply.

Craig jerked erect and whirled. A middle-aged woman was glaring at them from perhaps twenty feet away. She had a sweater thrown over her shoulders and a cordless telephone in one hand. Her thumb was ostentatiously posed over one of the phone's quick-dial buttons.

Before Craig could do more than flush, Mikey

stepped forward smiling—far enough to establish contact but not close enough to be threatening. "Yes ma'am," he said as if he was genuinely glad to see her. "My name is Ralph Simmons. I'm Judith Conally's supervisor. This is Craig Scott, a friend of Judith's. We've just come from the hospital and Judith asked us to bring her a few things."

Some of the venom left the woman's stare. "I thought she was in a coma."

Mikey positively beamed. "Oh, she's come out of it. She'll be in the hospital a while, but she's already talking about going back to work. I don't mind telling you that's a relief to me—I mean aside from being happy she's going to be all right. Judith is the only one who really understands that code. Just between you and me, we've been hurting without her."

The woman shifted her stance and her finger moved away from the call button. "Hadn't she quit to write or something?"

"We'd brought her back on a consulting contract. You know, just for a few hours a week. You don't just let someone like Judith walk out the door."

The woman nodded reluctantly. "She always seemed like a real dedicated person."

"Very dedicated," Mikey agreed. "And a very good worker." Then he frowned every so slightly. "But we seem to have a little trouble here. Judith told us she left a spare key under a rock in the planter, but we can't seem to find it."

"Oh, I took that in after the accident. Didn't seem safe."

"That was very thoughtful of you, ma'am. I wonder if you could see your way clear to let us use it for a few minutes. You see, Judith wanted to look over some of the listings and the doctor thought it would be good for her. Kind of therapy, you know."

"Well . . ."

Mikey turned up the wattage on the smile. "Oh, I

know it's a lot to ask, but they never did find Judith's keys after the accident. Naturally if you'd like to call the hospital . . ." again the trace of a frown, "only Judith's not supposed to have phone calls and they'd probably have to track the doctor down."

"Just some papers, you say?"

"Yes, ma'am. She won't be needing clothes or anything for a while."

"I don't suppose it would hurt. I'm Mrs. Mapelthorpe, the manager. I can let you in on my pass key."

"Yes, ma'am. If you'd like to come in with us, just to make sure . . ."

Mrs. Mapelthorpe smiled. "Oh, I'm sure that won't be necessary." She fished in the pocket of her sweater and brought out a key ring. "Just stop by 102 and check with me before you leave. Oh, and if you could, remind her that her lease is up next month. She needs to decide what she's going to do about the apartment then."

Mike flashed that winning smile, again. "We will. Thank you."

The place smelled of dust and cool, stale air. Someone had obviously tidied up after the accident, but apparently no one had been here since. The place had the feel of being not-quite lived in.

"This is weird," Craig said looking around the apartment. Mikey made a beeline for the desk.

"If we're going to see the old bitch on the way out I don't guess we'd better take anything except the papers—unless she kept that gold here?"

"No, that's in a safety deposit box."

"Bingo!" Mikey said, holding up a thick notebook triumphantly. "Right on top of the pile." He looked at the papers stacked beneath it. "And here's some more." He started scooping up the papers and stacking them on top of the notebook. "And some disks too. Find me a box to carry this shit, will you?"

They couldn't wait to get back to Mikey's apartment, so they took a corner booth in a coffee shop and set their box of plunder on the seat while they spread the papers out to study them.

"Boy, I didn't think that would work," Craig said. "When the old lady showed up I was sure we were dead."

Mike looked at him contemptuously. "All you have to do is act sincere and be polite. Then people will believe any bullshit you feed them. Especially the old farts."

Neither of them said anything as they studied the papers and notebook. Their coffee arrived and Craig hardly looked up to add extra sugar and nearly a whole pitcher of creamer. Mikey sipped his black, apparently oblivious to the heat.

"It looks like the whole damn language is here," Craig said finally. "Weird looking stuff, though."

"You expected maybe ANSI C? Of course this shit's weird. Look at what it does."

Craig put his hand down on the stack of papers and leaned across the table to Mikey, eyes glowing. "You know what this is? I mean really? It's the road to your heart's desire. Anything you want."

"So, what do you want?"

Craig hesitated. "I guess a better world. Where people really care about people, you know?"

Mikey looked amused. "No, I don't know. Tell me."

Craig fidgeted. "I dunno. But we went wrong here. I mean with all the pollution and shit. We've just squeezed the beauty out of the way we live. There's no magic in the world."

He toyed with the spoon in his coffee. "Maybe with magic we can build something better. Something that uses magic and technology both in the way they were supposed to be used."

Outside the traffic rushed by.

"What about you? What's your heart's desire?"

Mike grinned lopsidedly. "That's easy. I want to be master of all I survey."

# Seven

# JOURNEY

*"Getting there is half the fun."*
### —Wrong-way Corrigan

"I thought we were going outside," Ragnar the dwarf complained as he puffed along under a pack nearly as large as he was.

"We are," Glandurg told him as he led his band up the sloping passageway. Each of the dwarves was nearly buried in weapons, food and other necessities for the journey.

"This doesn't lead to the gate. The only things up here are the watch posts."

"You will see," Glandurg assured his men. "Step lively now."

The corridor grew steeper until finally it challenged even the surefootedness of the dwarves burdened as they were. The way was narrower here above the highest of the workshops and habitations and the walls and floor rougher. The tunnel began to turn more frequently as the very mountain narrowed toward its peak. Several times they passed doors leading to lookout posts on the mountain itself. The dwarves guarding the doors did not salute them as they passed, but they didn't try to stop them either. That was reassuring to Glandurg's followers, who still had trouble believing that King Tosig had trusted his ne'er-do-well relative with an important mission.

Finally, just when it seemed the trail couldn't get any steeper or the mountain any narrower, Glandurg stopped in front of an iron door set in the rock. Fumbling in his pouch he produced a large key and turned it in the lock. Soundlessly the door swung open and blinding daylight flooded into the tunnel.

Hard on each others heels the dwarves tumbled

out onto the mountain top. They were standing on a broad, flat expanse of dark gray stone. Squinting off in the distance they could see the other peaks of the Southern Forest Range, most of them lower than they were now. Beyond the mountains in every direction stretched the dark green of the Wild Wood, cut here and there with the meandering silver thread of a river.

None of them had ever been this high on the mountain and most of them had been outside their home tunnels perhaps a half-dozen times in their lives. It was an intoxicating sight and they peered in every direction, jabbering excitedly as they pointed out features to one another.

Glandurg ignored his unsophisticated comrades and strode toward the edge of the open space. He reached into his pouch and produced a polished bone whistle, elaborately carved in dwarvish fashion. Placing it to his lips he blew loud and hard, but no sound came from it. He scanned the skies and then blew again.

The response came not from the air as he expected, but from behind him. There was a scrabbling sound and a griffin leapt lightly down into the center of the ledge.

There was a gasp from Glandurg's followers and they shrank away from the apparition which had appeared in front of them. Glandurg gulped, terribly aware that the griffin was between him and the door to safety. But he put on his best leader's manner and strode toward the beast in what he hoped was a good imitation of fearlessness.

The other dwarves were under no such burden. They moved back against the doorway, ready to vanish down their tunnel to safety at the first sign of a hostile move.

The griffin managed to look smug, amused and dangerous all at the same time. The dwarves were on her turf and they all knew it.

Dwarves and griffins shared the mountains in an

uneasy truce. The griffins nested on the uppermost crags and the dwarves tunneled through the rock. Dwarf mothers frightened their children into obedience with tales of dwarf children who had wandered away and been seized and eaten by griffins. By the same token dwarves were known to enjoy the occasional griffin egg surreptitiously taken from the nest.

"I told you we would ride," Glandurg said as he strode to the griffin.

The griffin hissed loudly and backed away.

"But you agreed to take us to the human wizard," Glandurg protested.

The griffin nodded.

"Well," said an exasperated Glandurg, "if we don't ride how will you get us there?"

The griffin smiled—as much as a creature with the beak of an eagle can smile—and flexed its claws.

Craig scowled as he riffled through the papers spread out on Mikey's coffee table. The clock display in the upper-right corner of the television set showed it was after midnight, but he paid no more attention to that than he did to the old movie on the screen. He took another pull on the can of grape soda and slammed it down, slopping sticky purple fluid on Judith's notes.

"We got a problem."

Mikey looked up from the recliner where he was curled up with Judith's notebook. "Like what?"

"How are we going to get to this other world?"

"Judith got over there, didn't she?"

"Yeah, but someone took her."

Mikey considered for a moment. "What about that first guy, the one she called Wiz? He got there on his own, didn't he?"

"No, he was taken over too. By one of their wizards." Craig drained the last of the soda and threw the empty can in the general direction of the waste-basket. "Great! So we've got all this magic and stuff and we can't do anything with it."

Mikey laughed and shook his head.

"What's so goddamn funny?"

"You. You're talking like a system administrator. If it's not obvious or it's not in the manual, it can't be done. What you need to do is chill out and keep working on this stuff."

"What good does that do?" Craig asked, half-sullen.

"The more you learn, the easier it is to make things happen. That's the secret of hacking. You don't worry if something seems impossible. You just keep watching and learning and pretty soon it's not impossible."

He stood up and stretched on tiptoes, leaning far back to work the kinks out of his spine. "Now here, we can't get over ourselves, but maybe we can get someone to bring us over."

"How?"

"We make something like a beacon. Something that says 'here we are, come get us.' "

"Can we do that?"

"Your friend thought so. She worked out a way to do it."

He flipped open the notebook and put it on the coffee table. "See?"

Craig studied the block diagram scribbled on the page. "I don't think that's gonna be easy."

Mikey grinned lopsided. "So? Nothing that's worth having is."

Craig was right. It wasn't easy. Judith's notes had no more than outlined the beacon spell. It was broken down into modules, but half the modules hadn't been written and several of the ones that had been needed modification.

Worse, they were flying blind. They had no way of testing anything because the magic compiler didn't work in their world. All they could do was check and re-check their work manually and hope they had everything correct.

They didn't have much in the way of tools. Judith had started work on a cross-compiler for the magic language that would run on an MS-DOS computer, but it was only a skeleton. She had written a sort of a syntax checker for the magic language that worked something like *lint* for C. But like *lint* it flagged all possible errors. Since there was no way of running a test compile, they had to be "more Catholic than the fucking Pope," as Mikey put it, and correct everything that the checker flagged.

Mikey ended up picking the basic approaches and doing the broad outlines while Craig did the detail work and coding. Partially this was because Craig wasn't very good at the big-picture stuff and partially because that was just the way it worked out, somehow. That meant that while Craig spent hours sweating over the grunt work, Mikey lounged around the apartment drinking beer and playing computer games.

Since both of them were system breakers they worked essentially around the clock, catching naps when they felt like it and ordering in from fast food joints when they got hungry. Thus it was nearly three o'clock in the morning when Craig came in to tell Mikey they were finished.

"I'll get some sleep and then we can go over the whole thing one more time," he said to Mikey's back. "What are you playing anyway?"

"Empire."

Craig nodded. He was familiar with the game. You explored an unmapped world, captured cities and built armies and fleets while the computer did the same thing. Eventually you met the computer's forces in a climatic battle for control of the planet.

"Looks like you've got him on the run," Craig said,

surveying the map on the screen. "One or two more turns and he'll surrender."

"He surrendered a while ago," Mikey said, maneuvering about thirty aircraft to attack the sprinkling of enemy armies in the upper left corner of the screen.

"So why are you still playing?"

"Because I want to crush the motherfucker," Mikey said as his legions of aircraft tore into the opposing forces. Most of the armies went down under the onslaught, but one beat off five separate attacks.

"Die, you cocksucker!" Mikey snarled as he used the mouse to mass even more air forces against the remaining red marker on the screen.

"I always quit when the computer surrenders," Craig told him as he watched over his friend's shoulder.

"I don't want surrender. I want him wiped out," Mikey said without taking his eyes off the confrontation.

Craig took a swig of soda. "Takes too long that way."

"Yeah, but when it's over I'm the only one left standing."

The computer beeped as its final army vanished under the combined attack of nearly twenty aircraft.

*This is extremely undignified,* Glandurg thought as he watched the green forest sail by beneath him. *Warriors should ride into battle, not be carried along like a sack of meal.*

Behind him came eleven more griffins, each carrying a dwarf dangling from its talons.

*Still, there are advantages,* he admitted. *It would be hard to hold on riding griffin-back.*

Craig looked at the stuff laid out on the coffee table dubiously. Some of them, like the sheets of typing paper with the spell written on them, were perfectly ordinary. Others, like the hibachi full of glowing coals

67

were ordinary but out of place. Still others, like the roots and powders he and Mikey had scoured Chinatown to find, were just plain odd. The table had been shoved to the center of the room and a circle drawn around it in blue marking chalk.

Mikey had just finished placing the black, white and red candles at the points of an invisible star outside the circle. He used the tape measure to check the distances between them and then did a quick calculation on his HP calculator.

"That should do it," he said, carefully stepping over the chalk mark to join Craig at the coffee table.

"Give me your hand."

"What do you want that for?"

Mikey picked up the Exacto knife lying next to the hibachi. "I don't, I want some of your blood."

Craig winced as Mikey drove the point into his fingertip. "Hey! Not so rough, okay?"

But the blood flowed freely and Mikey held Craig's hand over the hibachi, letting the dark red drops drip onto the glowing coals.

Craig wrinkled his nose at the odor, but Mike didn't seem to notice. He reached into the coffee cup, picked up a four-finger pinch of the powder there and cast it onto the coals where Craig's blood still sizzled. The powder sparkled as it hit the charcoal and heavy sweet-smelling smoke boiled up out of the hibachi.

Craig coughed and his eyes watered, but he grabbed Mike's outstretched hands in his across the glowing coals. Then he looked down at the notes to the side of the hibachi and both of them began to chant, reading the words in unison.

The smoke got thicker and thicker until Craig could hardly see the paper and the sweetish, pungent odor made his head swim. He shut out the discomfort and chanted for all he was worth as the room began to shimmer and dissolve around him.

## Eight
# THE OLD ONES

*The enemy of my enemy is my friend.*
                    **—Old Arab proverb**

*So with friends like these, who needs enemies?*
                    **—Old Jewish proverb**

*Smoke and fire and candlelight . . .*

At first Craig thought the place was on fire. There was smoke or fog everywhere and a dim red light coming from the wrong angle. Between the smoke and the dim red light, Craig couldn't see very well and somehow he was very glad for that. What he could see was *wrong*, like an optical illusion.

They were in a cave, or maybe on a mountain crag. The ground under them was rough rock, kind of, and it sloped away so steeply that Craig was afraid to take a step. The air was thin and hard to breathe, or maybe just so full of smoke there wasn't much oxygen in it. His chest heaved as he sucked great, unsatisfying lungs full. He clutched Mikey's hands tight in his own. Mikey squeezed back so hard Craig's hands hurt.

Craig was scared. For the first time in his life he was so afraid the very marrow of his bones chilled. He didn't care about treasure, or adventuring, or magic. This place played on dark half-realized places in his psyche in ways that were horrible. He just wanted *out*.

Then he realized they were being watched.

It loomed above them in the fog, tall and manlike. There was a hint of distance about it as if it was enormous, but there was no way to tell. In the smoky red haze Craig could make out the outline, including the pointed ears. There was a suggestion of body hair, or maybe fur. Worst of all, it seemed to twist and flicker like an image in a mirage. Looking at the thing made

69

Craig's eyes hurt, but he couldn't make himself look away.

Craig wanted to moan in terror, to yell a warning, to scream, but he couldn't get his breath to do any of it. All he could do was stare at the half-seen creature and cling to Mikey's hands for dear life.

"Who are you?" Mikey finally got out.

*We are what was and what might be.* The voice filled Craig's head like ringing thunder until he wanted to clap his hands to his ears to shut it out. *We are what will be again.* The voice pressed on. *We are the dawn and nightfall and deepest night. We are . . . Ur-elves.*

"We, ah, we weren't expecting this."

*We know,* the voice came again and there was amusement in the rolling words. *But you called and we answered.*

"Why did you bring us here?"

*To serve.*

"Then you want to make a deal, right?" Mikey said, the words low and fast, as if he was desperate.

*We have a bargain,* the voice thundered inexorably. *Sealed in blood.* Craig thought of his finger, still throbbing where Mikey had pricked it, and moaned aloud.

*Your talents will serve us. Your magic will be the spearhead of our power. You will bring down those who stand between us and our fulfillment and lay waste to their world.*

Craig closed his eyes tightly and moaned again. The thing and its words were awful and terrifying and . . .

Attractive.

*Come closer*, the thing said. *Come closer and watch.*

As if moving through a zoom lens Craig and Mikey were sped to the side of the Ur-elf. Craig still couldn't form a clear impression of what it looked like and for that he was just as glad.

Craig had the impression of two huge, shaggy hands cupped before him, hands with claws for nails. There was something glowing in the hollow, like a living coal. The radiance expanded and grew brighter until his face was bathed with yellow light. The light turned cloudy. Then it cleared and they were looking down on a world held in the Ur-elf's palms.

There was deep blue ocean and spotted through it were islands. As Craig watched the islands formed as faceted images, then smoothed and took on color and texture. Vaguely he sensed that one end of this place connected to his own world and the other end to the world of magic.

Again the zooming effect and they were falling toward a large island in the center of the ocean. The place was long and narrow, with reddish brown desert shading from mountains at one end down through brown-yellow plains in the center to lush gray-green at the other end.

Faster and faster they fell, closer and closer to the mountains at the desert end. Craig sucked in his breath as the mountain peaks rushed up toward them.

Then suddenly they were standing on the tallest peak of all, looking out over the mountains and desert.

*In this place the magic of both worlds works*, the voice inside their heads told them. *It is yours for now. Make good use of it.*

And then they were alone on the crag.

Craig tasted bile on his tongue. His head hurt with a roaring, throbbing ache that threatened to take the top of his skull off with every beat of his hammering heart. Mikey didn't look too much better.

The two looked at each other for a long moment while the chill mountain wind whipped around them and tugged at their clothing.

"Come on," Mikey said at last. "Let's get to work."

The amazing thing was, Craig realized, he already *knew* this stuff. He didn't have to think about how to do it, he could already make magic.

Working alongside Mikey, he sketched out the form of their new home, the citadel and fortress which would be their base for the attack into the new world.

Shadowy cloud forms hovered around the peak as the pair pushed and shaped the outlines of their castle. It would be small at first, covering no more than the top of the peak. But already Craig could visualize its spread as a great stronghold and arsenal to pour forth the sinews of conquest.

It was somehow *right* that they should conquer this world of magic. It was the natural order of things, meant to be. As he shaped and formed, Craig realized in the back of his mind he hadn't always felt that way. But that was immaterial, like a long-ago dream. This was fated and he would bend all his talents to seizing this other world.

Something told him that those talents were now considerable.

A push, a twist, a sudden shimmering coalescence and their magic castle was *done*! Craig breathed a sigh and admired their creation.

The walls soared straight up out of the sides of the peak. Towers and turrets sprouted everywhere, flags flew from the staffs and whipped in the incessant wind. It was magnificent!

At least it was magnificent for a first effort. He had to admit that the walls leaned askew in a couple of places and that some of the towers slumped as if half-melted. Some of the windows were funny shapes too. And somehow it wasn't as *big* as he had imagined it would be.

"Needs a lot of work," Mikey said.

"It's pretty good for a first effort."

Mikey shrugged. "Come on. Let's get the hell out of this wind."

Together they strode over the canting drawbridge and through the lopsided gate of their redoubt.

Craig looked at his handiwork sitting in the flagged stone courtyard and suppressed a pang of disappointment. It was smaller than he had thought it would be, maybe ten feet from wingtip to wingtip. The color was a nice battleship gray, just like a real F-15 and the twin tails stood proudly above the jet exhausts, but somehow it didn't look just right. It looked kind of like an F-15 Eagle, or maybe a Russian Foxhound or Flanker interceptor, or maybe even a Navy Tomcat. He tried to remember just exactly what an F-15 looked like and found he couldn't separate the images of twin-engine, twin-tail interceptors in his mind.

Well, all right, it would have to do. They needed air defense, didn't they? This might not be exactly right, but it could fly and it could fight. That was good enough.

Anyway, there was some good stuff. The conformal fuel tanks along the sides of the fuselage under the wings were right. And the missiles and drop tanks hanging from the pylons beneath the wings and body looked right. Who cared if it wasn't perfect? It was wicked and it was all his.

"Hey Mikey," he yelled, "look what I've got."

"Yeah?" Mikey came out of the main keep, wiping his hands on a rag.

"There," Craig gestured proudly. "It's a robot F-15."

Mikey walked over to the plane. "Bullshit."

"Huh?"

"Bullshit. Look, you've got a missile under the left wing and a drop tank under the right."

"So?"

"So what happens if you drop the tank or fire the missile? You've got an unbalanced load on the plane. And anyway, that missile isn't off an F-15. It looks Russian or something. And you've got the center drop tank painted with a red nose, like a bomb."

"So who the hell cares? It will fly and it can fight. All right? That's what's important, isn't it?"

"Who's it going to fight?" Mikey demanded. "We're the only people in this world. You think the Russians are going to come swarming in here or something?"

"We're here to fight someone," Craig said stubbornly. "*They* told us so."

"Oh yeah," Mikey agreed. "We're gonna have to fight all right. But shit like this," he gestured at the plane, "isn't going to be what decides that battle."

"Oh yeah? Well, what will decide that fucking battle, hotshot?"

Mikey got that sneering smile Craig had come to hate. "Something a lot more powerful than any robot airplane. You'll see when the time comes."

*Well, fuck you very much!* Craig thought as Mikey disappeared back into their lumpy castle. He picked up a loose stone and threw it against the castle wall with all his strength.

He needed a better way to do this. He'd created the F-15 just by imagining it, but the problem with that was that you had to imagine all the details at once. That was too hard.

74

Okay, so what about breaking it down? Suppose you could imagine something one part at a time, like drawing it out on paper? Or on a computer screen! Yeah. Like a workstation!

What he needed was a magical workstation. Already the image was forming in his mind. He'd never seen a jet fighter up close, but he knew exactly what a workstation was like. Of course, he'd want to make a few improvements.

Craig left the misshapen fighter sitting in the courtyard. He'd do a hell of a lot better the next time, but he was going to build that fighter anyway. Squadrons and squadrons of them, just on principle.

It took him nearly three days, but at last Craig had his workstation. The "screen" was a gently glowing rectangle nearly a yard across. There was a keyboard and a mouse, of course, but the system also had voice input. If he really wanted he could just think hard at the screen and make things happen.

The display was an engineer's dream. Infinite resolution, at least sixteen million colors, three-dimensional, fully shaded modelling and redraws at better than sixty frames a second. He could design anything on this baby!

Craig stared at the glowing surface and tried to think of his first project. Maybe jet fighters were a little old fashioned for what they needed to do. They needed weapons that were more far-out, more science-fictional.

Like giant robots! Yeah, now there was something he could really get into. He'd always liked Robobattle, where the gamers slugged it out in twenty-fifth-century robot war machines. Now he could actually build something like that.

Instinctively he reached for the mouse and began to sketch designs on his super-workstation. More accurately, he tried to remember what the warbots in

Robobattle were like. They were nice and impressive and in the game they had a lot of firepower. Then there were the giant intelligent tanks from Orc. And magic! Yeah, what would it be like to have a couple of hundred megaton/seconds of firepower and the destruction spells of a Seventh-Level Mage? That would be really something.

Working with bits and pieces from computer games, role-playing games and old television shows, Craig began to fashion his engines of destruction. It never occurred to him that he had the power to do something original.

"See?" Craig said eagerly. "I can design stuff here on the screen and then build it magically."

Mikey looked over Craig's workstation and didn't say anything.

"I don't have to imagine it all in one piece. I can work on it a piece at a time, and . . ."

"So build me a planet buster."

"Huh?"

"Come on. Whip me up something that can blow up a whole planet." He smacked his fist into his palm. "Pow! Just like that."

"It doesn't work that way," Craig said uncomfortably.

"Why not?"

"You've got to have at least a general idea of how something's supposed to work before you can build it."

"You mean we've got to sit down and fucking design all this shit?"

"No, not that bad. But we've got to know how the stuff functions or it won't work."

"Jesus fuckin' Christ," Mikey muttered. "What a pile of shit."

"You wanna go back and tell them that?" Craig snapped. "I sure as hell ain't gonna."

76

Mikey grinned in that nasty, superior way of his. "Maybe I will do that the next time I talk to them."

Craig's jaw dropped. "You've been *talking* to them?"

"They're around, if you want to make contact."

"But Jesus, I mean . . ."

"They're real interesting too. I'm learning a lot from them."

The way he said it made Craig uncomfortable. "You mean magic and stuff?"

Mikey grinned again. "Oh, I'm learning lots of things."

Craig knew he needed to learn more about how magic operated, but the thought of even seeing an Ur-elf again made him weak in the knees.

"Look, suppose you concentrate on the theoretical stuff and I'll keep working on the robots and shit."

"Okay," Mikey said with a little smile. Craig had the uneasy feeling he'd been outmaneuvered again.

Mikey stopped at the doorway and turned back to Craig. "Oh, if you want to do something useful, redesign this fucking castle and make it more livable."

*Okay,* Craig thought, turning back to his workstation and away from thoughts of Ur-elves and magical theory. *Let's really turn this sucker into something!*

Craig stood at the topmost point of the highest tower, surveyed his work and found it good.

The skimpy, saggy little castle they had formed out of pure magic was long gone. Now the entire top of the mountain had been terraced and leveled. What had been the original castle was now just the central piece of an elaborate structure. Even it was much changed.

*Caermort—the Castle of Death*, he thought. *That's what we'll call it.*

It certainly looked deadly enough. Energy cannons poked their ugly snouts out of domed turrets on the stone ramparts. The central tower of gleaming steel soared to neck-craning height, glittering like a mirror in the afternoon sun. Several of the courtyards had been roofed over with domes of crystal. Random bolts of lightning flew between towers and played over the domes. Further up the air sparkled and flickered as the protective magical shell around the castle interacted with random dust motes which were wafted into it.

Within the castle itself hordes of servants, robots and living creatures, hurried to do his bidding. In the caves dug into the mountain giant robots worked with monster tools to assemble more of their kind and other engines of destruction to boot.

It still wasn't absolutely perfect, he admitted modestly. If he did not work a thing up in complete detail on his screen the details were likely to be filled in haphazardly.

But all in all it was a marvelous engine of destruction. All this power aimed at a single goal. Conquest. Already his drones scouted the limits of this world and his robot legions formed in the huge caverns beneath the mountain or exercised on the desert plains. Mikey might sneer, but he'd stop when Craig's mechanical armies marched across the border between the worlds.

The border between *both* worlds, he amended silently. Why limit himself to the one where magic worked? There was no army on Earth that could stand against his creations.

Better to be Lord of Three Worlds, than Lord of Two, he decided.

# Ten
## WRECK'S WARNING

The programming team was up to its elbows in source code when Arianne came into their workroom.

"Forgive me, my Lords, my Lady," the tall blonde lady said as she entered the room. "Are you occupied?"

Wiz turned toward the door. "Occupied, but not super busy. What's up?"

"Bal-Simba sent me to request your presence."

"Sure. In his office?"

"At Oak Island off the south coast. A strange thing has washed ashore at the village. Bal-Simba asks that you examine it."

Wiz looked over at the pile of scrolls and the shimmering letters hanging above his desk and paused. A summons to meet Bal-Simba here was one thing. A jaunt to a distant village to look at something was another matter. Even walking the Wizard's Way, such a trip would probably eat the rest of the day.

"Can't we just send one of our searching units?" he asked. "We do have to get this stuff done before—"

Arianne hesitated. "Lord, I think you had better see this personally."

"What is it?"

"We do not know. But from the description I think it owes more to your world than ours."

Wiz smelled salt and mud. They were in a hollow between two sand dunes. Gray-green sand grasses and little twisted shrubs grew here and there around them and even in this sheltered spot a breeze ruffled the vegetation and their clothing.

There was a man waiting for them, a rough, grizzled fellow dressed in the bulky knit sweater and canvas trousers favored by the folk who made their living upon the Freshened Sea.

"My Lords, welcome," he said, bowing perfunctorily, as if unused to the exercise. "I am Weinrich, the mayor of Oak Island."

Moira curtsied and the rest bowed. "Well met, Lord. I am Moira and these are the wizards Sparrow, Jerry and Danny."

Weinrich's face cleared, as if a burden had been lifted from him.

"Ah, well met indeed. They said you might come."

"Well, we're here," Wiz said a trace sharply. "Let's see the thing that's causing all the fuss."

With the growing importance of Wiz's new magic, and the spreading word that he was from beyond the World, there was a growing tendency to ascribe anything out of the ordinary to the new magic. Normally Arianne and Bal-Simba did not take the villager's reports this seriously, still . . .

As they climbed the dune Wiz saw four dragons flying complex figure eight patterns off the beach, obviously on guard.

"If this is another piece of driftwood," he muttered to Jerry as they toiled up the sand dune, "I'll . . ."

Then he came over the rise and saw what was down on the beach.

The villagers had dragged it further up the beach, above the tide line. Now they clustered in knots at a respectful distance.

Off to one side the village hedge witch conferred nervously with a blue-robed wizard of the Mighty. Occasionally he would look over at the thing as if to make certain it had not moved under its own power.

It was worth looking at, Wiz had to admit. To the fisherfolk of this isolated island it must have seemed strange beyond all imagining.

One wing was crumpled under it and the other canted into the air. The front of the body was stove in, apparently from hitting the water. As they got closer Wiz could smell the sharp chemical reek of gasoline.

"An airplane," Danny said.

"Perhaps, but there is magic here as well," Moira said.

Wiz didn't have his wife's nose for magic, so he fished out the magic detector he carried in his pouch. The crystal glowed a strong green as he pointed it at the craft.

Magic all right. But gasoline as well. He felt the hair begin to rise on his neck. Whatever this thing was, it was very, very wrong.

"Moira, you and the others stay back. Jerry and I will go in for a closer look."

Moira nodded. "Be careful, love."

"Very careful."

Wiz and Jerry half-stumbled, half-slid down the seaward face of the dune, oblivious to the sand that was trickling into their shoes. As they got onto the beach, they split up. Wiz approached from the tail and Jerry eased toward the crushed nose. There was no sign of movement.

The sea breeze swished through the grasses at the edge of the beach, drowning out the villagers' whispers and dulling the wizards' conversation to an unintelligible murmur.

"Look at this!" Jerry called. "It's got a gasoline engine."

As Wiz ducked under the wing of the plane to join him, Jerry reached out and gave the cowling fasteners an expert twist. Then he flipped the cowling back to expose the power plant.

"High output two-stroke," he said looking it over. "That thing probably puts out ninety horses in spite of its size." He looked further. "No muffler. If that thing was a two-stroke the villagers should have heard it coming for miles."

"It had to be running," Wiz said. "But that's impossible."

"Maybe not," Jerry pointed to the front of the plane. "Look at the prop. Only one blade bent. That means it wasn't turning when it went in."

Wiz knelt down beside the propeller. "If it crashed here it's not surprising. That engine couldn't possibly run in this World."

"Do you think it was sucked through from our world?"

Wiz shrugged. "Maybe, but how? And why? Anyway, the thing's obviously not dangerous now. Let's get the others down here."

Moira and Danny quickly joined them at the wreck. The other wizards kept their distance.

"It's our technology, all right," Wiz said as the other came up. "No cockpit, so it was a drone of some kind."

"What about the magic?" Moira asked.

Wiz looked at his magic detector. "That seems to be concentrated in the boxes in the mid-section."

"If I didn't know better I'd say that was an instrument bay," Jerry said, ducking under the up-tilted wing and squatting down beside it.

"Don't be too sure you know better."

Jerry popped the fasteners and lifted the covering. Inside was a wild tangle of wires and printed circuit boards leading back to several oddly carved lumps of pearl-gray material.

"Cute," Jerry said at last. "Some of this stuff is obviously electronic, but the guts of it," he pointed to the pearl-gray lumps, "are obviously magical."

"We can probably untangle the electronics, but the magic?" He looked over at Moira.

"That is likely to be difficult, my Lord. We do not know who made those things or what they are supposed to do." She frowned and concentrated. "I can tell you that the spells are most powerful, however."

"So the magic's fine," Jerry summed up. "It's the engine that doesn't work."

"Of course the engine doesn't work," Wiz said irritably. "It couldn't work here. The whole thing's impossible."

"Oh yeah?" Danny retorted. "Take a look at those exhaust pipes."

Wiz followed Danny's pointing finger and saw that the pipes were discolored where they came out of the cylinders.

"Heat did that. That sucker ran and it ran for a while."

"But if the engine worked, then the guidance system and the imaging stuff wouldn't. They're based on magic."

"Wait a minute," Wiz said. "Let me try something. **emac!**" he commanded.

"?"

"**list**"

The Emac took the quill from behind his ear and scribbled furiously in the air. Lines of fiery symbols appeared and scrolled upward from the Emac.

"**carat S**" Wiz pronounced and the Emac froze in mid-line.

"Hey, I recognize that!" Wiz peered closely at the glowing letters of fire. "Not only are they magic, they're *our* magic. These spells were written with our magic compiler or something damn like it."

Four pairs of eyes met over the wreckage and no one said anything.

"This will do," Glandurg puffed, looking around the grove.

"High time too," Thorfin wheezed, coming up behind him nearly bent double by the climb and the weight of the enormous pack he carried.

One by one the other dwarves filed into the clearing and dumped their packs. The griffins had left them off at dawn on the other side of the forest and they had been walking ever since. The wooded land was a collection of craggy hills cut by little valleys and laced with brooks and streams. Generations of firewood gathering by mortals had left the woods open and parklike under the spreading trees, but it was still hard going, even for dwarves.

Glandurg had led his band almost entirely through the forest to a wooded bluff overlooking the river that ran by the base of the Capital mount. Just a few hundred yards and a stretch of placid water now separated the dwarves from the enormous bluff that bore the capital city of the North on its back and the Wizard's Keep at its very tip.

As his followers rested behind him, Glandurg surveyed the scene. From here they could watch the Wizard's Keep and the comings and goings of their quarry and stay concealed in the forest. A perfect spot to plan an ambush.

"How are we supposed to know this wizard when we find him?" Gimli asked from where he lay against his pack under a spreading tree. "Mortals all look alike."

"No they don't," Snorri said with a superior air. "There's men mortals and there's women mortals. You can tell them apart easy."

"That only cuts it down by half," Gimli said. "We can't go around killing all the male mortals we meet, can we?"

Glandurg turned back to his band. "That will not be necessary," he said loftily. "I thought of this before we left and I obtained from my uncle the King a means to infallibly identify this mortal."

He drew from his pouch a handful of hazelnut-sized lumps. "Each of you will have one of these. They will always point the way to this foreign sorcerer, be he a hundred leagues away."

Each of the dwarves came forward and took one of the seekers from his hand.

"It's dark," said Thorfin, staring into his palm.

"Mine's not pointing any way at all," Snorri chimed in.

Glandurg scowled and grabbed for the more powerful version of the device that hung around his own neck. Cupping his hands to shield it from the light he saw that it glowed only very dimly. The arrow within pointed waveringly south.

"He must be more than a hundred leagues from here," Glandurg said weakly.

"We aren't going to fly after him, are we?" Thorfin asked with a dangerous edge to his voice. The other dwarves muttered in agreement.

"No. There is no need for that. He will return soon enough. Meanwhile we will scout around us and wait."

Bal-Simba was waiting for them at the crest of the dune. Outlined against the sky with sea breezes whipping the edges of his leopard skin loin cloth the big wizard was a most impressive sight. Wiz, who was a little chilly in spite of his travelling cloak, wondered how he managed to keep warm.

He heard their breathless report gravely and without comment. "We will have the thing taken back to the Capital for study," he told them. "Unless you think it is unsafe?"

"No reason to think that, Lord," Wiz said. "Although since we don't even know where it came from I can't guarantee anything."

Bal-Simba pursed his lips. "I think we may have a clue as to that. I have been talking to Weinrich and the other villagers. They say there has been a change in the weather recently."

"The weather?" Wiz said blankly.

"Folk who live by the sea are always sensitive to the weather. This far south on the Freshened Sea the pattern of wind and weather is constant, year to year."

"Village folk are usually wise in the ways of the immediate surroundings," Moira agreed. "But you say a change?"

"A fog bank about a day's sail to the east. A fog that does not lift and does not move. A place where a sailor can get lost because neither compass nor magic works properly."

"And they think this thing came out of the fog?" Wiz asked.

"It seems to have come from that direction."

"Lord, if I were you I'd search the hell out of that fog bank."

"That is already in train, Sparrow," Bal-Simba said.

Dragon Leader looked over his formation again and then turned his eyes back to the sea below. Two days ago his entire wing of almost fifty dragons had been brought together from their scattered patrol bases and sent hurrying south to Oak Island. Yesterday had been spent frantically setting up a makeshift base among the fisherfolk and putting out the first hasty patrols to try to define the edges of this strangeness.

Now Dragon Leader was taking his flight into the heart of this new thing. Every rider and dragon was at the peak of alertness. He could tell from the way they were flying that none of them liked it at all.

Even the formation reflected that. Instead of putting his dragons in line abreast or an echelon to cover the maximum territory, he had his first element above and behind his main formation for top cover. The rest of the patrol was pretty much line abreast, but they were closer together than normal so they could support each other quickly in case of trouble.

Every man and woman in the patrol understood the significance of that. This was a fighting formation, not a scouting one. Dragon Leader was going into this strange place loaded for bear.

Dragon Leader and his troopers were used to flying into the unknown. In a world where maps were components of spells rather than guides to terrain, he had often struck out over uncharted territory. He was used to magic as well. Save for the death spells on their iron arrows and a few odds and ends, dragon cavalry did not use magic. But they dealt with it constantly and most of them had faced it on more than one occasion.

Not that they had seen any magic here. So far he had seen nothing but sun-dappled sea and the occasional wheeling sea bird. Just what they should have seen, in other words.

But it wasn't right. There was something odd about this stretch of ocean, something that made his eyes hurt to look at it and made him queasy the deeper the patrol penetrated. It was like trying to look at two things at once, he decided. Two pictures that were almost but not exactly alike.

His dragon sensed it too. Whatever there was about this place, his mount didn't want anything to do with it. He signaled his patrol to extra alertness and pushed on. Then he reached for his communications crystal to report.

There—again there was strangeness. He managed to reach the Watcher on Oak Island, but the voice was weak and there were gaps, requiring several repeats to get the message through.

*Interference?* he thought as he replaced the crystal. But that didn't seem right either. He knew the effects of jamming spells on communications crystals. He had felt them often enough during the years of war against the Dark League. But this was more as if someone had substituted a poorly ensorceled crystal for his own. It was as if the spell on the crystal had suddenly become much weaker, less competent.

He noticed that the rhythm of his mount had changed as well. The dragon's wingbeats had increased, as if they were climbing instead of flying level. The beast wasn't exactly laboring, but he was definitely working harder. He did a quick calculation and decided that if this continued, the extra effort would reduce his patrol's flying time by one-third.

Down below the sea seemed the same, but this place was definitely different.

Off to his right one of the dragons flying top cover waggled its wings to attract attention. The riders on the right wing caught it as soon as Dragon Leader did and used hand signals to pass the information on to their commander.

Dragon Leader kneed his mount gently and his dragon banked gently left and right to acknowledge. Craning his neck he saw the rider rise in her saddle and raise both her arms above her head in the signal for land.

Dragon Leader hesitated for an instant and then signaled the entire patrol to turn toward the land.

The patrol was barely halfway into their turn when three gray shapes hurtled down on them out of the clouds.

"Break! Break!" Dragon leader screamed into his communications crystal. The warning was unnecessary, already the squadron was scattering like a flock of frightened chickens as the screaming intruders dived on them. Riders fumbled for their war bows as they twisted and dove in every direction, trying desperately to get away from their attackers.

In the end it was biology rather than maneuvering that saved them. Dragons have poor radar returns and the targeting radars on the robot fighters were unable to get a lock. Craig hadn't thought to equip his creations with cannon, so the planes were impotent against the dragons.

Of course the dragons were equally impotent against the planes. The aircraft were too fast and too unexpected. They swooped through the formation before a single rider could draw a bow or a single dragon could breathe fire. The planes made a tight curving climb back into the clouds and then they were gone.

The dragons didn't hang around either. The entire squadron dove for the wavetops and ran for home as fast as their wings could carry them.

"That," said Wiz grimly, "is definitely a jet fighter."

The recording had been frozen at the moment that the plane was climbing away from the dragon squadron. The view was almost from directly above and the outline and details were unmistakable.

"Looks like it was drawn by a fourteen-year-old," Danny said contemptuously. "It's a combination of a bunch of different planes."

"Notice that it's unmanned," Jerry said, sticking his finger into the image to point at the place where the cockpit should be. "Either these guys are real cautious about risking their necks or there aren't very many of them. Maybe only one or two."

"The main thing," Wiz said, getting up from the table, "is that we've got both dragons and jet fighters in the same air at the same time." He turned to Arianne, who had brought them the recording.

"You say the dragon riders were having trouble communicating?"

"Their voices were weak. And they said their dragons tired easily."

Jerry gestured and the image started moving again.

"Those planes don't look like they're doing any too well, either."

"Basically then," Wiz said, "both magic and technology work in that place, they just don't work very well."

"Sounds like an IBM shop," Jerry said.

"Whatever. Anyway that explains the drone. It was

only designed to work in that world and it got in here by accident."

"But it does not tell us who sent it," Moira said. "Or why. Those are the things we most need to know."

"It seems to me," Bal-Simba rumbled, "that we have two ways to find out. We can sit here and wait for whoever or whatever is sending these things to come to us or we can send our own scouts through to spy out this new world."

"Lord, that's not much of a choice," Wiz said. "So far these things aren't hostile, but they're sure not friendly. If we wait we may not like what we get."

"My thinking precisely, Sparrow. So we must go and see."

"Forgive me, Lord," Moira said, "but might that not be taken as an unfriendly act? True, they have not sent us embassies, but they have done us no harm either."

"Unfriendly, perhaps. But no more so than what they have done already. If you have a better suggestion, Lady, I am anxious to hear it."

"No, none, Lord. But I would not have us blunder into war unnecessarily."

"Fear not, Lady. We shall be very circumspect."

## Eleven
# A WALK IN THE WOODS

Across the river from the castle mount a line of hills ran down to the water's edge. Because the land was so rugged it had never been farmed. Instead it was left as a source of firewood, mushrooms and herbs for the denizens of the Capital.

It also made a pleasant place to walk on an Indian summer afternoon. Which is why Wiz, Danny and Jerry were picking their way through the woods as the sky started to darken from twilight to evening.

"I still think we ought to try to catch one of those drones," Danny said as the trio made their way down a trail that skirted the edge of the bluff.

"For the tenth time, no," Wiz told him. "And watch your step here, it's steep."

"We already have one drone," Jerry said, stepping to the side of the trail away from the cliff. "What do we need another one for?"

"Yeah but . . ."

A small black-clad shape hurtled out of the trees above them, screaming and waving a samurai sword as he came. The trio watched open-mouthed as he passed a good four feet to their left, missed the path completely and went over the edge of the cliff.

There were a couple of bounces, a thud and then something that sounded like a particularly inventive brand of profanity.

"What was that?" Jerry asked, peering over the edge.

"I think it was a ninja dwarf," Wiz said wonderingly.

Danny frowned. "That sounds like a character out of a D&D game." He thought for a second. "A *bad* D&D game."

*    *    *

Bal-Simba looked up from the scrying stone and blinked as if to clear his vision.

Wiz leaned across the table eagerly. "Well?"

"I sense malign influences aimed at you and a definite violent intent." The big black wizard rubbed his temples. "It appears, Sparrow, that someone is trying to kill you—again."

"Who?" Wiz asked. "And why? And why a dwarf, for Pete's sake?"

"That I could not discover," Bal-Simba said. "There is deadly intent and fixity of purpose. There are indications that non-mortals are involved, but that is all I know."

"Lisella?" Jerry suggested.

"Perhaps," Bal-Simba said slowly.

Wiz shook his head. "I don't think so. Lisella is subtle. There's nothing subtle about a dwarf jumping out of a tree waving a sword."

"Nothing very effective either," Danny said. "He missed us by a mile. Well," he amended under Wiz's glare, "a good six feet."

"Maybe that was Duke Aelric protecting you."

Wiz snorted. "More likely it was incompetence."

Bal-Simba stood up. "Whatever it was, I think it would be best if you stayed within the Wizard's Keep for a space."

"Fine by me. I've got more than enough to keep me busy for a couple of weeks."

"It may be longer than that," Bal-Simba told him. "Until we know who or what is behind this attack, you should stay where we can protect you."

"How long then?"

"I do not know. But my magic tells me whoever is after you is not easily discouraged. Until we have found the guiding hand you are in danger."

"You had to go after him yourself," Glandurg said disgustedly. "You couldn't wait for the rest of us."

"Well, you said he had to be slain quickly," Gimli said defensively. "There he was coming along the trail and there I was, so . . ." He shrugged.

"You're lucky he didn't turn you into a rabbit," his leader told him, "instead of just throwing you over the cliff."

"Didn't throw me," Gimli said sullenly.

"You jumped, I suppose?"

"Well . . ."

Glandurg looked around at the other dwarves. "Listen to me. No more striking half-heated, do you understand?"

"Not much chance of that," Snorri said. "The foreign wizard hasn't stirred from his castle for days."

"Then we have run him to earth and trapped like a rat!" Glandurg gloated.

"Begging my Lord's pardon, but how do we get him out of the trap now that we've got him in it?"

The dwarf leader frowned. There was more to this business than he had imagined and some of the details were proving quite annoying.

"We could tunnel in," one of the other dwarves suggested. "That whole bluff's nothing but limestone."

The others shifted and murmured approval. Tunnelling was something dwarves were comfortable with.

"How long would that take?" Glandurg demanded.

The dwarf who had made the suggestion eyed the distant cliff and castle.

"If we can sneak in close and drive the shaft steep up from the river level—oh—not more than two, three years, I should think," he finished brightly.

The leader shook his head. "That will not do, then. Our king promised the trolls speedy action." Besides

93

he knew in a general way that two or three years was a long time for a human to stay in one place.

"You got a better idea then?" the other challenged.

"Of course I have."

"What then?" the other persisted.

The leader reddened. "Don't be impertinent!"

"I'm not being impertinent, I just want to know what your idea is."

"I . . ." Over the shoulder of his questioner, the leader saw a flight of river swans glide down to the smooth river surface, their wings extended and motionless. As the swans touched down he had an inspiration.

"Backwards!" he proclaimed. "We will come at this alien wizard backwards!"

# Twelve
## PICNIC

Wiz paced to the window, looked down into the courtyard, paced back to his chair, sat down, picked up the scroll, got up and strode to the window again.

"I've got to get out of here," he said turning to face his wife.

Moira kept her eyes on the blouse she was embroidering with a pattern of moss rose and holly leaves. "So go."

"No, I mean I've got to get away from the Wizard's Keep."

Moira looked up from her work. "You never wanted to go outside the castle before."

"Yeah, but I knew I could do it any time then. Now I'm cooped up here and it's getting to me. I'm going stir crazy."

Moira put down her needlework and frowned. "With assassins about that is not safe, but if you feel you must, I can summon a troop of guardsmen . . ."

"No. That would be worse than not going out at all."

"Then you must stay in, I am afraid."

"Look, I could rig a spell that would protect me."

"Against what? Dwarves are clever and we do not know when or how they will strike again."

"We don't even know if they'll strike at all," Wiz said. "That may have been a fluke."

"Bal-Simba does not think so."

Wiz growled.

Moira took his hands in hers. "I am sorry, my love. I do not mean to sound unsympathetic. It is just that here you are safe. Outside the castle you cannot be protected."

"I feel like I'm wrapped in cotton wool and it's suffocating me," Wiz protested. "It's affecting my work. I just want to get away from everyone for a while."

Moira twisted her mouth sideways as she thought.

"I will speak to Bal-Simba," she said finally, "and see if he thinks it is safe."

"Where are we going anyway?" Wiz asked for the fifth time as Moira threw a light cloak over her new dress.

She smiled at him in the mirror as she adjusted the cloak on her otherwise bare shoulders. "To a special place. You will see."

Wiz stepped up behind her and put his hands around her waist. "Darling, any place is special with you. Especially in that dress."

"I am glad you like it, my Lord. I had it made specially for today." Then she turned practical in a flash. "But come, we do not want to be late for our own picnic. And bring the basket."

Moira didn't tell Wiz where they were going even when she took them on the Wizard's Way, so Wiz was completely unprepared for the place where they popped up.

A familiar flash of darkness and they were in a sunlit dell. Clear water leapt off the rocks above and splashed musically into the pool beside them. Sunlight poured into the open space about the pool and dappled through the trees and bushes around. The grass was bright green and tiny orange and red flowers spangled the meadow. In a quiet side of the pool, sweet blue irises reared above swordlike stands of green leaves. The bushes were blooming in clusters of pink and white and sometimes blood red. Where it was not stirred by the fall, the water was so clear Wiz could see minnows darting among the pebbles on the bottom.

"This is beautiful," Wiz said looking around him.

"Thank you, my Lord. Bal-Simba suggested it as a favorite picnic spot for those in the castle."

She forbore to mention Bal-Simba had also suggested it because it was easy to defend. Nor did she tell him the area had been swept by a troop of guardsmen and wizards only moments before their arrival. Nor did she mention the other precautions which had been taken.

Watching from the hilltop, Snorri the dwarf could not believe his luck. When they weren't working on Glandurg's contraptions, the dwarves had been scouting through the forest and surrounding countryside, hoping for something that would give them any entry into the castle. He had suspected something when he saw the guardsmen searching the dell. He had hidden himself among the bushes and now his patience had been rewarded.

Their quarry himself! Without guards and completely at his ease. The dwarf's hand crept to the sword strapped across his back. A quick charge and . . .

Then Snorri paused and frowned. There was magic about this strange wizard, and powerful magic at that. He did not recognize the spell, but its import was clear enough. Not only was the wizard shielded from violence, but any attempt at it would bring swift and deadly retribution. Protected as he was he could not be shot, cleaved, hacked, bashed or in any other wise attacked.

The dwarf bit his lip in frustration. He was closer to his prey than any of the party had been since the first day when that idiot Gimli tried. Yet he was as blocked from overt violence as if the wizard was still within the castle.

But that was only *overt* violence! Slowly, very slowly, Snorri put his hand into his belt pouch and felt the small tightly wrapped packet at the bottom. Then he turned his attention back to the protection spell.

Finally he smiled. If his face had not been hidden by his hood it would have been a most unpleasant smile.

A fraction of an inch at a time, Snorri began to crawl forward toward the pair on the blanket.

Even if Wiz had been looking for the dwarf he couldn't have seen him and Wiz's mind—and eyes—were on other things.

Moira had laid aside her cloak and was bustling about spreading the blanket and laying out things from the hamper. As she came past, he reached out and pulled her to him for a long kiss.

"I thought you said you were hungry," Moira said, slipping from his grasp.

Wiz looked deep into his wife's green eyes. "There are all kinds of hunger."

"Food first," the hedge witch said firmly. "Then we shall see what else this blanket is good for."

She settled herself on the blanket with Wiz beside her and took out a green bottle.

"Currant wine for me," she said as she set the bottle to one side, "and for you, blackmoss tea." She wrinkled her nose as she pulled the earthen jug from the hamper.

"How you can stand to drink that stuff is beyond me," she told her husband, as Wiz poured the dark brew into a mug. "Especially when it is cold."

"Iced tea is a tradition where I come from. And it really isn't that bad once you get used to it."

"Ugh!" said Moira.

Wiz raised his mug. "To us."

Moira raised her goblet in response. Both drank and their eyes locked. Wiz eased closer, gazing deeply into his wife's wonderful green eyes.

"Pigs feet!" she said suddenly.

"Huh?"

"Pickled pigs feet." Moira turned and reached into the basket. "Shauna sent some along."

"And you don't like blackmoss tea," he said, setting his mug down.

Moira unwrapped Shauna's contribution. "But blackmoss tea is disgusting," she said seriously. "Shauna's pig's feet are delicious."

"Ugh," said Wiz firmly.

Neither of them noticed the black gloved hand that snaked stretched out of the bushes behind them and passed over Wiz's mug. Nor did they see the surface of the tea roil briefly and then settle back into oily stillness.

Worming his way backwards Snorri kept his eyes on the couple. Wizard the Sparrow might be, and lucky he certainly was, but neither wizardry nor luck would save any mortal who consumed the powerful corrosive in that cup. Even gold itself would dissolve under the puissant acid formed when the magic powder met water.

Snorri was clever, but common sense wasn't his strong point.

"Well," said Moira, "I also brought along some of those meat pies you are so fond of."

"Now that's more like it. Darling, I don't know how to thank you for setting this all up. It's wonderful."

Moira picked up her goblet and took a sip. "I am glad you are enjoying yourself. And as for thanking me, perhaps we can think of something."

Without taking his eyes off Moira, Wiz picked up his mug and raised it toward his lips.

At which point the bottom fell out of the mug and the tea splashed all over the blanket.

"I think I made it too strong," Wiz said dumbly.

"Wiz, look!" Moira pointed at the blanket where the tea had splashed. The fabric was dissolving in smoking ruin and bare black earth was showing through beneath.

99

"Definitely too strong."

"You ninny, it's been poisoned!" Moira raised both her arms and gestured. Instantly five guardsmen and a blue-robed wizard popped through about them. The guardsmen surrounded Wiz and Moira and the wizard swung his staff over his head, throwing a glittering circle of protection around the group. Already Moira had started the spell to take them back to the castle along the Wizard's Way.

Back in their quarters Wiz and Moira surveyed the ruins of their picnic. The guardsmen had brought the basket and utensils back, but the food and drink had been disposed of as possibly poisoned. The remaining contents of the basket had tested safe, Arianne assured them. But somehow it didn't make up for the rest.

Moira looked sadly at the still-smoldering remains of the blanket. For a moment Wiz thought she would cry.

"I'm sorry about the blanket, darling."

Moira looked up at him, smiled and clutched his arm. "I'm glad it was only the blanket."

# Thirteen
## AIR ATTACK

Glandurg put his hands on his hips and surveyed the results of his men's labors. The forest clearing had been converted into an impromptu woodworking shop as dwarves dragged felled trees into position, rived them into billets and shaped the billets according to his direction.

His original idea had been to have the griffins fly them into the castle, but the griffins had flatly refused. Well, so be it. This would work just as well and in truth he had more confidence in dwarvish craftsmanship than he did in griffins.

Already four frames lay scattered about under the cover of the trees, complete except for their covering. The covering had arrived this morning, borne by griffins from the hold of the Mid-Northeastern Dwarves of the Southern Forest Range. The bolts of spider silk had been accompanied by a letter from King Tosig complaining about the expense, but Glandurg had barely glanced at that. It was just like his quasi-uncle to be preoccupied with such trifling details.

Glandurg moved among his companions, instructing them, pointing out defects and in general making a nuisance of himself as the other dwarves fitted and tied the pieces together. He paused to inspect the hide glue soaking in a cooking pot off to one side of the clearing and for the twentieth time that morning congratulated himself on his plan.

"Brilliant," he said to no one in particular. "They will never expect us to attack from the air!"

"Bloody good reason for that," muttered one of the dwarves as he bound a rib to a wing spar. The leader glared at him but he did not raise his head to meet Glandurg's eyes.

\* \* \*

For several hours after their return, Wiz and Moira moped about their apartment. It was like going on a picnic and being rained out, Wiz thought glumly.

"Look at this," Moira said ruefully, "I have stains on my gown."

She held the garmet up for Wiz to see. Sure enough, the back and one of the sleeves were stained with the red wine that had slopped out of her goblet.

"Looks like a job for a cleaning spell," Wiz said.

"Alas, the gown itself is magical."

"I wondered how that thing stayed up."

She smiled roguishly. "Men are supposed to wonder, my Lord." Then she looked down and sighed. "But the magic of this gown interferes with the spells we use to clean clothes. My Lord, do you know any cleaning spells?"

Wiz considered. For the mightiest wizard in all the world his repertoire of magic was rather limited. He could think of a dozen ways to incinerate the gown, but offhand he didn't know a single one to clean it.

"Well, I haven't been looking for one." He stopped and snapped his fingers. "Wait a minute, I know what you need. A detergent!"

"What does it deter?" Moira asked blankly.

"Not a deterrent, a detergent. Something that will lock onto the particles of stain and bind them to water so they will rinse away. I'll need to talk to Danny and Jerry. But we should be able to whip something up."

In a few minutes of quick conversation and some scribbles on the ever-present slates the three programmers had worked out a spell to make a detergent.

"We need something to mix it in." Wiz started toward the kitchen.

"You are not experimenting in one of my pots," Moira said, stepping in front of him.

"How about a bucket?" Danny suggested. "There's one out in the hall."

"One of the maids must have left it there," Moira said. "Honestly, I think they become more slovenly every day."

"In this case it's a good thing," Wiz said as he made for the door.

The bucket was half-full of dirty water, but that didn't bother Wiz. "After all, when we get done with the spell it won't be water," he explained to the others.

A few quickly done spells, a quick call for an Emac and the spell was under way.

"You know, this gets easier all the time," Jerry said. "I don't ever remember being able to whip up programs this fast back in California."

Wiz shrugged. "Superior tools."

Jerry looked unconvinced.

"I think the system is actually helping us," Danny said. "Sometimes when I'm putting a spell together it's like the magic is reading my mind."

"In your case that's scary," Wiz said. "Whoops. Here's the operating demon."

The demon was small but muscular. It was clad in a white T-shirt and tight-fitting pants. Its eyebrows were white, its head was shaved and a gold earring dangled from one pointed ear.

"This is like watching old television commercials," Jerry said.

"Just be glad it wasn't a big arm punching out of the bucket," Wiz said.

The demon nodded at them and dived into the bucket. There was a trace of a splash and suddenly the dirty water had turned to something clear and viscous. There was no sign of the demon and the stuff looked like machine oil and smelled like nothing in particular.

"That's it?" Moira asked.

"I guess so."

Danny dipped his forefinger into the liquid. He tried to force his thumb and forefinger together and they slid over each other quickly and silently.

"Boy," Danny said admiringly, "that stuff's slicker than greased owl shit."

"Detergents generally are," Jerry said.

"So we use this in place of water?" Moira asked.

"Good grief no! You'll only need a dear little bit of it, maybe a few drops, in a whole bucket of water."

Moira frowned. "At that rate, I think we have enough to clean the entire castle for the next year."

"Oh," Wiz looked abashed. "That's not a problem, is it?"

"Not really. I will get a bottle from the stillroom tomorrow and for now we will leave the bucket in the alcove with the mops and brooms." She nodded to a tapestry hanging in the corridor near their apartment door. Such hangings were used to conceal this World's equivalent of broom closets. "It will be safe there on the shelf."

"It's simple, you see," Glandurg said, gesturing to the newly completed wing. "We'll just fly over the walls of the castle, as easy as birds."

"We're not birds," said Thorfin.

"Anyway we don't know how to fly them," Snorri added.

"You built them, didn't you? You can fly them."

"I built a cradle once," another dwarf said. "That doesn't mean I know how to have a baby."

"All right then," said Glandurg in disgust. "We'll practice until you do know how to fly them."

All the dwarves looked expectantly at their leader and Glandurg realized he had just backed himself into a corner.

"Here we are," he said with more confidence than he felt. "You pick it up like this, grab the holding bar like this and you maneuver by shifting your weight or twisting the bar. Now what could be simpler?"

"Telling isn't showing," Thorfin said dubiously.

"Well, keep watching," Glandurg snapped. He hoisted the wing, ran forward and leapt into the air.

The result was a sort of grotesque hop that carried him perhaps two feet up and six feet forward. He barely got his feet down in time and half-stumbled on landing.

"Not much flying there," said Snorri.

"Well, I didn't get going fast enough. Here, let me show you again."

This time Glandurg went to the far end of the clearing and came pounding across the open space at a dead run. He reached the top of a small hillock and again jumped into the air. The result was a flight of perhaps a dozen feet.

"There, you see," he puffed triumphantly as he came back to join his followers.

"Not very well," Snorri said. "Can you do it again?"

Glandurg glared at him. "I will not. You do it."

"Don't know how," Snorri replied.

Glandurg glared at him. "Not enough, is it? Very well. I'll show you some flying." He turned and made for the largest tree at the edge of the clearing. "Come along," he flung over his shoulder. "You'll see right enough."

When he reached the base of the tree he started to climb. With a lot of grunting and heaving he managed to reach the branches about thirty feet up. From there he swarmed upward until he was nearly a hundred feet above his fellows.

"Pass the wing up," he shouted down.

"How?" Thorfin shouted back.

Glandurg bridled. "Don't be insubordinate."

Finally, with the aid of a line thrown to Glandurg, they were able to get the wing up to him. The others watched as Glandurg wormed his way into the contraption while balancing precariously on a branch.

"Watch," he commanded, and launched himself out into empty air.

Considering he had never flown in his life, it wasn't too bad. He dived too steeply and had to pull back sharply to keep from ploughing into the ground. He overcorrected and soared up again, slipping off to the right as he lost longitudinal control. He managed to bank sharply left, thereby avoiding the trees at the edge of the clearing and he was still turning when the ground came up to meet him. He moved further back to bleed off more airspeed, brought the nose up too far and came down in something that was more a poorly controlled stall than a landing.

The shock rattled Glandurg's teeth and drove him to his knees. It also snapped the left wing spar just outboard of his left shoulder.

"You see?" Glandurg said as he staggered to meet the pack of dwarves running toward him. "You see how easy it is.

"Here now," he said to Thorfin. "You try it."

"Will not."

"What?"

"I ain't going," Thorfin said stubbornly.

Glandurg marched over and stuck his face in Thorfin's. "I'm the leader here and I say you bloody are going!" he roared.

"You can be the leader all you want and I'm bloody not going," Thorfin said in the same unyielding tone. "No way I could handle one of them things. I'm scared of heights."

" 'S truth," Gimli said. "I watched him on the flight here. Fair like to mess his pants, he was."

Thorfin glared at the purveyor of this unsought bit of support, but he stood firm. "I ain't going up in one of them things. Not even for practice."

"You would betray your oath?" Glandurg heaped scorn into his words.

"I ain't going back on my oath, but the oath didn't say anything about playing at being a bird."

Glandurg sensed that he was facing his first command crisis. He decided to resort to his ultimate threat.

"You will or you'll be sorry."

"You can't make me sorrier than I would be if I took one of those things. What could you do to me that's worse?" The other dwarves shifted uneasily and one or two murmured support for Thorfin.

Glandurg considered the question. It dawned on him there really wasn't anything he could do. The members of his band were sworn to kill the wizard, but Glandurg had not sworn them to obey him—in part because he doubted they would take such an oath.

However a successful commander remains flexible in the face of unexpected opposition.

"All right then, you won't have to fly. You and anyone else who feels the way you do can create a diversion by attacking the castle from below. There won't be as much glory in it, of course." He let the scorn drip from his voice. "But when the attack starts you can swim the river and climb the castle walls."

Thorfin nodded. "That suits," he said stolidly.

In the event two other dwarves decided they'd rather swim and climb than fly. That left Glandurg and eight others to practice gliding out of trees.

By the end of the day each dwarf had made five flights. It was a most successful training session, Glandurg decided. They were all alive and they still had half the wings undamaged. They could even land in the general direction of their target most of the time.

They needed more training. But meanwhile they could continue to practice with the remaining gliders and work on repairing the damaged wings.

It wasn't the woods, or even the streets of the Capital outside the castle, but there was solitude in this place, and a lovely view.

*Well*, Wiz thought to himself, *at least I'm safe up here.*

Glandurg shifted uneasily and grasped his holding bar even tighter. This had seemed like a brilliant inspiration when he had both feet on the ground. Now, dangling hundreds of feet above the river, he was less certain.

The wind whipped loose a strand of hair from under his hood and slapped it across his eyes. Instinctively he reached to push it away and for a heart-stopping instant he nearly lost his grip. He clutched the holding bar and squeezed his eyes tightly shut to blot out the scenery passing below him. Above him the griffin flew on, oblivious to his cargo's antics.

*I am the leader,* Glandurg reminded himself. *I must see where I am going.* He forced his eyes open. The castle was coming up fast. Carefully he reached into his shirt and removed the indicator. The glowing arrow inside the crystal sphere pointed straight at the battlements. Glandurg squinted through the wind. Yes, there was a lone figure high on the castle walls.

For an instant the dwarf was so exhilarated he forgot to be afraid. The Sparrow himself and out in the open! Truly this was his lucky day.

"Release the wings," the dwarf commanded.

Off to the west Wiz saw a flock of pigeons or turkeys or some other kind of heavy-bodied birds. As they came closer to the castle he could see they were too large to be pigeons. Turkeys then.

*Hey, wait a minute! There aren't any turkeys in this World!* Not only that, but each one seemed to have two sets of wings. *Biplane birds?*

Then each of the birds seemed to split in two and half of each bird dove toward Wiz.

The dwarves had taken good care to build their wings strong and light. They had taken less care to learn how they reacted in flight and no care at all to understand the mass of thermals, updrafts and cross currents that swirled around the castle on a warm autumn afternoon.

Nine dwarves aimed themselves straight at the lone figure on the parapet without hesitation or thought for consequences. So naturally the nine dwarves went everywhere *but* to their target.

In his eagerness to reach his prey Glandurg had dived too steeply. He came in fast and low, headed straight for the castle wall. Frantically he pulled back on his control bar in an effort to avoid smashing into the stone. His wing swooped up, lost airspeed and teetered on the verge of a stall as it approached Wiz. Then Glandurg hit the updraft along the face of the wall, rose like an elevator and sailed majestically over the wall a good twenty feet above his gaping prey to drop into the courtyard behind.

Ragnar took a lesson from his leader's approach and set his height correctly. But his griffin had been well behind Glandurg's and he had to turn to the right in order to come in on Wiz. The turn brought him into the turbulence in the lee of one of the wall towers and he was tossed like a leaf to land nearly a hundred yards further down the wall, almost at the feet of an astonished guardsman.

By the time Ragnar had untangled himself from the wreckage of his wing the guardsman had drawn his sword. The dwarf scampered off with the guard in hot pursuit.

Meanwhile the other flying dwarves had arrived. Some went left, some right and some high. One or two threatened to smash into the wall and had to abort, hauling their wings around in tight turns and then dropping away into the valley.

The Wizard's Keep was boiling like an overturned anthill. Alarm horns rang out from the towers along the walls, guardsmen raced frantically to their stations, dragon cavalry poured out of their cave aeries and Wiz was surrounded by guards and wizards and hustled away to safety.

Off in the distance the griffins circled in a tight knot, watching intently and making noises that sounded suspiciously like laughter.

Thorfin wrinkled his nose in disgust. The wind must have shifted and now he would have to breathe dragon stink all the rest of the way up the cliff.

Nasty beasts! No one but a mortal would think of keeping them. And as for riding them . . . He shivered involuntarily. Still, the dragons were all in their caves and his target was above him.

He levered himself up onto the outcrop and found himself nose to nose with a dragon.

It was not a very large dragon, but then Thorfin was not a very large dwarf. More to the point, the dragon was safely resting on a ledge and Thorfin was clinging to the cliff face by his toes and fingers. His sword was strapped across his back in a position more picturesque than practical and the blade wasn't designed for dragon slaying anyway. All things considered, the dwarf was at a serious disadvantage.

Thorfin did the best thing he could think of. He squinched his eyes tightly shut, turned his head away and pressed himself as tight against the cliff as he could manage.

Because they are both greedy for treasure, dwarves and dragons are natural enemies. However like cats and dogs, this is learned behavior. Thorfin had enough experience to know about dwarves and dragons. The Little Red Dragon had never even seen

110

a dwarf before. It divided its time between roaming the programmers' quarters of the castle and sunning itself on the ledges on the cliff beneath the castle walls.

The dragon nudged the black-clad figure experimentally. It went "whoof" in a satisfying fashion.

Little Red Dragon nudged harder. This time he was met by a louder "whoof" and a string of interesting words.

This was more fun than annoying the castle cats! The dragon braced all four feet against the rock and pushed with all his strength.

Under the impact of the head butt Thorfin lost his grip on the rock and went hurtling down toward the river, screaming curses as he fell.

"We chased six of the little buggers out of the castle, Lord," the guard captain told Wiz as they made their way back to his quarters that evening. "Plus a couple more that never made it over the walls. That was all of them, we think."

"You think?"

"That's why we are here, Lord."

"This is weird," Wiz said. "I've never even *met* a dwarf, I mean socially, and now there are a bunch of them trying to kill me. Why?"

"Ask us after we capture one. But by tomorrow this castle will be dwarf-proof."

Wiz knew that Jerry, Danny and several of the Mighty were already erecting a dwarf-repellent spell around the Wizard's Keep. "I just hope it works," he said as they came up the back stairs and into the hall that led to his apartment. "I've been jumped, poisoned and attacked from the air—or they've tried to do all that anyway. I'm getting tired of it."

*Fear not, mortal*, thought Ragnar as he watched the party approach from the curtained alcove where he lay hidden. *You will not be tired of anything much longer.*

With so many mortal soldiers about there was no

111

hope of fighting his way clear. So be it. He would fulfill his band's vow at the cost of his own heart's blood. They could kill him but not even twice that number of mortal warriors could protect the strange wizard from a pantherlike spring from his hiding place.

Ragnar crouched and drew his sword with a flourish that knocked a bucket off the shelf above him. The humans started at the noise, but Ragnar, oblivious to the liquid that drenched him, leaped forward with his sword brandished above his head. The guardsmen went for their weapons, but the dwarf was already in their midst and his blade was flashing toward his sworn foe.

His blade was still flashing when his feet shot out from under him and he went scooting between the startled guardsmen flat on his back with his arms and legs waving in all directions. His sword made glancing contact with one guardsman's mailed thigh and then he was through them and sliding down the corridor, his passage lubricated by the super detergent that had soaked him and his clothes.

Wiz watched stunned as the dwarf whisked down the corridor, trailing curses, until he reached the stairs, where his cries ended in a *bump bump bump*.

One of the guardsmen moved to follow and immediately went to his knees in the trail of detergent Ragnar had left behind. Two others went more cautiously, hugging the walls of the corridor. Four others pushed Wiz back against the wall and stood shoulder to shoulder around him, protecting him with a wall of living flesh.

"It seems there were seven dwarves, my Lord," the guard captain said sheepishly. "Perhaps we had better stay with you until the wizards finish their spell."

"Yeah," Wiz said shakily. "Perhaps you had better."

It was a battered, dispirited group of dwarves that met in the clearing that night. Ragnar was the last to return, stripped to his loincloth to rid himself of the effects of the super-detergent and undwarvishly clean from swimming the river with traces of it on his body. While he dried himself by the fire and swilled down a mug of steaming soup, his companions considered what their next move should be.

"We learned much today," Glandurg said as he paced up and down before the fire.

"We learned dwarves are not meant to fly," came a voice from the edge of the circle.

"We learned the plan of the castle and of our enemy's defenses," Glandurg shot back, determined to put the best possible face on the day's events. "If we did not accomplish our objective, at least we gathered valuable knowledge."

"And how do we use that knowledge?" asked one of the other dwarves.

"We will find a way, but first we need a new strategy."

"We need a new leader," Snorri muttered.

Glandurg reddened. "Someone who attacks with poison and kills the cup no doubt."

It was Snorri's turn to redden.

"Can't we just say we tried and go home?" asked Gimli, the youngest of the dwarves.

"*No!*" Glandurg roared. "We are sworn to this quest. Our honor and the honor of all dwarfdom rests with us. Others may turn and run, but I will pursue our pledge to the bitter end."

"Bitter it is likely to be," said Thorfin sourly, nursing an arm in a sling.

"That is as it is," Glandurg said loftily. "The important thing is how we may fulfill our vow."

"Well, we're not going to fly in," Ragnar said from the fire.

"The human wizards have been busy," Thorfin said. "Now the whole castle is closed to us."

113

"Unlikely it is that this Sparrow will venture beyond the walls," Snorri added.

"We must think," Glandurg said. "We must await our opportunity and think in the meanwhile." He dropped down on a stump and ostentatiously rested his chin on his fist in a pose meant to suggest to all deep thought. In their own ways all of his followers imitated him.

It was a very imposing sight, but none of them had the faintest idea what to do next.

# Fourteen

# VIRTUAL UN-REALITY

"This is hopeless," Wiz said finally. "We've just got to have more information."

The dusty smell of hay and cattle still clung to the programmers' workroom, legacy of its days as a cow barn. Most of the stalls along the walls were no longer used as programmers' cubicles and the people who were left could have fitted into a room inside the keep proper, but the programming team kept the Bull Pen, partly because it was easier than moving and partly because of the aptness of the name. In a little while they were settled around the long plank table down the center. "We can't very well go knocking on the gate," Wiz said.

"Perhaps we can do exactly that," Moira said slowly. She turned down the table to Arianne. "Lady, does magic work within that castle?"

Arianne's brow furrowed as she considered. "As best we can tell. We cannot see through their barriers, but they seem to use magic within it."

"Then perhaps someone can go knocking at the gate of the castle. Or at least the semblance of someone."

Arianne's jaw dropped. Then she beamed and nodded. "Of course! Yes, Lady, I think that would work very nicely."

"When I proposed this, I did not have you in mind," Moira grumbled as she watched the preparations. She, Wiz and Arianne were jammed into Arianne's workroom off the main courtyard of the keep.

As one of the Mighty, Arianne rated a tower to herself, but as Bal-Simba's assistant she spent most of her time doing administrative work and she preferred a place closer to the meeting halls of the main keep.

"Come on, darling, you said yourself this isn't dangerous," Wiz said from the stool in the middle of the room.

"She said no such thing," Arianne said sharply, looking up from her work table. "She said you cannot be harmed physically. But there will be a psychic link between you and the simulacrum."

"Not like a video game, huh?"

"Not a game of any sort," Arianne repeated firmly. "So be very careful and pull out at the first sign of trouble."

"That's right about now."

"There are many others who could go."

Wiz shook his head. "Nope. We need someone who knows enough programming to understand what he sees. That's me or Jerry. I'm higher ranking so they're more likely to talk to me."

Arianne nodded. She reached under the workbench and produced a bag of black velvet.

"Put this over your head."

Wiz looked at the hood dubiously.

"Is this necessary?"

"Not absolutely. But it will help you concentrate."

"Let's do without it then. That looks too much like what they put on someone before they hang him."

Arianne shrugged. "Your choice, Lord. But I will leave it around your shoulders should you want it."

She stretched to reach a shelf above her workbench and took down a carved wooden box about the size of a cigar box. Opening it, she hesitated over the contents before reaching in and removing a gnarled, forked root about the size of her hand.

"I have never seen one so large," Moira said as she came from her place by the door to get a closer look.

"Plucked from the earth by the full moon of mid-Winter," Arianne told her proudly. "It is the best I have."

116

"The bigger the root, the better, eh?" Wiz said from his stool.

"There are other factors, but basically yes. Now, if everyone is ready?"

Wiz nodded, Moira stepped back to the door and Arianne laid the root on the stone floor. Then she produced an ebony wand decorated with silver leaves and jeweled flowers.

Suddenly she spun and jabbed the wand at Wiz. He started and flinched at the unexpected move. Slowly and carefully she brought the wand away from Wiz and pointed it at the mandrake root, all the while keeping it perfectly level as if balancing an egg on the end.

Wiz looked down at the root. It seemed the same, but he felt dizzy and lightheaded, as if he hadn't eaten all day. He thought about trying to clear his head and decided against it.

Again Arianne turned and jabbed the wand at Wiz. Again a wave of lightheadedness rose up in him. As she turned back toward the root he could hear the spell she was muttering more clearly, although she had not raised her voice.

A third time she jabbed and pointed at the root. Wiz felt as if he was dividing like an amoeba. He saw the workroom from two perspectives at once, as if his vision had doubled. He closed his eyes, but both sets of eyes closed and he was completely in the dark. For a moment he felt nauseous and he took two deep breaths at once to try to settle his stomach.

With his eyes kept tightly shut, he reached up with all four of his hands and groped for the hood. He pulled it over his head and opened his eyes to darkness and to light.

He turned and faced himself and the two women.

"This is sooo weird," he said wonderingly in reverb duet.

"You will get used to it," Arianne said. "Concentrate on the simulacrum and try to ignore your body."

Wiz tried to move around the workroom to get the feel of his new body. At first both his standing body and his body on the stool tried to move together. He concentrated fiercely on the standing body and bit by bit his other body relaxed. Finally his "vision" fused completely into his new body. Distantly and dimly he could feel himself sitting on the stool and his breath sucking through the black velvet hood but he had to concentrate to feel it.

It wasn't a perfect illusion. His sense of touch worked very poorly and his sense of smell seemed to work not at all. But he could see and hear perfectly and his balance was good enough.

He faced his audience and spread his arms.

"Ta-DAH," Wiz said. He made a low bow and instantly regretted it as a wave of dizziness washed over him. He barely managed to avoid falling on his face.

"Can you move all right?" Arianne asked.

"I'm still kind of clumsy." He took another turn around the room, more confidently this time. "Okay, let's do it."

With Arianne and Moira trailing, he stepped out into the bright sunshine of the courtyard. He was particularly proud that he didn't trip over the raised sill of the workroom.

Jerry was waiting in the chantry with Bal-Simba and a couple of other blue-robed wizards. They had decided to have someone else send the simulacrum to the castle because Wiz was afraid he might transport himself instead of his image if he tried to walk the Wizard's Way unaided.

As "Wiz" and the others came into the room Jerry squinted at him.

"Gee, it really isn't you, is it? I can't tell even this close."

"Let us hope no one else can either."

Bal-Simba reached out and clapped the image on the shoulder. Then he grinned broadly at Arianne, showing all his pointed teeth.

"It even feels right! A work of art, Lady."

The usually unemotional wizardess dimpled and dropped a curtsey in return.

One of the other blue robes, a lean man with thinning dark hair named Juvian, bustled forward. "Everything you see and hear will be recorded." He tapped the glowing blue sphere he held in his palm. "It will not be necessary to stare or to overtly memorize anything. Keep your eyes moving and try to see as much as you possibly can."

Arianne stepped up beside him. "You know the recall signal. Use it at any sign of danger. We will be watching and if we see anything we will pull you back." She laid a hand on his shoulder and her brown eyes bored into his.

"Remember Sparrow, even though your body remains here you can be hurt. Do not become careless."

Wiz gulped and nodded.

A flash of darkness and Wiz found "himself" standing in front of the huge gate of the castle.

The doors were gigantic. Throwing his head back and squinting up, Wiz estimated they were at least a hundred feet high. They were made of some greenish metal with a zig-zag crack down the center where they met. The portal they were set in was made of some smooth pale blue substance with softly rounded forms and no joints anywhere, as if it and the walls of the castle had been cast in a single piece. The whole thing reminded Wiz of something out of a 1930's comic strip.

There was no sign of a knocker or a doorbell. He thought about knocking, but if the thing was as thick as it looked he doubted he would be heard inside.

*Well, nothing ventured . . .*

He stepped up to the door and pounded three times with his fist. The door boomed and rang from the blows in a way that made Wiz's whole body shiver.

For a minute nothing happened. Then he stepped back from the door and a motion on the portal caught his attention.

What he had taken as parts of the rounded decoration were futuristic gun turrets. The barrels poking out of the turrets were equally futuristic, with cooling fins and streamlined muzzle brakes. There were at least six of them and all of them were pointing directly at him.

*Okay, so now they know I'm here.* He decided the best thing to do was to act nonchalant, as if he went calling on strange castles every day. He thought about trying to whistle, but he wasn't sure he could. So he settled for folding his arms and looking around.

Around him the red sand desert stretched away in gentle folds. The landscape was dotted here and there with dark green spindly bushes and an occasional clump of something that looked like it might have been cactus if it had known what a cactus was supposed to be. The sun was high in the sky and the reflection off the greenish metal of the gates was enough to make him squint.

Oddly, when you got this close to it the castle wasn't very impressive. Standing next to it was like standing next to a mountain instead of something manmade. Even the gate was huge and impersonal. Somehow that made it less imposing, not more.

*Well, it's not their taste in architecture I'm concerned about.*

Wiz couldn't sense temperature very well through the simulacrum, but the glare of the sun and the bright reflection off the gate told him it had to be hot out here. He wondered if he was sweating.

Then the door started to move. Wiz opened his mouth and nearly choked on his carefully prepared greeting when he saw what was behind it.

120

The robot was eight feet tall with glowing red eyes and a glossy black skin. It was human-shaped, but it wasn't what Wiz would call reassuring.

"You rannggg?" it asked in a voice like the bell of doom. It would have been even more impressive if the robot had been talking to the visitor instead of the gatepost.

Wiz dredged up the last of his nonchalance. "Yeah. I'm Wiz Zumwalt and I'm here to see the boss."

The robot paused as if considering the information. A crackling blue nimbus played over its head and down its right shoulder.

"Commeee," it commanded.

The head cocked to one side and jerked upright. The arms jerked up, elbows bent, bringing the hands to shoulder level. The robot spun on its heel, nearly lunged into the gate, recovered and strode off, weaving from side to side like a drunken sailor.

"Lead on, Lurch," Wiz said to the robot's departing back, then hurried after him. The guns tried to track him even inside the portal.

The hall beyond the gate was so gargantuan that Wiz couldn't make out the other end. High above shafts of sunlight washed down through the haze that hid the ceiling.

A rather thick haze, Wiz noticed as he strode along after his jerking, zig-zagging guide. It wasn't just that the place was big, it needed a good vacuuming. He noticed that both he and the robot were leaving footprints in the film of reddish dust on the marble tiled floor.

After a few hundred yards they turned off into a side corridor. Its proportions were more to human scale, but it was round and a trickle of water down the center made the going harder. The robot splashed along unconcerned, but Wiz tried to keep his feet dry by staying to the side. He had to hurry even more to keep up with the robot.

Even though Wiz's temperature sense didn't work very well, it was so cold he shivered a bit. The metal walls of the tunnel were filmed with condensation which trickled down and accumulated at the bottom of the corridor.

*That's where the water comes from,* he thought. *They need a little work on their climate control system.* He looked down at the water in the center of the tunnel and saw it was slimed with green algae.

*Not to mention their housekeeping.*

A short way down the corridor was a door, round and massive like a bank vault's. The robot stopped short and waited as Wiz came up beside him.

Just as Wiz reached the robot the door popped open and clanged against the corridor wall. Wiz jumped back to keep from being crushed. His guide remained impassive even though the door missed him by a fraction of an inch.

*A few other little things they need work on, too.* As he set off in pursuit of the robot he wondered if that was supposed to have been an automated door opener or a man trap.

Another few hundred feet brought them to a bank of elevators that looked like something out of a New York office building—if you ignored the remote controlled machine guns covering the lobby and the gargoyles perched over the elevator doors.

After a brief wait one set of doors banged open and Wiz and the robot stepped into an elevator—more accurately, they stepped *down* into an elevator, since the car had stopped about a foot below the floor.

It took a long, long time to reach the top. Wiz wasn't sure whether that was because they were going so high or because the elevator worked about as well as the robot guide. They jerked, lurched, sputtered, speeded up and slowed down until Wiz lost all sense of how far they had come. He wasn't even too sure they had gone straight up.

122

At last the doors flew open and they stepped out into another corridor. This one was broad and clean, at least. The floor was tiled in jade-green material, the walls were malachite and the ceilings and wall decorations were in polished gold. It was like being inside a Faberge Easter egg and it removed any last lingering doubts Wiz might have had about his hosts' taste.

The robot lurched drunkenly down the corridor and caromed off the wall, knocking off chips of malachite and bending a golden wall sconce.

At the end of the hall was a bronze portal. The robot stopped before it and made a motioning gesture with its arm that nearly took Wiz's head off. Then it froze.

Wiz recovered from the accidental assault, realized his guide had signaled him through the door, saw that the robot wasn't likely to make any other dangerous moves, and stepped past.

The room was as out-of-scale as everything else in the castle. One whole side and half the ceiling was picture-window-size panes of glass giving a panoramic, eagle's-eye view of red desert and sere mountains. The place was fitted out like a laboratory, or perhaps a control room, with panels of dials and switches everywhere, the odd arc of electricity here and there and huge pieces of unidentifiable apparatus scattered about. The whole room reeked of electricity and danger.

There were two humans waiting for him there.

The younger one reminded Wiz a little of the way Danny had looked when they first met, kind of soft and unformed. The other one was a few years older, harder and leaner. He was sitting on one of the control consoles with his legs dangling. Even though he was relaxed, there was something predatory in the way he looked at Wiz.

For a minute no one said anything.

"Uh, hi. I'm Wiz Zumwalt. From Cupertino." His voice was almost lost in the huge room.

"We know who you are," the older one said. He reached behind him, picked up a beer bottle and took a swig. No one made a move to offer Wiz a drink.

"Lurch there is really something," Wiz said brightly.

"He's an early model," the younger one said. "The ones we build now are a lot better."

His companion grinned nastily. "*Much* better."

"Very impressive."

The silence stretched on.

"I'm Craig Scott," the young one said at last. "This is Mikey Baker."

"Craig talks too much," Mikey said conversationally. "Don't you, Craig?"

Craig wilted.

"Pleased to meet you," Wiz said.

"Yeah?"

Again the silence stretched out.

"Anyway, I thought we should meet, you know, talk."

"So talk."

"You know you upset a lot of people when you showed up."

Mikey smiled. A not at all pleasant smile. "No shit? Well, we're going to upset a lot more people, aren't we Craig?"

"We sure are."

"What are you going to do? What do you want?"

"We're going to build a whole new order," Craig said. "We're going to combine magic and technology into a system that really works for mankind. When we get done things will be better than they have ever been."

"Only you won't be around to see it, man," Mikey said.

"We're going to . . ."

"You talk too much, Craig," Mikey repeated

without heat. "Now shut up and let the grownups talk, will you?"

He took another pull on his beer.

"You see, you're squatting on a prime piece of real estate, you and your friends. Now it so happens we need that place. So in just a little while we're going to come over and take it."

Wiz went cold. "Hey look, we can negotiate . . ." But Mikey cut him off with a sharp bark of laughter.

"What's to negotiate?" he said, sliding off the table and stalking over to Wiz. "We're here and you're history." He jammed his face into Wiz's, so close Wiz could see the pores on his skin. "We're gonna get your whole fucking *world* before we're through, baby, and there's not a damn thing you can do about it."

"The hell there isn't," Wiz flared back. "Technology doesn't work over there, remember? And we've got magic the likes of which you've never seen."

Mikey smiled. "Wanna bet?"

Then his expression softened. "But maybe you're right. Maybe we should negotiate this thing like adults." He smiled again, a more relaxed, gentle smile. "After all, there's plenty for both of us. Two whole worlds, right?"

"Well . . ." Wiz didn't want to break the moment, but he didn't like the idea of giving away half the World. "I'm not empowered to negotiate directly, but I can take an offer back to the Council of the North."

Mike nodded and his smile grew wider, almost radiant. "Of course. So here's the offer I want you to take back to your Council."

He flicked his hand up and a wave of fire washed over Wiz.

Wiz screamed as the flames hit him. He dropped to his knees and then fell to the floor, the center of a white-hot ball haloed in orange. Thick black smoke roiled off the body and disappeared.

Then the inferno vanished and nothing remained

but a tiny blackened thing lying on the laboratory floor.

Craig was white with shock at what his friend had done. "It wasn't him," he said dully. "He wasn't really here after all."

"Shit!" Mikey picked up the charred bit of root and threw it against the wall. "Shit, shit, *shit!*"

# Fifteen

# FIRE WITH FIRE

*Reverse engineering is the sincerest form of flattery.*
  **—Engineers' saying in Silicon Valley**

Wiz screamed.

His very eyes were on fire. Heat singed his hair and beat on his brain through his skull. The flesh melted and ran off his face. The palms of his hands and the soles of his feet throbbed with pain as the awful, searing heat destroyed the nerve endings.

Somewhere far beyond the wall of terrible pain he was aware of Arianne gesturing wildly. Then waves of coolness washed over his body.

"Oh my God," Wiz moaned. "Oh my God."

Arianne held him in a way that combined professionalism and compassion. "You will be all right, my Lord," she said soothingly. "Try to relax."

Wiz relaxed one tiny, knotted muscle. The expected flare of pain did not come. He relaxed a few more muscles and still no pain.

"Jesus," he breathed out raggedly. Arianne released him to another's arms. Moira. Instinctively he reached out to touch her hair.

"I warned you that the psychic effects could be painful," Arianne said.

"Yeah, but . . ." He gasped for breath again. " . . . my God." Moira hugged him to her and he felt her tears on his cheek.

"I'm all right now, darling," he said with a smile he did not feel.

"*They* will not be if ever we meet," his wife said fiercely.

"I am sorry we did not get you out sooner, my Lord," Arianne told him, "but we did not realize what was happening."

127

Wiz sucked another racking breath. "Sucker punched. That son-of-a-bitch sucker-punched me."

The tall blonde sorceress shrugged. "Name it as you like. They have no honor."

Wiz was still shaking a few minutes later when the programmers and such of the Mighty as were in the castle assembled hastily in the chambers of the Council of the North. They took their places haphazardly around the long oak table without regard for the carefully established rules of place and precedence. That alone told Wiz how seriously the wizards took this.

"They're programmers, all right," he told the group. "From our world or one very much like it."

"Do your people make war against us?" demanded Juvian.

"Definitely not. I could tell that much just by looking. But they're trained in the same discipline we are."

"That's bad," Jerry said.

"Worse than you know, perhaps," Bal-Simba rumbled. "They have some powerful magical force behind them."

"The Dark League again?"

Bal-Simba snorted. "Much more powerful than that. Non-human I think, and mighty even for non-humans."

"Elves?"

"Perhaps."

"That must be what they've been up to," Danny said. "They've been stalling the negotiations while they got this thing set up."

Wiz frowned. "I don't know. There was magic all over the place, but it didn't feel like elf magic."

"May I remind you, Sparrow," Bal-Simba said, "that you have not met many elves?" Then he shook his head. "But you are correct. Elves can make time and space run strangely, but I have never heard of them creating a whole new World."

"Well, whoever it is has found themselves a couple of people who understand programming. They seem to be pretty good at it."

"They are," Danny said.

"You know them?" Wiz demanded.

"One of them. Mikey Baker. Well, I didn't really know him but I used to see him around on the nets. His handle was 'Panda,' you know?"

"No, we don't know. Tell us."

"Well, he was into hacking and phreaking—system breaking and shit like that."

"Don't call it hacking," Wiz said sharply. "People like that aren't 'hackers,' they're worms."

Danny shrugged. Unlike Wiz and Jerry he didn't have the true hackers' deep contempt for computer vandals who used their skills to break into computer systems. Nor was he offended that the media insisted on calling those criminals "hackers."

"Whatever. Anyway, no one liked him much."

"I can see why. But was he any good?"

"Oh, I guess so. But he was like nasty-nice, you know? Real sweet and easy-going on the surface and just rotten underneath."

"He sure as hell wasn't sweet to me!"

"He wasn't like that before. It seems like he's changed a lot."

"Well, what else do you know about him?"

"Not a lot. The people I knew didn't like him so I steered clear of him. There's a rumor he had something to do with the Jesse James Virus."

Wiz looked puzzled. "The Jesse James Virus?"

"That was after you left." Jerry shook his head. "A variation on the Panama Virus. Very sophisticated and real nasty. If this guy was behind it, he's got talent."

"I'd say there's a lot of talent behind that place,"

Wiz said. "Face it. We're not unique. There are a lot of competent programmers who could do pretty much what we've done if they knew about this place and how to get here."

"Yeah," Danny said, "but *how* did they find out about this world?"

"Perhaps they did not," Moira said. "Perhaps they were brought here as the wizard Patrius brought you here."

"Mikey told me they came here voluntarily."

"I wouldn't trust anything that guy said," Danny put in.

"Maybe, but someone turned them on to magic programming and our magic compiler. They didn't pick that up on their own."

No one said anything for a minute.

"There's only one place they could have gotten the compiler," Wiz said at last. "It had to come from here."

Bal-Simba frowned like a thundercloud. "A traitor?"

"Not exactly," Jerry said. "I've been studying the code from that recon drone we found. The compiler they're using isn't exactly our compiler. It doesn't have the extensions we've added in the last year and it's got a couple of features we don't."

"So they got an earlier version of the code and they've been working on it independently," Wiz said. "Can you tell roughly when they got their version?"

"No 'roughly' about it. I know exactly when. They're working with the last version the full programming team worked on."

"One of the programmers after all," Wiz said. "But we'd ruled that out."

"I fail to see how," Bal-Simba said. "That—ah— 'non-disclosure agreement' you had them sign is not enforceable in your world."

"Meaning we can't sic that demon named Guido on

them," Wiz agreed. "But we thought of this before and we checked."

"Between Worlds?" Bal-Simba looked skeptical.

"Even in our world there are ways of checking, although they aren't absolutely accurate."

"We had to make a couple of phone calls," Danny said.

Arianne looked at him strangely but said nothing.

"And you checked everyone?"

"Not everyone. One person, Judith Conally, is very ill. She was hurt in an accident a few months back and she's still in a coma."

"She's out then," Wiz said. "People in comas don't talk."

"That's not true, you know," Bronwyn said from where she sat at the end of the table.

"Huh?"

"People in comas can sometimes talk. It is not common, but . . ." She shrugged.

"If she talked," Moira said slowly, "there might have been ears to hear."

"Well, we pretty well know that no one else did," Jerry said.

"I think," Bal-Simba said, "it is time for another Great Summoning from your world."

## Sixteen
# RESCUE

Three A.M. is a bad time in hospitals. Normal life processes are at their lowest ebb. If it is busy it is because things have gone to hell and if it's quiet it's hard to stay alert. Fortunately things were quiet on Neuro, so the nursing supervisor was having trouble staying awake when Sheila came up to the station.

"We've lost Conally." Sheila's voice was so low and tight the supervisor had trouble understanding her.

The super looked up from her charts. "What?"

"Conally, the patient in 314. We've lost her."

The supervisor looked sharply at the young nurse. She seemed to be taking this one very hard.

"Too bad," the supervisor said sympathetically, reaching for the phone. "I'll get a resident up here to pronounce and then we'll . . ."

Sheila shook her head. "You don't understand. She's not dead, she's gone! Not in her room."

It was the supervisor's turn to go white.

The bed was in place, the bedclothes rumpled but not thrown back and the bed was empty.

"Did you check the other rooms?"

"I've looked everywhere in the ward. I can't find her."

It wasn't unknown for Neuro patients to get out of bed and wander around. That was why the unit was built secure. Except for emergency exits with alarms, the only way in or out was past the nurse's station and the door could not be opened from the inside unless someone at the nurse's station buzzed you out.

"Well, search again."

"I've already got Doreen and Lupe doing that."

"We'd better alert security to search the rest of the hospital," the supervisor said at last.

As she turned away from the empty bed she

thought regretfully of the cigarettes she had left in her locker. This was going to be a bitch of a night.

Bronwyn looked up from the still form, her lips pressed into a tight bloodless line. "What have those damned barbarians done to her?" she demanded.

"How should I know?" Wiz said. "I'm not a doctor."

"Neither are any of them by the look of it. They kept her clean and fed, but they did nothing to heal the damage to her brain."

"I don't think we can," Wiz said. "Head injuries are hard for us to handle."

"Barbarians," Bronwyn repeated and motioned her assistant to her. "Now leave us. And don't expect to talk to this one for a couple of days at least."

In the event, it was three days before Bronwyn would let Wiz and Moira in to see her patient.

Judith was laying in bed propped up with pillows. She still looked terrible, but she was conscious.

"Hi, Judith. How are you feeling?"

"Wiz, Moira," she said weakly. "I dreamed about you." Then she frowned. "I feel funny. Arms and legs don't move right and my eyes don't wanna focus."

"That is normal," Bronwyn said. "Magic can only do so much safely. You must heal the rest of the way naturally. That will take time and work on your part."

"Not complaining," Judith said muzzily.

"You said you dreamed about us," Moira said gently.

"Dreamed about this place a lot. I think."

"Do you remember answering questions about this World?"

Judith's eyes flicked from side to side, as if searching. "I, I might have. It seems like I went over and over things about this place."

"She will never have complete memory of that time," Bronwyn whispered in Wiz's ear. "There was too much damage."

133

"Did you have any notes about our system of magic?" Wiz asked.

"Notes?" Judith seemed confused. Then she pressed her fingers to her forehead in an effort to think. "Yes, I did make some notes after I got back, but I didn't show them to anybody. They're in my apartment."

"We'll check on that," Wiz said.

"What's wrong?" Judith asked.

"We think you talked while you were in the hospital," Wiz told her. "We think someone got most of the system of magic out of you. I'll bet we won't find those notes in your apartment either. Do you know a guy named Mikey Baker?"

"No."

"What about Craig Scott?"

"Yes," Judith said hoarsely. "He's a friend of mine. We furp together all the time."

"Furp?" Moira asked.

"FRP—fantasy role playing games," Wiz explained absently.

"What's happened? What's wrong?"

"Craig and this Mikey character are here. They're raising all kinds of hell."

Judith went even whiter. "No! I couldn't have!"

"That is enough," Bronwyn said firmly. "She needs to rest."

"Right," Wiz said. "Listen, you just concentrate on getting well and don't worry, okay." He patted her hand and left.

"Moira?" Judith said weakly as the hedge witch turned to go.

"Yes, my Lady?"

"I screwed up, didn't I? I really screwed up."

Moira smiled at patted her shoulder. "It is all right," she told her. "It doesn't really matter."

Then she turned away so Judith would not see how much that statement cost her.

## Seventeen
# A NEW ALLY

Wiz was in the middle of analyzing a module from the crashed recon drone when Bal-Simba found him in the Bull Pen.

"My Lord, you have a visitor."

There was something in the way he said it that made Wiz snap around, the intricacies of the code forgotten.

"Who?"

"Duke Aelric."

Wiz's jaw dropped. Only once before had the elf duke sent his image into the Wizard's Keep. The times Wiz had met him it had been in his own elf hill. No mortal understood how the elf hierarchy worked, but Aelric was called "duke" and stood high among the elves. Whatever this was, it had to be important.

Without another word Wiz left his code and hurried out the door of the Bull Pen, but when he turned toward the main keep and the Watcher's Hall, Bal-Simba placed a hand on his shoulder.

"Not there. The main gate."

"Why did he send his image there?"

Bal-Simba looked at him strangely.

"He did not send his image, my Lord. He is here in person."

There was no room in the Wizard's Keep deemed grand enough for receiving an elf, but the Wizard's Day Room was quickly put right, Malus was awakened from his afternoon nap and shooed out, and Wiz and Duke Aelric retired there.

Even in leather breeches, boots and a simple tunic of dark blue velvet brocaded in silver, Duke Aelric was as out of place as a president in a pig sty. But he contrived to put Wiz so much at his ease in the short walk from the main gate that Wiz didn't notice—almost.

"What can we do for you, my Lord?" Wiz asked after his guest had been seated and refused refreshment.

"It is more a question of what I can do for you, Sparrow," Duke Aelric said. "Or perhaps what we can do for each other."

"Oh?" was all Wiz could think of to say.

"You have already met the new arrivals from your world?"

"Mikey and Craig?" Wiz said grimly. "Yeah, I've met them."

"Then you agree they must be dealt with?"

"Yeah. That's what you might call at the top of my to-do list."

"I also want to see them dealt with. And what is behind them. Better to work together on this, do you not agree?"

"I'd be honored, Lord. But why . . . ?

Aelric cocked a silvery eyebrow. "Why am I interested? Because what you are doing is important. And because I think you will need my help. In fact, you will need all the help you can get."

The way he said it made Wiz's blood run cold. He knew the business with Craig and Mikey was serious, but if Duke Aelric was interested it had to be even more serious than he imagined.

*You will meet your greatest challenge*, Lisella had said. He forced the rest of the prophecy out of his mind.

"Okay, what do you suggest?"

"First, I think, we must pool our knowledge. There are things I can tell you which will help and other things I wish to learn from you."

"Sure." Wiz reached for the silver bell to summon a servant. "Let me get the rest of the team in here."

Duke Aelric made small talk while they waited. Wiz was too astonished by the whole situation to do more than respond half-heartedly. He was very glad when Jerry burst into the room.

"They said you wanted to . . ." He stopped short and goggled at the guest. Duke Aelric rose and bowed exquisitely, obviously amused by Jerry's reaction.

"This is, uh, Duke Aelric," Wiz said lamely. "I've told you about him."

"Honored."

"Ye . . . yeah," Jerry replied weakly. "Uh, forgive me. They didn't tell me . . . I mean, they just said Wiz wanted to see me."

The door opened behind him and Danny came in with June beside him.

"And this is Danny . . ." Wiz began, but he was cut short by June's shriek. She shrank back against Danny, white and open-mouthed.

Aelric bowed again. "My Lord, my Lady."

June turned away and buried her face in Danny's shoulder.

"Uh Danny, why don't you take June back to your room?" Wiz said desperately. "I'll talk to you later, okay?" Danny threw Aelric a venomous glance and led his shaking wife out.

"Now then," Wiz said, turning back to Duke Aelric, "here's what we know so far."

It was several hours later when Wiz hunted up Moira.

"How is our guest?" she asked as soon as he came into their apartment.

Wiz kissed her perfunctorily. "You heard, huh?"

Moira looked at him. "Not much of a greeting, my Lord."

"I've got a problem. You know June saw Aelric and nearly went into hysterics?"

Moira nodded. "So I had heard."

"It's the same thing that happened the last time she met an elf," Wiz went on. "At the time I thought it was

137

just Lisella. The way she popped up was enough to scare anyone and June's easy to frighten. But Aelric was just sitting there and she's more afraid of him than she was of Lisella."

Moira nodded. "Certainly she is terrified of elves. But you are concerned about more than June's feelings, I think."

"I'm concerned about making this thing work. Right now Danny wants to tear Aelric's heart out because of the effect he has on June. We can't build a team with something like that going on."

"What can I do to help you, love?"

"You're closer to June than anyone. Do you have any idea why she's so afraid of Aelric?"

"Nothing specific," the hedge witch said slowly. "June is afraid of many things." She smiled ruefully. "She is hardly what you would call normal in the best of circumstances."

"Amen to that!"

"But still . . ." Moira trailed off and stared away. Then she looked up at her husband. "You know her history. She was found wandering on the Fringe of the Wild Wood a few years ago, much as she is now. No one knew her or whence she came and she cannot, or will not, tell us."

"So?"

"She is terribly afraid of elves. Perhaps she has had dealings with them before."

"That doesn't make sense. Elves don't deal with humans."

"They deal with you."

"So I've got an elf magnet in my pocket. June sure doesn't."

"There is one case where elves do deal with humans regularly. They take human children to act as bond servants within elf hills."

"And you think June . . ."

"Time passes strangely under an elf hill. It seems

138

like a season or two but when the servants have fulfilled their bond and are released centuries have passed. Their family, their friends, even their villages are dust and gone."

"It makes sense," Wiz said at last. "It would explain where she comes from and a lot about why she is so strange."

Moira said nothing.

"What else? There's something you aren't telling me, isn't there?"

"My Lord, I do not know any of this. It is all surmise."

"But you suspect something. Out with it."

Moira stared into her lap. Wiz waited. "Do you know why June needs Shauna to help nurse Ian?" she asked at last.

"I never really thought about it."

"Because she does not produce enough milk."

"As flat-chested as she is, I can believe it, but so what?"

Moira snorted. "My Lord, contrary to what lechers like you believe, the size of a woman's breasts has little to do with her ability to feed an infant. No, June does not produce enough milk because her breasts are damaged. There are scars around both her nipples. Many little scars, as if she had been bitten repeatedly."

Wiz went cold. "Meaning what?"

"You recall I once told you elves prefer human nursemaids for their infants? It is said that elf babies are born with all their teeth."

Moira looked at him levelly, green eyes intent and serious. "It is also said those teeth are sharp enough to draw blood."

Duke Aelric was on the castle wall, watching the setting sun turn the clouds orange and the hills purple. In his own unearthly way he was as magnificent as the

139

sunset and Wiz watched both for several minutes before he got up the courage to approach him.

"My Lord, I need to talk to you."

Aelric turned from the sunset and inclined his head. "Of course, Sparrow."

"It's about June, Danny's wife."

A graceful frown knitted the elf duke's brow. "Ah, the one who was so upset? Forgive me, I thought she was a servant."

"Was she?" Wiz asked harshly.

"I beg your pardon?"

"Was she one of your servants?"

Duke Aelric made a throw-away gesture. "I really do not know, Sparrow. There have been so many."

"She was some elf's servant. Now she's terrified of elves because of something that happened to her."

Duke Aelric said nothing.

"Doesn't that bother you at all?" Wiz demanded.

The elf duke raised a silvery eyebrow. "Why should it? If she did serve the ever-living I can assure you she was not deliberately mistreated. If she was a servant it was because she was offered a bargain and she accepted. I assure you the bargain was kept." He cocked his head. "Forgive me, but I do not see the relevance of an old bargain with one mortal—if bargain there was. Nor do I understand why you are so concerned about it."

"Some bargain," Wiz said bitterly. "Parents would 'foster' their children into elf hills in return for the protection they needed to survive."

"Nonetheless, she would have entered our domains as all mortals enter them. Of her own will."

"And came out to find that centuries had passed."

Aelric cocked his head and said nothing.

Wiz could only stare. When they had met before Duke Aelric had been gracious, even charming, if somewhat frightening. Wiz knew that elves could be cold and cruel, but this was the first time he had ever seen it in Aelric.

And the worst of it was, Wiz realized, he wasn't being cruel at all. He honestly did not understand why what had happened to June should be any of his concern. He began to appreciate, vaguely, just how un-human elves really were.

"Now she's terrified of you and her husband would just as soon murder you as look at you and I've got to work with both of you."

The elf turned to Wiz and gave him a look that rooted him where he stood. "Her husband cannot find the necessity one-tenth as distasteful as I do." Aelric's fine features drew up in a sneer. "Sparrow, do you think I *like* coming here; associating with mortals?"

"Then why did you come?"

"Sparrow, listen to me. There are *things* in this World that are not of it. Ancient things whose very nature you cannot comprehend." His eyes bored into Wiz. "I told you once that you had upset a very delicate balance. Even after all that has happened I still do not think you understand what you have done.

"Magic in the hands of mortals is dangerous, Sparrow. Unlike the ever-living, you are not inherently magical. You do not really understand magic.

"But your new magic is very powerful. That arouses certain—things—" He trailed off, as if thinking. Then he resumed briskly. "Now those things must be dealt with. For this we will both need to bend all the powers we possess to the task."

He was afraid, Wiz realized. Duke Aelric was actually afraid of whatever it was they were facing! Something cold and hard grew in Wiz's stomach.

It was fully dark by the time Wiz went to visit Danny. He was alone in his room, Shauna having taken June and Ian off someplace to try to calm her down.

"Has he gone yet?" Danny demanded sullenly.

"No, and he's not going."

Danny bounced up off the bed. "Fuck that shit! He's going if I have to throw him out of here on his goddamn ass!"

Wiz moved in front of the door. "You're not going anywhere. You're going to sit down and we're going to talk."

"Fuck that." Danny tried to force his way past Wiz, but Wiz grabbed him and pushed him back into the room.

"Listen to me. This is a war, not a popularity contest. Right now we need all the help we can get and he's about the most potent help we're likely to find.

"Maybe something happened between June and Aelric once. But that's over. Now we need each other. That means if you're going to be part of the team you're going to have to work with him." He looked hard at Danny. "Right now Aelric is a lot more valuable to this project than you are. If you can't handle it, I'll have to replace you."

"With who?" Danny sneered.

"With one of the wizards we've been training. Malus, maybe. He may not be as talented as you are, but he can get along with Aelric."

Danny didn't say anything.

"Well?"

"I still don't like him," Danny said sullenly.

"You don't have to like him. You have to work with him. Now, can you do that?"

"Yeah, I guess so. Just keep him the hell away from June."

Wiz released Danny's shoulders. "He doesn't have to come anywhere near June."

"Okay then," Danny said. "Anything else?"

"Not now. We'll have a staff meeting at noon tomorrow to figure out approaches."

Duke Aelric did not stay the night in the Wizard's Keep but he returned early the next morning. Again they met in the Wizard's Day Room: Wiz, Jerry, a sullen but cooperative Danny, and Bal-Simba as the head of the Council of the North. The huge wizard said little and Aelric generally ignored him.

Yesterday Wiz and Jerry had done most of the talking as they filled Duke Aelric in. Today it was the elf duke who dominated.

"Lord, it sounds as if the simplest approach would be to close off the gate into our World somehow," Jerry said when Aelric had finished.

"Simple indeed," Aelric said with a trace of amusement, "if we but had the key."

"Is there a key?"

In response Aelric lifted a finger and an elaborate, convoluted shape blossomed in the center of the table.

"That is a simple representation," he told them. "There are actually eleven directions, not just three. The narrow part at the top represents the situation when the gate was first opened. Here at the bottom," he gestured at the wildly intertwined strands that seemed to grow out of the table top, "is the situation as it is now. If I knew the total shape, it would be possible to construct the key and so close the door beyond opening again. But . . ." He smiled slightly and shrugged.

"Wait a minute!" Jerry said thinking hard. He scribbled frantically on a slate while the others watched in silence. "That's a fractal!"

"I do not know that word," Aelric said.

"It's a self-similar figure with fractional dimensions."

Aelric arched an eyebrow.

"Just a minute," Wiz put in. "Are you sure that's a fractal?"

"Pretty sure. Look." He passed the tablet over to Wiz.

"Yeah," Wiz said slowly. Then he looked back at the elf. "Look, when you say 'know the shape,' do you mean 'describe mathematically'?"

Aelric frowned. "I do not understand you, Sparrow. When I say 'know the shape,' I use the words as mortal magicians do, I think."

Wiz turned to Bal-Simba. "Lord . . . ?"

"If the Sparrow means what I believe he means, then yes. A mathematical description is sufficiently precise."

Aelric turned back to Wiz. "Can you do this?"

Wiz nodded. "Fractals have another characteristic. They are generated by iteratively applying a function—that means applying the function over and over—and a lot of those functions are pretty simple."

"There are image compression systems that use fractals," Jerry said. "Rather than store the actual image they store functions that generate fractals to mimic each part of the picture and then combine them. You can compress an image ten thousand to one or more that way."

"Show me," Aelric commanded.

The elf was leaning forward looking at them so intently Wiz almost thought he was going to spring at them like a lion at an antelope.

Slowly and carefully Jerry and Wiz led Aelric through the process that would yield the solution. Although mathematics was an alien language to the elf, parts of it he grasped intuitively. Other parts had to be broken into tiny pieces and gone over and over.

At last his face split into a broad smile. "Brilliant. A whole new way of looking at such things. Thank you both." Then he sobered. "Yes, I think this," he tapped the slate, "is a fair representation of the problem of closing that door. But if I understand you, it is a problem almost beyond solution."

"Almost isn't the same as impossible," Jerry said. "There are ways you can simplify something like that. In principle it is solvable. It is just a matter of putting enough computer power to work on it."

"Now that's something we can do," Wiz said. "Our spell compiler isn't adapted to solving mathematical problems but demons can be made to calculate as well as work magic."

Danny shook his head. "I dunno. This isn't going to be easy." It was the first thing he had said all morning and he looked at the glowing model rather than Aelric when he said it.

"So it's not easy," Wiz told him. "We can do it anyway."

"Okay," Wiz said three days later, "I was wrong."

The same group, less Aelric and with the addition of Moira and Arianne, was assembled in the Bull Pen to review the project. After the initial flurry of writing code, things had settled down to running the program. It had been running day and night for the last two days and as they met the Emac controlling it sat on Wiz's desk in a stall behind them, scribbling away furiously at line after line of glowing "printout."

"This isn't going to work," Wiz said tiredly. "We can't do the calculations fast enough. The problem with the magical compiler is it's slow. We're getting maybe 200 MOPS, absolute tops."

"MOPS?" Moira asked.

"Magical Operations Per Second."

"Two hundred spells a second does not sound slow to me," Bal-Simba said.

"It is for this kind of work. What we're doing here isn't so much spell casting as it is mathematical analysis and that takes a lot of computing power, magic or no."

He sighed. "Back home I used to work on machines that could do five or six million instructions per second and we had access to some that could do two hundred million."

"That is a great deal of calculation," Bal-Simba said.

"The fractal resembles a Mandelbrot set in some respects, although it's defined by a completely different function," Wiz told him. "What that means is there is not an analytic equation which will give us the boundary—which is what I was hoping for. What we do have is a procedure for calculating whether a given point is inside or outside the set."

"I will take your word for it," Bal-Simba said.

Wiz sighed. "What it comes down to is that we can find the shape of the key to any desired degree of precision, but we have to do it by calculating one point at a time. That takes computing power."

"Wait a minute!" Jerry said. "What about parallelism? Each of those points is calculated independently of the others, right? So why don't we get a bunch of copies of the program working on the problem simultaneously and feeding results to each other?"

"Well, machine resources are essentially free," Wiz said. "But it would mean rewriting part of the compiler to handle the parallelism."

Jerry nodded. "That's doable. But before we do that we can test it with just a few copies active and one copy acting as supervisor. Kind of like running multiple virtual machines."

"Virtual machines?" asked Moira, catching a phrase in the mass of technobabble that almost sounded familiar.

"That's like a computer that isn't there," Jerry said helpfully.

"It's something that acts like a computer only it isn't," Wiz added.

Moira regarded both of them coldly. "I see. Like your explanations."

Wiz shook his head. "No, our explanations are real. A virtual explanation would be something that acted like an explanation, but wasn't."

Moira nodded. "I rest my case. Well, never mind. Just tell me what you will need to make this machine that is not a machine and I will see about getting it for you."

Wiz looked at the setup and nodded. This wasn't going to be pretty, but it was strictly a proof-of-principal device.

Ranked in front of him were twenty-one Emacs, all sitting cross-legged on the floor of the Bull Pen. All of them had their quill pens out and poised expectantly.

"This will take a while," he told Jerry and Danny quite unnecessarily. "We've only got twenty processors here and that key is a twelfth-order function. On the other hand, our algorithm will converge on that function. We'll start seeing a representation almost immediately, but it will be real fuzzy."

"And the more processing time we put on the sharper the image will get," Danny interjected. "We helped you write the damn thing, remember?"

Wiz blushed, nodded, and raised his staff.

"You know . . ." Jerry said slowly.

"What?"

"I don't know. I have a feeling about this. Like the one I got in the City of Night just before we used the digging spell."

Wiz lowered his arms. "What is it that bothers you?"

"I can't put my finger on it. But there is something about this whole business." He thought hard and then shook his head. "No, I guess not. Go on with the spell."

Wiz looked around for a convenient cover in case he needed it. Then he raised his staff again.

"**backslash**" he proclaimed.

"**?**" responded the first Emac.

"**fractal_find exe**," Wiz said. The Emac on the far left turned to the others and began to gabble at them. The other twenty Emacs bent to their tasks immediately.

The air above the Emacs began to thicken and take on a bluish tinge. It grew denser and bluer until a neon blue cloud hung over their heads.

"It's working!" Danny said.

Wiz just stared at the slowly coalescing shape and wondered why everything the Emacs turned out was in such violent colors.

As the cloud solidified it began to show hazy lumps and hollows. It wasn't even solid enough to be called a shape yet, but already Wiz could see similarities between it and the thing Duke Aelric had called up on the conference table. The process was slowing as the algorithm had to work harder and harder to discover which points were part of the shape and which were not.

The form began to pulse and Wiz realized he was getting a headache. He looked away, but the afterimage remained burned in his retinas. His vision grew dark around the periphery and everything seemed fuzzy. He shook his head to try to clear it but that only made things worse.

"Do you guys feel all right?" Wiz asked.

"I feel fine," said a large Saint Bernard dog with Jerry's voice. To his left a six-foot-tall cockroach waved its feelers in agreement.

"Well, I don't," Wiz sang with two of his mouths, creating a bell-like harmony. Vaguely he realized they were standing not in the Bull Pen but under an enormous crystal canopy that shimmered with pastel highlights. And wasn't he supposed to have only two arms and one body segment?

As he watched, dog, cockroach and canopy all began to melt and run together. He felt his own body grow indistinct at the edges and begin to flow.

"SIGTERM!!" Wiz screamed.

The universe, canopy, cockroach and dog all froze in a half-melted state.

"UNDO!" he commanded. Instantly Wiz, Jerry and Danny were standing in the Bull Pen again.

"My God," Danny said shakily. "I mean, well, my God!"

"I think we have a problem here," Jerry said. His voice was calm but he was white and breathing in long, deep gulps.

"I think we just got closer to being inside a system crash than I ever wanted to be," Wiz replied, collapsing onto a bench before his legs gave out.

"You know," Jerry said, "this may not work after all."

Danny collapsed on the bench next to Wiz. "Right now, I'm just glad everything's back to normal."

"Oh yeah?" Jerry said, "look."

Wiz followed his pointing finger. Where the Emacs had been stood twenty mice, all dressed in blue and red band uniforms, complete with frogged jackets and plumed shakos, and carrying musical instruments. The twenty-first mouse, wearing a tall bearskin hat, raised his baton. The mouse bass drummer struck three quick, sharp beats and the entire mouse marching band charged into song.

*Who's the leader of the club . . .*

"UNDO!" Wiz, Jerry and Danny yelled simultaneously.

It was afternoon the next day when a tired, dispirited team of programmers met with Moira, Bal-Simba and Duke Aelric.

" . . . and we still don't know what happened," Wiz concluded. "One minute everything is fine and the next minute the world goes crazy."

Aelric looked at him strangely. "You honestly do not know?"

Suddenly Wiz had the feeling they had missed something very obvious.

The elf duke sighed. "Forgive me, Sparrow. I had forgotten I was dealing with mortals and I simply assumed . . ."

"What did happen?" Jerry asked.

Aelric paused, weighing his words. "The object we call the key is in some sense a representation not only of the gate, but of this World as well. As your spell moved closer and closer to producing the shape of the key it began to have an ever-stronger effect because it became an ever-more exact replica of the World."

"And by the Law of Similarity, like things affect each other," Wiz put said. "So it began to affect the universe."

"That is—ah—a not incorrect way of putting it. Quite frankly I wondered how you would deal with the problem. It never occurred to me you had not realized what would happen."

"Why didn't the shape have any effect when you showed it to us?"

"What I showed you is powerful enough, believe me, Sparrow. But it was incomplete; only the part between the Bubble World's creation and that moment. I did not attempt to reproduce the entire shape of the key."

"I told you guys it was a hardware bug," Danny said, running his hand through his disheveled hair.

"The question is, how do we fix it?" Jerry said.

"I know of no way to fix it," Aelric said. "Any spell

150

which can produce that shape must inevitably affect the World in a chaotic fashion."

For a minute no one said anything.

"You know," Jerry said finally. "This thing acts like some kind of quantum effect at a macro level."

"So maybe we need a quantum mechanic," Wiz said. Jerry groaned, Danny scowled and Moira and Bal-Simba looked blank.

"Just trying to lighten the mood a little. Sorry."

"You should be," Jerry told him.

"Sparrow, there are times I think it is a blessing I do not always understand you," Bal-Simba rumbled. "But I take it that this approach is not practical?"

"I guess not," Wiz said. "Damn! And it looked so perfect."

"Just a minute," Jerry said. "You say that it is the *spell* which affects the World?"

Aelric inclined his head. "Just so."

"Well, suppose we did it without using a spell?"

Aelric thought hard. "You mean using no magic at all? Yes, I suppose that would be possible."

"The calculations could be done by hand," Jerry said.

Danny snorted. "Man, there isn't that much time in the universe. What we need is a Cray or something."

"Computers won't work here," Wiz protested. "Nothing high-tech works in this world."

"Craig and Mikey seem to be doing all right."

"Yeah, but they're not in *this* world, they're in that bubble universe."

Danny shrugged. "So we get ourselves a supercomputer and we set it up in our own bubble universe."

"Do you know how to create such a thing?" Bal-Simba asked.

"No," admitted Danny.

"Nor do I," said Bal-Simba.

Everyone turned to look at Aelric.

"It, ah, would not be practical for us to do it either."

"Whoever is helping those two is powerful indeed," Bal-Simba said.

"Well, there's gotta be a way," Danny said a bit sullenly.

"Maybe there is," Jerry said. "Suppose we help ourself to a corner of their universe?"

Wiz, Moira and Bal-Simba stared hard at Jerry.

"My Lord, how long has it been since you slept?" Moira asked.

"Twenty-eight hours or so, but what's that got to do with it?"

"If you get a good night's sleep, I suspect the connection will occur to you," the hedge witch said tartly.

There was a lull in the conversation while everyone considered.

"Well, it does seem to be a pretty big place," Wiz said at last. "Lots of islands and no one in most of it."

"We've been able to set up scout bases for our dragon patrols," Danny pointed out. "Why can't we just take over one of the deserted islands?"

"You can't be serious!" Moira snapped. "You mean hide like a mouse in the corner while you do your work?"

"Hey, it's there and they're not using all of it," Danny said. "Why not?"

"For a beginning you could all get killed. None of you know what lurks in that place nor how it is guarded."

"I do not believe it is guarded at all," Bal-Simba said. "Our scouts have found no sign of watchers or guardian spells. Indeed, their biggest problem seems to be to keep from straying into that universe unintentionally."

The hedge witch's mouth dropped open. "You are actually serious! My Lord, I cannot believe that you are actually considering this."

"My Lady," Bal-Simba said gravely. "In times like

these we must consider many things we would rather not."

She turned to Aelric in mute appeal, but the elf only shrugged. "It does seem to present a solution, Lady."

"There's another little problem," Wiz said. "Where are we going to get a supercomputer?"

"We can't just issue a purchase order, can we?" Jerry said finally.

"I don't think Dun and Bradstreet has a current report on us."

"I take it," Bal-Simba said, "we cannot simply pay for this in gold, as we paid the programmers?"

"Not that simple," Wiz told him. "First, I don't think they'd take gold. Second, these things are built to order and most manufacturers have backlogs. Third, they're still under export controls and there is a lot of paperwork you have to fill out before you can buy one."

"Well," Jerry said slowly, "the regulations have gotten a lot looser since you left. Anyway, legally we *are* entitled to an export license. We're not on the list of proscribed countries, after all."

Wiz looked at him. "You want to fill out the application? And then explain it to the State Department?"

"Just a thought."

Danny shrugged. "So we swipe one."

"I don't think so. At five million a copy, people would talk."

"So what? The Russians do it all the time."

"We're not . . ." Wiz started and then stopped. "You know, you may have something there, in a back-handed sort of way." He stared off into space for a minute and chewed on his lower lip.

"Assuming we can make our searching demons operate . . . yeah."

"We're gonna swipe one?" Danny asked eagerly.

"If we can find the right one," Wiz told him. "After

all, a fair robbery is no exchange—or something like that."

"And then you are just going to walk into this bubble universe and set it up," Moira said disgustedly. She picked up the jug of fruit juice and sniffed it. "Are you sure you did not turn this into something stronger when I was not looking?"

# Eighteen

# INTERNATIONAL COMPLICATIONS

Generals are not known for their sunny dispositions. Just now this general's disposition was as frigid as the Alaskan snowbanks lining the runways outside. His staff didn't look like they were having much fun either.

"Okay, so whatever these things are, we haven't been able to get good radar signatures on them. Are we even sure they are real?"

The other officers in the room shifted uncomfortably. At last the intelligence officer spoke up.

"Sir, we're not sure. But they act like they are."

"Analysis shows there's about an eighty-five percent chance they are real," said the officer responsible for the base's powerful radar chain.

The general glared as if he wanted to kill someone. Now.

"Well, if they're real why the hell can't our pilots find them?"

"By the time we can get there they are always gone," the intelligence officer said. "Besides, that whole area is a fog bank."

"That's unusual in itself, isn't it?"

"No, sir, not exactly," the base weather officer put in. "As you know fog's not unusual in that part of the Bering Sea. More like the normal thing."

"Is it normal for the same patch of ocean to stay fogged in for weeks?"

The weather officer shrugged. "Not quite so far north, no. But it's not unheard of either."

"What's causing that?"

"Cold air moving over warm water. Telemetry shows the water's somewhat warmer there than in the surrounding parts of the ocean."

"Why?"

Again the shrug. "We don't understand the weather patterns in this part of the world that well. An upwelling current, a vortex breaking off one of the regular warm currents, we just don't know."

"And you don't know what's playing hide and seek with our radar?"

"Whatever it is, it's not meteorological."

The general turned to his radar officer.

"And you don't know either?"

"No, sir. I can tell you something is showing up intermittently and whatever it is is probably not an artifact of the equipment, but that's all I can say."

"And patrols through that show nothing?"

"Nothing but fog. Sometimes our equipment works perfectly. Sometimes everything goes to hell. Radar, radios. I even had one case where the inertial navigation systems started acting up."

He scowled at the thought. This far north compasses were unreliable. If the INS failed, the pilot was reduced to dead reckoning and quite possibly a very chilly bath.

The general nodded again. In peacetime the base only kept one pair of F-15s sitting as CAP—combat air patrol—and they were not launched except at definite targets. They were well positioned to intercept something coming in to the Alaskan mainland, but not to go chasing things out over the Bering Sea.

He looked over at his intelligence officer, who merely shook his head. "It doesn't match anything we know of."

The general thought hard. "Thank you, gentlemen." The officers rose to go, but the general motioned his intelligence officer back into his chair. "Matt, stay behind for a minute, will you?

"Now," the general said when the others had filed out and closed the door behind them. "What do you think this thing is?"

The intelligence officer frowned and shook his head.

"I don't have the faintest idea. If it is Soviet, it's stealthed well beyond what we thought they could do and it's carrying one holy hell of an electronic counter-measures suite. I don't know anything that could produce returns like that, or the kind of interference that's coming out of that area." He paused significantly. The northern border was so sensitive that if the intelligence officer at this base didn't know, no one in the Air Force knew.

"I'll tell you something else," he went on at last. "From what I'm hearing, I don't think the spooks know what those things are either. CIA and NSA don't tell us everything, but the reactions I'm getting tell me they're in the dark and they're plenty worried."

It was the general's turn to frown. "Why so?"

"The arms control talks. If the Soviets can produce something that good without our having an inkling of it, then our 'national technical means of verification' aren't worth a damn. If we can't catch them with our satellites and spy planes then we can't make sure they aren't cheating." He made a throw-away gesture. "Poof, no treaty."

The general didn't say anything for a long, long time.

"Would they really blow a treaty over some anomalous returns?"

"It sure as hell wouldn't help."

"But why the hell would the Soviets take something like that out over the ocean? Haven't they got enough places to test it where it would be secure?"

The intelligence officer shrugged. "Ask me another one. But don't be surprised if we get some company before long. Important company."

The general cracked the knuckles in one fist and then the other, like a man preparing for a fight. Then he smacked his right fist into his left palm and stared out into space.

"All right," he said finally, "what you're telling me is that it's vital to the security of the United States that we find out what the hell these things are?"

The IO chewed that over for a minute and then nodded. "Not 'vital' maybe, but damned important. Yessir, that's my assessment."

The general slammed his palm down on the desk. "Then we're by damn going to find out, and soon! I want some F-15s prepared with long range ferry tanks and recon gear up the wazoo. Damn, I wish I had some EF-111s!" He looked over at his intelligence officer.

"The next time that thing shows its nose we're going to be ready. We're going to find out what this sucker is and we're going to nail him!"

# Nineteen

# MOUSEHOLE

"Behold, the Mousehole!" Wiz Zumwalt said, standing in the lobby of his new secret headquarters and gesturing grandly. Moira, who was standing beside him, only sniffed.

The Mousehole—no one could remember who came up with the name—was a one-story complex of glass and stone raised overnight by magic. It meandered beneath the trees in a small valley like a giant's game of dominoes. In addition to the labs and workshops, the complex included wings of private quarters for the programmers, wizards and their servants and helpers, storerooms and, most importantly of all, a room for their soon-to-be-acquired computer.

Wiz put his hands on his hips and surveyed the scene. With its airy spaces, hidden fluorescent lighting and non-static carpeting, the complex would not have looked out of place in a Silicon Valley industrial park. Of course, it did have a few features most Silicon Valley complexes lacked—such as windows that opened and the smokeless torches in brackets along the walls because the electricity wasn't hooked up yet.

"You know," Wiz said, "the Wizard's Keep has a lot of atmosphere, but this is still pretty neat."

"This is still madness," Moira responded grimly. "I just hope we do not all live to regret this."

"You mean you hope we *do* live to regret it."

"You know perfectly well what I mean!" the hedge witch snapped. "And *here* on this island, of all places!" She growled in frustration, crossed her arms and turned away.

Wiz came up behind her and put his arms around her. "I don't like it either, darling. But we've got to be able to use a computer and that means taking risks."

He felt her stance begin to soften. "And they don't

patrol this island regularly. So we're safer here than anywhere else. Besides, we've taken precautions."

In fact the precautions had taken more time than the buildings. Not only was the glass carefully dulled to avoid any hint of reflection and the stone colored to match the surrounding rock, but powerful blocking spells had been erected over the place. From the air the valley appeared as simply another hill. Magical emanations were blocked. Even infrared, UV and radar signatures were tightly controlled.

Moira sighed. "Oh, I know, love. But on the same island as our enemies!"

"It's a big island. We're nearly a hundred miles away from them. As long as we don't have dragons flying in and out of here or something we'll be safe enough."

"I suppose," Moira said in a tone that suggested she supposed nothing of the sort. But she relaxed and turned back toward Wiz.

He smiled down at her. "Besides, look at the bright side. In this world there are no dwarves trying to kill me."

Glandurg was bent over his locating talisman. For two days there had been no sign of the Sparrow even on his searching device. Now he was attempting a difficult spell to increase its power temporarily.

His followers were crowded around the stump where he sat, watching as he poured all the magical energy he could muster into the device. The sweat was running down Glandurg's brow and even Gimli was uncharacteristically quiet.

The device pulsed, flickered and then lit with a faint blue glow. Within it a shadowy arrow pointed south.

Glandurg jumped up off the stump so quickly he almost knocked Ragnar over. "South! The alien wizard has gone south." His face split in a wide smile.

"Excellent. We have driven him from his hole and now we can follow him. He will not be so well protected in his new lair." He jumped up on the stump and struck a heroic pose.

"This time we shall not fail!" he proclaimed in ringing tones.

The other dwarves listened politely, but with a notable lack of enthusiasm.

"This means the griffins again, doesn't it?" Thorfin asked glumly.

"I don't see why we don't just grab the thing now," Danny complained as he and Wiz made their way back to their quarters. "It's been nearly a week since we got here and we can't do anything until we get that computer."

It was well past midnight and the halls were deserted. The support staff was small and was not on duty around the clock. Even Jerry had turned in an hour ago, leaving Wiz and Danny to finish reviewing the results of their search for a "candidate" computer system.

"Because it's still legal," Wiz told him. "They haven't done anything they aren't supposed to yet."

"But we know they're going to."

"But they haven't. So we don't touch it."

"Like, the KGB is really going to use a supercomputer in the United States."

"It's the GRU—military intelligence—and they're still legal."

"Bullshit!"

"Maybe," Wiz said firmly. "But that's the way we're going to play it."

They walked on in silence. Their feet made no noise on the carpeted floor and the dim light from the ceiling panels had a bluish cast that made it seem even dimmer.

As they came around a corner, they saw movement

161

ahead. Instinctively they both froze. Then Wiz realized it was June.

June was always cat-quiet when she moved, edging along the walls of a room as if she was afraid something would grab her. Now she was moving even more stealthily. She kept her back to the wall and stepped sideways with large cross-body steps that carried her along utterly without sound.

Danny moved to say something, but Wiz put a cautionary hand on his arm. As silently as she had come, June disappeared down the cross-corridor.

"What's June doing sneaking around like that?"

"She's not sneaking!" Danny fired back.

"All right, she's not sneaking. What's she doing?"

Danny dropped his eyes and didn't say anything.

"Danny . . ." Wiz began dangerously.

"She's . . ." He took a deep breath. "Well, she's watching."

"Watching who?"

"That elf dude. She doesn't trust him."

"That's obvious. Any special reason?"

"Because he's dangerous. Because he doesn't belong here."

"He's our ally."

"How do we know that? Because he says so?"

"Because he is," Wiz told him with a lot more firmness than he felt.

"Look man, June knows elves. She lived with them for hundreds of years, right? She doesn't trust him and that's good enough for me."

"He's saved my life a couple of times and that's good enough for me," Wiz retorted. "Look, I told you once before you don't have to like him, but you're going to have to work with him. If you or June can't handle that, I'll have to send you back to the Capital."

Danny just snorted and turned away.

The only thing worse than flying over the ocean,

Glandurg decided, was flying over the ocean at night. It was bad enough to look down and see nothing but water beneath you, but it was worse to look down and not see the water you knew was there.

This whole trip was worse than anything he had imagined. He was cramped and sore after hours of hanging from a griffin's talons. He was mortally tired, but he could not get any sleep. He was chilled nearly to the marrow from the night cold and wind. He was still half-airsick from the terrible fog bank they had gone through a while ago where everything was suddenly *wrong*. Now the griffin that bore him was laboring and wheezing as if from exhaustion.

Well, at least Thorfin had stopped moaning and Gimli wasn't retching any more. *The next time I make a journey like this I will insist on a flying carpet,* he declared to himself. *It costs more, but the extra comfort is worth it.*

The truth of the matter, he admitted to himself, was that he didn't want to make a journey like this. Not ever again. Not even the quest was worth this misery. He would have gladly ordered the griffins to turn around and take them home if it didn't mean flying for hours and hours more.

A sudden move by the griffin jerked him out of his misery and sent a new thrill of terror through him. The griffin had banked and seemed to be losing altitude. Glandurg's heart jumped into his throat at the thought of going down in the ocean.

Then his dwarvishly keen nose caught a new smell mingled with the iodine-and-salt odor of the ocean. A smell of mud and decay that was like perfume to him. Land! There was land ahead.

Glandurg fumbled with half-numb fingers for the thong around his throat. The talisman was glowing brightly and the arrow pointed sharp and clear straight ahead of them.

\*       \*       \*

"We have got to do something about June," Wiz told his wife the next morning over breakfast. "Now she's taken to sneaking around after Duke Aelric."

"I know," Moira said calmly.

"Huh?"

Moira laid down her slice of bread. "Love, not everyone is as oblivious to what goes on around them as you are. And more importantly, Duke Aelric knows as well."

"He said something?"

"He is an elf. He knows."

"Great!" Wiz sighed. "All we need to do is insult Aelric."

"Has he told you he is insulted?"

"No, but you know how touchy he is."

Moira reached from the jam. "Just so. If he were insulted, you would know it. I take it he has said nothing?" She cocked her head. "No? Then it does not concern him and should not concern you."

Wiz grunted. "Anyway I'm going to send June back to the Capital."

"Danny will not like that."

"Then Danny can go back too. Dammit, she's not supposed to be here in the first place!"

Moira looked amused. "Perhaps not. But do you seriously think you can keep her and Danny apart?"

Wiz considered that. "With a moat full of crocodiles, maybe."

"I would bet on June over the crocodiles. No, love, I am not sure even death could separate those two."

"So I send them both back."

"Wiz, I do not mean to tell you how to mind your business," his wife said in a tone indicating she was about to do exactly that, "but I think that would be unwise for two reasons."

Wiz started to say something, but Moira held up her hand to stop him.

"First, what can Danny accomplish back at the

Capital? He needs to be with you and Jerry to be effective, does he not?"

"Yeah, but . . ."

"And second, do you think anyone at the Capital can control him?"

Wiz thought about that. "Right. He doesn't listen to anyone except Jerry and me and half the time he doesn't listen to us." He sighed. "Okay, he stays and that means June stays. But for Pete's sake will you use whatever influence you have with her to get her to lay off Aelric?"

"I have already spoken to her and I will do so again. But I fear she is even more resistant to direction than Danny. Besides, in this case she has a very strong motive for following Aelric."

"Danny says it's because she doesn't trust him."

"I am sure that is true. But I think there is more to it. She spies on him because she fears him."

"And that's why she doesn't trust him."

Moira shook her head. "Again, I think that is true in part. But mostly I think she follows him because it is a way to rise above her fear. She somewhat controls the thing she fears, you see."

"Not exactly, no."

"Nevertheless it is so."

"Sheesh! I dunno. This whole thing used to be so simple. There were good guys and bad guys and it was easy to tell the difference. Now . . ." He shrugged.

Moira reached out and took his hand. "You have managed well enough so far."

"Yeah, but you'd think this saving the world business would get easier with practice. It just seems to get harder and more complicated every time."

"Let us hope this is the final time, love."

"Yeah," Wiz said fervently and squeezed her hand.

"Besides," Moira went on brightly. "There is a positive side to this, you know. You said we needed to do something about June. June is doing something about herself. It is helping to heal her."

"That's something, I guess."

They ate in silence for a while.

"Moira?" Wiz said at last.

"Yes, love?"

"Do you trust Duke Aelric?"

The redheaded witch considered. "Not trust, exactly. I think that as he says, his goals and ours run together on this thing. Besides, Bal-Simba says he is worthy in this and I trust Bal-Simba."

Wiz hesitated. "You really don't like him, do you? Aelric, I mean."

Moira paused. "Nooo," she said at last. "I do not like him."

"You seemed to like him well enough when we met him in the Wild Wood."

"He saved our lives in the Wild Wood."

"But you never said anything that indicated you don't like him."

Moira sighed and bit into her bread and jam. "Liking or not-liking an elf is like liking or not-liking a mountain," she said around the mouthful of food. "An elf or a mountain simply *is* and you must accept that."

"Well, *I* like him," Wiz said firmly. "And I trust him too."

He turned back to his own breakfast. *Just maybe not as much as I used to*, he thought as he reached for the butter.

Even for humans, the place was strange looking, Glandurg thought as he crouched on the hill looking down on his enemy's new lair. It was only one story, even if it did run out in all directions. The stone of the walls looked solid enough, but the place had windows as big as doors! Not a moat or a crenelation to be seen.

166

Not even a log palisade. He snorted silently. The place was defenseless.

There was a tiny noise in the bushes and Ragnar slithered back into view. Glandurg and the others crowded around him.

"Dwarf-proof!" he said disgustedly. "Whole bloody place is spelled against us."

Glandurg wanted to beat his fist in the dirt in frustration. But it would not do to lose control in front of his followers. "Then we will wait and watch," he said between gritted teeth. "The wizard cannot stay within forever."

# Twenty

# MEETING BY MOONLIGHT

Unlike the Wizard's Keep, the small staff at the Mousehole did not work around the clock. By nine P.M. the hallways were deserted and by midnight the place was as silent as a tomb.

It was well past midnight when a shadow slipped into the lobby and paused at the main door. A remarkably well-dressed shadow.

Aelric's cloak was blue at the shoulders fading to purple and finally to black at the hem. Here and there upon it gems sparkled like stars in fading twilight. As he turned June saw his tunic was dove gray and his hose pure white. He turned fully and she caught her breath and shrank back into the shadow. But his face remained as serene as always and he gave no hint that he knew she was there.

Then liquidly, noiselessly, he opened the door and slipped out into the night. June waited for a moment and then followed, not nearly so graceful but just as soundlessly.

Aelric did not sneak, but nonetheless he moved quickly and gracefully in an odd twisting fashion that was hard for a human eye to follow.

About a half mile from headquarters the path wound through a thick patch of ferns and then dropped into an open glade. June hesitated for a moment and when Aelric did not emerge on the path that came out of the depression, she dropped to her hands and knees and crept forward.

She knew the glade well enough. By day it was a pleasant spot and once or twice she and Danny had come this way to picnic and make love. Under the full moon their pleasant little picnic spot was transformed into something completely different.

Through a break in the lacy foliage June caught a

glimpse of movement in the glade. Oblivious to the damage to her dress, she pressed herself flat to the earth and slowly wormed her way forward through the overhanging ferns.

The moon was high and its silvery light poured into the clearing. Duke Aelric stood in the middle of the open space and he was not alone. There was another cloaked figure beside him, nearly as tall as he was. Then Aelric moved and June saw it was Lisella.

She was near as pale as the moonlight itself and her hair cascaded down her back dark as the forest shadows. Like Aelric she was wearing a cloak with the hood thrown back. To a normal mortal she would have been heartbreakingly beautiful, but June dug her fingers into the soil and pressed herself flatter at the sight.

Neither of the elves spared a glance for their surroundings. They were deep in conversation. The liquid tones of elf speech did not carry well, but June could see clearly enough.

Lisella was speaking quickly, her eyes focused on Duke Aelric's face. Aelric heard her out without changing expression and then said something with a half-smile that made her draw back and bite out a retort.

From her hiding place June watched intently. Normally elves were impassive or half-mocking when they spoke to each other. She had never seen them talk together like this.

Lisella faced Aelric square on and said something. Aelric half-nodded, as if agreeing with her, and then responded calmly. Lisella seemed to have trouble controlling her temper. She said something short and sharp.

Aelric made a chopping motion with his hand and turned away, as if to leave. Lisella's voice caught and held him. He turned back to her. Without moving

closer he spoke firmly to her. She looked at him closely and then shrugged.

Lisella cocked her head and said something with a
mocking little smile. Aelric nodded.

She arched an eyebrow slightly but he said nothing
and stood firm. At last she nodded and spoke. He
bowed formally and she responded with a half-
curtsey. Then she turned and swept out of the
clearing. Aelric stood watching her for a moment and
then took the moonlit path back toward headquarters.

June remained flat on her belly under the ferns for
a long time before she rose cautiously and slipped
back to the fortress.

Wiz got an early start the next morning and by the
time Danny arrived in the lab he was deep in his latest
project.

"You know your buddy, the elf dude?" the young
programmer said as soon as he stepped into the room.

"It's elf *duke*," Wiz said without looking up from the
code he was debugging.

"Whatever. Anyway you know Lisella, the one you
said was trying to kill you?"

Wiz looked up cautiously. "Yeah?"

"Did you know Aelric's meeting her here?"

"What? How do you know that?"

"June saw them out in the forest last night. She says
it looked like they were arguing about something."

"So June's still following Aelric."

"You ought to be glad *someone* is," Danny snapped.
"Didn't you hear what I said? He's meeting with the
one who's trying to kill you!"

"She's not trying to kill me anymore."

"She sure wasn't trying to do you any good when
she showed up at the City of Night."

Wiz laid down the scroll he was holding. "Look, I
don't know why Aelric's meeting Lisella. But right

now we can't afford to alienate him. So tell June to lay off, will you?"

Danny stared at him, hard. "Man, you're goddamn blind! You just don't want to see, do you?" With that he turned on his heel and stomped out of the lab.

In the next hour Wiz got maybe two lines of code written. Finally he gave it up and went to find Moira.

Moira was in the storeroom, overseeing the stocking of a load of supplies which had been brought over the Wizard's Way that morning. While the servants bustled about, Wiz took her off in a corner and told her June's tale.

"A human spying on elves?" she said when Wiz had finished. "It seems unlikely. They can pass unseen by mortals as easily as they breathe."

"Yeah, but if anyone could do it, it would be June. Besides, magic doesn't work as well here, remember?"

The hedge witch wrinkled her brow. "To be sure it is an unlikely tale for her to concoct. Well, if it is true, then we must be even more careful with our elf duke."

"I thought you trusted him, more or less."

"Less now than before."

"I don't know, though. If he wanted to harm us there are a lot easier ways to do it. Why go through all this rigamarole of pretending to ally with us?"

"Well," Moira said, "it is said that elves are tricksome and strange."

171

## Twenty-one
# THE GREAT PLANE ROBBERY

Ivan Semonovich Kuznetsov, major in GRU, snapped awake and sought groggily for the thing that had awakened him.

The four big Ivchenko turboprop engines on the wings of the AN 12 transport beat steadily as the plane bore east and a little north toward Leningrad. His cheek was slightly numb from the cold and vibration where it had rested against the metal side of the cabin.

But there had been something . . .

He shook it off. Too much vodka last night, that was all. Truly it was a terrible thing to grow old. Not that thirty-three was old, but he could no longer drink the night away and rise fresh with the dawn.

But this dawn there was cause enough for celebration. Snug in the belly of the aircraft was the newest, fastest graphics supercomputer the Americans made. In a few hours it would be in Leningrad and Major Ivan Kuznetsov could expect to share in the rewards of a job well done.

The computer had travelled a long and shifty path from the factory in Texas. It had originally been ordered for a research institute in England, but by a carefully staged "coincidence" it had been diverted to Austria and from there on to what had been East Germany where the Soviet intelligence service still had friends. Kuznetsov had some small part in all of that. Now he was accompanying it on the last leg of its trip to the Soviet Union.

Where it would go once it reached Soviet soil he did not know and would never have dreamed to ask. There were many important projects in the motherland that required computers which were beyond the current abilities of the socialist nations to build. Since the Americans still would not sell such computers openly, the nation relied on the GRU, the intelligence arm of the Red Army, to acquire them in other ways.

"Comrade Major . . ." Kuznetsov jerked fully awake. Whenever one of his subordinates addressed him as "comrade" he knew something had gone wrong.

"Yes, Sergeant?"

"The computer . . ." Vasily began. In a flash the GRU major was out of his seat, thrusting the man out of the way and diving headlong through the door into the cargo compartment.

"It's gone," the sergeant's voice echoed after him.

Kuznetsov didn't need Vasily to tell him that. The webbing that had bound the computer tightly in place was a tangled limp mass on the floor. The wooden pallets were exactly as they had been, but the crates were gone.

"Yo momma!"

Like a wild beast Kuznetsov spun and sprang for the cockpit door. His sergeant pressed against the bulkhead to let him pass as he squeezed into the cockpit. Before the pilot could turn to him he grabbed the man's shoulder and tried to twist him around in his seat.

"The cargo door," he demanded. "When did it open?"

"It didn't open," the pilot, Volkov, protested. "There's an indicator . . ."

*"The devil take your fucking indicator,"* the GRU man roared. *"When did that door open?"*

"It didn't! We would have felt it in the controls. Comrade Major, I swear to you on my mother's grave that door did not open."

*"Don't lie to me!* That door opened. *Now when?"* He took a deep breath, pulled his pistol from its holster and pressed it against Volkov's head, just in front of

his earphones. "If you do not tell me the truth immediately I will blow your brains all over this cabin."

The co-pilot and flight engineer had their eyes studiously glued to their instrument panels. The pilot looked at the pistol out of the corner of his eye and Kuznetsov jammed the gun against his head even harder.

"Major," Captain Volkov said with quiet dignity, "you may arrest me. You may shoot me here and now. But that door did not open. It could not have."

"Very well," Kuznetsov said softly, so softly he was almost inaudible over the roar of the engines. "Very well, the door did not open." He took the gun from the pilot's head. "Then would you please tell me *where is the fucking cargo?*" His voice dropped again to a near whisper. "That is all I want to know."

Volkov blanched and started out of the pilot's seat. Kuznetsov moved to block him and then thought better of it. He nodded curtly. "Sergeant, accompany him."

As the two scrambled aft Kuznetsov stared moodily at the cloudscape below him. They were somewhere over Estonia, he knew, and the Estonians were notorious through the USSR as the biggest thieves of state property in all the republics. The Georgians were bigger black marketers and the Azerbijaniis were more violent, but over the years the Estonians had stolen everything from a freight train to an entire fleet of fishing trawlers. "Well, this time those damned Estonians have gone too far," he muttered to himself.

"Sir?" asked the copilot. Then he withered under the GRU man's glare.

"Sir, should I radio Leningrad and declare an emergency?"

"No, you idiot! The last thing we need is to have Leningrad Center shouting questions at us."

Although the questions would come soon enough, he realized. Chill fear clutched at his stomach as he thought what those questions would be like.

Just then the intercom squawked. "Major," Vasily's voice came over the loudspeaker. "Major, I think you'd better come down here and take a look at this."

Kuznetsov looked down at the co-pilot and flight engineer and decided he was not going to leave them alone in the cockpit to do God-knows-what.

"Come with me," he commanded. The co-pilot opened his mouth to protest and Kuznetsov touched his holster. "Now," he ordered, "immediately." Wordlessly the men slid out of their seats and preceded the major down to the cargo deck.

Volkov and Vasily were squatting over the heap of webbing where the computer had been, staring intently at one of the pallets. As Kuznetsov made his way back to them, bracing with one hand against the side of the plane, he saw there was a small pile of something shiny and metallic in among the straps and buckles.

"When we looked closely we found this," Vasily shouted to make himself heard over the din of the engines. He handed Kuznetsov an object off the stack, an object that glinted like summer sunlight even in the gloom of the aircraft deck.

Kuznetsov had never seen gold before, but no one had to tell him this was gold.

"But where did it come from?" Volkov asked, bewildered.

"That is a very good question," Kuznetsov said, kneeling down to study the pile of gold bars. They were surprisingly tiny, each one fitting neatly in the palm of his hand and weighing about two kilograms. There were no identifying marks of the kind usually found on bar gold, not even assayer's marks.

"How much do you suppose it is worth?" asked the co-pilot.

"If I had to guess, I would say perhaps ten million American dollars. That was the value of our cargo."

"What was our cargo, anyway?" the pilot asked.

The GRU man glared at him. "That is none of your concern."

Volkov did not flinch. "If my career is to be ruined I would at least like to know what over."

Kuznetsov considered and then nodded. "Very well. It was an American supercomputer. The latest model of supercomputer and one that took us nearly two years to acquire."

The pilot's mouth dropped as he realized the enormity of the loss. "Boishemoi!" he breathed.

The GRU man nodded curtly. "Just so."

"What I don't understand," the co-pilot said, "is why go to the trouble of leaving the gold after stealing the computer?"

"That too is a very good question," Kuznetsov said sourly as he braced himself against the plane's gentle bank to the right. "Does anyone have any more good questions?"

"Just one," Vasily said hesitantly as the craft began to bank more steeply. "Who is flying the plane?"

Volkov and Semelov gaped at each other and both dashed for the cockpit.

"Well," Wiz said at last for want of anything better to say, "there it is."

Sitting under the lights on the concrete floor were two dozen boxes full of computer and supporting equipment, all cocooned in foam and cardboard, wrapped around with clear plastic and bound with metal straps.

Moira followed the programmers' admiring looks and tried to be enthusiastic, but it all looked so *ordinary*. The way Wiz and the others had been talking she expected a nimbus of power around the boxes, or lightning bolts or something.

None of the programmers noticed her disappointment. They were too busy swarming over the pile, touching cabinets and opening boxes.

"I hope the installation instructions are complete," Danny said dubiously. "I've never installed anything bigger than a 386 PC."

"Voila!" Wiz stood up from a newly opened box waving a black oblong. "A complete installation course on video tape. Just sit ourselves down with some popcorn and get educated."

"Wiz."

"Yeah, Jerry?"

"Where are we going to get a VCR?"

"Lift one out of a store the same way we lifted the computer," Danny said.

Wiz frowned. "I dunno. That would be stealing."

"Wiz."

"Yeah, Jerry?"

Jerry gestured at the $10 million pile of crates. "What do you call this?"


"Well," Major Ivan Kuznetsov said, hefting the bar of gold absently, "what do we do now?"

The occupants of the cockpit looked at one another and no one said anything. By now it was painfully obvious they would all share the same fate.

"Think, comrades," Kuznetsov urged. "Think as if your lives depended on it." *As they well may*, he didn't have to add. "What could have possibly happened to that computer?"

"It was fine when we loaded it aboard," Vasily said. "I checked and rechecked it myself."

"And I also," Semelov put in. "The webbing was secure and there was nothing unusual about it."

The pilot and the major nodded. They had also checked the cargo and the mountings before takeoff and Kuznetsov and Vasily had been on the cargo deck for takeoff.

"And there was nothing out of the ordinary when you left to go to the latrine?" Kuznetsov asked Vasily.

"Not the least little thing."

Kuznetsov said nothing. Technically both he and the sergeant were supposed to have been on the cargo deck at all times. But rank has privileges and he had chosen to ride up front where it was warmer and quieter. Abstractedly he realized that would be seen as dereliction of duty by his interrogators, but he did not think it would matter much. He turned to the pilot.

"And you are sure the cargo doors did not open in flight?"

"Major, I swear to you on my mother's grave that none of the aircraft doors opened after we left the ground," Volkov said. "For that matter the load did not even shift. We would have felt the alteration in the center of gravity."

Kuznetsov looked at him with contempt. "So one moment it was there and the next it vanished like winter fog?"

Volkov shrugged and spread his hands helplessly.

"It was there when I left and gone when I returned, not two minutes later," Vasily said.

"Where does that leave us?" asked the co-pilot.

"As traitors to the Motherland," Kuznetsov snapped. He furrowed his brow and grimly, desperately, tried to think.

"What are our options?" Volkov asked.

"We should call Leningrad Center and report this immediately," Vasily said when no one else spoke up. "It will go harder on us the longer we delay."

Kuznetsov shook his head. "Report what, Sergeant? That our cargo seems to be missing and we have acquired a pile of gold instead? Perhaps we had better consider the situation first."

*Besides,* Kuznetsov thought, *it can't go any harder on us than it will already.*

"At least we have the gold," Semelov pointed out.

Kuznetsov snorted. "Leningrad Center isn't expecting gold. It is expecting a computer. May I remind you, comrades, computers such as this you cannot buy at a hard currency store?"

"I don't suppose there is any chance they will believe us?" Volkov asked tentatively.

Kuznetsov snorted again. "Would you? Besides, it makes no difference. The computer was in our care. We lost it. We are responsible."

Volkov licked his lips. "What do you think they will do to us?"

For a moment there was only the roar and vibration of the engines. "I doubt they will shoot us," he said at last. "Not when we give them the gold. But we will undoubtedly be interrogated—rigorously." He paused, remembering the courses he had had on interrogation techniques. Then he tried to shove those images out of his mind.

"They will doubtless conclude we sold the computer for gold. Nothing we could say or do will convince them otherwise. Then they will want to know who we sold it to. Eventually we will tell them."

"But we haven't sold the computer!" Volkov protested.

Kuznetsov grinned mirthlessly. "My friend, you do not appreciate scientific socialist interrogation. By the time they get done with us we will have confessed anyway—over and over again. Eventually we will come up with a confession they will choose to believe."

"And then?"

"Then we will spend the rest of our lives at hard labor in a prison camp. I understand that under Perestroika conditions in even the severe regimen camps have improved greatly. Now the average prisoner lives as long as seven years."

No one said anything.

"I have a wife . . ." the co-pilot began.

"She is disgraced," Kuznetsov cut him off. "She will doubtless be arrested and interrogated as well, probably sentenced to prison." He thought of his own Yelena and tried not to.

"Comrade major . . ." Vasily began.

"Yes?"

"Sir, I . . ." He stopped, licked his lips and took a deep breath. Then the words came with a rush. "Sir, they do not imprison the families of defectors do they?"

All five men froze, not even breathing. Then their eyes darted around to the faces of the others, seeking some sign of their thoughts. Finally the other four looked straight as Kuznetsov.

"No," the GRU man said slowly. "They are disgraced and interrogated, but not rigorously. They are not imprisoned."

"And," Volkov added eagerly, "if we landed someplace in the West, they would assume the Americans had reclaimed their computer and were lying about it not being aboard."

Kuznetsov said nothing at all.

"There are even," Volkov went on carefully, "places in, say, Sweden, where you can land an aircraft like this and not be discovered for, oh, long enough to hide something in the woods before anyone arrived."

Kuznetsov hefted the gold bar thoughtfully.

"Comrades," he said finally, "I understand Sweden is lovely at this time of the year."

Volkov looked at Kuznetsov, Vasily looked at Semelov and the co-pilot looked at his charts. Then they all looked at the bar of gold in Kuznetsov's hand.

Without another word, Volkov reached up and flipped off the radar transponder. Then he pushed the wheel hard forward and shoved on the rudder pedal, sending the plane diving for the deck and, as soon as they were below radar, turning north toward Sweden.

## *Twenty-two*
# INSTALLATION

"Hey Moira," Jerry called. "Can you come in here and help me for a minute?"

"Of course," Moira said. "But what are you doing?"

Because the room had no windows the only light came from a torch on the wall. Jerry was on his hands and knees with a string and a piece of chalk. With exaggerated care he marked a tiny dot on the concrete.

"Did Wiz ever explain to you about 220-volt single-phase 60-cycle AC?"

"No."

"Then I'm drawing on the floor. Anyway, I need to mark out a pentagram. Can you stand in the center and hold the line exactly on this dot while I swing a circle?"

"Of course," Moira said as she took the string and stooped to hold it on the point Jerry had marked, "but why do you need to be so precise?"

"This spell multiplies a mass times a length and divides it by time. I've got to get the units exactly right or we won't get the output we need. So the pentagram has to be just the right diameter."

"Forgive me, My Lord, but that is a circle, not a pentagram."

"Special kind of pentagram," Jerry grunted.

"It is *not* a pentagram. It is a circle."

"A pentagram approaches a circle for sufficiently large values of five. Now, step out of the way, will you? And don't muss the lines."

As Moira moved out of the way, he deftly sketched a shape in the center of his creation.

"That is not any kind of pentagram," Moira insisted. "That is a circle with a sideways S in it."

"It does the job of a pentagram," Jerry said. "Stand

back." He turned to the Emac which was standing nearby.

"**backslash**," he commanded. "**power_up exe.**"

A puff of bright blue smoke billowed into the diagram on the floor, coalesced, condensed and solidified. The demon was about two feet tall and looked like a stick figure. Except instead of straight lines, its arms, legs and body were composed of neon blue lightning bolts. Its nose was a 150-watt light bulb.

*"bzzzzp bzzzzp ready,"* it said in a buzzing voice.

Jerry nodded and flipped the switch on the wall. The fluorescents in the ceiling flickered and caught, bathing the room in a cold bluish glow.

"Okay. Douse the torch, will you? We've got power."

"Of that I make no doubt," Moira said, eyeing Jerry's creation dubiously.

# Twenty-three
# GREMLINS

"Where does this go, Lord?" asked one particularly lanky guardsman as he and his fellows rolled a tan metal object through the opened double doors.

Wiz looked up from the sea of packing material, pallets and computer parts scattered across the floor of the computer room.

"Oh, that's part of the air conditioning. It goes in that room over there. And be careful of the stuff on the floor. There's metal strapping all over the place."

Moira looked over the slowly growing computer in the middle of all the litter. It still wasn't very impressive. There were four tan metal cubes, each about waist high, that stood all in a row. Next to them were a couple of taller cabinets. At the other end was a large desk with a workstation sitting on it—the "console" the programmers called it, although what consolation it might be Moira couldn't imagine. There were a half-dozen other workstations, a thing Wiz told her was a printer and some other equipment scattered around the room.

"Forgive me darling, but the problem with your world's magic is that it just doesn't look impressive."

"It's not supposed to," Wiz told her. "If it looks impressive it scares the suits."

Moira thought about that and then did what she usually did when the conversation lapsed into incomprehensibility. She changed the subject.

"What does that part do?" She nodded toward the box being maneuvered through the just-big-enough doorway.

"That's the climate control system. It's not really part of the computer at all. It just keeps the room at constant temperature and humidity. These things are picky that way."

"This could be done by magic, you know."

"I know, but the computer is designed to work with this system and as long as we have electric power, why not use it?"

"Magic would be more reliable," Moira said dubiously.

"Magic doesn't work as well here as it does at home. Besides, machinery can be just as reliable as magic."

Moira arched an eyebrow skeptically, but she said nothing.

"Hey Wiz," Danny called out. "I think I've got the cabling problem whipped. Come look at this."

Danny had several sections of the raised floor up to expose one of the cable runs. "You know you said it would take us a couple of days to get all the cabling spliced right? Well, I found a way around it."

"emac" he said, and one of the yard-tall editor demons appeared beside him.

"?" said the Emac.

He reached behind him on the floor and handed the demon the wiring manual and printout of the installation chart. The little demon staggered under the pile of paper nearly as tall as he was. Then Danny gestured down into the hole and commanded "**backslash untangle exe**". A foot-tall demon wearing work clothes and a tool belt popped up in the cable run. The Emac flipped open the wiring chart and started to gabble furiously. The demon in the cable run whipped out his tools and began splicing wires so fast its hands were a blur.

Wiz shook his head in admiration. "Danny, that is a truly tasty bit of work."

The younger programmer shrugged, but his face lit up at the compliment. "I figure it will take maybe a couple of hours to get the cabling done."

"What does that do to the rest of the schedule?" Moira asked.

Wiz thought for a minute. "We should be able to

hook up the climate control this evening. Once we turn it on that's about all we can do tonight. We need to let the temperature and humidity stabilize before we try to bring the system up. That'll take six or eight hours."

The programmers were in fine fettle the next morning. They were days ahead of schedule and best of all, the hardware installation was almost done. All of them were much more at home with software and they were looking forward to the next phase.

"Well," Wiz was saying as they came down the hall, "if everything passes the hardware checks we should be able to start loading system software by this evening."

"That'll be a relief," Danny said. "I'm getting sick of messing with hardware. What's the matter?"

Wiz had stopped dead and was frowning off into space.

"Is it my imagination or is it humid in here?"

"Humid," Moira said.

"Definitely," Jerry said.

Wiz looked at the others. "Come on." He wasn't quite running as he headed toward the computer room, but he wasn't far from it. The others were right behind him.

Smoke was pouring out of the computer room.

"What the hell?"

"The place is on fire!" Wiz shouted.

Danny ran forward as if to dash into the room. "That's not smoke," he exclaimed. "It's cool and wet."

"Fog," Jerry said wonderingly. "The room's full of fog."

Wiz took a deep breath and charged into the computer room. The air was so clammy he could hardly breathe and the fog swirled around him like the special effects in a bad monster movie. Batting at the swirling mist he fought his way to the back of the room. Thick white clouds of vapor were pouring out of the air conditioning duct at the rear of the room.

"Shut off the climate control," he yelled over his shoulder. "And get a fan in here to clear this stuff out."

Almost instantly a wind rushed through the room, sucking the fog out faster than it could pour in through the vents. By the time Wiz reached the door again, the air in the room was clear. The relays clicked over and the air conditioning died.

Moira was standing in the doorway with her staff in her hand and the wind she had raised tugging at her skirt and tousling her coppery hair. As Wiz emerged she gestured and the winds died away instantly.

"My Lord," the hedge witch said with a smug little smile and arched eyebrow, "explain to me again how reliable mechanical contrivances are."

She looked so lovely with her hair in disarray Wiz forgave her.

It took the programmers and their helpers nearly two hours to get things under control. Water had to be vacuumed out of the soaked carpet, books and papers had to be spread out to dry and a dehumidifying spell was used to help dry out the equipment. Fortunately there wasn't much damage, but there was a lot of work to be done.

"Okay," Wiz said grimly. "Somehow the air conditioner and the humidifier both got stuck on. The low temperature turned the high humidity to fog."

"We're lucky we didn't take two days off," Jerry said. "We probably would have had ice all over the equipment."

"I'm damn glad we hadn't powered up the computer," Wiz replied. "That would have been a real mess."

"Hey guys," Danny called from the back of the room. "These things didn't get stuck on. Someone reset the thermostat and the humidity thingie."

Wiz and Jerry crowded around him quickly. Sure

186

enough inside the clear plastic box covering the controls both dials were at their maximum positions.

"I could have sworn I set those properly," Jerry said.

"You did," Wiz told him. "I double-checked before I left the computer room last night."

"Someone must have messed with them," Danny said.

"Inside the locked cover? I don't see how."

"Magic," the young programmer retorted.

"From where?" Wiz asked. "Moira, did you . . ."

"Certainly not!" the hedge witch said indignantly. "Nor did any of the other wizards here. Believe me, my Lord, if there is one thing any apprentice learns early it is not to tamper with another's magic. Those who do not learn it do not live long enough to become magicians."

Wiz put his hand on her arm. "Of course you didn't darling, it's just that . . ." Then he stopped as he caught sight of something over Moira's shoulder.

A line of seven little figures marched across the top of the computer console, their arms swinging and their bodies swaying in time to the song they were bawling out at the top of their tiny lungs. Their voices were so shrill that the words were lost, but the tune came through clearly, as if hummed by a chorus of mosquitoes.

*eee-eh, eee-eh*
eee-eh heh heh heh heh
eee-eh heh heh, eee-eh heh heh
eee-eh—heh heh heh heh

As Wiz watched, the creatures disappeared through an open inspection panel into the guts of the computer. The last one, evidently realizing it was being watched, waved gaily to Wiz before it dived after its fellows.

"Uh, folks," Wiz said just a shade too calmly. "I think we've found our problem."

For a moment no one said anything. For a long moment.

"What in the World was that?" Jerry demanded finally.

"I have seen their like before," Moira said. "The mill in my village had one. How the miller would curse when the thing played tricks on him! He had me down there nearly every new moon to try to rid the mill of it."

"I take it you didn't have much luck?"

"No. Sometimes it would quiet down after I came. Sometimes not. Once it dumped near a barrel of flour on the miller and me as we left the mill after the exorcism."

She paused and shrugged. "I do not know what to call them. They are so rare they do not have a name."

"Gremlins," Wiz supplied. "We have gremlins in our computer. Wonderful."

"Gremlins?" Moira asked.

"Little magical creatures that live in machinery and cause trouble." He jerked a thumb at the infested computer. "You know, gremlins."

Moira frowned in the especially pretty manner she had when she was confused. "Love, how is it you have names for these things if they do not exist in your world?"

"They didn't exist so we had to make them up."

Moira raised an eyebrow. "That makes less sense than most of what you say."

"That's because you've never worked around complicated equipment. Believe me, it's enough to make you believe in gremlins even when you know they don't exist."

The hedge witch sighed. "I will take your word for it."

"The real question is, how do we get rid of them?" Jerry asked.

"I do not know. I was not very successful with the one in the mill. Perhaps one of the Mighty will know more."

"What can you tell us about them?"

Moira pursed her lips and tried to think. "Not a great deal, I fear. They are very uncommon."

"You said there was just one in the mill," Wiz said. "I just saw seven of them go into the computer."

"That is very unusual. I have never heard of more than one at any place."

"I'm surprised you don't have them around the Capital with all the magical apparatus there."

"Only mechanical things attract them. Aside from that," she shrugged, "I know only that they are somewhat like the other Little Folk, the ones you call Brownies."

"Wait a minute," Wiz said. "Do you think Brownies could give us some pointers on handling these pests?"

Moira considered. "I do not know. We have no Brownies here to ask."

"No, but there are Brownies at Heart's Ease. Lannach and his people, the ones I rescued in the Wild Wood."

The hedge witch nodded. "They are in your debt then. It is worth a try, yes."

The brownies arrived the next day, brought along the Wizard's Way by Malus.

"We are here, Lord," Lannach said, hopping down from Malus's pack onto the table and bowing deeply.

Wiz bowed back to the little manlike creature. "Thanks, Lannach. If you can help us we'd really appreciate it."

Behind Lannach, Brechean, Loaghaire and Fleagh jumped down to the table. Then Meoan climbed out

189

of the pack and Brechean and Fleagh helped her down.

Wiz's eyebrows went up. "Meoan too?"

The little woman looked up. "Am I unwelcome then, Lord?"

"No, not at all. I just thought you'd stay at Heart's Ease with your baby."

"Lord," Meoan said gravely, "we owe you our lives. Small we may be, and with scant powers. But we do not forget our debts."

"Well, if you can keep these little bleeders under control you can consider the debt paid in full."

" 'Twere best we were about it then," Lannach said.

While Wiz and the others watched from across the computer room, Lannach knelt by a ventilation grill in the base of the console. He called out in a language that sounded like an excited mouse. Then he cocked his head and listened intently.

Although Wiz heard nothing, Lannach apparently got a reply. While Wiz and the other humans fidgeted Lannach conducted a long and seemingly involved conversation in mouse-squeak. Finally he stood up and dusted his hands on his moleskin breeches.

"Your device is inhabited, Lord," he reported, hopping up on the table next to Wiz.

"We know that."

"They thank you most gratefully. They say they have never seen a more fitting home for their kind."

"So we've got seven of them living in there?"

The brownie's tiny face creased in a frown. "Seven? Oh no, many more than that, I think."

"We only saw seven."

"Ah, well they are shy creatures so doubtless you did not see them all. Besides, they multiply quickly when they are in a place to their liking."

"Look, we don't mind them living here, but we can't have them interfering with our work. Is there any way to keep them in line?"

190

The little creature shook his head. "We can try, Lord. But they are flighty and chancy beings. They will not keep their word even if they can remember from one minute to the next what they have sworn to."

"I don't suppose a repulsion spell like **ddt** would do any good?" Wiz asked hopefully.

"Little, I fear," Lannach said. "As you may know, Lord, non-mortals differ in their susceptibility to such things. These are especially resistant. They are hard to dissuade and they would even be hard to kill by magic."

"Great," Wiz muttered.

"We can do this, Lord. If my kin and I work together we can probably dissuade them from their worst mischief."

"That would be something anyway," Wiz sighed. "Okay, Lannach. Do your best. Meanwhile Moira will show you your quarters and fix you up with something to eat."

"We have a place for you in the kitchen," Moira said as she led the gaggle of brownies out the door, "and bowls of milk for you all."

"Wonderful," Wiz said as the brownies left. "We got cockroaches. Insecticide-resistant cockroaches."

"Just think of it as working with beta version hardware," Jerry said helpfully.

Wiz glared at him. "Is that supposed to make me feel better?"

"No, it just puts the problem in perspective."

Wiz groaned.

Ozzie Sharp drained the last of his cold coffee and paced down the line of radar and communications operators. He briefly considered going forward and getting another cup, but his tongue felt like it had grown fur, his stomach was starting to go sour and the combination of the coffee and the cabin noise of the aircraft was making his bladder twinge already. Better save it until he needed the caffeine.

He looked for a place to set down the cup, but most of the flat, stable surfaces in an AWACS aircraft are for work. He kept the cup clinched in his brown fingers and turned his attention back to the radar displays.

Ozzie wasn't a big man, but he was built like a fireplug. There were traces of gray in his curly black hair, but he still moved in a way that suggested that if there was a brick wall between him and where he wanted to be it was too damn bad for the wall. Like the crew, he wore a dark blue Air Force flight suit. But there was no insignia of rank on Ozzie Sharp's flight suit because he had no rank.

"Anything?" he asked the operator at the end of the line.

"Not a thing," the operator said, never taking his eyes off the screen. The operator didn't add "sir" and Sharp understood the significance of that perfectly.

Well, fuck 'em. Ozzie Sharp had been sent here from Washington because he was one of the best trouble shooters in the agency. This was trouble and he meant to get to the bottom of it.

So far he was just a passenger. The general had set this operation up before he arrived and all Ozzie had to do was ride along. The general might be content to command from the ground, but Ozzie Sharp wanted to be where the action was.

The AWACS was further west than usual. Whatever was out there was tricky. Moving the plane out over the Bering Sea made it easier to burn through the jamming and pick up the weak radar returns.

Orbiting nearby were two F-15 Eagles with conformal fuel tanks for extra range and Sparrow and Sidewinder missiles to deal with whatever they encountered. Perhaps more importantly, the fighters also carried a variety of sensors including special video cameras to record what they found.

Back at the base were more Eagles, two KC-10 tankers on alert. and another AWACS, ready to take up station when this group reached the end of their endurance. They had been doing this for four days now, but no one was getting bored.

The operator, a skinny kid with a shock of dark hair, turned to his passenger and tapped his screen. "Ivan's out in force today."

"What's that?"

The radar operator grinned. "Our opposite number. An Illuyshin 76 AWACS."

"Observing a test?"

The operator shrugged. "Maybe. But if I had to guess I'd say they're looking for something in that fog bank—just like us."

"With just the AWACS?"

"Nossir, that's not their style. But they like to hold their interceptors on the ground until they've got a target and then come in like gangbusters. Their birds are probably faster than ours but they don't have the range."

Sharp nodded. It was a well-known fact that the Soviets were years behind the West in jet engine technology. What the Americans achieved by sophisticated engineering and advanced materials, the Russians got by brute force at the cost of higher fuel consumption.

But high-tech or low-tech, the effect was the same,

Sharp reminded himself. When those interceptors came they could be damn dangerous.

"Make sure our people know about this," he told the operator.

"Already done," the operator replied, pleased he had anticipated the civilian.

The operator turned back to his screen, scowled at it, then reached over and fiddled with the controls.

"Hello, hello," the operator said to himself. "Looky here." Then he thumbed his mike.

"Okay, we've got contact. Bearing 231 and range approximately 220 nautical miles. Height 500."

The pilot's voice squawked in his earphones. "Five thousand?"

"Negative. Five hundred."

"Understood," the pilot came back. "Five hundred feet."

"Eagle Flight," the flight controller's voice came on the circuit, "you are cleared. Now go!"

"Eedyoteh!" Go!

Senior Lieutenant Sergei Sergovitch Abrin of the PVO—the Soviet air defense forces—eased the throttle on the Mig 29 Flanker forward. The plane rolled down the rain-slick runway gathering speed as it came. In his rear view mirror he could see his wing man behind and to his right. He was vaguely conscious that the second pair of his flight was taking off on the parallel runway several hundred meters to his left.

The weather was abominable, fog and occasional flurries of snow and rain. But that was nothing out of the ordinary and Senior Lieutenant Abrin had nearly a thousand hours flying out of this base.

As they passed the critical point, he eased back on the stick and the powerful interceptor lunged into the air. Even as he climbed into the overcast, Sergei Abrin ran another quick check of his systems.

A Mig 29 had the range for this mission and no Soviet interceptor carried a more powerful or sophisticated radar than the one in the nose of his Flanker. Whatever those things were they were damn hard to pick up on radar and he would need all the power he had.

Satisfied, he watched the altimeter wind up and considered what he and his men were heading into.

For weeks now the powerful warning radars along the coast of Siberia had been getting anomalous and faint returns from out over the narrow sea that separated Russia and Alaska. Recon flights had shown nothing and previous attempts to intercept these things had failed. After the usual dithering and indecision, Moscow had decided to make a serious effort to discover what was happening on this most sensitive of borders.

An early warning aircraft had been assigned and interceptor squadrons were given permission to depart from their regular training plans to investigate in force the next time something was cited. They were also fitted with long-range fuel tanks and given full loads of fuel—a departure in the defection-conscious Soviet air force. If that wasn't enough to convince the pilots how serious this was, the KGB showed up and installed a number of very black boxes in each aircraft.

Senior Lieutenant Abrin thought of himself as a man of the world, as befitted the son of a medium-high party official. He had his own theory about this thing.

It was no accident that nearly invisible aircraft were flying along the US-USSR border. Obviously the United States intended this series of provocations as a tactic to wring further arms concessions from the Soviet negotiators in Vienna.

Well, they would learn the folly of their ways. For longer than Sergei Abrin had been alive, the men and machines of the PVO had stood between the Motherland and the Capitalist aggressors. If they wanted to play games over this narrow sea they would find that the Red Air Force could play also—and far better.

Still, he thought as his interceptor raced out over the ocean. This was a bitch of a day to be flying.

"Go!"

Patrol Two kneed the dragon and pulled on the reins. In response the beast swept into a wide, gentle turn. He was obviously happy to be going home and so was Patrol Two.

The squadron leader's instructions had been explicit. Head out on this track for four day-tenths, then reverse course and return to the temporary base the dragon riders had established on one of the small islands. Each rider had set out alone on a slightly different course to cover as much of this strange new world as they possibly could in the least amount of time. The squadron leader didn't want to stay on the island too long for fear of discovery and for once Patrol Two fully agreed with him. They would pause another day to rest their dragons and then they would leave this ill-begotten place.

This particular corner was worse than most, Patrol Two admitted as the dragon's strong wingbeats bore them along. Not only was there the strangeness here that made dragons uncomfortable and dampened the effect of magic. Here there was also constant fog mixed with freezing rain and snow from thick, low-hanging clouds that forever darkened the sky. Were it not for the dragon's homing instinct and the fact they had flown a straight course out, Patrol Two wasn't at all sure they could find their way back to their fellows.

A weak sun broke through a ragged hole in the clouds, turning the sea the color of fresh-beaten lead. Patrol Two frowned. The sun seemed to be in the wrong place. Then a shake of the head. Well, it wasn't the only thing that was wrong here.

A window popped up on Craig's screen. In it, in full color and three dimensions, was a robot.

"Ready, master," the robot intoned.

"Ready for what?" he snapped. All his worker robots looked alike. Then he saw the designation in the status line under the window. "Oh, the jammer! Then turn it on!"

The robot nodded and winked out while Craig turned his attention back to the warbot he was designing. But now he was smiling.

He had suspected all along that the dragon riders who flitted around the edges of his realm had some kind of communications system. It was magic rather than radio and it had taken a lot of work to discover just how it worked. Once he knew, he had set his robots to work building jammers. Now he had just cut his enemies' communication link.

*Maybe that will clear those damn dragons out of my airspace*, he thought as he went back to work on the warbot.

"Now go!"

Major Michael Francis Xavier Gilligan grunted and broke out of the holding pattern. A quick check of the cockpit panels, a fast glance to the right to make sure Smitty, his wingman was still in position and he concentrated on his descent. Five hundred feet wasn't a lot of altitude for a high performance fighter in this kind of weather. A few seconds inattention and you'd fly right into the water.

*Bitch of a day to go flying*, Gilligan thought to himself. Then he turned his full attention to the job at hand.

Patrol Two looked down at the now-useless communications crystal and swore luridly. Between the

197

winds and the fog, the rider and dragon were perilously close to being lost. And now this!

*This*, thought Patrol Two, *is turning into one bitch of a day.*

Sharp hunched over the operator's shoulder, staring at the big screen as if he was about to dive into it.

"Incoming aircraft!" one of the other operators sang out. Sharp jerked erect and hurried to the man's console.

"We got four, heading our way from the East." The operator looked at the screen again. "Probably those tricked-up Flankers." He studied the radar signature analysis. "Yeah, four Flankers incoming."

"Are they after us or Eagle Flight?" Sharp demanded.

"They're heading into the area Eagle Flight is going for. Uh oh!" The operator spoke quickly into his mike. "The Soviets just lit up their air intercept radars."

"Are they after our guys?"

The operator studied the screen intently. "They're headed in that direction. No, wait a minute. I don't think so. They seem to be after the same targets we are. The IL-76 must have picked them up just after we did."

Ozzie Sharp scowled mightily at the screen. All of a sudden the air over that God-forsaken patch of ocean was getting awfully crowded.

"Smitty, check your ten," Gilligan called to his wingman. "Do you see that?"

Off to their left and slightly below them, something dark was threading its way through a canyon between two banks of clouds.

"What the hell is it?" Smitty demanded a few seconds later.

"I don't know. I don't think it's doing a hundred knots and it keeps ducking in and out of those clouds."

Gilligan touch-keyed his mike to transmit the report, but there was silence in the earphones.

He tried again. Still nothing. He switched radios. Nothing. He tried different frequencies, he checked the circuit breakers, he ran the radio checklist. Still nothing. He could get Smitty but that was all. Meanwhile the thing appeared out of another cloud.

"Smitty, can you raise anyone?"

"Negative, sir."

Gilligan considered for a minute. Whatever this jamming was it apparently wasn't strong enough to block him from talking to his wingman, but there was no way to reach anyone else. It had been made crystal clear to him that one way or another the information he collected *had* to get back.

"Smitty, have you been getting this on tape?"

"Yessir."

"Then make sure you've got a good image and then split off. I'm going in for a closer look."

"The hell you say!"

"As soon as you're sure you've got a good image, split off and get the hell out of here. That information has got to get back."

There was a long crackling silence on the radio.

"Am I supposed to say 'yes sir'?" Smitty said finally.

"You're supposed to get that damn information back. Anything else is up to you. Now, have you got it?"

"On the tape."

"Then go. Remember. No matter what happens to me, you've got to get that data home."

Gilligan watched as his wingman broke off. Since his first day in flight school he had been drilled that a fighter never, ever, flies alone. Suddenly it was awfully lonely.

*Well, the sooner I do this, the sooner it will be over.* Reaching down, he activated his camera. Then just to be on the safe side he armed the two Sidewinders hanging under the fuselage. He left the Sparrows unarmed. That thing might have a fuzzbuster tuned to the targeting radar's frequencies and he didn't want to fight unless he absolutely had to. Finally he checked the status of his 20mm cannon.

*One good pass,* Gilligan told himself. *One pass so close I can see the color of their eyes.*

It was the sound that first alerted Patrol Two. The hissing roar that sliced through the eerie silence of the fog banks. The dragon rider had only a brief glimpse of something moving up behind and to the left. Something very, very fast and headed straight at them.

To a dragon rider that meant only one thing: Dragon attack! No time to turn into it and fight fire with fire. Patrol Two grabbed an iron seeker arrow out of the quiver and brought the bow up with the other hand. Twisting around in the saddle even as the arrow fitted into the bow and not waiting for the seeker to get a lock, Patrol Two got off one shot. Then the rider pressed flat against the beast's back and yanked the reins to throw the dragon into violent evasive maneuvers. The dragon, unsettled by the roaring monster, responded enthusiastically and dropped into a writhing, spiraling dive into the fog.

The arrow's spell wasn't capable of making fine distinctions. It had been launched at a moving target and that was sufficient. The arrow flew straight to its mark and hit the plane's right wing about halfway out toward the tip.

As soon as the point penetrated the thin aluminum skin the arrow's death spell activated. It didn't know it was trying to kill an inanimate object and it was as incapable of caring as it was of knowing.

Like most things magic, the spell didn't work perfectly in this strange halfway world, but it worked well enough.

*"What the fuck?"* Mick Gilligan yelled, but there was no one to hear. His radios, like every other piece of electronic equipment in his Eagle had gone stone dead.

Unlike the F-16, an F-15 does not have to be flown by computers every second it is in the air. But everything from the fuel flow to the trim tabs is normally controlled by electronic devices.

As a result Major Mick Gilligan didn't fall out of the sky instantly. But everything on the plane started going slowly and inexorably to hell.

One of the things that went was the automatic fuel control system. Normally the F-15 draws a few gallons at a time from each tank in the plane to keep everything in trim. When the electronics died, Major Gilligan's plane was drawing from the outboard left wing tank. Rather than switching, it kept draining that tank, lightening the wing and putting the plane progressively more out of trim.

Gilligan didn't notice. He was too busy dealing with the engines. Losing the electronics meant they were no longer automatically synchronized. Almost immediately the right engine was putting out more power than the left. By the time Gilligan had taken stock of the situation, the exhaust gas temperature on the right engine was climbing dangerously and the left engine was going into compressor stall.

He didn't waste time cursing. He put both hands on the throttles and started jockeying the levers individually, trying to get more power out of his left engine and cut back the right before the temperature became critical.

It wasn't easy. Without the electronic controls the throttles were sluggish and the engines unresponsive. Gilligan was like a man trying to take a shower when the hot water is boiling and the cold water is freezing. It's painful and it takes a lot of fiddling to get things right. Gilligan was fiddling furiously.

Gilligan looked up and saw the windshield was opaque with dew. The windshield wipers had quit working along with everything else. He also saw by the ball indicator that the plane was banking right and descending. Instinctively he corrected and put the throttles forward to add power and get away from the water. The engines seemed to hesitate and then they caught with a burst of acceleration that pressed Gilligan back into his seat.

It almost worked. In fact it would have worked if Gilligan hadn't forgotten one other automatic system. When the power came on, the Eagle's nose came up. Too far up. The Boundary Layer Control System that is supposed to keep the F-15 from stalling at high angles of attack was also dead. The nose went up and then back down as the Eagle stalled and plummeted toward the ocean.

Senior Lieutenant Abrin had lost contact with his base and the rest of his flight, but his radar seemed to be working perfectly. He watched on the screen as the Americans performed the highly unusual maneuver of splitting up and one of them turned back. Then he saw the other plane make a pass at something and then disappear from the screen.

That was enough. He quickly turned his plane in that direction to see what had happened.

Patrol Two broke out of the clouds almost in the water. Frantically the rider signaled the beast to climb for everything he was worth. The dragon extended its huge wings fully and beat the air desperately to keep from smashing into the sea. Spray drenched dragon and rider alike, but somehow they avoided the ocean.

The dragon beat its wings strongly to climb away from the water and suddenly roared in pain.

*Fortuna!* Patrol Two thought. Somewhere in the last minute's violent maneuvering the dragon had injured himself. The rider touched the communications crystal worn on a neck thong, but the bit of stone remained cold and dead.

Gilligan reached for the yellow-and-black handle next to his right leg. *I hope to Christ this still works*, he thought as he pulled the ejection lever.

The ejection seat was designed as a fail safe, electronics or no. The canopy blew off and Gilligan was blasted into the air scant feet above the water.

There was a whirling rush and then Gilligan was kicked free of the ejection seat. Suddenly he was dangling under his parachute floating down in a clammy fog to the water he knew had to be below him.

Below and off to one side he saw a tiny splash as his ejection seat hurtled into the Bering Sea. Then the fog closed in around him and all he could see was cottony grayness.

Gilligan cursed luridly. In the personal effects compartment of his ejection seat was his map case and in that map case were several letters he had intended to mail—including the alimony check to his ex-wife which was already a week overdue.

*Sandi's lawyer is going to kill me!* he thought as he floated soundlessly through the fog for an unknown destination.

Patrol Two was in no better shape. The dragon was favoring its right wing in a way the rider knew meant the beast would not be able to bear them up much longer.

*Pox rot this place!* Patrol Two swore silently and then concentrated on trying to remember the way to the nearest land. It was a terrible place to set down, but from the way the dragon's chest muscles tightened with each wing beat Patrol Two realized they would be doing well to make it at all.

Lieutenant Smith hadn't seen Major Gilligan go in, nor had he heard the distress cry from the F-15's transponder. But the major was supposed to make a quick pass and come back to join him. As the minutes ticked by, the lieutenant became increasingly worried. Something had to have happened to his commander.

Smith hadn't gotten a good look at whatever it was, but he knew his video camera had it all down. That part of the mission was over. Now all they had to do was get back safely. He concentrated on guiding his plane back on what he was pretty sure was a reciprocal heading while he kept running through the channels on his radios. Mick would be along, he was sure. And if he wasn't then that video tape was doubly important.

Suddenly Smith's radar and radios were working again. Quickly he shifted to his assigned frequency, keyed his mike and began reporting what had happened.

Lieutenant Smith wasn't at all sure what he had seen down there, but he was reasonably sure the Soviets didn't have anything to do with it.

Patrol Two stayed in the open to make searching for land easier, but the rider also kept close to the clouds to hide quickly if need be. Off on the far horizon, the rider saw a thin line that seemed to be land. The dragon saw it too and surged forward, its wing beats picking up strength as it flew.

Patrol Two was just starting to relax when another of the roaring gray monsters burst out of the clouds above and in front of them less than half a bowshot off.

Instantly, the rider rolled the dragon right and

ducked into the clouds. As the misty gray swallowed them up, Patrol Two had a quick glimpse of the thing rolling into a turn to follow them.

*So stiff,* Patrol Two thought. *Its wings don't move even in a turn and the rest of the body stays rigid as well.* Whatever the things were, they weren't dragons.

Senior Lieutenant Abrin spent the next ten minutes dodging in and out of the clouds looking for the thing again. Although his plane did not have a video imaging system like the F-15s and it had all happened so quickly he hadn't had time to turn on his gun cameras, he had gotten a good look at the object before it disappeared.

Lieutenant Abrin had no such doubts about what he had just seen. His most prized possessions were a Japanese VCR and a bunch of bootleged American movies. The more he thought about it the more obvious it was to him what was going on.

"Comrades. Do we have any information on Spielberg making a movie in this area?"

## Twenty-five
# MAROONED

*Warm!* Mick Gilligan thought as he spluttered his way to the surface. *The water's warm.*

By rights it ought to be nearly freezing. But it was nearly as tepid as the Caribbean.

*Nothing but surprises,* he thought as he pulled his seat pack to the surface with the cord attached to his leg. *At least this one is pleasant.* He unsnapped the cover on the top half and inflated his raft.

*Wait a minute! There are sharks in the Caribbean.* He redoubled his struggles to get into the raft.

It wasn't easy. An Air Force survival raft is about the size of a child's wading pool and it is designed to be stable once the pilot is in it, not to be easy to get into. Gilligan was encumbered by his arctic survival suit, his G-suit and his flight suit. He wanted to hurry for fear of sharks, but he didn't want to splash too much for fear of attracting them. If there had been anyone to watch, it might have been fairly amusing. But there wasn't and Gilligan himself wasn't at all amused.

Once he had flopped into the raft he tried to orient himself. The one thing that hadn't changed was the fog. It was dense and thick everywhere. The air was a good deal colder than the water, so that wasn't astonishing, but it didn't explain *why* the water was so warm.

He pulled the seat pack into the raft and set it on his lap while he undid the catches on the bottom. Inside was a standard Air Force survival kit, including food, medical supplies and a lot of other necessities. Right now he was most interested in the radio and the emergency transponder.

The radio was about the size of a pack of cigarettes.

Eagerly Gilligan extended the antenna and trailed the ground wire over the side into the water. Then he tried the radio. Only a hiss and crackle of static came out of the speaker.

Grimacing, Gilligan carefully clipped the radio to the breast pocket of his flight suit. Next he pulled out the transponder and examined it.

The transponder was bigger than the survival radio, but it did more. When it received a signal indicating an aircraft was in the area it transmitted a powerful homing signal. Just now it was silent as the grave.

Gilligan punched the self-test button on the receiver and watched the LED indicator light up. Then he studied the other indicator for a few minutes and his expression got grimmer and grimmer.

Every military aircraft and almost all airliners and business aircraft carry beacons which would trigger his transponder. Gilligan knew for a fact that an AWACS and several other aircraft should have been within range. If even one plane was above the horizon, the device should have been screaming its little electronic heart out. Yet the self-test said it was working.

Either the self-test was lying or there were no planes above the horizon. Considering what the rest of this business had been like, Gilligan didn't think the transponder was broken.

He pulled out his compass. He didn't expect it to work this far north and he wasn't disappointed.

There was one very non-standard item in Major Michael Francis Xavier Gilligan's survival kit. A 9mm Beretta automatic with three fourteen-round magazines and a black nylon Bianchi shoulder holster to match. He inspected the pistol, slammed one of the magazines home and jacked back the slide. Then he struggled into the shoulder holster's harness.

Then he felt a lot better.

Back at the base the people were feeling worse as the minutes ticked by.

The general wasn't happy, Ozzie Sharp wasn't happy, the squadron commander wasn't happy and unhappiest of all was the young captain who ran the base's rescue operation.

"We got on his last known position quickly and flew an expanding spiral search," the captain explained. "Then we did it again with a different aircraft and crew. We have had aircraft on top almost constantly. There is no voice communication and no transponder signal."

"What about the Russians?"

"They say they haven't seen any sign of him."

"And you believe them?"

"It's credible," Ozzie Sharp said. "The Russians returned to their base with all their missiles still on their wings." No one bothered to ask how he knew.

The general grunted. Then his head snapped up and he transfixed the young captain with a steely-eyed stare.

"Why the bloody hell can't you even find the area where he went down?"

"Sir, this is a very unusual situation. He had sent his wing man back, so we don't have as much information as we normally do." The captain thought about explaining how well they were doing to have gotten this far in the few hours since the missing pilot's wingman had broken out of the dead zone. Then he caught the general's eye again and decided not to.

"Have your crews found anything unusual?" Sharp asked. "Any unusual readings or problems with your instruments?"

"None, sir. As far as we can tell, there's nothing in that fog but more fog."

The expression on Sharp's face made the general seem mild by comparison.

"We're going over the area again," the captain offered quickly. "But so far there's no sign of Major Gilligan or his plane."

"Nothing on the transponder?" the general asked.

"Nossir," the officer said.

"Captain, I thought this sort of thing wasn't supposed to happen."

"It isn't, sir."

*It's as if he dropped off the face of the earth,* the captain thought. But it was bad form to say something like that.

Major Gilligan drifted through the fog and tried to figure out what the hell had happened to him. He didn't have the faintest idea where he was, but increasingly he doubted it was anywhere near Alaska. There was still fog all around him, but when the sun broke through it was bright, warm and too high in the sky, totally unlike anything he had experienced in Alaska.

He could hear the sound of surf off to his left. Surf usually meant land of some kind, so that was as good a direction as any. Besides, the fog seemed to be marginally thinner that way.

Major Michael Francis Xavier Gilligan began paddling grimly toward the sound of the waves.

# Twenty-six

# GILLIGAN'S ISLAND

Gilligan saw the land almost as soon as he broke out of the fog bank. One minute he was paddling along surrounded by whiteness and the next he was out under sunny skies with only an occasional puff of fleecy white clouds. Behind him the fog looked like a wall.

Ahead of him he could see a shore fringed with trees, and hills behind. Between him and that shore waves beat on a reef, making the noise that had drawn him here.

Gilligan studied the situation as best he could sitting in his raft. Fortunately the current wasn't strong here and the tide was high. He thought about trying to find a channel, but he decided that would cost him more energy than he could afford. So he picked the best-looking spot and paddled toward it.

It took perhaps an hour for Gilligan to negotiate the reef and another forty-five minutes or so to cross the lagoon behind it. As he crossed the lagoon, Gilligan had a chance to admire "his" island. It was worth admiring, he had to admit. The black sand beach was smooth and unmarred. The trees behind it were tall and tropic green. The place looked like a travel poster.

*A travel poster for a deserted island,* he thought. There was no sign of footprints, tire tracks, roads or trails. The detritus along the tide line included not one beer can, plastic jug or bottle.

Reflexively he scanned the sky for contrails. There were very few places in the world where you could not see jet tracks in the sky, but apparently this was one of them. Except for the clouds and the fog on the water behind him there was nothing in the sky but the bright tropical sun.

*Wherever I am, with scenery like this there's sure to be a Club Med or something close by.*

After pulling his raft up on the beach above the tide line, Gilligan stripped off his life vest, arctic survival suit and G-suit, stowed his gear, checked his radios again and started off down the beach. Either this place was as deserted as it looked or it wasn't and he stood a better chance of finding either people or food if he stayed on the beach.

After almost an hour of walking he found nothing to show that the place was or ever had been inhabited. He had stopped twice to empty the sand out of his boots. Finally he tied the laces together and slung them around his neck so he could walk barefoot through the fine black sand.

Crabs skittered across the beach, gulls wheeled over the water and an occasional brightly colored bird flashed through the trees. But there was not a single sign of human life.

*Damn it*, he thought, scanning the sky again. *Places like this just don't exist any more.* He looked down the long, pristine stretch of beach. *And if they do, I want to retire here!*

He had been walking perhaps half a mile barefoot when he found a place where a boat had pulled up. *Not a boat*, he corrected, *an amphibious tractor.* The signs were clear enough. The place where it had come out of the water had been washed away by the tide, but he could clearly see where it had pulled up above the tide line and then the tread marks where it had churned over the soft sand and in among the trees between the tread marks was a furrow as if the vehicle had not retracted its rudder. Following the line he could even see where several branches had been broken off in its passage.

Gilligan paused and considered. An amphtrack implied military. Even in backwaters like this civilians

211

didn't own them. That meant there was an element of risk in meeting the tractor and its crew. On the other hand, there was also the possibility of rescue.

He studied the marks carefully. Although he was no expert, he knew that the amphibious tractors of the U.S. Marines drove through the water on special treads with extra-deep cleats. Soviet equipment used regular treads and either propellers or water jets. But the sand was much too fine and soft to give him any clue. He could only see that something big and not wheeled had come this way.

*What the hell, this is the era of glasnost. We're all supposed to be friends these days.* He sat down on a tree root and put his boots on. Then he checked his pistol. *Still, it never hurts to be careful.*

Cautiously, Major Mick Gilligan set off into the forest in pursuit of the vehicle.

The trail was surprisingly difficult to follow. The amphtrack had not torn up the forest floor as much as he expected. There were no clear tread marks and in many places broken branches offered clearer indications than the tracks. Still, you can't move something that big through a wooded area without leaving a plain trail.

Except for the breeze in the trees and an occasional bird or animal call, the woods were silent. There was no sound of an engine, which made Gilligan even more cautious. But there were no voices, either. Perhaps they were too far ahead for him to hear.

Gilligan was a pilot, not a woodsman. He had to divide his attention between trying to follow the trail, trying not to walk into a tree and trying to scout ahead. So it wasn't surprising he stepped into the clearing without seeing Patrol Two standing in the trees on the other side.

Then the dragon rider shifted. Gilligan caught the motion and looked up. Then he stared—first at the weapon and then at the wielder.

The bow was nearly as tall as she was and the limbs were of unequal length. Gilligan remembered seeing something like that when he had been stationed in Japan and he had gone to a demonstration of traditional Japanese archery. But the person carrying it was anything but Japanese.

To Gilligan she looked like something out of a Robin Hood movie. She wore thigh-high boots of soft brown leather, tight breeches that bloused out at the thigh and a fleece-lined vest over a close-fitting tunic. She was tall, nearly as tall as he was, and slender. Her hair was cornsilk blonde and freckles dusted her nose. The eyes were pure, pale blue and very, very serious. The arrow in her bow was aimed straight at his midriff.

"Uh, hi," Gilligan said.

## Twenty-seven
# ENCOUNTER

Karin studied the stranger carefully without shifting the aim of the arrow. He was a big man, broad shouldered and apparently well muscled, although it was hard to tell through his clothing. He wore a drab green coverall with straps, pockets and strange black runes scattered over it. The thing in his hand was black and shiny and he handled it like a weapon, although Karin had never seen its like.

In all their patrolling, the dragon riders had never seen a human in this place. Indeed, they had been told there were only two humans among the enemy and they never left their castle. Where did this one come from?

He didn't act like one of the enemy, she thought. In fact he seemed more confused than hostile. Still better to be safe, so she simply nodded to him without moving the bow.

"I'm Major Michael Gilligan, United States Air Force. I, ah, had a little trouble back there and I need to contact my unit." He stopped, as if expecting a response. "Um, I don't suppose there's a phone around here anywhere?"

"Air Force? You are a flier then?"

"Yes, ma'am. Only, as I say, I had a little trouble and came down in the water."

"And your mount?"

"Down at sea."

The poor man's dragon had drowned! To Karin, who had only narrowly avoided the same fate, the tragedy was doubly poignant.

"I'm very sorry," she said, lowering her bow. "I am called Karin and I too am a flier."

Slowly and with exaggerated care, the man put the

black metal thing in a pouch under his armpit. "Pleased to meet you, ma'am. Ah, about that phone . . . ?"

"I do not think you will find one here," Karin told him, not quite comprehending what a "phone" was.

"I kind of figured that," he said. "Where are we, anyway?"

"I am not quite sure," she admitted. "I think it is the western shore of the main island in the Bubble World."

"Bubble World?" he asked blankly.

"The World between the Worlds. I do not pretend to understand it, but our wizards say that it is connected at one end to our World and at the other end to the World from whence came the Sparrow."

"Sparrow? Excuse me, ma'am, but I'm just plain confused."

"Of course! You must be from the other World, the Sparrow's World." She smiled. "This must all be very strange to you, I know."

"Yes, ma'am!" he said fervently. "It certainly is that."

"Well, come back to my camp then and we can talk. Oh, and stop calling me ma'am. I am neither a witch, a wizard or an elder and I am called Karin."

He looked at her in a way Karin found rather pleasant. "No ma'am—I mean, Karin—you are definitely not an *old* witch!"

*This*, Major Mick Gilligan told himself firmly, *has gotta be a hallucination*. He was probably lying in a hospital bed somewhere drugged out of his skull after being fished out of the Bering Sea. He wondered if his nurse looked anything like Karin.

*Still*, he thought, *hallucination or not, I've gotta play it like it's real*. So far it hadn't been too bad. Stuck on a deserted island with a beautiful girl, even a beautiful girl who thought she was William Tell. No, that wasn't half bad for a hallucination.

"My camp is just over there," Karin said, pointing toward an especially thick clump of trees.

"Where's your vehicle?" Gilligan asked.

"No vehicle, only Stigi and myself," Karin told him as they stepped into the camp.

"But we've been following . . ." Gilligan began.

Then he saw the dragon.

Stigi was only average size for a cavalry mount— which is to say he was eighty feet long and his wings would probably span as much when fully extended.

An eighty-foot wingspan on an airplane wouldn't have impressed Gilligan particularly. Eighty feet of bat wings on a scaled, fanged monster who looked ready to breathe fire at any second was *very* impressive.

Gilligan's jaw dropped and he licked his lips. "That's, that's a . . ."

"That is Stigi," Karin supplied, strolling over to the monster and patting its scaly shoulder just in front of its left wing.

The dragon raised its head about ten feet off the ground and regarded Gilligan with a football-sized golden eye.

"Does it fly?"

"Of course he flies," Karin said. "How else would we get here?"

"Hoo boy," said Major Mick Gilligan. "Oh boy."

Karin's camp was well off the beach, in a fold in the ground well-shaded by trees. The dragon took up a good half the space, but there was still room for a small fire and a simple canopy made with something like a shelter half.

"This is pretty cozy," Gilligan said as he looked around.

"I am a scout," Karin explained. "There is always the possibility of being caught away from my base and

216

having to forage. So," she shrugged, "we are prepared."

"There aren't many places we can land away from our bases," Mick told her. "If something goes wrong we have to bail out."

"Bail out?"

"Use our ejection seats."

"Ejection seats?"

He looked over at the dragon. "Yeah, I guess you don't have much call for those."

"Now," Karin said, settling herself on a log by the fire, "what happened to you, Major?"

"It's Mick, as long as we're on a first name basis."

Karin frowned prettily. "I thought you said your name was major."

"No, that's my rank. My first name's Michael, but everyone calls me Mick."

"Ah," Karin said. "When Stigi and I are in the air we are called Patrol Two."

"That's like a call sign. I was Eagle One on my last mission."

"What happened to you?"

Gilligan sighed. "Kind of a long story. Basically we were getting some peculiar—ah, indications—from an area out over the ocean and they sent us out to look. My wingman and I found something, but we couldn't communicate with our base. I sent him back and went on in for a closer look. There was a little tussle and I came out on the short end."

It was Karin's turn to sigh. "That is more or less what happened to me. I was out on single patrol, near the great fog bank where this World connects to yours, when I was attacked from behind. I managed to avoid the attacker and I even got a shot off at it, but in the maneuvering Stigi sprained his wing."

"Sprained it?"

"Our dragons seldom hurt themselves so, but this is

a strange place and things are not exactly as they are in our world."

"They're not as they are in our world, either," Gilligan said, looking over at Stigi. The dragon's head was resting on the ground but one unwinking yellow eye was fixed on Gilligan.

"What jumped you, another dragon?" he asked as he turned so he didn't have to look at the dragon looking at him.

Karin frowned. "Something strange. It was all gray and roared as it came. I did not get a good look at it."

*Uh-oh,* Gilligan thought. *Gray and roaring and came at her from behind. Hooboy.*

To cover himself he asked the first non-personal question that came to mind. "You keep talking about different worlds. What do you mean?"

"There is our World, where magic holds sway. There is your World, where I gather magic works poorly or not at all?" He nodded and she went on. "And there is this World, where both the things of our world and the things of your world work after a fashion. But this World is new. Some say it was created by our enemies."

"Your enemies?"

"Powerful wizards who command legions of non-living beings," Karin explained. "It is said they prepare war against both your world and ours. But surely you know this?"

"All we know is that there's something funny going on out over the ocean. We thought maybe it was someone from our world. That's why I was sent to investigate."

The dragon rider frowned. "If that is all your people know then surely you must return to bear word to them."

"That's my plan."

Karin sighed. "I wish I could contact my base, but

my communication crystal stopped working just before I was attacked. I am sure my squadron commander would know what to do."

"You seem to be doing all right," Gilligan said, looking around the camp site.

Karin smiled. She had a wonderful smile, Gilligan noticed. Then she sobered. "Thank you, but I feel so inadequate. I have been a rider for just two seasons. I have never been in combat before. In that time there has been no one to fight."

"I know the feeling," Gilligan told her. "I've been in for ten years, I've got about 1800 hours in F-15s and I've never been in combat either." He had missed Iraq because he'd been in the hospital with hepatitis, but he didn't tell her that.

Karin looked astonished. "Ten years and never a battle?"

"We've been at peace all that time," Gilligan said. *Well, more or less.* "Actually we've been at peace for almost twenty-five years and we haven't had a major war in nearly fifty."

"Forgive me, but if that is so then why do you maintain fighting fliers?"

"Because for most of that time we've been close to war. My nation and another great nation were ready to go to war at a moment's notice."

"Yet you did not? You must be remarkably peace-loving in spite of it."

Gilligan grinned mirthlessly. "Not peace-loving. Scared. We got too good at it. We developed weapons that would let us destroy cities in an eyeblink. Weapons we had no defenses against. All of a sudden a major war didn't look real cost effective."

Karin shivered. "I do not think I would like to see war in your world."

"Neither would we," Gilligan told her.

"But," Karin said thoughtfully, "with such weapons you would be powerful allies against our enemies."

"Maybe. I don't make policy, but I'm sure willing to carry the word back to the people who do."

"We must get you back to your World, then."

"You mean you can get me home?"

"The Mighty at the Capital certainly can. The Sparrow knows how."

"But first we've got to get to your Capital. Are they going to come looking for you?"

Karin shrugged. "Probably. But they dare not search too long or too hard. Magical methods work poorly here and we are too close to our enemies' hold to risk many riders and dragons."

"So they aren't likely to find us."

"No, but I do not think that will matter. Once Stigi's wing is healed, he will be able to carry us back to my people."

Gilligan looked over at the snoring dragon. "You mean that thing can really get us out of here?"

"In easy stages, of course. Stigi can carry two for a ways and there are many reefs and islands where we can rest."

"That's something to look forward to, anyway."

"Meanwhile," Karin said, getting up. "It is late and morning comes early. Let us to bed."

Mick Gilligan fell asleep that night and dreamed about flying and girls with blonde hair and freckles.

*Quite a collection of brass,* Willie Sherman thought to herself. It wasn't the biggest group she'd ever worked with and it wasn't the highest ranking, but it was still two generals, a gaggle of colonels of both types and a brother who was obviously some kind of high-up spook. Pretty impressive.

Not that Master Sergeant Wiletta Sherman was impressed. After being in for eighteen years there wasn't a lot left that could impress her.

Less than twenty-four hours ago she had been at Edwards AFB in the California desert helping to test a new filmless imaging system. She had been ordered to Alaska so quickly she'd just had time to throw a winter uniform into a suitcase and grab a few toiletries.

Unfortunately whoever was responsible for this building had never heard of the DOD energy conservation guidelines. It had to be eighty-five degrees and she was already sweating in her heavy blue wool uniform.

If it weren't for all the brass she would have taken her jacket off. But no one else had, so she just sweated.

"Everybody here?" asked the ranking two-star. "Okay, pull it up and let's see what we got."

Willie hit a couple of keys to call up the file on the screen. Before she got here someone had already gone through the tape, picked out the best images and digitized them. So all she had to do was the processing.

The workstation she was using wasn't much bigger than a personal computer tied to a compact refrigerator, but it had cost the government nearly a million dollars. She didn't know how many millions had gone into the software, but it obviously hadn't been cheap. For Willie, who had started her career analyzing photographs of North Vietnam with a binocular microscope, it was a lot more impressive than her audience.

After a couple of seconds the image flashed on the screen. Willie looked at it and her eyes went wide. Some asshole was playing tricks, in front of the goddamn generals, no less!

The picture was obviously taken at long range but it was clear enough. Against a background of fleecy gray clouds a dragon sailed along with its wings extended. There was a rider on its back just forward of the wings.

Beautiful job, though. There was no sign of a matte line or the kinds of shadow inconsistencies that usually trip up faked photographs—not that that was going to save the poor bastard who was responsible.

Willie braced for the inevitable explosion. It didn't come. All the generals and colonels were staring at the picture as if it made sense. Some of them looked sideways at each other, as if they wanted to say something, but none of them opened their mouths.

"Hmm, ah yes," the major general said. "You're sure this is, ah, correct?"

"I unloaded the tape and digitized the image myself," said the colonel in charge of the base's imaging section.

"And this is the best image that was on the tape?"

"Ah, yes sir," said the colonel. "None of them are any better and they all, um, show the same thing."

The major general looked over at the black man in the flight suit with no insignia and the brother looked back at the general. Not a muscle in either man's face moved.

"Well then," the general said briskly. "We'll have to use this one." He peered at the screen again. "Although it is a little out of focus."

*It's a dragon, you fucking moron!* Willie Sherman thought. But in the Air Force there are times when you protest and there are times when you keep your mouth shut. In her climb to master sergeant she had learned which was which and this was definitely a time to shut up and soldier.

"Let's check it against known aircraft first," the head of the image processing section said.

*Try checking it against Saturday morning cartoons,* Willie thought. But she entered the command anyway.

Quickly the machine ran through the profiles of Soviet and NATO aircraft.

"No match, sir," Willie reported without taking her eyes off the screen. Even smiling would be bad form and she wasn't sure she could keep a straight face if she met someone's eyes.

The major general nodded. "A new type then."

"That's what we suspected all along," the man with no insignia said.

"Let's see if we can get some more detail," the imaging colonel said. "Try stretching the contrast."

Without comment Willie used the mouse to indicate the new contrast range. Instantly the dragon and rider seemed to fuzz and smooth out as every shade of color broke down into sixteen closely related shades.

"Look there along the trailing edge of the wing," said one of the other colonels. "That's obviously some different kind of material."

"Radar absorbing," said the spook. "If you look at the way the trailing edge is scalloped you'll see that it has some resemblance to the trailing edge of the B-2."

"Might also be radiators to dump infrared," one of the other colonels said.

The brigadier general rubbed his chin. "Plausible. Okay, assume they're radiators. They'd be flat black, wouldn't they?"

The imaging colonel nodded. "That gives us a color reference. Make them flat black."

*I can't believe you people are taking this seriously!* Willie thought. But what she said was, "Yes, sir."

Making the rear of the wings flat black changed the colors on the rest of the image, muting them and fuzzing the details even further.

"Okay," the two-star general said. "Now, where are the tail surfaces?"

"If you look closely at the tail boom you'll see it's somewhat flattened," the imaging colonel told him. "The entire thing is apparently an empennage."

"Enhance that, will you?" the brigadier asked. "Let's see if we can bring out the detail along the boom."

"Try compressing the tones there," suggested the imaging colonel.

Willie marked out the tail with her mouse and compressed the colors. Now four or five shades on the tail were rendered as one. The thing on the screen didn't look like a dragon anymore, but it didn't look like much of anything else either.

Slowly and gradually, one change at a time, the gaggle of officers used a million-dollar workstation to enhance a clear picture of a dragon into something they could accept.

By the time they broke for dinner they were arguing over the serial numbers on the tail.

It was still cool and gray when Mick awoke, but Karin was already stirring. She had taken the quiver from the pile of harness and slung it over her shoulder.

"What are you doing?" he asked, throwing back the blanket.

"I must hunt to feed my mount," the dragonrider said, holding her bow horizontally and sighting down the string.

Mick Gilligan compared the monster before him to his dog at home and then computed the amount of dog food it would take to make a meal for a fifty-foot-long golden retriever.

"An elephant a day?"

"Not so much," Karin shook her head and then brushed a wisp of golden hair off her forehead. "Dragons are related in part to lizards and magical besides. They do not eat as much as you would suppose."

"Still, it's going to take a lot of meat."

"I know where to find that. There is open country not far from here and large game to be had. Will you hunt with me?"

At home Mick had gone deer hunting occasionally, without much luck. On the other hand the thought of being stuck in camp all day with an overgrown iguana with a sore wing didn't appeal to him either.

"Sure," he said. "Let me get boots on."

Karin led off at a brisk pace through the forest. Trailing behind her Gilligan found himself admiring the way she moved lithely through the undergrowth—and the swing of her hips in her tight riding breeches. He shook the thought off and tried to concentrate on business.

Gradually the trees thinned and the underbrush

diminished until the forest became almost parklike. Once a herd of deer or something like them went bounding away at their passage. Karin ignored them, obviously intent on bigger game.

After perhaps three miles the forest petered out altogether and they moved out onto a broad plain. The trees were reduced to occasional clumps and the grass varied between knee and waist high.

Karin stopped and raised her head as if she was sniffing the air. Then she pointed off to their left and, motioning Gilligan to silence, she started off in that direction.

Gilligan heard their prey before he saw it. The wind brought crackling and crashing as if a number of large animals were moving about. As they got closer he could smell them as well, a faint odor that reminded him of nothing so much as the elephant house in the zoo.

The dragon rider moved through the grass silently with a grace that made it seem effortless. Gilligan, trying to move quietly, found it wasn't effortless at all. He had to keep his eyes on the ground in order to keep from stepping on dry leaves or twigs. He was so intent on trying to move quietly he almost ran into Karin when she stopped suddenly. Then he looked up and saw what they were hunting.

*Dinosaurs!* Gilligan thought. There were about a dozen of them in a clump of trees perhaps a hundred and fifty yards off. They were bipedal and balanced themselves with their long tails while they used their smaller forearms to pull branches down to the small heads on their snakelike necks and then nipped off the leaves and buds. They were striped dusty gray and green and they didn't look like any dinosaurs he had ever seen pictures of. But they were definitely large and reptilian.

While Gilligan had been staring at the animals, Karin had slipped to one side and dropped down on one knee. Slowly and carefully she drew the bow to full extension, string and arrow kissing her lip. Then she released.

Suddenly an arrow sprouted from the flank of one of the dinosaurs. The beast stopped feeding, looked down at its tormentor, honked once and then dropped like a sack of sand.

Instantly the other dinosaurs fled, honking and bellowing, knocking over a small tree in their flight.

As the noise of the herd faded into the distance Karin and Mick moved up to the carcass.

"They have no fear of humans," Karin said, surveying her kill. "If all the beasts on this island are like that I will have no trouble keeping Stigi fed."

"As long as they don't stampede toward you when you shoot one," Gilligan said.

"Such animals almost always run upwind when frightened," Karin told him. "That way they can smell what is ahead of them."

"Great," Mick said, looking at the kill. "Now, how do we get it back to camp?"

"That will not be necessary. Stigi can walk. I will go and get him. Can you stay here with the kill?"

"Sure."

"Oh, and do not let predators get at the carcass. Stigi expects to be first on a kill and it upsets him when he is not."

Mick thought of Stigi angry. "Right," he said.

Karin nodded and strode off the way they had come.

"Hey, wait a minute! How do I keep predators off this carcass?"

Karin turned back to him. "Use your weapon," she called and then disappeared in the brush.

Mick drew the 9mm automatic and looked at it sourly. Then he looked over at the elephant-sized monster he was supposed to be guarding. Then he thought about the kind of thing that was likely to prey on something the size of an elephant.

"Right," he said again.

The sun was close to the horizon when Stigi waddled out of the forest with Karin alongside. Mick moved to meet them, but Stigi drew back his head and hissed like a jet engine starting up. Mick took the hint and backed off.

"He does not like you," Karin said, quite unnecessarily. "Perhaps it would be better if you gathered wood for a fire. It looks as if we shall have to camp here tonight." Mick noticed that both his and Karin's pack were tied to the saddle.

Mick retrieved the hand axe and started gathering firewood. After he saw Stigi tear into the carcass he spent as much time as he could with his back to the dragon. Stigi's manners ran to the enthusiastic rather than the polite and Mick, who hated the chore of field dressing a rabbit, was a little put out by the sight.

By the time Mick had a double armload of firewood Stigi had finished his meal. The dragon followed docilely behind Karin and settled down near the fire with a belch that smelled like smog in a butcher shop.

Their own dinner was a thick stew of parched grain, dried fruit and jerky from Karin's pack. By mutual agreement they had decided to save Gilligan's rations against future need.

While they ate Stigi washed himself with his tongue like a giant cat and then curled up and went to sleep. With his belly full he snored even more loudly.

Around them the plain was alive with the sounds of night birds and the roars of hunting predators. Gilligan took to running his thumb over the butt of his pistol and searching the darkness.

"Nothing will come close to us," Karin told him,

catching his expression. "They are afraid of Stigi and the fire."

"What about scavengers after the carcass?"

Karin shook her head. "Especially not the scavengers. Besides, if something did approach Stigi would sense it instantly and waken."

"What's left of that carcass is going to get pretty ripe in a couple of days."

"We will not be here that long. Indeed, we would not have camped here tonight if darkness had not caught us. We need to be back among the trees for safety."

"Doesn't that just make it easier for things to sneak up on us?"

"Not the predators." Karin pointed outside the firelit circle. "That."

Mick followed her arm with his eyes. Off in the distance there was a greenish glow against the sky, as if there were a city lit entirely by mercury vapor lamps just over the horizon.

"What is that?"

"Our enemies' hold," Karin said grimly. "A great castle and fortress."

"So close? They must be on the next island over."

"No," Karin told him. "They are on this island."

Mick started. "Then what the hell are we doing sitting around a campfire?"

"Keeping off predators," Karin said sharply. "Without the fire they would be a danger, Stigi or no."

"Besides," she added, relaxing slightly, "those of the castle do not hunt by night."

"If you say so," Mick said neutrally.

"Such has been our experience."

Despite the roaring and the snoring, Mick finally got to sleep that night. But he didn't sleep easily or comfortably and his dreams weren't nearly as pleasant as they had been the night before.

Craig looked down from the balcony and out over the serried ranks of his handiwork.

The narrow valley was full of rank upon rank of war machines. There were warbots ranging from two-ton Fleas to 200-ton Deathbringers, there were tanks and armored cars and artillery and jeeps and scout cars and missile carriers and on and on. They were there by the companies and battalions and regiments, by the hundreds and the thousands. They packed the valley and spilled back through the enormous portal at the valley's head into the very bowels of the mountain. And over it all, perched on a reviewing stand carved out of living rock, was their creator.

Looking them over, Craig reflected he had come a long way since those first crude robots.

Now for the test. He had marked off hundreds of square miles of desert south of the castle for a proving ground. There he would pit his creations against each other to test his tactics and designs. When the battles for the control of the new world began he wanted his armies to be perfect.

Flanked by his robot servants, Craig shifted in his elaborately carved chair. The other chair on the platform was empty. Mikey had sent word at the last minute that he would be too busy to watch the show.

*As if he's done anything since we got here,* Craig thought. Aside from a few robots he had whipped up for his own use, Mikey had never touched his engineering workstation. Craig seldom saw him anymore and he palmed him off with vague explanations when he tried to ask about his work.

*Even if he was busy, he could have taken a couple of hours to see at least part of the parade,* Craig thought. He realized that part of it was disappointment. He was sure

Mikey would be impressed when he saw the super-weapons he had whipped up. *But no, he's too busy even to come to the damn parade.*

Well, it didn't matter. He'd created all this and now he'd work out the winning tactics on the game board of the desert. When the time came Mikey would be plenty impressed with how his armies performed in battle. That was really all that mattered.

He turned to the robot to his right. "Move out," he commanded.

The valley filled with the ear-splitting noise of ten thousand engines starting up. Clouds of dust roiled over the scene as Craig's army began to move.

On wheels, on tracks, on legs and on cushions of air, the forces Craig had fashioned out of magic and engineering began to pass by their creator in review. In spite of the noise, the choking dust and the diesel and gasoline fumes, Craig hung over the balcony rail and watched entranced for hours.

## Thirty-one
# PICNIC ON PARADISE

Karin was as good as her word. They were breaking camp at dawn and by the time the sun was full up they were back in the forest. By mid-day they had found another camp site. The hillside Karin chose was not far from the plain and its plentiful supply of dragon fodder, but the trees were tall and broad enough to provide cover even for a dragon. There was a rock outcropping with an overhang that would shield their fires from prying eyes and could serve as a lookout spot as well. At the foot of the hill a small stream wound through the forest.

By the time they had returned to their old camp site and brought their goods to the new spot, it was late in the afternoon. This time Karin insisted on gathering the firewood and she brought in several armloads of dead branches.

"The wood is neither green nor rotten," she explained as she threw down the third load. "It makes almost no smoke."

Dinner that night was a stew of dried meat, grain and dried fruit, all from Karin's rations. Tomorrow they could explore and see what kinds of food they could find in the forest. For tonight it was easier to eat what they had.

"So tell me about dragon riding," Gilligan said as they scraped the last of the stew out of their bowls.

"It is much the same everywhere, is it not?"

Gilligan shrugged. "I wouldn't know. We fly airplanes, not dragons."

Karin looked at him strangely.

"Machines," Gilligan explained. "Non-living flying things."

"I see," Karin said slowly and then seemed to gather herself. "Well, it takes several years to become a flier. You must bond with your dragon, of course. Then you must learn how to maneuver, how to fly in formation and combat tactics."

"You mean you actually fight air to air combat on those things?"

"Yes."

Gilligan whistled. "That must be something to see. I imagine your tactics aren't anything like ours."

"Well," Karin said slowly, "there are many things to consider. In general, the rider who starts with the best position will win. That usually means diving on your enemy from above with the sun at your back. But of course there are many other things you must consider. Relative strength, level of training."

"It's the same with us," Gilligan told her. "If we get in close we try to have the advantage in height and position. Diving out of the sun is a favorite tactic."

"We do that also," Karin said.

"Do you break off after one pass?"

"We might. It depends on numbers and your dragon's fighting potential. Some dragons, like Stigi, are very strong and fierce. In a melee I would have a considerable advantage." She paused and frowned. "Still, there are a great many things which can happen in such a situation. Diving on an enemy and past him is surer."

"Have you ever been in a dog fight?"

"Crave pardon?"

"That's what we call short-range air-to-air combat. Dog fights."

Karin considered. "I see. Yes, the expression is somewhat apt. But no, I have never been in battle of any sort."

She hesitated for a minute. "Mick, may I ask you something?"

"Sure."

"Are you bonded to another?"

Mick looked up from the fire. "I beg your pardon?"

233

"Bonded? I do not know your customs, but do you have a life companion, a mate?"

"We get married," Gilligan told her. "I was. Not any more."

"Your wife died? I am sorry."

"No, we're divorced—that means we ended the marriage."

Karin grew solemn. "Among us that is not a thing done easily."

"It isn't easy with us either," Gilligan said, thinking of the lawyers, the interminable conferences, the constant phone calls and the months of aching, gaping hurt.

"Forgive me for asking, but how did your wife displease you?"

Gilligan smiled mirthlessly into the campfire. "She didn't displease me. I displeased her. I think. Or maybe we just displeased each other. Anyway, she had her choice of rotating to Alaska with me or leaving me, so she left." He snapped the twig and threw it into the fire.

"Look, it was nobody's fault. Okay? It's just that I'm a pilot and an Air Force officer and she couldn't handle that."

For a while neither of them said anything. "I understand, somewhat," Karin said slowly. She sighed. "I was to be married once, while I was in training. But Johan wanted me to give up flying. I could not do that."

The fire turned the pale skin of her cheeks ruddy and painted reddish highlights into her blonde hair.

"I couldn't either. God knows I loved Sandi, but I just couldn't give it up."

Karin looked up at him and smiled slightly. "We are two of a kind then."

"Guess so," Gilligan agreed.

They sat by the fire for a while in companionable silence.

*   *   *

The next morning Karin took Stigi out into the open and carefully exercised him. She was frowning when she led him back into camp.

"How's the wing?" Mick asked, seeing her expression.

"Not good. It is healing, but only slowly. It may be another half-moon before Stigi is strong enough to bear us away."

"Is it infected or something?"

"Nothing like that. It is simply taking more time than it should to heal. If I did not know better I would think he was not properly fed." She sighed. "As it is, I suspect it is simply the nature of this place. It is harder for dragons to stay aloft here, you know."

"I hadn't noticed."

She led Stigi back to his resting place and spent the next hour or so grooming him and talking to him. To Mick, lounging under the overhang, the sight was remarkable. *Beauty and the Beast,* he thought.

Karin was still frowning when she left Stigi and came to sit beside him in the shade.

"Something else wrong with Stigi?"

"No. Nothing like that." She dropped down beside him.

"What then?"

Karin bit her lip. "Mick, there is something else you should know. After last night . . . The way you describe your mount . . . I think I am the one who brought you down."

"I know."

She turned to him wide-eyed. "You knew? And you did not tell me."

"I pretty much figured it out the first day. I got a better look at you than you did at me and unless there were other dragon riders in the area it pretty much had to be you."

"And you made me gather up my courage to tell you! Thank you very much, I am sure."

"Hey," he said, laying a comforting hand on her shoulder, "I was the one who hurt Stigi. I wasn't sure how you'd take that."

"Yes, but you did not mean to."

"And you didn't mean to shoot me down." He grinned. "We're even. By the way, how did you bring me down?"

"With this," Karin said, reaching behind her and drawing an arrow from the front part of the quiver.

"Do not touch it," she admonished as she held it up for his inspection. Gilligan saw the whole arrow, from head to fletching, was made of iron.

Karin pointed to two black dots, one on each side of the broad arrow head. "These crystals on either side of the head are eyes," she explained, pointing to the shiny black buttons. "When both can see their target the arrow's aim is true. There is a spell to keep the target centered in each crystal."

"Like a guidance head," Gilligan nodded. "But that still doesn't explain how an arrow brought down a twenty-eight-million-dollar aircraft with triply redundant everything."

"The death spell," Karin told him. "It paralyzes anything the arrow strikes."

"So that's why my electronics went to hell." He shook his head and handed the arrow back to her. "I'm damn glad Congress is never going to hear about this."

There was very little they could do. They did some exploring, hunted a bit and gathered berries and other wild foods from the forest. But that did not take much time. Karin spent an hour or two working with Stigi every day and another half hour or so grooming him. Mostly they lazed around camp and talked while they waited for Stigi's wing to heal.

There was one chore that needed to be done regularly. Stigi was very efficient at converting dragon food into dragon droppings. Although he was partially housebroken and used a spot down hill from the camp, the spot had to be shoveled out and spread around, well mixed with earth. Otherwise the smell and insects would have made the camp uninhabitable.

Using her hand axe, Karin made them two wooden scoop shovels. They looked a little odd to Gilligan and the handles were too short for his tastes, but they were much better than using hands.

Every two or three days Karin or Gilligan would "clean the catbox," as Gilligan insisted on calling it. It was hard, dirty work but it was at least something to do.

"Well, this part of the woods should be green next year," Gilligan said, stretching backwards to try to get the kinks out of his back. "You know this is one thing we never had to worry about with an F-15."

Karin tamped down a mound of mixed earth and dragon dung and looked up.

"Back at the Capital the grooms and stable hands would take care of such chores. But it is part of dragonriders' training to be able to care for our mounts in the field."

"Does that include making shovels out of expedient materials?"

"Expedient . . . ? Ah, I see." She smiled in a way Gilligan found utterly charming. "No, I learned that from my uncle when I was growing up on the farm. He would make such implements to take to the village and sell." She looked down at the scoop beside her. "I think he would find these a little crude, though."

"You grew up with your uncle?"

"My parents died when I was young," Karin said. "A hard winter, not much food and some malevolent magic." She shrugged. "Life was hard before the Sparrow brought us new magic."

"Who's this Sparrow?" Mick asked, as much to keep her sitting beside him as to keep from going back to shovelling.

She turned to him, her blue eyes wide. "You must know the Sparrow. He comes from your world."

"The only sparrow I know is an air-to-air missile."

"This Sparrow is a mighty wizard. Near four years ago he broke the entire Dark League of the South in a great battle of magics. Since then his new magic has spread across the land, driving back the dark."

"From my world, you say? Do you know where?"

"'Tis said from a place called the Valley of Quartz."

"Silicon Valley? Yeah, I suppose if we had wizards that's where they'd be. Have you ever met this guy?"

Karin shook her head. "I am not stationed at the Capital. I have seen him once, though. He and his fellow wizards, Jerry and Danny." She stopped. "Are those more of your air-to-air missiles?"

He smiled. "If they are I never heard of them."

"Well, no matter," the dragon rider said with a glance at the horizon. "It grows late. If we do not finish soon we will have to bathe in the dark."

Gilligan stood up. "I guess you're right." He reached down to help her up and when she stood up they were almost nose to nose. He held on and their eyes locked. Then Karin dropped her hands and broke away.

"Quickly, " she said with a breathless little laugh. "We would not want to have to finish on the morrow."

Even working at their best pace, it was still nearly dark when they got back to their camp. Karin went to the stream to bathe first and Mick stayed behind to build the fire and start dinner. Once the fire was going and the stew was bubbling in its pot, he had nothing to do but stare into the flames and think.

Karin came back from the stream with her clothes over her arm and her blanket wrapped around her.

238

"I feel cleaner without them," she explained. "They need to be washed."

"I wish to God you'd put them on," Gilligan said tightly, keeping his attention riveted on the fire.

"Why?"

"It's easier to take." He looked up at her. "Dammit, lady! Do you have any idea how hard it is on me to keep my hands off you anyway?"

"Then why try?" Karin asked softly, letting the blanket drop.

The flames traced out the curve of her hip and the swell of her breast and the light put a ruddy glow in her cheek and highlighted the pale strands of her hair.

Mick sucked in his breath at the firelit vision before him. Then he stepped forward and clasped her to him.


"I never did get my bath, you know."

Karin giggled and nuzzled the pit of his shoulder. "You smell all right."

"And if you keep that up, I'm not going to get any sleep either."

"Are you complaining?"

Gilligan leaned over and kissed her. "Hell no. Just observing."

The fire had long since died and the only light came from the stars that powdered the sky. There was not enough light to see, but that didn't matter and hadn't mattered for hours. Being shot down, the dragon, none of it mattered. He hadn't felt this good since Sandi . . . well, not in a long time. And maybe not even then, come to think of it.

As he bent to her again he noticed that Stigi had very ostentatiously turned his back on them.

At last they both relaxed, soft and sleepy and warm in each other's arms.

"What is it?" Karin said, feeling Mick tense suddenly.

"I've got to go back, you know," Mick said softly. "If I can find a way out, I've got to go back."

Karin shifted and snuggled more closely to him. "I understand. I too have my duty."

"So where does that leave us?"

"It leaves us with meanwhile," Karin told him. "We have meanwhile."

"Yeah," Mick said, reaching out to caress her. "We have meanwhile."

Karin giggled. "Remember today is a hunting day. We will be walking and away from camp almost the whole day."

"So?"

"So you said you needed sleep."

"Right now," Gilligan said into her ear, "there are things I need more."

## *Thirty-two*
# THE ULTIMATE WATER BALLOON

Craig was deep in the design of a new kind of battle armor when one of Mikey's robot servants came for him.

"The Master commands your presence," the robot said in a Darth Vader voice of doom.

"You mean Mikey?"

"The Master. Come." With that the robot pivoted on its heel and marched out the door with Craig hurrying along behind.

Mikey was up on the battlements, standing next to a troughlike contraption and looking out over the valley.

"What's shaking, dude?" Craig said as he puffed up with the robot guide.

"Shaking? A whole lot. I want you to see my latest invention."

Since Mikey had ignored everything he had done since he made the giant robot, Craig didn't think this was quite fair. But he didn't object. Instead he bent over and inspected the device.

"What is that thing?"

"It's a water balloon. The best goddamn water balloon you've ever seen."

It didn't look much like a balloon to Craig. Just a featureless silvery sphere, like those mirrored balls people used to put on pedestals in gardens. The sphere was resting in the trough and there were some springs and some other, less identifiable, bits of machinery underneath.

"What does it do?"

"Watch," Mikey told him. "But put these on first." He snapped his fingers and the robot stepped forward and proffered a couple of smashed ham sandwiches.

241

"Not those, you fucking moron!" Mikey said. "Give him the goddamn goggles!

"Jeez, Craig you need to do something about these robots. They're so fucking stupid."

Craig started to tell him it wasn't one of his robots, but Mikey had already slipped on a pair of dark goggles and was looking back out over the valley. Craig took the pair of goggles the robot was holding out to him, wiped the mustard and mayonnaise off the lenses and slipped them on.

Mikey threw a lever on the side of his device and the silvery ball whisked down the trough and out over the valley in a high, lazy arc. Craig watched the ball shrink to a dot and then lost it in the sun.

Suddenly the world exploded.

Castle, valley and mountains all disappeared in a blaze of blinding radiance. Craig squinched his eyes shut but the sight was burned into his vision. He opened his mouth but he was bowled over backwards as if he had been slapped by a giant hand. Sand and bits of rock stung his skin and the wind whipped insanely about him. The parapet shook beneath him until he was sure the castle was coming down. The noise shook him like a terrier shakes a rat. All he could do was lie curled up in a ball and scream at the pain in his ears and the red after-images in his eyes.

Then it was over. As suddenly as it had come the noise and the shaking stopped. Cautiously, Craig opened his eyes and tried to climb to his feet.

Mikey was standing at the battlement braced like a sea captain facing into a storm. His hair was blown back and his clothes had been whipped about, but he stood firm and unrelenting, looking out over the valley. As he gazed on the roiling clouds of dust and debris below his smile reminded Mikey of a picture he had seen once in Sunday school, of Moses looking out over the Promised Land.

Craig shook himself and looked around. The pennants on the castle towers had been torn to shreds by the blast. Half the roof tiles had been blown off the conical roof of the nearest tower and the chamber below gaped up. His robot guide lay in a twitching heap, unable to rise.

Mikey said something, but it didn't register on Craig's numbed and ringing ears.

"What?"

"I said, 'Neat huh?' " Mikey half-shouted.

"What in the hell was *that*?"

"Like I said, a water balloon."

"Like hell!"

Mikey's smile grew broader. "Nope. Take a sphere of water—just ordinary water—and squeeze it real hard. Pretty soon the atoms disassociate into hydrogen and oxygen. Then if you squeeze it hard enough those hydrogen atoms are forced close enough together that they fuse." He threw up his hands. "Poof! Instant H-bomb."

"Jesus Christ," Craig said. Then he looked out over the dust-filled valley. "Jesus H. Fucking Christ on a goddamn rubber crutch!"

"Hey, that was nothing. The castle's shields took most of the blast so we only got a little of it. And the best part is that the spell to compress that water is so simple I can make my H-bombs any size I want. A hundred megatons, two hundred, even a thousand megatons, no problem."

Craig leaned against the battlement to ease his shaky knees. "That's some water balloon. You ought to put one of those things in the nose of an ICBM."

"ICBMs? We don' need no steenkin' ICBMs. Combine that with the teleportation spell. What do you think would happen if you shoved a mother big bomb down into the planet's crust?"

"Jesus," Craig breathed. "You could sink half a continent!"

Mikey's smile grew wider. "If you do it right you

should smash the world." He looked out past Craig, past the fortress and past the dissipating cloud.

"The whole fucking world," he repeated dreamily.

## Thirty-three
# A FRIGHTENED DRAGON

In spite of the night's activities, Karin and Mick got an early start. Mick caught a quick bath in the freezing stream at first light while Karin spent time with Stigi. Then they set out on the hunt as dawn turned the sky red.

The pickings weren't as easy as they had been. The dinosaurs had learned to be wary of the humans and keeping Stigi fed now involved more stalking. Fortunately Karin was adept at hunting with a bow.

Still it was nearly noon before they found a likely looking herd and moved into position downwind for the stalk.

Karin was just sizing up the situation when a second sun blossomed in the northern sky. In an instant the world turned overexposed blue-white with stark black shadows, as if a gigantic flashbulb had gone off behind them.

"*Get down!*" Mick yelled and pulled Karin down beside him.

"What . . ." The dragonrider tried to look back toward the source of the flash, but Gilligan reached out and forced her head down.

"Don't look! Keep your head down and close your eyes."

"I . . ." Karin begin, but her voice was drowned out when the shock wave hit.

Gilligan pressed his face into the dirt and screamed at the top of his lungs as the wall of dust and flying debris passed over them. The wind yanked at his flight suit and the wind-driven sand stung his exposed skin. He kept his head down and his eyes screwed shut until the gale ceased.

When he opened his eyes Karin was staring at him in shock. She tried to get up but at that instant the

245

ground shock wave hit them and she was knocked first to her knees and then flat as the earth trembled beneath her. She lay on her stomach and clutched at the ground with clawed fingers as if she was afraid the shaking would throw her off.

Gilligan waited until everything was still and probably quiet—his ears were ringing so he couldn't tell—before he climbed shakily to his knees and looked around.

Dust stained the sky an ugly mustard yellow and dimmed the sun to a reddish disk. One of the nearby trees had been blown down and limbs had broken off several others. In the distance a herd of reptiles stampeded blindly, bellowing their panic across he plain.

"Okay, you can get up now."

Karin's face was white where it was not smudged with dirt and her freckles stood out starkly.

"Mick, what was that?" She clung to his forearms to hold herself erect.

"Let's get out of here," Gilligan said grimly.

"But Stigi needs to eat."

"He'll have to hunt for himself if we both die of radiation poisoning. Now let's get the hell out of the open!"

She bent and retrieved her bow. "He will be frightened," she said by way of agreement.

*He's not the only one*, Gilligan thought.

Karin was right. Stigi was blundering around roaring in fear and pain. The campsite was a wreck where the dragon had lumbered through it, flattening shelters and mashing things into the dirt.

The dragon rider set about the task of trying to calm her mount while Gilligan gathered everything of value and flung it under the overhanging rock for protection from fallout. He kept his eye on the skies, looking for rain clouds.

"Karin, get over here!"

"But Stigi needs me."

"Bring him here then. But get the hell under cover."

She led the dragon over to the rock shelter, still patting his great scaled neck and talking to him in soothing tones.

"Get in here with me and have him lay down next to the overhang so he blocks the entrance," Gilligan commanded.

For once Stigi did not object to Gilligan's proximity. It was hard to imagine an eighty-foot monster cowering, but this one was shivering from fang to tail tip. Karin kept patting his back and talking to the dragon even after it lay down.

Gilligan checked his shoulder holster and found that about a handful of sand had gotten into it when he hit the dirt. Rummaging through the haphazard pile of equipment he found his cleaning kit and proceeded to field strip and clean his Beretta.

Objectively it didn't help much, but it made him feel better.

"You said you would tell me what that was later," Karin said after a time. "Is now later enough?"

"It was an air burst," Gilligan said tightly. "I don't know how big because I don't know how far away."

He looked out around the quaking dragon at the sky. "Pretty far, I think. There's no sign of blast-induced rain."

"It wasn't natural, was it? I mean it isn't something that just happens here?"

"No, it's manmade. Or *something* made anyway."

Karin eyed him sideways. "And you have seen them before?"

"Never. I always hoped I never would." He slid the pistol back into its holster. "You remember I told you that we would fight an all-out war with weapons that could destroy a city in the blink of an eye? That was one of those weapons."

"Then your people . . . ?"

247

*"No!"* Karin jerked back as if she had been slapped at the violence of his reply. "I told you we'd never use them unless we were attacked. Nobody would. We're all too afraid of them."

"I can see why."

"Besides, if we did use them we wouldn't set one off over a deserted plain like that and we wouldn't use just one of them."

"But you are expecting more of them. You make us stay under the rocks."

"If there were going to be more we never would have gotten off the plain. We're here because of fallout."

"What is that?"

He turned to her. "Nuclear weapons don't just make a big explosion. They produce all kinds of poisonous byproducts. Even if the blast doesn't get you you can still sicken or die. That stuff will be coming out of the sky for the next few hours and it will be dangerous for the next few days. That blast was a pure air burst so there won't be as much fallout as there could have been. The wind is generally away from us so the plume may not reach us. We may be safe, but I don't want to take chances."

"What about Stigi?"

"You see any place around here that could shelter him?"

Karin shook her head reluctantly.

"Besides, he may not be as affected by this stuff as we are." *For all I know he's got a nuclear reactor in his gut,* Gilligan thought. He wondered if anyone had ever worked out the dose response tables for a firebreathing dragon.

There was no rain that night, and no more explosions. Sometime on toward dawn Gilligan finally drifted off into an uneasy sleep. He dreamed of ruined deserted cities and Karin with her hair falling out.

He awoke numb and muzzy headed. The sun was above the horizon, Karin was gone and so was Stigi.

He cast about frantically for a moment, but Karin's pack and Stigi's saddle were still where he had piled them. Obviously Karin expected to be back soon. Gilligan forced himself to sit down under the overhang and wait.

Perhaps an hour later Karin led Stigi back up the path and into the wrecked campsite.

Heedless of the possibility of fallout or Stigi's steamwhistle snort, he raced across the clearing to meet them. "Karin, I was worried about you," Gilligan said as he took her in his arms. They kissed deeply and then Karin broke away.

"Stigi was restless so I took him to the stream for a bath," she explained. "It always calms him."

"That wasn't safe. We don't know we're out of the fallout plume."

"Oh, but that thing did not leave poison here," Karin said almost gaily.

"What makes you so sure?"

"This," she said, digging into her pouch and producing a small object apparently carved out of jet. "Scouts carry these because sometimes we must forage abroad. It tells us if something is safe to eat or drink. I checked everything I could find and there was no sign of harm."

"I don't know how good it is at detecting fallout," Gilligan said dubiously.

Karin returned the amulet to her pouch. "It has never failed us."

Mick nodded. It was possible serious fallout hadn't reached this far and they had nothing to worry about. If the fallout had reached them they were already facing a bout of radiation sickness. Logically there was no reason to believe Karin's magic rock was telling the truth, but it felt better that way.

He hugged her again "I was worried about you,"

he said with his nose and lips buried in the hair on her neck.

"I am sorry, love."

"That's the first time you called me that."

Karin pulled her head away and laid her fingertips on his cheek.

"Well?"

"Well, I like it." He kissed her again.

After a long moment Karin pulled away. "Mick, we have to talk."

"Okay, about what?"

"What happened yesterday. We cannot stay here now."

"You got that right. The best thing would be to move to the opposite end of the island, as far away from that castle . . ."

"No," Karin cut him off. "I need to go the other way. I need to get as close to that castle as I can to spy out its defenses."

Mick dropped his arms to his sides.

"One of those 'defenses' you're talking about is nuclear weapons. That's crazy!"

"Nevertheless," Karin said quietly, "I must."

"Look, at least wait until Stigi's wing is healed. That's, what, another week?"

"Longer than that, I fear. He apparently tried to fly yesterday in his panic and re-injured it."

"So you're going to walk?"

"I have no other choice."

"The hell you don't! You can stay here like a sensible person. Until help arrives or until that dragon can fly."

"And meanwhile the ones in that castle will be brewing up who knows what kind of horrors," Karin blazed back. "No. I have my duty as a scout and flier and I will not shirk it to lie around here while my very world is threatened."

"I don't know how it is in the dragon cavalry, but in

the Air Force a recon pilot's first job is to get the information back to his base."

"A scout's first job is to gather information. Having no way of getting anything back, I can only gather more."

"I'll bet you've got some kind of regulation against this kind of behavior," Gilligan said with a shrewdness born of desperation.

"There is also a regulation saying regulations are guides and must be applied with wisdom. This is an unusual situation and I must take unusual action."

*Like me sending Smitty back and pressing on alone*, Gilligan thought. Somehow he felt that the universe was getting even with him for that.

"What about Stigi?"

Karin frowned. "That is the thing which made it so hard. I will take Stigi with me. He can walk and dragons can keep a fairly good pace."

"Okay, you feel you've got to scout ahead. You could do it faster once Stigi's wing heals."

"It will heal just as well on the march as here."

"And if you're caught in the open?"

"That is a chance I must take."

Gilligan opened his mouth and found he didn't have any more arguments. Karin obviously wasn't thinking straight, but that didn't matter. She was driven by an overpowering urge to do something, anything, except the intelligent thing, which was sit and wait.

Intellectually he could understand that. He felt the same way. But the kind of training it takes to fly a high performance jet had drummed the value of patience into him. Dragon riding didn't demand the same qualities, or maybe Karin was still too inexperienced to have learned them.

Gilligan considered knocking her out and tying her up. But Karin was lithe and strong. Then he considered Stigi's likely reaction if he tried it and quickly discarded the notion.

The dragon rider set her jaw defiantly. "You have your own rations and equipment. I am sure that you will have no trouble reaching the far end of the island. I will give you a note so that your story will be believed should you meet one of our patrols. Then you can send help on to me."

"You're crazy, you know that?"

Karin shrugged. "I have my duty."

Mick stepped forward and grasped her hands in his. "I'm not going to let you do this. Not alone." Karin looked at him and then smiled.

*Hell of an expeditionary force*, he thought as he pulled her close and kissed her hard. *Two crazies and a gimpy dragon.* Then he opened his eyes and looked at the woman in his arms.

*Still,* he thought, *there are compensations in being crazy.*


They spent the rest of the day packing and headed out across the plain the next morning. Karin took the lead with Gilligan beside her. Stigi followed at her heels like an overgrown hound.

The morning was bright and the sky was painted pastel blues and pinks by the rising sun. Except for an occasional broken limb or an uprooted tree there was nothing to suggest what had happened here two days ago. The plains animals had returned to their normal habits and several times they passed herds of them grazing in the distance.

Once Stigi bridled and snorted as though an animal had come near, but he quickly relaxed and resumed walking. Either there had been nothing there, Gilligan decided, or whatever it was had gotten a look at Stigi and decided not to try anything.

## Thirty-four
# RECON BATTLE

For three days they trekked across the plain. The tree-studded veldt gave way to grassy savanna and the grass grew shorter and sparser. The soil was brick red now and vegetation grew poorly. Water was something you found in greenish sinks instead of rivers or streams and trees became a memory.

Several times they saw large columns of dust to the north, as if distant armies were on the march. They tried to go between them and saw nothing. The herds had been left behind them on the veldt and now even the antelopelike runners were scarce.

There were signs, however. Twice they crossed ground which had been torn up by treads. Once the tread marks were accompanied by what appeared to be enormous footprints, as if some unimaginable two-legged beast had been following the vehicles.

On mid-afternoon of the third day they were approaching a low ridge of reddish earth when Karin called a sudden halt.

"Wait." She held up her hand and dug something out of her pouch. "There is magic ahead of us."

Gilligan reached for his gun. "What kind?"

"It doesn't tell me that, only . . ."

With a thundering roar a tank burst over the hill. Beside it came three two-legged robots, springing forward on back-flexing limbs. While the tank nosed up and over the hill, the robots leaped over the ridge like giant grasshoppers.

Stigi reared back, wings spread and neck extended, and roared a challenge. Karin dropped to one knee and had the bow off her shoulder and an arrow nocked in one fluid motion. Without seeming to aim she fired at the tank.

The arrow hit the tank's armor without seeming effect. With a roar of its engine it continued down the hill straight at the party.

"Run for it!" Gilligan yelled and dashed to his left to try to circle the attackers. Seeing his action, Karin broke right.

Stigi had a different idea. The dragon inhaled and blasted a gout of flame straight ahead, bathing the tank in fire. The flame splashed off the tank, but here and there it caught. A tiny tongue of orange licked out of the deck behind the turret. It spouted thick black smoke and grew larger. The tank stopped and the tongue turned into a gout of orange and black as something in the machine's engine compartment caught.

Meanwhile Karin had dropped to her knee and fired another arrow at one of the robots. Again her aim was true and again the robot continued to advance apparently unheeding.

Karin tried to run again, but as she rose she got tangled in the lower limb of her bow and went sprawling into the sand. She rolled to the side and threw her arm up in a futile attempt to shield herself from the advancing robot.

The robot never noticed. It continued unerringly straight toward the place where she had been. Then it emitted a despairing whine and toppled into the sand beside her.

Karin looked up, shook sand from her eyes and tried to locate Mick and Stigi.

Mick's sudden dash had attracted the attention of two of the robots and now he was frantically dodging blasts of energy from their snout cannon. By a combination of broken field running and dive-and-roll, he had managed to stay ahead of them so far, but the robots had split up and they were coming at him from different directions.

Karin grabbed another arrow, but Stigi reached Mick first. With a roar, the dragon charged full on into one of the robots, catching it at knee level in a way that would have earned him a clipping penalty if they had been playing football. The robot lurched forward onto its snout, then got its feet under it and tried to rise.

It got halfway up when a whipping blow from Stigi's tail hammered it to the ground again. This time the robot didn't try to rise. It swiveled its body around to face the on-rushing dragon and let loose with a bolt from its cannon.

Fortunately energy cannons don't work any better than regular ones when the barrel is full of sand. There was a muffled "whump" and the cannon barrel glowed cherry red and went limp. Stigi grabbed the fifteen-foot-tall robot in his powerful jaws and shook it the way a terrier shakes a rat, slamming it into the ground and tossing it into the air until pieces began to fly off.

Meanwhile, Karin's arrow had found the third robot. It took two more steps and collapsed with the iron arrow sticking straight out of its back.

Craig frowned at the glowing display. He had sent a light scout force scooting along the southern edge of the play area to try to get behind his opponent's main body. Now something had knocked them out.

Sending a stronger force south to engage whatever his scouts had hit was bad strategy. It would dilute his main strength. He decided to send a recon flier south to check it out. Then he turned his attention back to the battle that was shaping up between his warbot columns and his enemy's main force. If he worked quickly enough he might be able to catch them in a pincer.

"Mick, are you all right?"

Gilligan put his hands on his knees and bent forward to take deep, heaving breaths. He was too winded to talk so he shook his head and made a waving off motion to Karin.

Mechanically, Karin walked over to the third robot and pulled her arrow out of its back.

"Stigi, release!" she commanded. With a clank and a clatter, the dragon reluctantly dropped its much-mangled new toy so Karin could retrieve her arrow.

By this time Mick had gotten enough breath back to stand up and look around. Off in the distance he could see plumes of dust rising into the burning sky. Karin was staring intently at the flaming mass that had been the tank.

"Come on!" Gilligan grabbed her arm.

"But my arrow!"

"We don't have time," he panted. "Let's get the hell out of here before reinforcements arrive."

She nodded and they set off, Karin at a fast walk, Gilligan at an exhausted shamble and Stigi, prancing from pride, bringing up the rear.

After about a half a mile, they stopped for a moment to get their bearings and let Mick catch his breath.

"Were those more of your people's creations?" Karin asked.

"The only place I've seen stuff like that is on Saturday morning cartoons." He caught her puzzled look. "No, we don't have anything like that."

"The enemy then."

"Whatever they were before it's a safe bet they are our enemies now." He looked out at the dust clouds in the distance.

"I'll bet they are not alone either."

"Probably not," Karin said in a small voice. Then she put her head up. "We must go more carefully and quietly," she added more firmly.

"What we must do," Mick told her, "is get the hell out of here while we still have the opportunity."

"You are free to go."

"Look, we dodged the bullet this time, but only barely. What do we do if we meet a bigger force? And another thing. That unit is going to be missed. This place has about as much cover as a billiard table and when they start looking we're going to stand out like bugs on a plate."

"We must find out more," Karin said stubbornly.

Mick threw up his hands.

"All right, but if we're going to commit suicide, let's at least do it intelligently. Let's find some cover and rest while we work out the best approach."

Finding cover turned out to be easier said than done. Finally they discovered a deep wash that offered some protection from ground level observation. Stigi hunkered down against the bank and made like a rock and Karin and Mick sat in the shade near his head.

"We had best move only at night from now on," Karin said as she dropped down next to Gilligan. "That way they cannot see us."

"Don't bet on it. There's a real good chance at least some of that equipment has infrared sensors. At night we will stand out even better."

"What do you suggest then? Aside from turning back?"

"I think we'd better look for cover. The land's been getting drier ever since we left our old campsite, so I don't think we're going to find any forests. But it's also been rising. I'd be willing to bet that there are places not far from here that are cut up by arroyos and canyons. That's not as good as trees but it will give us some cover."

Karin nodded. "Since the land rises off to the east, that is the way we should go then."

She stopped and frowned. "What is that sound?"

Gilligan's hearing was damaged from years around jet engines, but he heard it too, a low, hissing whine. Unlike Karin he knew what it was.

"Get down!" he shouted.

The black bat shape glided over the gully without stopping or turning. There was no time to hide. Mick and Karin froze where they were. Stigi opened an eye and for an awful moment Mick was afraid the dragon would stick his head up to see what was going on, but there were no interesting smells or sounds so the dragon decided it wasn't worth the effort.

Eventually the flier meandered off to the south and finally over the horizon. They stayed frozen a long minute more and then relaxed.

"A scout?" Karin said shakily.

"Probably. Trying to find those things we knocked out."

"Then we had best move quickly. Perhaps we can reach those hills you spoke of by nightfall."

She signalled Stigi to his feet and Gilligan shouldered his pack.

"What the hell is that?" Mikey demanded. He had taken his time coming in answer to Craig's urgent summons and he obviously wasn't happy about being called to give a second opinion on a piece of metal.

"I think it's an arrow. We found it sticking in the hull of a burned-out tank on the edge of the wargame area," Craig told him. "I don't know how it works yet, but it's magic somehow."

"And all metal, too. What have you got out there? Robot Indians?"

"Whatever it is did a number on one of my Troll class tanks and three Springer Warbots. One of them was all messed up, like it had been run over by a bulldozer."

"So what do you want me to do?"

"I just figured you should know about it."

"All right, I know. What are you going to do?"

"I'm going to send some more patrols down that way. And mount more sensors on the stuff I'm testing." He paused. "Oh yeah, I'm going to send drones out to map and scout this whole fucking island. Maybe there's something out there we ought to know about."

He looked at Mikey. "I thought maybe you had some magic or technology or something that could help," he said hesitantly.

"Shit," Mikey said informatively.

"Huh."

"I said shit. S-h-i-t. Shit. That's what all this robot stuff is. It's shit."

"How are we going to fight without weapons?" Craig demanded.

"And you call those weapons?" Mikey sneered. "Things that can be wiped out by arrows."

He came around the table and moved close to Craig. "Listen to me, little man. The ones who brought us here have got power you can't imagine. They gave us the ability to create fucking anything and what do you do? You waste your time with comic book toys."

"They're not toys!" Craig yelled. "They're the most powerful weapons man has yet devised!"

"*Man* has yet devised," Mikey mimicked. "That's how limited your thinking is. This hasn't got anything to do with *man*. We're beyond *man*." He stepped back and grew calmer. "You were a mistake, do you know that? Instead of spending your time really learning about how to dominate worlds, you hide down here with your *toys*. Why don't you come up to the real world and let the Ur-elves show you what power is?"

"I don't like them," Craig mumbled. "They make me uncomfortable."

"And because you're uncomfortable you won't take advantage of what we're offered. Christ Jesus! Play with your toys. You're too fucking pathetic to do anything else!" With that he turned and stomped off.

He stopped at the door. "Oh yeah. From now on, if you've got anything to say to me, you come see me."

"*Goddamn motherfucker sonofabitch!*" Craig screamed at the door. That arrogant bag of shit! Just tossing it off like all the work he'd done was nothing. Just didn't count next to *his* high and mighty projects.

He grabbed the iron arrow off the table and threw it against the wall. It clanged off and the wastebasket scuttled under it to catch it as it fell.

Goddamn that sonofabitch! Why, he could take on NATO and the Warsaw Pact and stomp them both with what he had here. There wasn't an army on earth that could stand against what was here in the castle and out in the wargame area.

With an angry gesture he turned on the scanner. The central display showed the arrays of forces in neat green and gold symbols. Around the edges were six smaller screens, each showing a view of part of the battlefield in full color. The units were poised and ready. Except for scouts nothing had moved since he found the destroyed patrol.

Looking at the main map he saw that a platoon of green tanks was just over a small rise from a battalion of yellow armor. Perfect situation for the kind of fast-moving ambush he loved. With the mouse he turned both units on and took control of the green force. Quickly he moved them into position hull down behind the ridge and opened fire on the advancing battalion at barely 200 yards.

Six yellow tanks died in the first salvo and four more before the yellows could return fire. Their first shots were ineffective but they were maneuvering for cover and the next green shots only destroyed two more tanks.

*Twelve to nothing.* It was the time to scoot, but Craig held his ground, firing salvo after salvo into the deploying yellow forces.

Now it wasn't all one-sided. The yellow battalion had taken cover and was returning accurate fire. The battalion's SP battery opened up, walking volleys of tank-killing shells toward his platoon's position. First one and then another of his green tanks blew up and turned dark.

"*Goddamn you!*" Craig yelled and ordered his remaining tanks to charge directly into the lead elements of the battalion, all guns firing. He lost two more tanks in the wild charge and then he ran the survivors head-on into the remains of the battalion's transport section. Tanks ground over jeeps, butted trucks off the road and smashed scout cars. Then the battalion artillery began firing into its own supply train and in seconds it was all over.

Craig screamed in frustration and scanned the board. There was a section of warbots in the next hex over, 130-ton monsters with limited flight capability. They were also on the gold side, but that didn't matter. Taking direct command of the unit, Craig sent them hurtling toward the armored battalion even as it reorganized for the march.

The battalion was massacred before it could even deploy again. Salvo after salvo of missiles tore through the armored column. Multi-gigawatt battle lasers raked it from end to end, blowing up tanks and simply melting smaller vehicles. Finally the warbots themselves closed, smashing tanks beneath their enormous feet and picking up vehicles and flinging them for hundreds of yards.

"*Yes!*" Craig yelled and hunched over the screen. As fast as he could move the mouse he ordered a general engagement. Everything was to attack everything else.

What had been a relatively well-planned large-scale exercise turned into a mechanical armegeddon. From one end to the other the central plain of the exercise area blazed with explosions, laser blasts and burning vehicles and robots. Artillery batteries fired on the units they were supposed to be supporting or

261

turned their guns on each other. Recklessly tanks crashed together. Warbots tore other warbots limb from mechanical limb.

Where the battle wasn't fierce enough or the destruction great enough, Craig took direct command of his units, overriding their carefully programmed tactics in an urge to slaughter. Blind and unheeding, robots charged forward in obedience to their master's command. They didn't even break stride when they reached laser range. Instead they slammed in to each other, flailing with their arms and butting their heads against each others' armored capraces.

Finally it was over. On all the plain there were no more units capable of movement. Every damaged unit had fired off every available round, even if it meant beating the bare earth senselessly with machine guns. The few units that had ammunition they could not fire set it off in the magazines in an orgy of self-destruction.

Looking down on the destruction he had caused, Craig felt more relaxed. His fury at Mikey had died to a dull resentment. The guy was an asshole, but hey, it didn't matter much. They'd go into battle soon enough and when they did, Craig would show him what this stuff was worth.

As he rose from his command chair Craig remembered about the scouts. He still needed to scout the rest of the island. Well, he'd start making more tomorrow.

## Thirty-five
# COSMIC SQUARE DANCE

The blue thing on the screen wove and interwove. It divided, branched and rejoined in a complex, twisting pattern that hinted at an order beyond human imagining.

"How goes the work, Sparrow?"

Wiz jerked his attention away from the screen and saw Duke Aelric standing behind him.

"About like you see. We're making progress, but it's slow going." He reached for the keyboard and called up a second program with a couple of quick commands. Now a yellow thing joined the blue one on the screen. It wove in a complex and elaborate pattern that almost matched the blue one. Wiz moved the mouse and the two shapes melded together into a single form that was mostly green. Here and there, however, patches of yellow and blue still stood out vividly.

"The blue is what we're producing. The yellow is the pattern you gave us," Wiz explained.

The elf duke nodded. "Very good, Sparrow. You make excellent progress."

They watched the shapes for a while without comment.

"Lord, you said there was something stronger behind Craig and Mikey," Wiz said. "What?"

Aelric took his eyes from the screen. "Does it matter, Sparrow? More to the point, do you think you would understand the explanation?"

"Yes," Wiz said levelly. "I think it does matter. As for the explanation, try me."

"Very well." Duke Aelric stared into the screen and stroked the line of his jaw with a long pale forefinger. "Perhaps it would be easiest to say that the World as it is today exists because of choices, a multitude of choices made since the first instant of primal chaos. But each of those choices meant that other things were not chosen. In that dance of choose and choose again, some became strong and flourishing while others were made weak or even nonexistent. The patterns of the dance are not to the liking of all and there are those who would alter them."

"So they've set themselves up against the caller in this cosmic square dance?"

"Cosmic . . . ? Ah, I see. No Sparrow, there is no caller to this dance. It is blind chance working itself out through the interaction of chaos and such forces as came out of chaos. But yes, there are—those—that would have things work another way and they seek to alter the pattern, given a lever to work through."

"And Mikey and Craig are the lever?"

"So it would seem."

"And we don't know what it is these others want?"

"I would not wager that they could be said to 'want' anything at all, any more than a river 'wants' to run downhill. However I doubt very much that the World could survive in a pattern that would be more to their liking."

They were both silent for a minute.

"Aelric," Wiz said at last. "My Lord?"

"Hmm?"

"If Jerry and Danny and I can match their programmers are you strong enough to fight the ones who are behind them?"

The elf duke looked down at him with eyes gray and cold as a winter's sea. "No Sparrow, I am not. Not I and all my kind could stand unaided against them."

"Oh," said Wiz in a very small voice.

"Nor is it needful that we do so," Aelric continued. "The World as it is exists because it is stronger and more stable this way than in any other form it could easily reach. To say that a thing came about by chance

264

is not to say that it can be altered effortlessly once it has happened."

"You can't unscramble an egg," Wiz agreed and then frowned. "Only here you *can* unscramble an egg."

"That does not mean it is equally easy."

"So there's something like an energy gradient these others will have to cross before they can settle the universe into another stable state."

The elf duke paused as if tasting Wiz's words. "That would not be an incorrect way to put it. Perhaps it would be more nearly right to say they seek to create the conditions necessary to tunnel through the gradient to another state."

"Where did you learn about solid-state physics?"

Duke Aelric smiled. "Where did you learn about magic, Sparrow? We teach each other, I think."

Wiz thought that Aelric knew a lot more about physics than he had ever taught Wiz about magic, but he didn't pursue the point.

"You know this sounds an awful lot like cosmology."

"What is cosmology?"

"One of our sciences. The branch of physics that deals with things like the beginning and end of the universe."

The elf duke smiled. "Then this is cosmology."

Wiz turned that over in his mind and then returned to the main point.

"What you're saying then is that we can take them."

"What I am saying, Sparrow, is that there is a chance that we can take them. But first and above all else, you must wrest this new lever from their hands."

"That doesn't sound very hopeful."

"It is not hopeless, Sparrow. Leave it at that."

He nodded with mock gravity. "Now, are there any other matters on which I may set your mind at rest?"

Wiz took a deep breath. "Yes. What does Lisella want?"

Again that marrow-freezing stare. "What the Demoselle Lisella wants is none of your concern, Sparrow. She has not bothered you again, has she? No? Then dismiss her from your mind."

"But you've met her here."

"How do you know?"

"Someone saw you."

"Sparrow, you would do well to concentrate on matters of import, not my intrigues by moonlight. What is between the Demoselle and myself is none of yours. Now, is there aught else?"

"Just one other thing. Are those dwarves who are trying to kill me part of the Others' plan?"

Aelric's laugh was like the peal of a silver bell. "Believe me, Sparrow, they are not." He sobered. "No, that is a matter between you and others of this world, mortal or non-mortal, I think. But be wary of them, Sparrow. They can be dangerous."

# Thirty-six

# A VISIT WITH MIKEY

Craig couldn't really name the impulse that drove him to visit Mikey. He hadn't seen him since Mikey had called his weapons "toys." He didn't really have anything he needed to talk to him about. But he still decided to go. Maybe he could explain to Mikey about his new robots. Maybe Mikey would apologize for the things he'd said. Maybe whatever, he hadn't talked to anyone but robots for weeks.

Craig hadn't been in Mikey's part of the castle for a while and Mikey had made some changes since then. Where Craig's work area was modelled on a laboratory, airy and brightly lighted, Mikey's wing was gloomy as a smoggy twilight. The further he penetrated the dimmer and redder the light became until he felt he was pushing his way through blood-soaked gloom.

He turned the corner and started climbing stairs. The walls fell away as he climbed until the staircase seemed to stretch up into a bleak, blood-lit, starless sky. *Come on,* he told himself, *this is just an illusion. You know you're still inside the castle.* But somehow that only made the illusion stronger. The wind whistled around him, tugging at his jacket and whipping his jeans against his legs. There were hints of shapes in the sky above him, huge dark-on-dark things that shifted and twisted in ways his eye couldn't quite follow.

Craig shivered and stayed close to the center of the railless staircase. He thrust his hands deeper into the pockets of his windbreaker and kept his eyes on the stairs under his feet.

Suddenly he was there. There was no door, no anteroom. Just a pool of light at the top of the stairs and Mikey hunched over a desk in the middle of it.

As he reached the top Mikey regarded him in a not-quite-hostile manner.

"What brings you here?"

Craig shifted uncomfortably. "Well, I hadn't seen you in a while and I just felt like coming to see you, you know?"

Mikey grunted and turned back to his work. Craig stood uneasily as the silence stretched out and the wind whipped and whistled around them.

"This is kinda spooky," he said at last.

"I like it," Mikey said without looking up.

The silence dragged out as Craig stared at Mikey's back.

"You look like you've been learning a lot." Craig tried to flog his enthusiasm. "It must have taken some real magic to put this place together."

"Yeah," Mikey said. "I've been learning. That and a whole lot more."

"Oh?" Craig asked brightly. "Like what?"

"Like philosophy, man. I've really clarified my thinking." He smiled and for an instant the old, charming Mikey flashed through. "You know who really owns something? The person who can trash it. Just fucking ruin it completely. That's how you know the real owner."

"But what about the guy who can use it? You know, build something with it?"

"So what? If he can't protect it, he doesn't really own it. It's like a computer. The name on the paper may say it belongs to IBM or Pac Bell, but that doesn't mean shit. The people who really owned those computers were people like me who could get at them any time we wanted to."

Craig laughed nervously. "Man, you're getting heavy."

Mikey smiled. "Heavy times. Our friends now, they understand that. You know what those guys are really? They're the greatest goddamn hackers of all!" The smile grew wider, dreamier. "Man, this is gonna be great."

"Yeah, but there are people out there, you know?"

"So? If they can't protect it, they don't own it. Simple as that."

"Yeah," said Craig desperately, "but you don't have to destroy something to prove you own it, right? I mean it's enough to know that you can do it, isn't it?"

"Yeah," Mikey said with the same dreamy smile. "Sometimes that's enough."

"So all this is really theoretical, isn't it?" Craig pressed. "I mean it's not like you're actually gonna destroy anything, are you?"

Mikey came out of his trance and regarded him closely. "Sure it's all theoretical." He turned away from Craig and back to the crystal thing on his desk. "Just theoretical."

Craig hesitated, torn between a desire to press his companion for more assurances and the fear he might not get them. Finally he turned away, mumbled something about needing to get back to work, and started down the dark and twisting stairs.

Mikey didn't even grunt goodbye.

*"Not only is the universe stranger than you imagine, it is stranger than you can imagine."*
                                        —J.B.S. Haldane

*"And so are all the other universes."*
                                        —Wiz Zumwalt

Jerry and Danny listened intently when Wiz related what Duke Aelric had told him.

"That's weird," Danny said when Wiz had finished. "I wonder how much of it is true."

Jerry leaned back in his chair and put his feet up on the console. "What I want to know is what stirred these things up. If they've been around forever why did they pick *now* to start causing trouble?"

"Duke Aelric talked about that some when he first joined us," Wiz said. "He thinks it's because of us. Our brand of magic apparently triggered something." He glanced past Jerry's feet to the console screen where the convoluted blue shape slowly rotated.

"I think the whole thing's crazy," Danny said. "Is he still around?"

"Aelric? I don't think so. I think he left again right after I talked to him."

"Pity," Jerry said. "I would have liked to ask him some questions about this."

"Bet you wouldn't get any straight answers."

Before Wiz could reply the door opened and Moira came into the computer room carrying a wicker basket with a cloth over it.

"Forgive me, my Lords, but I thought you might enjoy some refreshment," she said as she put the basket down on the console.

Wiz started to object to covering up the stacks of papers, but then Moira folded back the cloth and he goggled instead.

"Doughnuts! Where did you learn to make doughnuts?"

"Jerry took me to a doughnut shop while I was in your world. I liked them, but it took me some little time to master the recipe."

Wiz grabbed a chocolate-frosted chocolate a fraction ahead of Jerry's and Danny's reaching hands. He took half of it in one bite and closed his eyes in bliss.

"You sure got it right. This is wonderful."

"You said it," Danny enthused, spewing crumbs from his second choice over Moira's skirt.

The hedge witch dimpled and bobbed a curtsey. "Thank you, my Lords. Now, if you will excuse me, I must see to the unpacking of our latest load of supplies."

"Won't you have some with us?" Wiz asked his wife.

"Thank you, no. I, ah, sampled several while I was making them. I fear I am more than somewhat full." She turned toward the door. "Do not eat too many and ruin your appetites. June is preparing something special for dinner." Behind her Wiz nodded and reached for his third doughnut.

For several minutes the only sound in the computer room was working jaws. Eventually a combination of sated appetites and an increasingly limited selection made the three more talkative.

"If she can whip up doughnuts why can't she make coffee to go with them?" Danny asked.

"She didn't like coffee when she tried it," Jerry told him. "She liked doughnuts."

"Okay, but why so many maple ones? Everyone hates maple."

"I think they were her favorites."

"Anyway," Wiz put in, "isn't there something about looking gift horses in the mouth?"

"Yeah. Sorry," Danny said perfunctorily.

"You know," Jerry said after a moment, "what Aelric said almost makes sense in a quantum mechanical sort of way."

Wiz looked around. "I'm not sure *anything* makes sense here," he said.

"They've been saying that about quantum mechanics for years," Jerry said. "Anyway, this might, if you looked at it right."

Wiz picked through the basket and selected a jelly doughnut as the best of the remaining batch. Then he turned back to his friends. "I'll bite. What does quantum mechanics have to do with these bad guys?"

"Okay, you know that in quantum mechanics you deal with the position of a particle in terms of probabilities? There's a probability wave and the particle is most likely to be found at the wave's greatest magnitude and less likely to be found at lower magnitudes. But the point is, you don't know exactly where it is."

Danny rummaged through the box. "So? Are there any more chocolate ones?"

"I think you ate them all, but as I was saying, we already know that something like quantum effects occur here on a macroscopic scale. Remember when we tried to play cards? The shuffled deck was in something like a quantum indeterminate state. We had to create a demon to collapse the state vector by looking at the cards before we could play. Otherwise the deck would respond to everyone's mental desires and you'd end up with everyone holding four aces or the like."

Jerry took another swig of tea from his mug. "It's as if the line between reality and unreality is drawn at a higher level here. Some things don't become real here until someone becomes aware of them."

Wiz took a bite of his doughnut and chewed thoughtfully, dribbling powdered sugar down his chin.

"How does that tie in with these—things—that want to destroy the World?"

"Well, there's an alternate interpretation of quantum mechanics from a guy named Everett which says that what we're really seeing is multiple worlds, all equally real. What collapsing the state vector really means is that we've chosen among them. One of them becomes 'real' because we've taken that branch of the skein of parallel universes and that makes the others unreal."

Wiz put his doughnut down on the console behind him and rubbed his chin thoughtfully, leaving white streaks on his cheek.

"That would explain a lot about this place. For instance, why there are some operations that seem to be basic that we can't use in our magic language because they're unstable."

"Yes," Jerry said slowly. "We've been beating our brains out because we thought they have to be composed of several simpler operations. Maybe there's some kind of uncertainty principle at work and those *are* primitives, they're just one thing one day and another thing the next."

"Well, the appearance of demons is sure influenced by the operator's mental state, unless you specify what they look like in the spell." Wiz wiped at the sugar on his cheek thoughtfully, smearing it out more evenly. "And so these things that Duke Aelric's worried about come from one of these parallel universes?"

"I suppose you could say that they represent a universe with a low-probability wave function that overlaps ours," Jerry said. Then he brightened. "Hey! If I work out the mathematics on this, will that make me the Neils Bohr of this universe?"

"You know . . ." Wiz began and reached behind him for the doughnut. When he couldn't find it he turned to look.

A mouse-sized gremlin was halfway down the desk

with the doughnut clasped in front of him. The prize was nearly as big as it was and the gremlin was bent backwards under the load as it staggered away.

"Hey!" Wiz yelled.

The gremlin looked over its shoulder at Wiz, grinned, and broke into a wobbly run. Right to the edge of the desk and several steps beyond into empty air.

Suddenly the grin faded. The little creature looked down and saw it was standing on nothing. Its face fell and its bat ears drooped to its shoulders.

"Uh oh," it squeaked. Then gremlin and doughnut plummeted to the floor.

As the gremlin scuttled away, Wiz walked over, picked up the doughnut, brushed it off and took a second bite.

"I don't know if that makes you Neils Bohr," he began again, "but if you're right I think Chuck Jones is the Erwin Schrodinger of this universe."

"Who's Chuck Jones?" asked Jerry

"Who's Erwin Schrodinger?" asked Danny.

Halfway to the hills Mick and Karin met a ruined army.

They smelled it before they saw it. The stink of burning rubber and insulation, of overheated metal and cordite. Of dust churned up in the heat of battle.

But there was no sound of combat. No artillery, no engines. Not even the shouts of men. Cautiously, Karin and Mick eased to the top of a rise and peered over it.

The panorama was so big and so torn up it was hard to tell what had happened here. Gilligan thought of the pictures he had seen of the destruction at Mitla Pass in the Sinai during the Six-Day War. But this was worse than any of those pictures. It seemed that the destroyed equipment spread over the plain for miles in front of them.

His first instinct was to go around, even if it meant walking for miles. But there was no hint of movement anywhere on that enormous battlefield, no contrails in the sky. Except for the occasional crackle of flame and the whistle of the wind there was nothing.

"Well?" Karin asked.

"I say go across. It's risky, but we're low on water. Besides, we'll be harder to spot out among all that junk than we would be out on the plain."

The dragon rider nodded and went back to get her mount.

It took hours to cross the battlefield.

They walked past a line of what looked like self-propelled guns—if self-propelled guns had barrels made of glass that would droop and melt under the effects of enemy weapons.

Here a half-dozen tanks in various stages of destruction confronted the remains of a fifty-foot-tall robot they had pulled down like wolves on an elk. Further on were the remains of a missile battery caught on the march and burned while trying to deploy.

But there were no bodies. The wind brought the smell of burnt vehicles but not a trace of the sweetish stink of burning flesh. Not even the carrion birds seemed interested in this plain of dead machines.

"Mick," Karin asked at last, "why do they do this? Do our enemies fight among themselves?"

"I think it's more likely they're just conducting live ammo practices."

"But they are killing their own creations!"

"These things weren't ever alive. They're machines, like my F-15, not living beings like Stigi. I doubt a single living creature lost its life here."

"Still, there is something . . . obscene about all this."

Gilligan shrugged. "For us, war is a material-intense business. You go through a lot of equipment."

But looking over the carnage, Mick tended to agree

with her. Even if these things weren't alive, it had taken ingenuity to design them and time and resources to build them. He had been taught that in a war you expended your equipment wholesale in an effort to win. If you struck hard and fast with overwhelming strength you minimized casualties, or so the reasoning went.

Gilligan had always accepted it unthinkingly. Now, wandering among acres of scorched and twisted ruins, he began to appreciate what that meant.

*Besides,* he thought, *this wasn't a battle. This was an exercise, a test. You don't need to wreck all this just to test it.*

"Mick?" Karin said after they had trudged on in silence for several minutes more. "The people who do this, why do they do it? Why like this?"

"I don't know," Mick told her sadly. "I don't understand their thinking at all."

## Thirty-eight
# TRAP

Wiz Zumwalt sat on a rock under a spreading tree and savored the experience. It was cool and pleasant here. The late afternoon sun did not quite reach down through the leaves and the forest around him was alive with birdsong and the skitterings of squirrels and other little animals.

Wiz wondered what season it was. It looked like late summer, but the Bubble World didn't seem to have seasons. *How can a world shaped like a burrito have seasons?* he wondered.

For once the pressure was off. The visualization program was running well, Lannach was keeping the gremlins under control and everything else he could think of to do was done. So he had slipped out of the Mousehole for a couple of hours to do a little exploring.

It was the first time he had really been outside the Mousehole since he arrived and he was enjoying it. No gremlins, no brownies, no elves and no dwarves.

Glandurg could not believe his luck. After all the weeks of hunting and the long weary days of waiting, there was the Sparrow, not two hundred paces away with his back turned!

And better yet, there was no sign of the protection spell Snorri had reported. Nothing that would do violence to an attacker. There was magic about him, of course, but after all he was a wizard.

Glandurg nearly hugged himself with glee.

He dropped to his belly and wormed his way forward through the fallen leaves. He moved with exquisite care as he eased his silent way toward the sitting figure. Fifty paces and still no move from his quarry. Twenty. Ten.

Glandurg rose with a rush, took two steps and leaped toward the defenseless Sparrow.

He didn't exactly bounce, but he certainly vibrated. Glandurg had leaped directly into the center of an enormous spider web that sprang up in his path. His sword fell to the leaves, but he remained thoroughly stuck in the mass of sticky strands.

Wiz turned around at the noise and gaped. There was a dwarf hanging upside down in a giant spider's web. The dwarf was struggling frantically and cursing luridly. Wiz didn't speak dwarfish, but it sure sounded lurid.

Wiz waited until the dwarf ran down.

"Now," he said. "Just what is this all about?"

"A protection spell," Glandurg spat. "I might have known."

"You didn't think I'd come walking in the woods without one, did you? I hoped I'd seen the last of you back at the Capital, but I wasn't taking any chances."

Actually Wiz had devised the spell against any wild animals that might be lurking in the forest. He didn't want to kill them, so he had settled for something that would immobilize an attacker.

"You know, I'm sort of glad you did show up," Wiz said. "Now maybe you'll tell me what this is all about."

Glandurg nodded and the gesture made his beard fall in his face. He shook his head to clear his eyes.

"Meet it is that you should know the cause and agent of your doom," he said in his best skaldic voice. Or at least the best voice he could manage suspended upside down in midair.

"I hight Glandurg; son of Megli, praised above all smiths; son of Famlir, who fell in the battle of Breccan's Doom; son of . . ."

"Yes, I'm sure you're from a very distinguished

line," Wiz cut him off, "but that doesn't explain why you're trying to kill me."

The dwarf glared. Mortals had no sense of family and no appreciation for skaldic recitation.

"My uncle is Tosig Longbeard, King of the Dwarves. To fulfill a debt he has commissioned me to seek your death. To this end I have sworn mighty oaths that my quest shall end in your death or my own."

"Uh, I don't suppose we can talk about this?"

The dwarf looked uncomfortable. "I am sorry, Wizard. You are brave and honorable and you are working for the good of all our World. But I have sworn a quest and you must die to satisfy it."

Wiz bent and picked up Glandurg's fallen sword.

"I can't very well let you go, you know. I can't be looking over my shoulder at every moment."

"Wait," Glandurg said quickly. "I cannot forgo my sacred mission but I can postpone it. If you release me, I swear to take no action against you," he made a motion as if to cross his heart, "until you have fulfilled your own work."

Wiz considered. He didn't have much stomach for killing anyway.

"All right," he said finally. "Swear to that and I'll let you go."

Glandurg moved his hands again. "I do swear that I shall not try to slay you until your battle with your enemies is over. I swear by the moon for as long as it is in the sky."

"Fine," Wiz said. He turned and started to walk away.

"Wizard," Glandurg called, "what about me?"

"Oh, the web will dissolve in six or eight hours," Wiz told him. "I'm sorry, but I can't get rid of it before that."

*Besides*, he thought as Glandurg's curses died behind him, *I'm not sure how far I trust you.*

"Well, that's one less problem anyway," Wiz said as he walked into the Mousehole's lounge. Aelric and the other programmers were nowhere to be seen, but Bal-Simba and Moira were there.

Bal-Simba looked up at him quizzically.

"The dwarves," Wiz said, plopping down on a sofa. "I just got them off my back."

"They are here?" Moira demanded.

Wiz nodded. "Their leader just tried to jump me. He ran right into my protection spell and before I'd let him go I made him promise he wouldn't try to kill me any more. At least," he amended, "not until this business with Craig and Mikey is finished."

"You made a deal with a dwarf," Moira said slowly.

"Uh, yeah."

"Sparrow," Bal-Simba said slowly, "what *precisely* did the dwarf swear to?"

"He promised he wouldn't kill me until this business is over."

"Can you remember his exact words?"

"Yeah. He said, 'I will not slay you until your battle with your adversaries is over.' Well, that's pretty close anyway."

Moira moaned.

"Is something wrong?"

Bal-Simba put a huge hand on Wiz's shoulder. "Sparrow, there are scant dealings between mortals and dwarves, but this much we have learned. A dwarf keeps only his exact, literal word. They are slippery as river eels and will wiggle through any least little hole left in an agreement."

"There's a hole in this one?" Wiz asked in a sinking voice.

"Sparrow, how many dwarves are we dealing with?"

"About a doz . . . oh," Wiz said in a small voice. "And he promised only for himself."

280

The black wizard nodded. "He only swore that he himself would not kill you. He did not even promise he would not help the others."

"Oh," Wiz said again.

It was almost nightfall by the time Glandurg's followers found him. The wait had done nothing to improve his temper.

"What happened to you?" Gimli asked in awe at the sight of his leader hanging enmeshed in sticky ropes.

"Never mind that, get me down!"

"He tried the Sparrow alone, he did," Ragnar told Gimli. "I recognize the signs."

"Now," the red-faced Glandurg ground out, "now I shall have him."

"Looks as if he had you," Ragnar observed. "Trussed you up like a spider to a fly."

"Just cut me down," Glandurg growled.

The dwarves set about it, but it was a sticky, tedious business. While they hacked and sawed Glandurg fumed and muttered.

"I will have his heart's blood."

"Can't very well do that," Thorfin said from the tree limb where he was cutting away at one of the last strands of the web. "You said you swore an oath you wouldn't harm him until after he's completed his own quest."

"I swore so long as the moon was in the sky," Glandurg amended.

Ragnar gaped. "He let you get away with that?"

"I am cleverer than any mortal wizard," Glandurg said smugly. "It was the first oath I offered and he took it."

Thorfin looked up at the darkening sky where a sliver of waning moon hung high. "And the moon has, what, eight, nine more days? Then it will be the dark of the moon and it will be gone completely." While he was looking up his knife severed the strand and Glandurg fell heavily to earth.

The dwarf rose and brushed off the last clinging bits of web. "Mark you, I shall use the time well. I have sent to my uncle the king for a thing which will finish this Sparrow once and for all."

*And maybe this time he'll let me have it*, Glandurg thought to himself.


Tosig Longbeard, king of the Mid-Northeastern Dwarves of the Southern Forest Range, fidgeted uneasily on his alabaster throne and waited for his visitor to get down to business. The smoky torches flared in their wall sockets, throwing distorted shadows dancing over the carved and inlaid walls of his audience chamber, but there were none but himself and his visitor to see. His court, his seneschal and even his guards had been withdrawn because Aelric, the most powerful elf west of the mountains, had "begged the favor" of a private audience.

Dwarves and elves have scant dealings and Tosig had absolutely no idea why one of the greatest elves should come to call. He noted his guest was carefully treating him to every shred of courtesy and respect to which he was entitled. Somehow that was not reassuring.

First there were the formalities to get through. Elves are notoriously punctilious and dwarves are sticklers for forms and honors, so that had taken time. Further, elves are as courteous and delicate as trolls are rude and direct. After half a morning's pleasantries, Tosig almost preferred the trolls.

At last, when Tosig was ready to scream, the elf turned to the subject at hand.

"I understand your nephew has undertaken a quest to fulfill a promise you made to the troll kings."

"He's not my nephew," Tosig snapped. Then he softened. "But, ah, yes, a minor kinsman of mine is off doing some small service for the trolls."

Aelric said nothing for a space. Tosig watched him warily. This elf was known to consort with mortals, including even this strange wizard the trolls wanted dead. Were he to take a hand in the business . . .

"The honor of dwarves in keeping their promises is well-known, " Aelric said. "It would be tragic if such an important promise were not kept because your relative was not given full support."

"I've supported that insufferable young pup to the limit of my purse and beyond!" Tosig burst out. "Oh, if you only know what this thing has cost me first and last. The supplies, the gold paid to griffins because he and his friends were too good to walk like ordinary dwarves. And always more demands. More supplies, more treasure. More gold to the griffins. More . . ." He stopped and beat his chest to relieve the burning pain. "I have supported him," he finished.

"But perhaps not with everything asked for?" Aelric murmured. "There was mention of a sword, I believe?"

"Blind Fury?" Tosig screamed. "Never! Never in a thousand lifetimes I tell you!" He dissolved into a choking fit.

"A great treasure to be sure," Aelric agreed. "And yet after all you have done it would be ironic if you were blamed for—lack of support."

"Greed," Tosig grated. "Say it outright! Dwarves are miserly and for my miserliness I would not risk giving Glandurg the sword Blind Fury."

"*I* would never say such a thing."

"But others would and you wouldn't correct them. Bah! Even for an elf you're mealy mouthed."

Aelric only nodded gracefully in a way that indicated he was much too well-bred to argue with his host.

Tosig drummed his fingers on the throne arm. He

283

could afford to turn his back on his debt to the trolls if he had Glandurg for a sacrificial goat. But to have an elf telling such a tale . . . Well, it would ruin his tribe's trade for generations.

"The thing's cursed, you know," he said at last. "And the boy's incompetent. He's had a score of chances at this alien wizard and muffed them all. Sword won't do him a bit of good."

Aelric made a throw-away gesture with one elegant hand. "As you say, I am sure. Yet the point is not whether your nephew . . ."

"Don't call him my nephew!" Tosig barked. "He isn't my nephew, rot him!"

"Your relative then. The point is not whether he accomplishes his mission, only that you cannot possibly be blamed for his failure." The elf arched a silvery eyebrow. "Besides, the wielder of Blind Fury is invincible in battle. Who knows what even your—relative—might accomplish with it?"

Tosig glared at the elf and continued to beat a tattoo on the throne arm. He was trapped and they both knew it.

"Why are you so interested in this anyway?" the dwarf king demanded. "I thought you had dealings with the wizard."

"Oh, I do," Aelric told him. "However there is the matter of a prophecy. It were best if it were fulfilled." A strange expression flashed across the elf's face. "Fulfilled in all its particulars."

"Behold the sword Blind Fury!"

Glandurg brandished the weapon aloft and the other dwarves crowded around. They had all heard stories of the great treasure of their tribe, but none of them had ever seen it before. Never in the memory of a living dwarf had the enchanted sword left the deepest, strongest treasury.

284

It was worth seeing. The golden hilt gleamed, throwing sparks and highlights where the sun's rays caught a bit of carving or granulation at just the right angle. The rubies and sapphires set in the hilt glowed with inner fires and the fist-size emerald in the pommel flashed and flamed.

In fact, it was downright gaudy.

That was fine with the dwarves, whose taste for gaudy is perhaps exceeded only by Las Vegas architects. But it was also deadly. The double-edged blade glittered in the sunlight with a sinister brilliance that threatened to outshine the hilt. The blade was as wide as a man's palm and nearly as long as a dwarf was tall and the magic of it twisted the air around it like heat waves in a mirage.

Glandurg could not conceal his glee. "One stroke! One stroke and the Sparrow is finished! Nothing can stop Blind Fury and he who wields it cannot be harmed in battle."

"Can we see?" Gimli asked eagerly.

"Yes," Ragnar said. "Show us."

The others took up the chorus. "Yes. Yes. Show us."

Glandurg smiled and nodded. Obviously the sword had gone a long way toward restoring his tattered prestige with his followers. He didn't tell them he had asked King Tosig for it before setting out and received a rebuff that singed his beard.

He marched to the edge of the clearing where a log nearly two feet thick lay against a head-high boulder.

"Observe the log," he said. He wound up and swung at the log with all his strength.

Blind Fury whistled through the air and Thorfin jumped back as the tip removed the bottom six inches of his beard. With an evil hiss the weapon missed the log completely and bit deeply into a boulder, cleaving the rock to the ground.

The dwarf looked around. Thorfin was fingering the end of his newly trimmed beard and several of the

285

other dwarves were looking at the newly split boulder with a combination of wonder and skepticism.

"I meant to do that," Glandurg told the watching dwarves. "Now stand back and give me room."

The others needed no urging. They backed off to give him a good twenty feet of room in every direction.

Glandurg hefted the sword. In the back of his mind it came to him that there were stories about how Blind Fury got its name.

"Now watch," he said. This time he did not specify a target.

Again he raised the sword over his head, braced his feet apart and swung a mighty blow. He was aiming at the boulder but the blade's arc flashed past the stone and on around and into the oak tree beside him. Glandurg was dragged along helplessly but Blind Fury sliced through the three-foot trunk as if it wasn't there.

Slowly, majestically, the tree rocked, teetered and began to fall—straight toward the watching dwarves. Dwarves scattered in every direction as the oak crashed down on them. The trunk itself missed Glandurg by scant inches where he stood holding the enchanted sword.

Wiz looked up from where he was checking some wiring in the computer room. "What was that crash?"

Jerry, who was closer to the window, looked out. "Just a tree falling up on the hillside."

"Oh," Wiz said, turning back to the wiring. "Nothing important then."

A curse! Yes, that was it, Glandurg remembered. There was a curse on the sword. Dwarfish faces began poking out among the still-shaking leaves of the fallen tree. Somehow they didn't show the respect they had a few minutes ago.

"Well, that's enough of that, isn't it?" Glandurg said. "Hand me the scabbard, will you?"

## Thirty-nine
# PROTECTION

It was just after dawn and Wiz was finishing up an all-nighter on a workstation when a shadow swept over the window. He jerked his head up in time to see a dragon land almost at the front entrance of the Mousehole.

It looked like a league dragon, but Wiz grabbed his staff and headed for the main door anyway. The dragon scouts were under strict orders to stay away from the Mousehole lest the coming and going of the dragons should attract attention.

By the time he reached the entrance Moira was already there. Of the other programmers or wizards there was no sign, but one of the guardsmen was holding the door for their unexpected guest. As he strode in, Wiz recognized Dragon Leader, the commander of all the League's dragon cavalry.

Dragon Leader was a bowlegged, solid little man with pale blonde hair and eyes like the fog off an arctic glacier. He was dusty and he and his flying leathers reeked of the snake-and-sulfur odor of dragon.

"My Lord, my Lady." His head bobbed in something more than a nod and less than a bow. "Forgive me for coming here, but we have a problem I thought you should hear of immediately."

"I understand," Wiz said. "We're still trying to find what's causing the trouble with the communication crystals."

"Thank you, my Lord. But now we have a new problem. In the past two days we have started to encounter enemy scouting demons over the island—well south of their usual routes."

Wiz gripped his staff tighter. "Do you think they know we're here?"

287

Dragon Leader considered. "So far as we know they have not tried to come this far south. But they are searching the island. That means you are in danger of discovery."

"Well, danger or not we can't leave."

Dragon Leader nodded. "Your decision, Lord. But understand we cannot protect you this close to our enemies' base."

"Understood."

"You should be safe for another ten-day or so. Their scouts are thorough but they do not move as quickly as dragons." He shrugged. "Perhaps they will not come this far south. Or if they do your disguise may fool them."

"But you wouldn't put money on it."

"As I say, Lord, their scouts are thorough."

"Anything else you can tell us?"

"Nothing not in our regular reports. There is constant activity around the castle, but no sign of any more great explosions."

"Okay," Wiz sighed. "Well, thanks for the warning. We'll do what we can."

"Will you stay for refreshment?" Moira asked. "Perhaps a bath?"

"Sorry, my Lady, but I have to rejoin my patrols." He sketched a bow, turned on his heel and strode from the room. A minute later they watched through the windows as man and dragon lifted off in a cloud of dust.

"What is that guy's name anyway?" Wiz asked as they watched their guest dwindle into a dot in the sky.

"Everyone just calls him Dragon Leader."

"Ardithjanelle, which means 'shy flower of the forest,'" Moira said. "The story is that his parents were expecting a girl child."

Wiz watched the dot for a second. "I think I'll just call him Dragon Leader."

It was less than half an hour after Dragon Leader

departed that the still-sleepy programmers, Moira and Duke Aelric met in the day room. Wiz outlined the situation to them and then posed the question on everyone's mind.

"Well, what do we do now?"

"How much longer do we need?" Moira asked.

"Maybe another two weeks, if Lannach can keep those damn gremlins at bay."

"There really isn't much we can do," Jerry said. "We have got to have this place to keep using the supercomputer."

"We could move to another island," Moira suggested, in a tone that indicated she didn't think much of the idea.

Wiz shook his head. "We'd have to stop work, get the system into a stable state, back up everything, move it all and then try to get up and running again. I know companies that have gone broke in the process and they could get spares from the manufacturer if they broke something. Besides, I think those patrols already cover the other islands." He grimaced. "Probably the best we can do is continue here for as long as we can and be ready to cut and run as soon as we're discovered."

"We may have more time than you think," Aelric put in from where he stood. "Our enemies seek something toward the middle of the island. I do not think they will come this far south."

"How do you know that?" Danny asked. Aelric shrugged elegantly.

"Anyway, we need to be ready to bug out if they do find us," Wiz said.

"We can put together some really righteous defenses," Danny said brightly. "I've been working on some ideas."

Moira shook her head. "Not as many as you might think. Defenses attract attention. Powerful ones are likely to shine like a beacon to anyone who can sense magic."

"We discussed this once before, Danny," Wiz said. "The logic still holds. Stealth is better than weapons."

"Shit," said Danny and scowled down at the table top.

"One thing we ought to do is to get as many people off the island as we can," Jerry said. "If we can't defend this place we don't need guardsmen and there is no reason to have as many support people as we have."

"We can all do our share of the cooking and laundry," Wiz agreed.

"Or do it by magic," Moira said to her husband. "Forgive me, Lord, but no one but a goat could stomach your cooking."

"Hey, I lived on it for years."

Moira leaned over and kissed him lightly. "I rest my case."

"In any event," Jerry said, "it's getting too dangerous to keep anyone here who isn't absolutely necessary."

He carefully avoided looking at Danny and so did everyone else in the room.

The brownies hadn't attended the council, so as soon as the meeting broke up, Wiz went to tell them. He found Lannach in the computer room, crouched on his haunches at the rear of the console and apparently talking to someone inside the computer.

"Lannach, we're going to have to pull your people out."

The little man stood up and dusted his knees. "Why, Lord? Are you dissatisfied with our work?"

"No, nothing like that. But Mikey and Craig are getting close to finding this place. We're sending everyone we can spare back."

Lannach frowned. "Forgive me, Lord, but you cannot spare us if you want your computer to work."

"We can't protect you if they find us and attack."

"Lord, we will not leave. Not just for our own safety."

"I don't want that on my conscience."

"It is not upon your head, Lord. It is our decision."

"Thanks, Lannach." Wiz held out his hand. Gravely Lannach took his first two fingers in both his tiny hands and pumped them up and down.


"Look, you've got to go."

It was late and the hall lights had long since dimmed, but Danny and June were still at it.

Again June shook her head so hard her mouse-colored curls beat against her forehead. "You come," she said with undiminished firmness.

"I told you, I can't. I've got to keep working."

June planted herself on the edge of the bed and crossed her arms. "You will not be rid of me," she said fiercely.

He pulled her up off the bed and held her in his arms. "Honey, I don't want to get rid of you, I want to save your life."

Ian stirred restlessly in his crib and started to whimper again. He wasn't used to hearing his parents argue and he had been crying off and on all evening.

June turned her back on her husband and scooped Ian out of the crib. For a moment all her attention was concentrated on soothing him while Danny tried to think of something more to say.

"Just this once," he promised. "Just this once you've got to leave me."

June shook her head wildly and clung to Ian.

"Dammit, you can't stay here," Danny said desperately. "If not for you think about Ian."

June looked down at the child and her eyes filled with tears but she shook her head again.


Wiz was trying to find a way to squeeze more speed

out of the algorithm when Danny came into the lab the next morning. His eyes were red, his skin was pale and blotchy, as if he'd been crying. Even his hair was a worse mess than usual. He looked like he hadn't slept at all last night.

"I had it out with June," he said dully.

Wiz put down the sheaf of papers. "Is she going back?"

Danny snorted. "Fuck no. That silly little bitch is determined to stay here and get herself killed." He growled in frustration and slammed his fist down on the desk. "God*damn* her and her stubbornness."

"I'm really sorry, man. I could ask Moira to talk to her."

"What for? She won't listen. She just rocks back and forth and shuts out the world."

Wiz couldn't think of anything to say. When he had come to this World Danny had been a self-centered twerp who did what he wanted and didn't care about any one. Now he had others to worry about and he was having to make hard choices. Wiz could sympathize. He'd had a fair measure of twerphood in his makeup when he first met Moira. But there wasn't anything he could do to make the choice easier.

"She's sending Ian back with Shauna," Danny said finally. "That's something anyway."

"But she won't go?"

Danny bit his lip. "It's real simple. Where I go she goes. And I've got to be here."

"Hey look, you could handle some of this stuff from the Capital."

"Bullshit," Danny said without heat. "The only place I can do any good is here."

"But the risk . . ."

"Moira's staying here, isn't she?" He looked up at Wiz with a ghost of a smile. "Besides, I want a World for my kid to grow up in." He looked down. "Shit. I left my notebook back in my room. I'll be back in a minute."

Danny brushed past Jerry as he went out.

"What was that all about?" Jerry asked after Danny disappeared down the hall.

"I think," Wiz said wonderingly, "that was Danny growing up."

By the time Danny got back Wiz and Jerry were hip-deep in trying to find something to make the algorithm work faster. By noon they considered and rejected at least four approaches.

Outside the computer center the Mousehole was abuzz with activity as nearly everyone else got ready to leave. Guardsmen, servants and wizards went back and forth in the hall carrying boxes, bags and piles of clothing. They finally took a break when Moira came in to discuss details of the move.

"You know," Jerry said as he pushed back his chair, "I could think a lot better if I didn't feel like I had a target painted on my back."

"Well, we're stuck with it," Danny said angrily. "We gotta stay and if they find us we can't fight. All we can do is hope we can get outta here in time."

"Wait a minute," Wiz said slowly. "Maybe there is something we can do."

"Like what?"

"Protection spells. Really heavy-duty protection spells. You know, like force fields in the science fiction movies."

Danny's eyes lit up. "Hey, cool!"

"Do you think that would work?" Jerry asked.

"It might. At least it would be better than nothing."

"Such spells are powerful magic that stands out strongly," Moira said dubiously.

"They stand out strongly in your World," Wiz said. "But magical senses don't work as well here. Besides,

Craig and Mikey don't use magical detectors the way your people do."

"We hope," Moira corrected. "And in any event, where do you propose to get the time to create such a spell?"

"Oh, I've got most of the groundwork done already," Wiz said. "I've been working on it off and on ever since I was rescued from the City of Night. Believe me, there is nothing like being nearly killed a dozen times over to make you think about ways to protect yourself."

"Voila!" Wiz proclaimed and placed five rings on the table like a handful of jacks.

"They look like something out of a Crackerjack box," Danny said dubiously.

"Well, as a matter of fact . . ." Wiz began. "Never mind. It isn't what they look like, it is what they do."

"They are certainly charged with magic," Moira said, eyeing the pile of trinkets. "Even in this place they have powerful auras."

"They've got more than that," Wiz said smugly. "This is a truly tasty hack, if I do say so myself."

Danny reached out and poked one of the rings with his forefinger. "So what do they do, shoot lightning bolts?"

"Nope, they generate a stasis field. Basically the spell is an amplified variation of that spell we used to stretch out a night and get more programming time while we were working on the magic compiler. Except instead of stretching nights out two-to-one, this spell stretches time out sagans to one."

"Sagans?" asked Jerry.

"Yeah, you know. Like 'SAY-guns and SAY-guns of light years.' "

"Oh, right," Jerry said, catching the imitation of the famous astronomer.

Moira frowned. "One moment. You say this spell slows down time enormously?"

"Yep."

"Then how can you move when the spell is active?"

"You can't. It freezes you solid. But nothing can hurt you."

"Still, the spell can be broken, can it not?"

"It automatically shuts off when malevolent magic goes away. Kind of like the protective spell I used against those dwarves."

"So at the first sign of trouble you slip on the ring and turn into a statue?"

"Well, no. We wear the rings all the time. They activate automatically when you're under direct attack and they stay active as long as you're in danger. The rest of the time they're inert."

"These things are like bullet-proof vests?" asked Jerry.

"More like an airbag in a car. Nothing happens until you need it."

Wiz passed the rings around and each of them slipped one on. Then Danny turned and held one out to June. But she hissed and shrank away as if Danny had offered her a scorpion.

"June, please." But June's face was white and she refused to touch the ring.

"It is not like the enchantment in the elf hill," Moira said, coming over to her and laying a hand on her arm. "It will serve only to protect you." Still June shook her head and turned away.

Danny held up his hand to display the ring he was wearing. "Look, if I wear this and your don't, we'll be separated if something happens. But if we both wear one we'll always be together. Please darling, wear it for me."

Hesitantly June reached out a shaking hand and clutched the ring Danny extended to her. With a sudden move she jammed the ring onto her finger and then jerked her hands back into the folds of her skirt. Danny grabbed her and hugged her to him.

"Oh yeah, I almost forgot," Wiz said a shade too brightly. "There's another way to turn the ring on and off."

He held up his hand and mimed twisting the stone. "If you want you can activate the spell by turning the stone in the ring a quarter turn to the right. You can deactivate the spell in the presence of danger by having someone turn the stone a quarter turn to the left."

"What kind of a moron would want to turn off the spell when he's in danger?" Danny asked.

Wiz stopped short. "You know, I never thought of that."

"Feeping creatureism," Jerry said.

"What kind of creature?" Moira asked.

"A feeping one," Danny explained. "That's one that has too feeping many . . ."

"What it means is that I've added features just to add features," Wiz interrupted. "It's a spoonerism on creeping featurism."

"If you expect me to ask you about spoons, my Lord, you will be sorely disappointed. Nevertheless I understand the idea."

"Yeah," Wiz said sadly, "and that took more work than all the rest of the spell put together."

"So now we can continue to work even under the strongest magical attack?" Moira asked, eager to get the conversation back to something that halfway made sense.

"Not under actual attack, but right up to the minute it begins."

Moira looked down at the ring on her finger. "I hope it works."

"I hope we never find out," Jerry said fervently.

The drone had come so far south only by accident, cut off from its base by a line of strong thunderstorms and blown well past the point where it should have turned for home. Nevertheless it kept recording what its sensors recorded and transmitting it back to the castle.

There wasn't much. This part of the island was mostly low hills covered with open forest. It had been hours since the drone had seen anything even as interesting as a herd of animals. Just the occasional bird, a motion in the branches that might be an animal and the mixture of trees and grassy clearings.

The sun was almost to the horizon and the shadows had lengthened and begun to blend together into the beginnings of dusk. The drone was already headed north, back towards its home when its infrared sensor recorded a patch of anomalous heat off to the right. True to its programming, it turned away to investigate.

A quick scan found nothing in the visual band to account for the heat, no sign of sun-heated rocks or hot springs. The machine was too simple-minded to be puzzled, but it did have contingency programming for something like this. It shut down its engine, switched on its full sensor array and turned to glide over the hot spot.

Beneath the trees and magical camouflage a lone guardsman was shifting the last of his troop's equipment into a neat pile for transport back to the Capital. He looked up as the shadow swept over him, caught a glimpse of something like a large bird and then bent again to his task.

He didn't even consider the incident worth reporting.

It took time for the drone's report to filter up the chain of command at Caermort. Craig had just finished a dinner of magically produced tacos and Coke when the notification popped up in a box on his screen. He glanced at it, frowned, and wiped the grease from his mouth and hands before he hit the key to get more information.

A strong source of IR and magic emissions under what appeared to be a perfectly ordinary hill at the far south of the island. Craig chewed at his lip. That wasn't that uncommon. There were a lot of centers of magic in this world and some of them had funny effects on the non-magic sensors.

But this magic fell off fast. Right over the site it showed up strongly on the drone's sensors. As soon as the drone moved off the spot it faded fast. A few hundred yards from the hill the magic was too weak to pick up.

Without taking his eyes off the screen, Craig balled up the taco wrappers and threw them in the direction of the wastebasket. The basket sensed the incoming object, saw that it would miss, and scurried over to catch it. Craig was too preoccupied to notice.

That kind of fall-off *was* unusual. Magic usually faded out evenly, following a kind of inverse square law. Still, it was more curious than anything else and a long way away besides.

"Ah, what the shit," Craig muttered at last. He had plenty of drones and besides, there were a couple of new types of recon robots he wanted to try out.

"Well, that's the last of them," Wiz said, looking at the spot where the guardsmen had just winked out.

"Gonna be lonely around here," Danny said from where he was lounging against the wall. June, who was standing at his side, bit her lip and nodded. Shauna had taken Ian back four or five hours ago and it was the longest June had been separated from her son since he was born.

The storeroom, which had been packed with equipment and supplies was mostly empty now. The departing guards and staff had taken much of the material back with them. Two of the three residential wings of the complex were completely shut down and only a few rooms in the other residential section were still being used.

"Yeah, at least until tomorrow night," Wiz agreed absently. Moira had gone back earlier to reorganize the supply effort to fit the new and much smaller operation. Only Wiz, Jerry, Danny, June and the brownies were left in the complex.

*And who-knows-how-many gremlins*, Wiz added to himself.

"Well," said Jerry, "now that we're alone what's for dinner?"

"Moira left us bread, cheese and cold roast beef in the kitchen," Wiz said. "I think we'd better enjoy it while we can."

He looked sourly at the stack of waxed cardboard cartons next to him. Each one was stenciled "Meals, Ready-To-Eat" and a lot of government-sounding gobbledygook. Wiz didn't know where Moira had gotten them, but he hoped she got back soon with some real food.

Noiselessly the metal spider crept toward the darkened buildings. At the edge of the tall grass it paused, bobbed slowly as if testing the air, and then skittered across the open space to the concealing shadows.

Carefully lifting only one leg at a time it eased its way along the wall, every sense alert for any sign of danger or alarm.

Danger there was none. The building's spells discouraged animals, kept away insects and were proof against dwarves. But there was nothing to keep away or warn of a robot.

There was a door halfway down the wall. Standing on its hind pair of legs and balancing itself with its left and right pairs, the robot stretched its front pair full out to try the knob. When it found the door locked, the robot retracted its legs and lowered its egg-shaped body to the ground. There it sat, listening intently for several minutes. A sliver of moon appeared through the scudding clouds, faintly illuminating the building. The robot stayed pressed to the ground, looking like a rock and a couple of sticks to the casual.

At last the moon disappeared into the clouds and the robot stretched up to the doorknob again. It swiveled its body and a beam of blinding red light lanced out of its underside to trace around the knob and lock.

If there had been anyone in the wing the brilliant light and the smell of burnt paint and scorched metal would have alerted them. But there wasn't. No one heard when the spider robot wrenched the lock free and no one saw when the thing pulled open the door a crack and slipped through.

It was pitch dark in the corridor, but that didn't matter to something equipped with image intensifiers backed by ultrasonics. Slowly, carefully the robot moved down the deserted hallways, its front pair of legs extended before it like antennae.

At the end of the third corridor, the spy droid detected a light far off to the right. It eased down the corridor, becoming more cautious as its sound sensors began to pick up voices.

" . . . and he used Interrupt 21h for error handling!"

There was a burst of laughter and then a second voice started to tell another joke.

Ahead was a doorway letting warm yellow light out into the hall. The robot pressed itself hard against the wall and crept ahead one tentative step at a time, moving sideways like a steel crab.

It paused again at the door and then with exquisite caution it eased a single leg around the corner so the video sensor in the "ankle" could scan the room.

Wiz was sitting in the console chair with his feet up on the console, tearing a bite out of an oversized sandwich. Danny was perched on the edge of the console drinking from a mug and Jerry was over at the table building himself another sandwich.

" . . . so, anyway," Wiz said around the half-chewed sandwich, "the physicist says, 'First assume a spherical chicken of uniform density.'"

Jerry roared and Danny broke up in a coughing fit when some of his drink went down wrong.

*Very funny*, Craig thought as he looked at the image his scout was sending back. *Laugh while you can.*


*Come on, damn you!* Wiz stared hard at the computer screen. *We're running out of time!* But the twisting, convoluted blue shape looked no different today than it had before.

"I *hate* asymptotically converging algorithms," he growled. "The closer you get to the solution the longer they take."

"If you've got a better algorithm it's not too late," Jerry said mildly.

Wiz just snorted. "I'm just on edge. It's a combination of being a little kid waiting for Christmas and the fact that the longer we're here the riskier it gets."

"Plus, Moira's not here," Danny said from the table where he and June were sitting. "When's she due back anyway?"

"She said probably late this afternoon." Wiz swiveled back to the monitor, but the shape still looked the same. Irritably he started flipping through the views, each of which showed three of the shape's dimensions at a time. But the effect started to give him a headache.

Suddenly June stiffened and grabbed Danny's arm. "Noise," she said.

"I don't hear anything," Jerry told her.

Danny was frowning and listening hard. "I do. Kind of a whine."

"Are we losing a bearing on the disk drive?" asked Wiz. He bent and pressed his ear to the case. "No, I don't think it's coming from there."

By now the whine was louder.

"I think it's coming from outside," Jerry said and all four of them moved to the window.

There was a flash and the window blew in with a roar.

Pieces of glass the size and shape of knives scythed toward them in a glittering rain. But they shattered or bounced off when they struck the four immobile figures. Clouds of dust from the explosion roiled through the empty window frames. But not one of the four moved so much as a muscle.

They stood still and silent as the doors to the computer room flew open and three hulking robots marched in, tracking mud behind them.

Then came Craig in a suit of power armor and lastly Mikey wearing jeans and a T-shirt.

"What's wrong with them?" Craig's voice was tinny through the battle armor's speaker.

"They were like that when I came in." Mikey looked them up and down and smiled nastily. "It's a spell of some sort." He turned his backs on the group and went to the computer console. The screen still showed the weaving blue form of the key.

"Son of a bitch," Mikey said, open-mouthed.

Craig stomped up to peer over Mikey's shoulder. "What is it?"

"Something that makes this whole business

302

worthwhile. Something that gives us just what we need."

Mikey smiled. Not one of his half-sneers or tight little mouth quirks, but a big broad smile like a child on Christmas Day.

He left the console and went around in front of the impromptu sculpture garden where he could stare directly into Wiz's eyes.

"Thanks for the computer. It will save us a lot of trouble."

He turned to Craig. "Have the robots pack all this up and load it on the ship. Then search the place and grab anything else that looks useful."

"What about them?"

Mikey looked at the frozen group. "Finish them."

Craig raised his arm and pointed the laser in his suit's right forearm at the group. A brilliant beam of red light shot out and played across Wiz and his friends. The wall behind them smoked and scorched but the four statues were unaffected.

"What the hell?" Craig raised both arms and two laser beams converged in a spot of blinding incandescence that moved over the forms. The concrete wall behind them pocked and spalled and the aluminum window frame with its remaining shards of glass melted and ran. But still Wiz and his friends were unharmed.

"Oh shit, just leave them," Mikey said. "Later we'll see how well that spell stands up to a nuclear fireball. If that doesn't work we'll just drop them in the Sun. But get the computer on board first."

With one last look at the object on the screen, he left the computer room.

Quickly Craig brought the system down, cursing the clumsiness of his armor's steel fingers on the keyboard. For a space there was no sound save the clicking of the keyboard. Neither the programmers nor the robots stirred.

Gradually the room began to fill with dense black smoke from a fire elsewhere in the Mousehole. Craig, protected by his armor, barely noticed.

After several minutes the system blinked and died. Craig ordered the robots to begin dismantling and removing the computer. Then he went over to stand in front of the four motionless figures.

"Greatest wizard in the world, huh?" he said to Wiz. "Man, you were easy." Wiz did not twitch. Not even the look in his eyes changed.

Craig turned from one to the other, savoring the moment. So this was what it felt like to be a winner, a real winner. He tried to burn the feeling into his memory so he could relive it over and over for the rest of his life.

But why have just a memory? Why not a souvenir to help keep the memory fresh. In fact, why not *four* souvenirs?

As the robots returned from moving the computer, Craig gave them new orders.

Outside the Mousehole was a ship, a golden cigar shape lying on its side and pressing into the earth. One by one the robots carried their burdens up the gangway and carefully stowed them in one of the holds.

"Okay," Mikey said as he came back into what had been the computer center. "Let's get going. Hey! Where's Zumwalt and the others?"

"On the ship. I'm gonna build a trophy room and they're going to be my first trophies."

Mikey snorted and shook his head.

"Have it your way. Just make damn sure they stay frozen. Now have you got everything? Then let's haul ass."

As soon as they were aboard the gangway withdrew into their ship and the airlock doors swung shut. With an ear-piercing whine the golden craft rocked slightly and then rose straight up.

In the cockpit, Craig and Mikey lounged back in their acceleration couches and watched the ground fall away. Once they were high above the valley, Mikey used the mouse to line the crosshairs up on the now-deserted Mousehole. Then he pressed the left button quickly three times.

"Bombs awaaaay," he called as three dots detached themselves from the ship and plummeted to Earth.

Three blinding, shattering explosions came as one, making the ship's screens darken for an instant and filling the world below them with boiling, churning dust. The ship rose and fell slightly in the blast wave and then sailed serenely out of the billowing mushroom cloud, made a right-angle turn and headed north.

The cloud of smoke rose high in the air behind them.

From the hillside where he lay, Glandurg cursed as the airship vanished in the distance. "Balked again!" Then he straightened. "Come. We must follow these strangers to their lair."

"Don't see why," Snorri grumbled. "Seems like this Sparrow is bloody well finished."

"He was alive when he was taken from his abode."

"Didn't look none too healthy," Thorfin said. "All stiff like that."

"But he was alive. To fulfill the quest we must kill him ourselves or make certain of his death."

"Lot of extra work, if you ask me," Snorri said.

Glandurg turned on him, red-faced. "Who's leading this quest, you or me?"

"Oh you are," Snorri said sullenly. The other dwarves stood in a silence Glandurg chose to interpret as assent.

"Too right I am! And I say we track the wizard down."

"How far do you reckon they'll taken him?"

"That's immaterial. We will follow our prey to the ends of the World."

"We're a good bit beyond those already," Thorfin muttered.

Glandurg ignored the remark. "Besides, I doubt these newcomers will have their lair ensorcelled against us. We should be able to penetrate easily."

"Does this mean griffins again?" the Gimli asked plaintively.

"We would be too easy to see. No, we shall follow on foot. Now quickly." He looked down at the cloud of smoke roiling out of the valley. "There is nothing left here for us."

Gathering their packs the dwarves set out toward the north, following Glandurg's magic indicator toward an unseen foe.

There was no sign of life in the room where Wiz had met Craig and Mikey. Now the glass wall showed the night sky clear but oddly devoid of stars. There were just a few sprinkled around, making it hard to tell where the sky left off and the shadow of the mountains began.

Aside from the weak starlight, the only illumination came from the console monitor which spilled a squarish puddle of pale light onto the tiled floor. The only motion was the slow ceaseless rotation of the strange shape on the computer screen as the system ground inexorably closer to the final solution.

The door opened and a robot guard clanked in, sensors swivelling left and right as it probed the darkness, the laser turrets on its shoulders tracking restlessly back and forth. It was the very picture of mechanized death, even if a thin stream of oil was leaking from a blown knee seal, leaving oily footprints in its wake. Every time the robot took a step the piston in the leaking hydraulic damper slammed against the stop, making a distinct "clank." But the noise only made the black metal thing more menacing.

Twice it circled the computer, alert for any sign of life or anything out of order. Finding nothing, it clanked around the room once more and left. The dim light glinted faintly off its shiny black carprace as it turned the corner and the sound of its passage faded into the silence and stillness of the night.

Long after the guard's last echo died something moved in the deepest dark at the base of the computer. Slowly and oh so cautiously a smaller patch of darkness separated itself from the computer's shadow. As it scuttled along the base of the wall a stray glimmer of light caught it and resolved the patch into a tiny manlike figure.

The gremlin squeaked inaudibly at the light and scurried back into the shadows. There it paused, casting this way and that, its leaflike ears flapping and its long pointed nose quivering.

Machines! It was in the middle of an enormous collection of machines with a variety and complexity it had never imagined. In every direction beyond these stone walls was a gremlin king's ransom of machines. The computer that had been such a regal home just a few days ago was shabby and threadbare by comparison.

A broad, snaggle-toothed and beatific smile spread over the little creature's face.

Suddenly it was a *very* happy gremlin.

## Forty-one
# LOSS

"Nothing?" Bal-Simba demanded. "Nothing at all left?"

Dragon Leader shook his head. "A smoking crater, Lord. We landed and searched for survivors, but we found only one."

He gestured at the brownie standing on the council table.

"Breachean, my Lord." The little man hung his head. "It is my great shame that when the invaders came I ran away."

"It is our good fortune that you did," Bal-Simba said kindly. "Else there would be none to tell us what happened."

"I cannot tell you much, my Lord. I was outside when the metal creatures arrived and I ran. From the top of the hill I saw them carry out the thing the gremlins loved and put it in their ship. But then I ran over the hill and saw nothing more until the explosion."

"The computer?" Moira demanded from her place behind Bal-Simba's chair. "They took the computer?"

"Aye, my Lady. The metal things carried it out."

"But you saw no people?"

"No, Lady, either yours or my own."

The giant black wizard was silent for a moment, his head sunk on his chest. Up and down the long table the wizards of the Council of the North simply stared. One seat at the table was conspicuously vacant.

"Very well," he said at last. "Thank you, Breachean. Dragon Leader, keep what watch you can on the area in case someone else did survive, but do not endanger your riders."

Dragon Leader saluted and left with the brownie at his heels.

Bal-Simba sighed and looked back at Moira. "Child, I am sorry," he said simply.

The hedge witch was white, her freckles standing out vividly. "They will pay for this," she said softly. "By the World, the sea and the sky above they will pay!"

"Indeed they shall," the wizard Juvian said from his place near the head of the table. "Lady, the Council extends its deepest sympathies to you in your bereavement."

"He is *not* dead," Moira said fiercely. "The others perhaps, but not Wiz. I would know if he was."

The wizards did not point out that psychic bonds worked poorly between the Worlds.

"Remember the elf Lisella's prophecy," another wizard said. "All would suffer great loss, the mightiest among them would perish and our enemy would gain his heart's desire."

"The first part is fulfilled," Bal-Simba said. "Let us see if we can prevent the rest from coming true."

"We still have the wizards and apprentices that Jerry was training," Arianne pointed out.

"Even the best of them is more promising than skillful," Bal-Simba told her. "They are but half trained and none of them is close to being a match for any of the off-worlders." He nodded to Malus and Juvian. "Meaning no offense, my Lords."

"None taken," Juvian replied. "You speak only the simple truth."

"What about the elf?" Honorious asked.

"Aelric? There is no sign. Perhaps he perished or perhaps he has returned to his own domains."

"Well then," Agricolus said. "We must still face these others. What chance have we?"

"If they have the computer they can take the Sparrow's work and turn it against us," Bal-Simba said grimly. "Now time is on their side. We must deny them as much of it as we can."

"You mean attack them now?" Arianne asked.

"As soon as we can. They will only grow stronger."

The wizards shifted in their chairs. Arianne opened her mouth as if to ask another question and then thought better of it.

"Well," said Juvian at last. "I see no way to better our position by waiting."

No one at the table was under any illusion about their chances. That was written in their faces. However cowards do not gain the magical power that lifts a man or woman into the ranks of the Mighty, still less are they chosen to sit on the Council of the North.

"Very true," said Malus with a completely uncharacteristic seriousness. "With the Sparrow and his friends gone there is no one left who is truly a master of the new magic."

"No, wait!" Moira shouted. "There is another!"

Judith was awake and sitting up in bed when Bronwyn and Moira came in.

"Hey Bronwyn, look at this." She held up her right arm, clenched a shaky fist and beamed. "Not bad, eh?"

Then she caught her visitors' mood and sobered. "Is something wrong?"

"A great deal, I am afraid," Bronwyn told her.

Moira stepped up to the bed. "My Lady, you know that Wiz and the others were hiding in the halfway world to use a computer?"

Judith nodded, eyes wide.

"They were . . ." Moira stopped and took a deep, ragged breath. "They were discovered there and apparently overwhelmed."

"Oh shit!" Judith breathed. Her eyes began to fill with tears. "I'm really sorry, Moira."

Moira reached out and patted her hand. Then she gathered herself. "Our one chance now is to strike quickly against these other two wizards from your world, but we have no one who is expert with the new magic."

"You have me," Judith said quietly. "I may not be in Wiz's league, but I helped write the compiler and I'm a pretty damn good programmer."

Moira sighed. "Thank you, my Lady. I had hoped you would say that."

"There is more," Bronwyn put in sharply. "Lady, before you can do anything, you must be further healed. The spells to do so are dangerous and could harm you."

Judith didn't say anything.

"I know this is difficult," Moira said sympathetically. "Craig is your friend."

"Ex-friend," Judith said coldly. She looked up at

Moira, her face white and her lips pressed into a bloodless line.

"Do you understand what he did to me?" she asked, her voice shaking. "He came to me when I was helpless and he *used* me! He pried things out of me I never intended to tell anyone. Then he took that information and he turned it against my friends." Her eyes glittered with a mixture of tears and rage.

"I feel like I've been raped. If there is anything I can do to get back at that son of a bitch, I'm for it."

"Even at the cost of your health?" Bronwyn asked sharply. "Understand Lady, this healing spell could leave you worse than you are now with no hope of recovery."

"I don't care if it leaves me confined to a goddamn iron lung! If I can take that slimy little bastard down with me it will be worth it."

Bronwyn nodded and motioned Moira to one side.

"Well?" Moira demanded. "She is willing."

"She is blinded by anger," Bronwyn said coldly. "She is not thinking rationally." She held up a hand to cut off the protest. "But nevertheless I will do it."

It was the work of a few moments to prepare for the spell. Bronwyn summoned her two most senior assistants and they prepared the brazier and candles while the chief healer traced the warding circle on about the bed.

Judith sat in the center of things and watched. "This isn't the spell you used on Wiz, is it?" she asked.

Bronwyn finished the warding circle and looked up. "You are more seriously ill, Lady." She stepped back and regarded Judith carefully. "You may still withdraw."

"Not on your life."

Bronwyn nodded. One assistant reached into the sleeve of his robe and pulled out a packet of herbs which he threw on the brazier. As the fragrant smoke billowed up, Bronwyn and her other assistant raised

312

their wands and began the chant. The first assistant joined in in a minor key. Judith's eyes widened and her mouth formed a little "O" of surprise as the spell took effect. She lay back on the pillows and jerked spasmodically, her breath coming in short gasps. Moira caught her breath, but Bronwyn and her assistants continued the chant uninterrupted.

The chant soared, dropped and finally died away like the after note of a great bell. Judith twitched once more and lay still. The smoke dissipated and Bronwyn ritually defaced the circle before stepping to the bedside.

"Is she all right?" Moira demanded.

"Only time will tell that," the healer said.

"But the convulsions . . ."

"Nerves knitting together and forming new pathways. I have seen worse."

Judith's eyes fluttered and she breathed in great wracking gasps. Moira reached to her, but Bronwyn placed a hand on her arm.

"Can you hear me, Lady?" the healer asked gently.

Judith opened her eyes and her mouth worked convulsively. "Wwww . . ." she gasped.

"Yes, Lady?"

"Wwwater," Judith forced out.

"Here, Lady," Bronwyn took a bowl from one of her assistants and held it to Judith's lips. "Sip, now. Just sip." Judith slurped the liquid in the bowl, choked and spluttered.

Bronwyn removed the bowl. "That is enough for now," she said. Judith sank back against the pillow and breathed strongly and regularly. In a moment she was asleep and snoring gently. The healer nodded and motioned for them to withdraw. Already her assistants were carrying out the brazier, candles and other paraphernalia.

"She will probably sleep for a few hours," Bronwyn told Moira as they left the room. "We will know more when she awakens."

"Do you have any idea?"

"Well," the chief healer said judiciously, "she is not dead. That is something."

Moira couldn't bear the thought of going back to the apartment she had shared with Wiz, so she went to her office off the programmers' quarters. She hoped that work would help, but after she went over the same list of supplies three times without being able to remember what was what from the top to the bottom of the tablet, she gave up the idea of doing anything useful. Instead she contented herself with trying to file some of the stacks of wooden tablets and sheets of parchment that had accumulated on her desk while she was in the Bubble World. Vaguely she realized she would probably never be able to find half the material again, but she didn't really care. At least it kept her from breaking down completely.

"Hi."

Moira looked up from her filing and saw Judith standing in the door of her office.

"Lady!" she whooped, knocking over a pile of files in her haste to get around the desk. "Are you all right?"

"Never better," Judith said as the hedge witch hugged her tight. "Hungry as hell, but I feel great and I don't think I've weighed this little since I was sixteen." She stood back and patted her now-concave stomach. "Hell of a way to lose weight, though."

"I'm so glad."

"Bronwyn says I'm fine, so I thought I'd come and surprise you. Now let's go get some dinner. I haven't eaten in—oh—fifteen minutes." Her voice hardened. "And then we need a council of war."

In the event, the council was combined with dinner. For the first half-hour or so, Judith tore into a heaping selection of meats, fruits, bread and cheeses laid out on the table in Bal-Simba's study while Moira, Bal-Simba and Arianne filled her in. Then as she started to dawdle over her food instead of wolfing it, she began to ask questions and contribute information.

"You say you have pictures of some of these robots Craig and Mikey have been producing?" she asked, polishing off another hunk of bread. "Can I see them?"

In response Arianne gestured at the tabletop and a miniature tableau sprang into existence among the bread crusts and fruit rinds. On a barren landscape of red hills and sand perhaps a dozen metal creations were locked in mortal combat.

"Well, what do you know?" Judith said wonderingly. "Warbots."

"You recognize them?" Bal-Simba asked.

"I'll say. That's a Murderer. That one's a Red Terror. That thing over there is a Fer de Lance tank. And a couple of King Cobras. I don't know what that one is, but it looks like a Preying Mantis with a couple of laser pods added."

She looked up from the display. "They're game pieces. Imaginary fighting machines. Only it looks like the little shit's made them real here."

"They are real enough, Lady," Arianne said.

Judith examined the display again. "I wish I had my rule books; then I could tell you exactly what they're capable of. But I can remember enough to do pretty good without them."

"They look powerful," Juvian said dubiously.

Judith twisted her mouth to the side and rubbed her chin. "Well, yes and no. They're sure nothing to mess with, but they have a lot of weaknesses."

Absently, she picked up a pear and bit into it.

"Look, I don't know this Mikey, but I know Craig. I know how he thinks and I know how he fights." She wiped a dribble of juice off her chin and took another big bite.

"When you do a long campaign with someone you get to know them pretty well. Craig is not very original. That's why we didn't let him DM. He was too predictable."

"DM?" Juvian asked.

"Dungeon Master. The person who sets up the game. Anyway, Craig's strictly a by-the-book player and he expects everyone else to be the same way." She stopped talking, demolished the remaining pear in three bites and wiped her chin before she went on.

"So maybe we can surprise them." She grinned nastily. "In fact, I know we can surprise them. And I have a few ideas on how."

"How long will it take you to—ah—arrange your surprises?" Bal-Simba asked.

"The longer the better, but I can have some stuff ready in a few days."

The black giant turned his attention to Moira. "And you said that Wiz believed we had at least two weeks?"

"So he said, Lord."

"Then we had best postpone our plans for an immediate attack. A few days will make us much stronger without appreciably strengthening our opponents, I think." He turned to Judith. "When can you begin?"

Judith took an apple out of the fruit bowl. "How does right now sound?"

In the event, it took a few hours longer than that to clear off her old desk in the Bull Pen and get started. It was after midnight when Malus and Juvian reported to her there.

"Moira tells me you're pretty good with the spell compiler."

"We are hardly what you might call skilled, Lady,"

316

Juvian said. Malus stifled a yawn. He hadn't been up this late in years.

"Okay, I want you to pick out the best of the apprentices and journeyman wizards. No, let that wait until morning. There are a couple of things I want you two to start on right away."

"You mean tonight?" Malus asked.

Judith smiled. "Get used to it. The time-expansion spell only works from sundown to dawn and we're going to need all the time we can get."

The morning sun was streaming into the Bull Pen when Moira came calling. Juvian and Malus had dragged themselves off to bed some time before, but Judith was still hard at work.

"My Lady, Bal-Simba sent me to see if you are in need of anything."

"Just fine, thanks. But if you could have the kitchen send over some more food, I'd appreciate it."

"And a quantity of blackmoss tea. It is already being prepared."

Judith leaned back away from her desk and put her arms behind her head. "Bronwyn told me the healing spell would make me hungry, but I didn't have any idea it would be like this."

"The healing process takes energy, Lady. The body must replenish itself."

"Anyway, I'm not tired and that's useful. Look what we whipped up last night."

Over on the center table sat a vaguely familiar object. Except instead of being made of coiled straw basketwork it was made of shiny metal. The shape was different, too. As if two of them had been placed bottom to bottom. The result was something like a football, if a football had been two feet long and made of steel finished to look like coiled straw.

"Malus did the critical part of the spell," Judith explained as she reached down on the object and

317

detached a tinier thing. This she held up for Moira's inspection.

It was a shiny piece of metal no bigger than the first joint of Moira's finger. She looked closely and realized it was a perfectly formed metal insect, a bee to be precise. She became aware of a muted buzzing coming from inside the larger thing, as if it was full of thousands of steel bees.

"They'll ignore you unless you're moving fast," Judith explained. "But they home in on anything going faster than about 800 feet per second and destroy it."

Moira handed the robot bee back to Judith. "That is clever, but I am not sure I see the purpose."

"That's because you don't know our weapons. The most common ones are guns that shoot pieces of metal at very high speeds."

"Wiz told me about those. He said they were very destructive."

"They are. And they're going to be one of Craig's prime weapons. But our little killer bees can destroy bullets and shells before they can hit anything. So when we attack, we saturate the area with a bunch of these beehive rounds."

"But that thing is not round," Moira said. Then she looked narrowly at Judith. "Or does it approach roundness for sufficiently large values?"

Judith looked blank. "I don't understand."

"Neither do I," Moira sighed. "It was something Jerry said."

She stopped and for an instant Judith thought she was going to cry. But instead she said, "If there is nothing more you need I will leave you to your work."

Judith leaned forward to her desk again. "You know," she said absently, "I've worked on mission-critical software before. But this is the first time I've had the whole world on my shoulders."

"How does it feel?"

318

Judith gave her a tight little smile. "I don't like it." She sighed and turned back to Moira. "People are going to get killed in this, aren't they? Probably a lot of people."

Moira nodded gravely. "This troubles you?"

"Yeah. A lot. Before when I've fought a campaign it's been a game. At the end you picked your pieces up and put them back in the box until next time. Here there won't be any next time and I'm sending people to their deaths on the strength of my bright ideas."

"They will go with or without you, Lady," Moira told her. "The best you can do for them is to give them the tools so they may win."

Judith grimaced as if she was tasting something sour. "Yeah, but that doesn't make it easier."

"I am told that it never is easy, Lady."

"Lady, this is fantastic," Bal-Simba said as he looked over the plans. "I am astonished that you have accomplished so much in so little time."

Judith shrugged. "Mostly it wasn't any harder than hacking out some simple BASIC subroutines. Besides, I had Malus, Juvian and some of the apprentices to help me."

"Still, I remember how long it took a dozen of you to produce what we needed the last time you were our guest."

"That's why it took so long. What we did then laid the groundwork for what I'm doing now." She smiled. "The secret of good programming is that you spend ninety percent of your time up front building tools and maybe ten percent on the actual job—plus the other ninety percent of the time it takes to debug everything, of course. Unlike most of the people I've worked for you were smart enough to stand back and let us spend the time on the tools. So now . . ." again the shrug, "it's easy."

"You said you also wanted to discuss strategy. My

guard commander tells me your suggestions are, um, somewhat unorthodox."

Judith smiled. "I'll bet he did."

"Well, he did put the matter—ah—somewhat more strongly."

"I can understand that. But I know Craig and Craig's a gamer."

Judith rested her elbows on the table and leaned forward. "Look, one of the problems most gamers have is they spend too much time worrying about hardware and not enough on C3—command, control and communications. If I know Craig, he's got some horrendously effective hardware. But he's weak on the things that will let him use it effectively.

"Now," she went on judiciously, "we could try to match him on the hardware. But we really can't because he's had longer to play with this stuff and he has control of the Bubble World. So mostly we won't bother. Instead we'll use pretty much the weapons and tactics your people already know—plus the new magic—and we'll primarily use technology to enhance the C3. We may not be as powerful as he is, but we'll be better coordinated."

Bal-Simba grinned. "Excellent, Lady." Then the grin faded. "But you have laid your plans in terms of only one of our enemies, this Craig. What about the other one? The one called Mikey?"

Judith's frown matched the wizard's. "I don't know. So far we haven't seen anything that isn't in Craig's style. Either Mikey is just like Craig or he's up to something that hasn't shown up yet."

"Ah," said the wizard Malus, "you sent for me, my Lord."

Bal-Simba looked up from his desk and eyed his tubby little colleague.

"My Lord," he inquired pleasantly, "have you ever flown on a dragon?"

Malus blinked. "A dragon, my Lord?"

"Yes. Have you ever flown on one?"

"Why, ah, no. No I haven't. That is . . ."

"We need wizards with the dragon cavalry in the attack. You are among the best qualified of the Mighty for the job." Bal-Simba forbore to mention that Malus's main qualification was his weight. In spite of his girth, he was the lightest of all the Mighty—save for Juvian, who suffered from an airsickness no spell could cure.

Malus half-bowed, torn between honor and trepidation. "Well, thank you, my Lord, but I mean, after all, a wizard on *dragonback* . . ."

"It is voluntary, of course," Bal-Simba said blandly.

"Oh naturally I volunteer, but, ah, wouldn't a levitation spell work just as well?"

"Dragons do not like to have other flying things near them when they are on the wing. Especially not something so unnatural as a flying wizard."

Malus deflated like a cold souffle. "Oh."

Bal-Simba beamed and clapped the smaller man on the shoulder. "Excellent. Now, report to the Master of Dragons in the main aerie. He will see to your training as a dragon rider. Later the Lady Judith will brief you on tactics and teach you the new spells you will need."

As the pudgy wizard bowed and turned toward the door he remembered that he was deathly afraid of heights.

Judith pushed a strand of dark hair out of her face as she bent over the map again. Her lower back ached from the time she had spent standing like this and she was hoarse from talking all morning, but at last the plan seemed to be coming together.

"Okay, that leaves the communications relay *here*." She stabbed her finger down on the three-dimensional map that occupied the whole table top. "If we

321

lose that we lose most of our ability to coordinate between the attacking force and the Capital."

Moira checked her stack of wooden tablets. "We have an entire squadron of dragons assigned to protect it. They carry your new weapons. The squadron leader is waiting outside should you wish to meet her."

Judith stood up from the map and stretched to try to get the kinks out of her back. "Yeah. There are a couple of things we need to go over." *And it'll give me an excuse to sit down.* She was still studying the map when she heard the door open.

"Reporting as ordered, my Ladies."

Judith looked up at the sound of the voice and gaped.

The squadron leader was a fresh-faced brunette with a fine dusting of freckles and one of those complexions that no one over the age of twenty can ever have.

"Have they explained your mission to you?" Moira asked, apparently oblivious of the effect the squadron leader was having on Judith.

"Yes, Lady. We have been running training exercises every day for as long as our dragons can fly."

"And the weapons?"

The dragon rider grinned. "Amazing, Lady. The dragons do not like them, but . . ." She shrugged.

"Okay," Judith put in. "Remember those things are most effective against metal—robots or flying machines. Don't use them against biologicals unless you have to. Also keep in mind there is a maximum and a minimum range. Also, the closer they get before you shoot the better your chances of hitting, but the fewer shots you can get off before they are too close."

"We have been practicing these things, Lady."

"Good. Now if we're lucky they won't detect the communications platform at all and you won't have to fight." The expression that flashed across the squadron leader's face showed she wouldn't consider that lucky at all. "If you do have to fight, you'll probably be in—ah—a target-rich environment. Keep in mind your job is to protect the relay, not shoot down attackers."

The girl nodded gravely. "I understand, Lady."

"Okay. Anything else? Then you're dismissed. I'll try to talk to you later about last minute details."

The squadron leader bowed and closed the door gently behind her as she left.

"Our apprentice squadron," Moira explained as Judith scowled at the closed door.

"Hell, she can't be more than fourteen!"

"Closer to sixteen summers."

"A goddamn kid!"

"What would you? The alternative is to send them into the thick of the battle. Besides, young riders and dragons are adaptable in ways that older ones are not. Believe me, my Lady, if they must use those weapons of yours, the dragons had better be the most adaptable ones we have."

### Forty-three
# YOU BASH THE BALROG,
# I'LL CLIMB THE TREE

The four frozen statues stood in a neat row, like the pieces in some gigantic game.

In truth, Craig's trophy room was only a storeroom off in one wing of the castle. Wiz and his friends were dumped there and left to gather dust against the day when Craig would have a proper trophy room to display them.

Once or twice in the succeeding days Craig came down to look at them and gloat. But mostly they were left alone to stare sightlessly at the stone wall across the room.

"Hhsst," a tiny voice squeaked. "Hhsst! my Lord."

But Wiz flicked not so much as an eyelid.

Lannach tiptoed into the room, keeping his back to the wall. He reached out to touch the hem of June's dress, he tugged on Wiz's pant leg. There was no response.

The protection spell! Of course. They were still in danger in this place so the protection spell still held them fast.

The brownie danced up and down in frustration. He and his companions had spent days searching for their friends and now they could do nothing for them. The castle was constantly patrolled by warbots and other strange creatures and Lannach knew it would only be a matter of minutes before he was discovered. Danger of discovery aside, any one of four was far too large for even all of the brownies together to move.

Then he remembered the rings and what Wiz had said when he gave them out. Lannach had been busy with the gremlins then and hadn't paid much attention, but he did remember that the spell could be turned off.

If he could get to the rings.

Lannach stepped back and considered. Both Danny and Jerry had their arms raised and away from their bodies. June had both her fists jammed in her mouth. Wiz's arms were down at his sides and slightly away from his body. Clearly it would be easier to reach his ring.

But even with his hands down, Wiz's ring was still easily at three times Lannach's height. The brownie looked around frantically, but there was nothing he could use as a ladder anywhere in the room.

Lannach reached above Wiz's boot and touched his leg. The fabric of his pants moved easily under his tiny hand. Not ideal, but it would have to do. Carefully he stretched up and grabbed Wiz's pant leg, pulling himself up to stand on the top of Wiz's boot.

He had just reached belt level when a shadow in the hall told him someone was coming. It was too far to jump to the floor and there was no obvious place to hide. But Wiz's jerkin was the kind that laced all the way down the front. Quickly he wiggled his way beneath the jerkin, clinging to the shirt for dear life.

The guard's little red eyes shifted back and forth as it scanned the room. Lannach pressed himself close and dared not to breathe. He knew he must make an unsightly bump on Wiz's stomach. He just hoped the guard didn't notice it.

Finally the creature gave a piglike grunt and shambled out the door, trailing his halberd behind him. Lannach closed his eyes and sighed in relief. He lost his grip and squeaked in terror as he almost slipped out of the jerkin. Then he resumed his ascent of Mt. Wiz.

A quick reach and grab gave Lannach a double handful of Wiz's shirt sleeve. Resolutely ignoring the drop below, the brownie swung his body out until he could wrap his legs around Wiz's forearm. Then he shinnied down the arm feet-first, locked his legs

325

around Wiz's wrist and reached out with both hands for the ring.

It was an awkward position and the stone was stiff. It took all of Lannach's strength to turn it.

Suddenly Wiz relaxed and dropped his arms, nearly dashing Lannach to the floor.

Wiz shook his head, felt the weight on his right arm and looked down to see Lannach clinging to his shirt sleeve for dear life. He put his left hand out to support the brownie's feet.

"Thanks, Lannach," Wiz said.

"We pay our debts, Lord."

Quickly he set the brownie down on the floor and moved to free his companions.

"Where are we?" Wiz asked the brownie.

"In your enemies' castle, Lord. They attacked the Mousehole, stole the computer and then destroyed the place."

"Damn!" Wiz breathed. "What about the rest of your people?"

"All here, Lord. Save only Breachean. We think he got away."

"Thank God for that."

"There is more, Lord," Lannach squeaked. "The Council is preparing to attack this place with everything they have."

"They'll be slaughtered!"

"Perhaps, but with you and the others dead, they saw it as their only chance."

"Can you get word to them that we're still alive?"

"Alas, Lord, their magic blocks us here."

"Damn!"

"Doesn't make much difference," Jerry said grimly. "If we don't stop Mikey and Craig right now we're cooked anyway."

"Damn!" Wiz said for the third time. He thought hard. "Okay, I guess our best chance is to do all the damage we can in here. The first thing we've got to do is take out that computer."

"That will not be easy," Lannach said dubiously. "It is heavily guarded. Besides, your enemies get little enough use of their prize. When they brought the computer they brought the gremlins with it. Now the whole castle is infested."

"The gremlins are here?"

"In greater numbers than ever, I fear."

"Hey Lannach," Danny said. "Do you think you could, like, stir those gremlins up a little?"

The little man grinned. "You mean encourage them to cause trouble? Easily, my Lord."

"Then do it," Wiz commanded. "Let's turn this place into a gremlin jamboree."

"With pleasure. But what will you do?"

"We," said Wiz, "are going to stage our own jamboree."

With Wiz in the lead the group made its way down the hall. Lannach had told them the computer was in the central tower and that meant they had to go to the center of the castle to reach it. That wouldn't be easy, Wiz knew. Not only was the place enormous, Lannach said there were guards everywhere.

*Don't think of it as a problem,* Wiz told himself. *Consider it a challenge.*

Their first challenges were just around the corner. Three of them, all nearly seven feet tall. Their faces were piglike with tusked snouts and red eyes that looked mean even as they laughed uproariously at something one of them said. They were wearing armor of fantastic designs and carrying an assortment of wicked-looking polearms. Curved swords and daggers hung from their studded metal belts, and nickel-plated machine guns were slung over their backs.

Wiz peered around cautiously and then jerked his

head back before they could see him. Danny, Jerry and June also peeked around.

June laid a hand on Danny's arm and looked at him quizzically.

"We're going to sneak up on them and knife all three of them when they're not looking," Danny whispered sarcastically.

Wiz signaled his companions into a huddle twenty feet or so back from the corner.

"We've got to go this way," he whispered to them. "Lannach says this is a blind corridor and there's only this one way out."

"Can we distract them?" Jerry asked.

"Without them raising the alarm? How?"

When they looked back, June was halfway down the corridor. All three motioned frantically for her to come back but June ignored them. Then she whipped around the corner.

"Oh shit! Come on." Danny set off at a dead run with Wiz and Jerry pounding after him.

As they came around the corner June was walking back toward them, wiping her knife on her skirt. Behind her were three large steel-clad forms lying in a heap.

"Now what?" she whispered to Danny.

"Uh, now we keep going," Danny whispered hoarsely. Wiz and Jerry just goggled.

Just past the guards was an open door leading to a room with masses of wires running down the walls.

"What do you suppose all this is anyway?" Danny asked, looking around the room.

"Hard to say, but if I was to guess I'd say it was a wiring closet for their phone exchange."

Wiz looked over the mass of wiring speculatively.

"I'd say it was a good place to start sabotage then." He raised his hands. "Let's see how long it takes this stuff to melt."

"I got a better idea," Danny said. "We've got a couple of minutes, don't we?"

Wiz looked down at the bodies of the three guards. "Uh, yeah."

Danny grinned. "Good. Let's see what happens when they get their wires crossed."

Wiz looked at the wall of hair-fine wires dubiously. "I said a couple of minutes, not a few hours."

"Oh, I'm gonna have help. **Emac!**"

Instantly one of the little demons stood before him.

"**backslash**," Danny commanded.

"**?**" the Emac responded.

"**list spaghetti exe**"

As Wiz and Jerry watched the demon scribbled furiously, filling the air with glowing symbols. Danny knelt down and began giving the creature commands in a low voice.

"You know," Jerry observed, "it's kind of handy carrying your own software development environment with you wherever you go. Kind of like having the world's niftiest laptop—except you don't get tired lugging it through airports."

Wiz eyed his friend. "I think you've been here too long."

With a final whispered **exe!**, Danny stood up. There was a quick swirl of air and another little demon stood next to the Emac. This one wore a blue denim work shirt, jeans and construction boots—much like the one Danny had produced to connect up the computer. However this demon bore a striking resemblance to Alfred E. Neumann.

Danny pointed at the wiring panel. "Kill!" he commanded.

The demon grinned and swarmed up the panel, clinging with its feet while it swapped wires with both hands.

"That was fast work," Wiz said as the quartet left

the wiring room. Behind them the demon was still furiously switching connections.

"It's something I've been kinda working on for a while," Danny admitted.

Wiz shook his head. "I don't think it's *ever* going to be safe to let you go back to California."

A line of dwarves came out of the desert. They were footsore, dusty, travel-worn and thirsty. Glandurg was in the lead, limping slightly and the rest were strung out behind him.

"Let us rest before the final assault," Glandurg commanded. His followers needed no second order. They threw themselves down in the shade of a red earth hillock.

While they rested, Glandurg and Thorfin crawled to the top and looked out at their target.

"Big enough," said Thorfin, craning his neck to try to see the top of the central tower.

"Our magic will let us locate our target no matter how big it is."

Thorfin looked ahead dubiously. The desert had been singularly unappealing and the castle before them looked less appealing than that.

"Not what I was thinking of," he muttered.

Glandurg started to say something but he was interrupted by one of the other dwarves.

"Hsst! Someone's coming."

Quickly the party concealed themselves as only dwarves can.

*What this time?* Glandurg thought. *More of those big metal walking things? Or the ones that roll over the ground?*

Then he heard the crunch of walking feet. The walkers again; two small ones from the sound of them.

But it wasn't the walkers. Instead it was two mortals and a dragon, looking as tired, dusty and footsore as the dwarves. While the dragon rested behind the hillock the humans climbed to the spot Glandurg and

Thorfin had vacated just moments before to spy out the castle.

"Now," said Major Mick Gilligan, "we can see the whole place from here. Is this close enough for you?"

Karin frowned. The trickles of sweat down her face left clean tracks through the reddish dust. "But we cannot see clearly. We must move closer."

Gilligan licked his lips and tasted grit. "From here on the land's flat as a pancake. We get any closer and we're going to stick out like three sore thumbs."

Karin smiled. "You only have two thumbs, silly."

Mick leaned over and kissed her on her dusty, sweaty cheek. "Two sore thumbs and a sore big toe, then. Anyway, we're not going to have any cover."

"I think we must risk it," Karin said seriously. "We won't learn much watching from here." She shaded her eyes and scanned the plain before them. "Besides, there is some cover out there. Enough to hide a person if you are careful."

Gilligan glanced back at Stigi and didn't say anything.

Karin scanned the plain. "At least there do not seem to be any robots out there."

*Fine,* Gilligan thought, *so it's a killing zone.*

"Okay, but remember what I told you. We keep spread out, drop at the least sign of trouble and be on the lookout for mines."

Karin nodded. They slithered down the hill, collected Stigi and started out onto the plain.

*Now what was that all about?* Glandurg thought as he watched the humans and the dragon go. He signaled his own group to assemble and they too started out on the plain.

The plain before them was not only flat, it was wired. There were pressure sensors in the soil, motion sensors concealed in rocks, capacitance sensors

331

masquerading as bushes and an invisible network of radar, laser and ultrasonic beams lacing back and forth so tightly not even a field mouse could move without being detected.

Neither group was more than a hundred yards onto the flat ground before they were picked up, marked as hostile and targeted.

In pillboxes disguised as hillocks of red earth, shutters slid off firing ports and machine guns poked out their ugly black snouts. Artillery buried in the base of the castle swung around as automatic loaders delivered shells and powder charges to their gaping breeches. Firing impulses raced at the speed of light along buried wires to fields of mines.

Suddenly the earth erupted in flame and smoke and flying pieces of metal.

"What was that?" Karin asked.

"Barrage," Gilligan told her shortly. "About a mile to our right. Come on. Let's move!"

"What was that?" Glandurg demanded as the explosions and gunfire rang out over the plain.

"Dunno," Snorri said. "But it's about half a league over yonder." He pointed to the column of smoke and dirt boiling up well to the dwarves' left.

"Well, let's not wait around to find out, shall we?"

The wiring closet had been heavily guarded because it was the concentration point for the sensors and fire control systems for the outer defenses of the entire southern quadrant of the castle.

The wiring was automatically monitored, but the computer doing the monitoring could only detect breaks and bad connections. It wasn't bright enough to realize that connections were being switched at the rate of hundreds per minute. So it didn't go to the backup.

Not that it would have mattered. The gremlins had been at the backup all morning.

"What the hell?" Craig muttered as the alert box popped up on his screen. Quickly he called up the display for the outer sensor array. The map showed possibly hostile contacts at half a dozen shifting points in the southern quadrant. They were being fired on but as fast as one winked out another appeared somewhere else.

*Not another herd of those damn grazing things,* he thought and called up the security camera displays. The cameras in the area showed a wild jumble of confused flickering images, but the ones mounted on the castle walls showed several tiny figures out on the plain. But they weren't any place close to the target zones.

"Shit!" The damn system was messed up again. He switched over to manual control and ordered a battery to fire on one of the groups of dots.

The guns fired, but the shells landed a couple of miles from where they were supposed to be. He tried to correct his aim and a different battery fired at a point well behind the targets. In rapid succession the same command fired other batteries.

Craig growled in frustration. He switched to his backup control system, only to get a message on the screen saying it was inoperative. He gritted his teeth and tried to sort out the mess by experimenting with the controls. But the demon in the wiring closet was changing connections at random much faster than Craig could fire ranging shots. At that point coincidence could be defined as the same command firing the same weapon twice in succession at the same target.

"Shit!" Craig yelled. Then he reached over and sounded the general alarm. The lights flickered and one wall of the room slid back to reveal a wall-sized

333

map of the castle and its approaches. "Guards to the perimeter," he barked into a microphone. "We have intruders approaching from the south."

Then he threw himself back in his chair, crossed his arms and watched the screens. "All right, suckers. Let's see you evade that!"

Slowly and cautiously Wiz and his friends made their way toward the center of the castle. They saw no more of the live guards, but several times they had to hide from heavily armed robot sentries. Fortunately they were so noisy the quartet could hear them coming and June was particularly adept at finding hiding places.

Finally they found the elevator.

Wiz eyed the number painted on the wall across from the elevator doors. "From the looks of this, we're pretty low in the castle. I'll bet what we want is further toward the top."

Off down the corridor there was a distinct clank clank clank.

"Robot coming. Everyone in quick." They piled in and Wiz pressed the button. "Okay, going up."

The elevator doors jerked towards each other, slammed back and then jerked together. The car twitched spasmodically, almost throwing its occupants into a heap.

"Maybe," Wiz amended. But the car began to rise, slowly and jerkily at first and then faster and jerkily. All four of them braced themselves against the sides of the car and tried their best to stay upright.

"Hey, " Danny said after a few minutes, "isn't there something about being trapped in an elevator?"

"Huh?"

"In the spy movies. Aren't people always getting trapped in elevators?"

"Don't be morbid."

"I'm not being morbid, I'm being practical."

"If you're so damn practical why didn't you think of that before we got on the frigging elevator?"

Danny just shrugged.

"Wait a minute," Wiz said, looking up, "there is something we can do. Jerry, see if you can reach the ceiling of the car."

Jerry extended his hand experimentally. "Sure. Now what?"

"See if you can find the service hatch."

Jerry prodded at the ceiling as the car continued its jerky climb. Finally one of the ceiling sections flipped back to reveal an opening perhaps two feet square.

"Okay," Wiz said, "we climb up on top of the car."

"Is that safe?" Jerry asked dubiously.

"Safer than meeting a reception committee. Now hoist Danny up, will you?"

With Jerry's help Danny easily wriggled through the hatch. June followed lithely with a slight assist from Danny. Wiz followed June with an easy leap and a quick chin up. That left Wiz, Danny and June on top of the elevator and Jerry in the car.

Since Jerry weighed nearly as much as Wiz and Danny put together this presented a problem. Since Jerry was not exactly light on his feet, it presented a serious problem. The first attempt to hoist Jerry through the opening nearly pulled Wiz and Danny back into the car. Finally, Wiz dropped back into the car to push from below while Danny heaved from above. With much tugging and shoving, they were able to get Jerry onto the roof of the car.

Then the elevator ground to a stop and the doors started to open.

Wiz leaped for the hatch and wriggled through just as the doors ground open. Before they could close the panel two goblin guards strode into the elevator with drawn laser pistols. As the four humans held their breath the guards looked around suspiciously, their weapons tracking their head movements.

One snorted like a bull and drew in a deep breath, as if testing the air. His companion grunted something to him and he exhaled with a grunt. They looked around again, but they did not look up.

Finally the pair backed out of the car and the doors closed. After a moment, the elevator creaked and jerked and started upward again.

Wiz let out a deep breath and nearly collapsed with relief.

"It's the helmets," Jerry said after a moment.

"What?"

"The helmets. They're so ornate the guards have trouble looking up." He shook his head. "Bad design. Like a lot of this place."

"Personally I think it's great design," Wiz said sharply. "It just saved our bacon."

"Aw, we could have taken them easy," Danny said. "A few lightning bolts and, hey—" He made a gun with his finger and mimed shooting at the door. There was a flash of blue spark from his fingertip and a large scorch mark appeared on the wall of the shaft.

Danny looked down at his finger in surprise. "I didn't know it was loaded."

"Well, holster it. And remember we're just a little bit outnumbered here. We don't start throwing fireballs until we absolutely have to."

"Get ready then," Jerry said, looking up at the indicator over the door. "We may have to. We're almost there."

Quickly the three magicians arranged themselves to have the best field of fire when the door opened. All three of them muttered preparation spells so they could come out shooting if they had to. Then they waited.

The elevator creaked and swayed, jerked twice more and then expired with a sigh. The doors started to open, slammed closed, and then slid all the way open with a despairing groan—leaving them looking at a blank stone wall.

Wiz looked down through the hatch and out the open door. At the bottom of the door there was a narrow slit of corridor visible, perhaps eighteen inches wide. The elevator had gone almost completely past their intended floor.

"Shit!" Wiz muttered and all of them quickly dropped through the hatch into the car.

Jerry reached out and punched the elevator button. The car lurched and groaned again, but did not move.

"Reminds me of the elevator at a Star Trek convention in Denver," he said.

"We'll have to squeeze out through that space then," Wiz said.

Jerry eyed the slit. "I don't know if I've got that much octopus blood in me," he said dubiously.

"Maybe there are working controls outside," Wiz said as he knelt to slip through the crack. He eased through the opening and felt for the floor with his feet. The elevator was just high enough that he couldn't keep his weight resting on his elbows in the car and touch the floor at the same time. He eased out further and for a terrible second kicked his legs over empty air in the elevator shaft. Then his left foot caught the floor and he eased himself down on solid footing. He sighed and turned around to face down the corridor.

And found himself face to face with a goblin guard.

The guard roared a challenge and swung his halberd two-handed. Wiz ducked and the halberd knocked chips of stone off the door jamb. Snarling, the guard swung the weapon back over his head and down toward the crouching programmer. Instinctively Wiz lunged forward as the blade descended. He hit the goblin in the knees just as the halberd came down with the full force of the monster's body behind it. The combination overbalanced him, and the guard went sprawling headfirst down the elevator shaft, screaming as he fell.

Wiz collapsed forward on his face, sucking great lungfuls of air. Somewhere in the distance a siren began to wail. Behind him he heard his three companions drop to the floor of the corridor. Then Jerry and Danny reached down and pulled him to his feet.

"How'd you do that?" Jerry panted, red-faced from the tight squeeze.

"I don't know," Wiz gasped. "Now run!"

The four of them pounded down the corridor, turned a corner and headed off in what Wiz hoped was the right direction. After several hundred yards they ducked into a side corridor to catch their breath.

All four of them leaned up against the wall gasping. Off in the distance, faintly, they could still hear the siren. Then another siren sounded and another and another until the castle reverberated to the sound.

"Guards to the perimeter," the speakers in the wall above them squawked. "We have intruders approaching from the south."

"What's that?" Danny panted.

"I think," Wiz said slowly between gulps of air, "that all hell just came unshirted."

# Forty-four

# FOR FAITH, FOR LOVE, FOR HONOR

The Wizard's Keep boiled with activity. From the tallest towers the trumpeters blew "Assembly" over and over. Down on the drill ground armored guardsmen fell in rank by rank while the drummers beat the Call To Arms on the great bass drums that hung by the reviewing stand. From the aeries below wing after wing of dragons rose and circled and grouped themselves into larger formations.

In the Watch Room every post was manned. The Watchers on the main floor murmured into communications crystals or peered into scrying glasses for some sign of the enemy. On the wall behind them glowed a huge map of the northern end of castle island, casting an eerie bluish glow over the proceedings.

On the dais at the opposite end of the room groups of wizards hovered over their own crystals and muttered spells and incantations. Bal-Simba was there, seated in his raised chair where he could watch and command everything. Judith was there, seated next to Moira at a small table to Bal-Simba's right. Arianne was at his left and next to her, the elf duke.

Aelric stood tall and terrible in shining silver mail of elven metal. His helm, intricately and carefully wrought, extended down over his cheeks and neck, unlike the conical helms of the Council's guardsmen. But save for the nose guard it left his face unprotected.

"Is there aught else?" Bal-Simba asked the people clustered around him. Arianne and Moira shook their heads and Aelric said nothing.

"My Lady Judith?"

"We're as ready as we'll ever be. The dragon riders have got the new spread-spectrum communications crystals so they can cut through the jamming, the guardsmen have the last of the special weapons and the scouting demons are deploying now." She took a deep breath. "It's going to be rough, but Craig's in a world of hurt unless he can make a saving roll."

"Saving roll?"

"Uh, unless he gets lucky."

Aelric smiled without warmth. "Fear not, Lady; luck they shall not have this day."

Bal-Simba looked around the group once more. "Aught else? Then we are ready."

Aelric bowed to the group. "If you will excuse me, I have my own part to play. This battle will not be fought entirely in the World you know and my own role comes—elsewhere." He started to go and then turned back. "One other thing. You may find you have acquired some unexpected allies. I would suggest that you simply accept such help as you are given." He picked his way off the crowded dais and strode toward the door.

Moira followed him and caught up with him in the corridor.

"You came back."

Aelric looked down at her. "Did you doubt that I would, Lady?"

She stopped. "Lord . . ." The elf duke turned back at the sound of her voice.

"Lord, I have not properly thanked you for your aid. I have been surly and ill-natured to you and," her eyes begin to fill with tears and the words came with a rush, "and I am sorry and thank you. That is all I wish to say."

"You are most welcome, Lady," Duke Aelric said, ignoring her tears. "Truly this has not been easy for any of us."

"I wish there was something I could do to make up for everything."

"Bend every power you possess to our victory," Duke Aelric said. "Then hope that it is enough."

The dwarves were panting and exhausted by the time they reached the base of the castle. The explosions and beams of burning light had never come close but they had taken them as a hint and crossed the plain at a dead run. Since dwarves are too short and stumpy for distance running they were pretty well worn out.

A dozen dwarves slumped down in a row beneath the towering walls of living rock and gulped great lungfuls of air. Out on the plain the explosions continued unabated.

"Now that we're here," Thorfin gasped after several minutes, "how do we get inside?"

"Place isn't spelled against us," said Snorri. "Don't see any gates, though."

"Gates would be guarded," Gimli pointed out.

"There are openings further up," Glandurg shaded his eyes and craned his neck. "Leave your packs here and bring only what we shall need for the final assault."

Thorfin and Snorri looked at each other and shifted uneasily. "You mean those openings that spout fire and explosions every so often?"

"You have a better idea? I thought not."

The wall was solid rock and so steep it was only a few degrees off vertical. But dwarves are creatures of the mountains and if they cannot run they can climb like flies.

Glandurg lifted Blind Fury high above his head with both hands.

"Forward!" he proclaimed. "For glory and honor!" Glandurg turned and began to climb the wall. Behind him his loyal followers hesitated and then started after him.

\*     \*     \*

It took Mick and Karin longer to cross the plain. Mick insisted on going flat every time the artillery came within a few hundred yards of them. Fortunately the fire never got really close and their only injury was to Stigi, who received a scratch from a shell fragment.

"Well, we're here," Mick said as they rested in the shade of the wall. "Now are you satisfied?"

"I wonder if we can get inside?" Karin said thoughtfully.

"Even for you that's a crazy notion. We've done too much already."

"Let us work our way along the wall and see if we can find a gate," she went on as if she had not heard him.

Mick looked at her, sighed and nodded.

*The things men do for love!*

"The scouts are in position," the Watcher reported.

Bal-Simba looked up at the display. Already it was beginning to show the information pouring in from tens of thousands of scouting demons like the ones Wiz and his company had used to locate the heart of Bale-Zur in the City of Night.

Unlike those demons, these absorbed everything that happened around them and transmitted the information back to dozens of concentrators floating well to the south out of the battle zone.

Circling off the southern end of the island was a thing like a gray tarp, a relay for communications and the concentrators. It absorbed the information, did some preliminary filtering and fed it back to the relay. The relay in turn passed the information back to the Watchers in the Capital.

As one, the controllers in the pit looked up at Bal-Simba. The giant wizard took a deep breath. Then he nodded.

The controllers turned back to their crystals and the attack was on.

## Forty-five
# BATTLE ROYAL

"Dragon Leader, you have an allied force approaching to your right. I say again, you have friendlies approaching from widdershins high."

*What the . . . ?* There were no more friendly forces. Save for a couple of squadrons on guard duty Dragon Leader had the entire cavalry of the North with him. Anything else in the air had to be hostile.

"Dragons at widdershins high," the scout on the right flank sang out.

"Can you identify?" Dragon Leader barked into his communications crystal. He hated surprises in the middle of a battle.

Silence.

"I say again, can you identify the dragons?"

"Uhhh . . ."

"Dammit, speak up!"

By now the formations were at almost the same level and closing fast as the newcomers pulled into a shallow dive.

Dragon Leader craned his neck to see the approaching force. Whoever they were, they had the most ragged-ass formation he had ever seen. They looked more like a flight of geese than a squadron of cavalry.

Dragon Leader's mount bridled and nearly bucked as the flight approached. It took a moment to bring the animal under control and when Dragon Leader looked up again the leader of the new force was flying next to him.

Dragon Leader glanced. Then he gaped. Then he nearly fell out of his saddle. Flying beside him was the biggest dragon he had ever seen in his life.

This was no adolescent cavalry mount. It was a full-grown, fully intelligent dragon and a monster of its

343

kind at that. It was easily twice the length of his own mount and might have reached 200 feet. Behind and above came dozens more wild dragons.

A great golden eye regarded Dragon Leader and his dragon with amused contempt. Then with a flick of its tail, the giant reptile winged over and dived for the deck. The rest of the wild dragons followed their leader down.

Dragon Leader licked lips suddenly gone dry. "Uh, central," he croaked into his communications crystal. "The allied forces have taken the lead position and are going in low."

"Allies lead and low," the controller's voice came back. "Acknowledged."

*Fortuna*, Dragon Leader thought, *what have we gotten ourselves into?*

Out on the edge of the plain the warbots waited. There were 100-ton Murderers, 30-ton Hellfires, Skysweeper anti-aircraft units, a couple of 200-ton Gargantua fire support models and a dozen or so Springer scouts, all in a loose grouping just behind the military crest of the ridge. They were being held as a mobile reserve, ready to sweep down off the ridge and deal any attacker on the plain a crushing blow to the flank.

The Springer nearest the crest of the ridge turned its head. Its sensors had picked up something....

With a rush the lead dragon swept over the hill scant feet off the ground. A blast of dragon fire destroyed the first robot before it could even face its foe.

The second warbot had time to half raise its laser before the hurtling mass slammed it to the ground. The warbot next to it had only half turned when the massive tail caught it in its midsection and sent it sprawling.

By now the engagement was general as a dozen

344

more dragons topped the ridge and piled into their metal enemies. Laser blasts and gouts of dragon fire lanced through the air and parts of robots and pieces of dragon bodies flew in every direction.

Then there were no more robots. Seven of the dragons lay motionless amidst the carnage and one dragged a wing.

As one, the unharmed dragons galloped forward and took to the air again. The one with the broken wing followed on foot.

Without warning clumps of guardsmen and wizards popped up all over the plain. Immediately they spread out into long, loose lines and started moving toward the castle.

Kenneth, at the head of his group squinted at what lay ahead. *Fortuna, what a mess!* he thought. The wizards had been able to bring them no closer than a league to the castle because of interfering magic. They would have to cross the distance on foot, possibly under fire and almost certainly against enemies.

Kenneth felt especially naked without comrades at either shoulder. But they had been warned that concentrations which gave defense against sword and spear would only serve as targets for the weapons of these foreign sorcerers.

Well in front of the attacking forces a half dozen football-shaped metal containers popped into existence and split open on the red sand. A dark cloud poured out of each of them and dissipated in the air.

That was the signal. Kenneth raised his arm and motioned his men to move forward.

*I wish I had a drink*, he thought.

"Mikey! Mikey!" Craig beat on the door frantically. Finally it opened a crack.

"Yeah?"

"Why the hell didn't you answer the net? I've been calling you for fifteen minutes."

"I told you. If you have business with me, you come to me. I'm not answering your goddamn pager." The door started to swing shut.

"Goddamnit, we're being attacked!" Craig yelled. "We've got dragons and infantry and shit all over the place."

The door swung open and there was Mikey wearing only a pair of pants. In the back of his mind Craig realized he looked terrible, all thin and sort of stretched out. He moved like a speed freak, all jerky, uncontrolled energy. There was a predatory gleam in his eye that Craig didn't remember seeing before.

"Yeah?" Mikey said. Then he paused as if listening to something that only he could hear.

"Come on, man! I need all the help I can get."

"You keep them busy. I've got something to set up."

Craig nodded and raced for his command center.


"We have isolated their control links," one of the Watchers called out to the group on the dais.

"Transfer the characteristics to my station," Judith called back. Instantly the Emac sitting cross-legged in front of her began to write in the air.

Judith smiled tightly. "Time to jam." She turned to the Emac.

**"backslash"**

"?" the Emac responded.

**"blackwatch exe"**

The Emac gabbled and several dozen demons appeared on the table. They were fashioned like men but each wore a skirt and shawl of dark green patterned with black. Several had drums and the rest had odd contrivances with several shiny black tubes extending over their shoulders. The leader carried a

346

silver-tipped staff near as tall as he was and wore an enormous hat made of some black fur.

"Give them The Black Bear," Judith commanded. "Then Scotland the Brave, The Highland Brigade at Maggersfontein, The Southdown Militia, The Earl of Mansfield and Lord Lovett Over The Rhine. After that use your imagination."

The tiny drum major nodded, turned to the demons behind him and raised his staff. The pipers inhaled as one, the drummer struck the beat and the skirl of the pipes reverberated off the stone walls.

"Let's see them even *think* through that," she said viciously.

"I hope it is as effective on the enemy as it is on us," Bal-Simba boomed over the noise.

Judith looked up and realized everyone in the command center had stopped work and was staring at the table. Several of them had clapped their hands over their ears. Judith made a gesture and the sound died to a whisper.

"Sorry Lord, I keep forgetting it's an acquired taste."

By the time Malus's dragon approached the castle the fat little wizard was half-seasick and thoroughly miserable. Normally a dragon could not carry two people for very long. But the wizards had added their magic to the animals' natural flying ability so they were able to keep up with the other dragons.

Not that it was much comfort to Malus. He was strapped into a second saddle back on the dragon's shoulders. The beast was too wide to straddle comfortably at that point and the insides of his thighs ached terribly. Although the straps holding him to the saddle were secure, the saddle itself had a tendency to shift alarmingly whenever the dragon maneuvered suddenly. For Malus's taste there had been far too many sudden maneuvers. The blue robe of the

Mighty, which was so impressive on the ground, was totally unsuited for dragon riding. The wind tugged at the hem and tended to flip it back above his knees. The cold air whipped up the robe and around his legs. Probably the only part of him that was still warm was his seat which was protected by the saddle. But he couldn't tell for sure because it had gone to sleep long since.

He tried to shut out the discomfort by concentrating on the back of the rider and not to look down. Above all, he didn't want to look down.

The castle erupted in flame and smoke as every weapon fired on the attackers. Artillery and mortars of every description fired and fired again as fast as the automatic loaders could feed them. Streams of tracers fountained up into the sky as anti-aircraft batteries sought their targets. Lines of laser light swept back and forth over the plain and sky.

Between the killer bees and the messed-up control system in the southern quadrant it wasn't nearly as effective as it should have been. What ought to have been annihilating was merely deadly. Men went down like tenpins and dragons fell from the sky under the impact, but still the others pressed on.

From ground and air the attackers returned fire. Lightning bolts and fireballs flew from the wizards' fingers destroying emplacements and blinding sensors. Then two squadrons of dragons peeled off and let fly with heat-seeking missiles. The missiles went for the hottest things in the castle, which were the barrels of the artillery and the firing tubes of the lasers. A series of explosions blossomed on the castle walls and here and there the secondary explosion of a magazine made a section of castle wall bulge outward and slump.

Still the attackers came on.

*   *   *

Circling above the battle Malus groped in the sleeve of his robe and brought out a crystal sphere just large enough to fit comfortably in the palm of his hand. It was held in a net that was tied to his wrist so he would not lose it and the netting made it harder than normal to concentrate. Still the picture was clear enough.

Peering into the crystal he saw that there were a number of other things in the air, but little enough magic.

Fumbling in his other sleeve he produced a light hazel wand. It wasn't as powerful or as impressive as his normal staff, but it was much easier to handle on dragon back. He kept his eyes fixed on the crystal as he raised his arm above his head and began to chant.


Craig's screen started to fill with magically generated hash. He quickly applied a filter function to the image and some of the interference faded, but what was left pulsed rhythmically and seemed to beat against itself like a badly tuned instrument, creating irregular patches of dark and light on his screen.

The magical sensors were worse. The screen filled with glowing blobs of amorphous color that made it look like a neon lava light. Craig swore under his breath and started combining the output of various kinds of sensors and tinkering with filters until he got his best picture.

Vaguely Craig realized he hadn't been smart in setting this system up. Everything flowed back to his command center, but he could only concentrate on a few facets of the battle at one time. There was too much happening for him to coordinate the defense. He would have to rely on the sensors and programming built into his warbots and other weapons. Which was fine, only there was no way for those weapons to coordinate without direct orders from his command center.

Still, he had a lot of weapons.


"What's going on up there?" Gilligan demanded.

Karin shaded her eyes and squinted. "I cannot see. No, wait! Those are dragons. Ridden dragons and they are attacking." She looked at Gilligan. "Those are my people."

"Can we signal them?"

"They are too high and too fully engaged." She picked up her bow and started back toward the castle. "Come on. We must help them."

"How?"

She looked over her shoulder. "We will think of something, now come if you are coming." She trotted off with Stigi humping along beside her. Gilligan had to run to catch up.


Thorfin looked at his leader's boot soles and scowled. It seemed as if they had been climbing for hours. First up the steep outer wall, then in through a gun port and finally up through the castle's ventilation ducts. There was plenty of room, but the wind was almost strong enough to pluck a dwarf from the wall and every few hundred yards they had to unfasten a grating that blocked the duct. Twice they had narrowly avoided the whirling blades of huge ventilation fans that threatened to turn the whole expedition into dwarf tartare. And still they climbed onward. Glandurg stopped every few minutes to check his locating talisman, but it always told them the Sparrow was above them.

*I never realized glory was such hard work,* Thorfin thought as Glandurg missed a foothold and kicked him in the face.

"Look," said Jerry. "Do you have any idea where we are?"

The four of them were standing at the crossing of four identical corridors. There were no floor numbers, room numbers or anything else to give them a clue.

"One of the upper floors of the castle," Wiz told him.

"In other words we're lost, right?"

"No, I know where we are. I just don't know where the computer is."

Jerry growled. "Okay, let's do this systematically. Lannach says the computer is in the room where you met Craig and Mikey, right?" Wiz nodded. "We know the room has an outside wall because it had a big window, right?" Again the nod.

"So let's go to the outside wall, put our left hands against it and follow it around, checking every door as we go. Eventually we've got to find the right room."

"There are hundreds of rooms on this floor," Danny protested.

"All the more reason we need a system."

"Okay," Wiz said. "There's the outside wall. Let's do it."

All four of them put their left hands on the wall and started walking single file. The first room they came to was empty. The second held a mass of machinery that was obviously not the computer.

"This looks more like it," said Wiz as they came to the third door. It was wider than the others and almost as high as the corridor.

Wiz opened the door and looked inside. Ranked along the walls in the dark were a dozen heavily armed robots, all motionless. Suddenly the lights came on, the robots jerked erect and a dozen metal heads swiveled toward the door.

The programmers didn't wait for the rest. Wiz

threw fireballs, Danny threw lightning bolts and Jerry hit them with some kind of spell that made them crumble to powder. A couple of laser beams flashed over their heads and left burning furrows in the wall behind them. The heat activated the fire sprinklers, drenching all four of them with water.

June looked up at the rain magically coming from the ceiling and laughed at the wonder of it all. Wiz choked on the smell of fried, electrocuted, powdered robot and shook his head to get the water out of his eyes.

He glared up at Jerry. "You and your system."

"There's nothing wrong with the system. It's just that if you follow it you are certain to find everything on this floor."

"Most of which we don't want to find. Okay, we'll keep following the wall, but from now on we don't open any doors unless they look really promising."

Karin stopped so quickly Mick almost ran into her. She turned, put her finger to her lips and gestured around the corner. Cautiously Mick peeked around. There was a door there, set at the end of a narrow corridor back into the wall. There were also six things out of someone's nightmare guarding it. They were big, ugly, armored, and armed to the teeth.

He ducked back and looked at Karin. Go the other way? he pantomimed and Karin nodded.

Just then Stigi decided to see what was so interesting. He stuck out his neck, thrust his head fully around the corner and snorted in curiosity.

With a wild yell the guards charged forward.

"Shit," Gilligan said, fumbling for his shoulder holster. Before Karin could draw her bow, he stepped around the corner, dropped to a semi-crouch and fired two-handed.

Eight shots rang out in the confined space and all six of the guards were down.

Karin's eyes widened at the sight.

"Well done," she said. "Now, shall we use the door they were guarding?"

At that moment the door flew open and a solid mass of the manlike monsters charged out waving swords, spears and other less identifiable, more nasty, weapons.

Instinctively Gilligan dropped into his shooters' stance, but Karin grabbed his arm and pulled him down.

With a *whoosh* and a roar Stigi let go with a blast of flame.

The effect on the packed mass was instant and appalling. The things shriveled, screamed, burst into flame, and died in the ranks.

Again the *whoosh* and another lance of dragon fire struck the remaining attackers. Black smoke boiled off charred flesh and the stink was appalling. Here and there came a series of explosions as ammunition in guards' bandoleers ignited.

And then there were no more attackers. Gilligan looked at the blackened mass in front of him and was almost sick. He'd seen people burned to death in air crashes before, but not on this scale. Karin had gone deathly pale under the layer of reddish dust.

"Let's get inside," he said. Carefully they picked their way through the grisly remains, trying to touch as little as possible.

"My God," Gilligan breathed, "will you look at this place?"

The room was enormous. The ceiling was at least a hundred feet above them and it stretched out proportionally in all directions. In the center of the brightly lit area were half a dozen huge robots in various stages of construction with smaller robots swarming over them like worker ants. As they watched a traveling crane maneuvered a torso section over the legs and hips of one of the robots.

"It's a factory," he said, awed.

None of the robots paid the least heed to their unexpected visitors. They kept right on working.

Gilligan motioned and led Karin and Stigi along the wall and around the assembly area.

"There's got to be another way out of here. No way those robots could get through the door we just came through."

They were halfway around the room when another giant robot stepped out of the shadows behind them.

Karin screamed, Stigi whirled, inhaled and spouted a gout of flame. The robot stepped forward inexorably and raised its laser arm.

Craig had designed the robot with a magic power source, a magically reinforced body and magic senors and control links. But the design was essentially technological. He hadn't considered what might happen if his creation stepped in front of a giant flame thrower.

The robot's first bolt went wild into the ceiling, knocking hot rock down on the three and burning a red afterimage in Mick's vision. Then the chips in the control circuits overheated and failed. The robot pinwheeled its arms wildly and its glittering torso twisted from right to left and back again. Then the seals in the hydraulic cylinders in its legs and hips failed from the heat and contact with the boiling hydraulic fluid. The thing lost hydraulic power in a gush of robotic incontinence, tottered and fell face-first into a puddle of smoking hydraulic fluid. The floor shook, but the robot workers paid no attention.

Stigi stalked forward and sniffed disdainfully at his kill. Then he stepped daintily around the puddle—or as daintily as you can when you're eighty feet long and in a confined space—and continued on his way.

The main door out of the assembly area was on the

same scale as the rest of the factory. Fortunately it was also open.

"Now, where do we go from here?"

"Up I would think," Karin said. "Their commanders would want to be as high as possible to see as much as they could."

Gilligan didn't bother to point out to her that it didn't work that way when you had radar and advanced sensors.

"Think we can get Stigi upstairs?" he asked.

"Oh yes, Stigi is not afraid of heights." She frowned. "Though this place is so tall it may take us hours to reach the top."

Remembering how high the fortress looked from the outside Gilligan thought that was a wild underestimate.

Then he caught sight of something. "Wait a minute, we may not have to walk. Look at this."

Set in the far wall was a freight elevator big enough to take a semi. "They must use this to move robots. If it will carry one of them it will sure hold Stigi."

It took a little doing to get the dragon into the elevator. If Stigi wasn't afraid of heights, he wasn't very fond of confined spaces and to him an elevator big enough to move the Space Shuttle was still a confined space. He started alarmingly when the elevator began to move and for a moment Gilligan was afraid he was going to crush them both. But Karin stood by his head, stroking him and telling him what a good dragon he was.

Stigi calmed down but every so often he would glare over at Gilligan in a way that said he understood perfectly well Mick was to blame for all this and some day he would get even.

The elevator lurched to a stop and the doors opened. "End of the line," Gilligan said.

He drew his pistol and peered out. They seemed to be in some sort of service area. The floors were bare concrete and the light fixtures were Spartan. Scattered about were a number of pieces of equipment Gilligan didn't recognize and a thing like a metal octopus that was obviously a cleaning robot of some kind. At least it had a floor buffer built into its base.

As Craig studied his screen, a new symbol sprang up at the very bottom. One of his scouts had located the attacker's main communications relay.

"Get that relay," Craig screamed into the screen. On the periphery of the battle a demi-wing of two squadrons wheeled and raced to do his bidding.

"Shield flight, you have sixteen enemy incoming. I say again, sixteen incoming."

"Understood. Sixteen incoming," Elke repeated into her communications crystal.

There were only five other dragons and riders at her back.

*What was it the strange sorceress had called this? A "target-rich environment."* To hell with that. She called it being plain old-fashioned outnumbered.

She signaled her command and the dragons wheeled and spread out into the attack formation they had practiced so many times at the Capital. Off in a far corner of her mind Elke realized she wasn't frightened, just terribly, terribly busy.

The fighters came in hugging the ground to escape radar detection, but that did nothing to shield them from magic. Elke and the Watcher both saw them coming.

Almost directly beneath their quarry the flight of metal shapes arrowed upward, jets thundering as they climbed toward their target.

Far above them Elke winged her dragon over into a steep dive. Out of the corners of her eyes she saw the dragons to her left and right fold their wings back and follow her down.

356

Her instructors might not have approved. The formation was loose and dragons were slowed by the objects they grasped in their talons. But it was closing with the enemy and that was all that mattered.

The targeting spell for the new weapons she carried began to sing. Before her eyes lines of glowing green merged into cross hairs and rectangle of her target sight. She kept staring intently at the specks below her, moving her head slightly to center them in the crosshairs, listening intently all the while. Then the squadron leader heard the bone-quivering hum in her ear that told her the weapon had locked on. She reached out and touched a stud on her saddle.

A trail of smoke sprang from the box in the dragon's claw as the air-to-air missile leaped free of its launcher. Beside and behind her other trails of dirty gray smoke streaked the sky as the rest of her flight fired.

The squadron leader eased back on the reins and hauled her dragon around into a tight spiraling turn. Below her fourteen missiles raced toward their targets. In spite of their magical components, the guidance systems were essentially technological. They looked for the brightest radar returns in the sky. Dragons and the relay they were guarding returned only small echoes but the climbing fighters stood out sharply.

The fighters were hardly sitting ducks. Their radar sensors picked up the missiles as soon as they launched and the attackers broke and jinked all over the sky in an effort to break the radar locks, scattering flares and packets of chaff behind them.

For half of the fighters it was enough. Eight of their companions exploded in balls of black and orange as the missiles found them but the others continued to climb toward the relay demon.

Elke counted the explosions and nodded to herself. Well, they'd been warned that some might get through. But the survivors had lost momentum. That gave her squadron opening enough.

Again she led her dragons into a screaming dive into the midst of the attackers.

The fighters filled the air with ECM, flares dropped free with magnesium radiance that briefly outshone the sun and chaff bloomed everywhere around them.

None of which mattered in the slightest. Dragons, even missile-armed dragons, don't carry radar and the forces were too close for missiles. Now the defenders relied on the traditional weapons of the dragon cavalry. Bursts of dragon fire ripped at the metal shapes. Then the great bows sang and iron arrows leaped toward their targets. Planes cartwheeled across the sky or dropped like stones as flames and death arrows found their marks.

One lone fighter pulled away from the melee, climbing toward the relay station. Elke lined her dragon up on the metal enemy and touched the second stud on her saddle. Again smoke streaked from the dragon's claws as a second missile sprang free. But there was no pulse of radar energy to warn the aircraft. Instead Elke held the missile on course by manipulating the stud with her thumb, always keeping it centered in the glowing orange rectangle. The missile traveled up the plane's tailpipe and blew it out of the sky before the aircraft or its controllers even knew it was there.

In his castle, Craig cursed and pounded his fist on the table. But he had other things to command his attention.

Well, it wasn't the first time he had lost heavily in the early moves and gone on to win the campaign. The enemy couldn't do jack shit unless they could penetrate his fortress. They hadn't hit his outworks yet. When they did things would be different.

358

Vaguely he wondered where the hell Mikey was and what he was doing.

The wind whistled and whipped like knives of ice around the high, dark spire where Mikey stood. He could sense rather than see the formless shapes that pulsated and moved in the freezing distance beneath his feet.

A single wan pool of yellow light illuminated his workbench. For the last time he checked the spell before him.

It was a complex shape about the size of his head and so dark as to be beyond black.

Mikey caressed the thing, oblivious to its piercing chill. At last it was ready.

*We are prepared.* The voice pulsed in his ears like his own blood. *We wait.*

With a gesture Mikey killed the light on the workbench. Then he clasped the sphere to him and started down from his high place.

The guardsmen and wizards advanced in loose order over the barren ground.

Actually, Donal thought, "loose order" was a misnomer. A "swarm of gaggles" was more like it.

But this was the formation they had been advised to use. Having seen pictures of their likely opponents Donal was all for it. Absently he reached back and touched the tube slung across his back. He hoped it was as good as advertised.

So far they had met no real opposition on the ground. The shelling had died down to a background rumble. Once a cluster of gray metal things swooped down on them with fire and explosions. But between their wizards' lightning bolts and the timely intervention of a wing of dragons there had been very little damage done.

Up ahead a door opened in the castle wall and several things shaped like men stepped out.

*Either we're a hundred paces from the castle*, Donal thought, *or those things are giants.* He signaled his squad to spread out and take cover. Seemingly oblivious to the oncoming metal giants, the guardsmen responded as they had been drilled.

A lance of fire slashed into the earth so close to him he could smell the ozone stink. Behind him bullets beat a tattoo into the dirt. Donal jammed the point of his sword into the ground and brought the dull green tube slung across his back around and over his shoulder. As methodically as he had been taught he flipped up the sights and lined them up on the giant robot.

The tube bobbed up and down as he followed his target and then he squeezed the trigger. The tube bucked slightly and Donal dropped and rolled just before another blast of laser energy rent the place where he had been standing.

When he looked up the robot was swaying uncertainly, its right knee a smoking ruin. Before he could get to his hands and knees two more explosions blossomed on the giant torso. It swayed forward once more and then toppled like a felled tree.

In his tower Craig swore viciously. His warbots were programmed to fight other warbots or dragons, not infantry with anti-tank missiles. He'd have to override and run this action himself. He slapped a button on his console, but nothing happened.

"Get me a control link!" he yelled into his microphone.

"We are trying, dread master," came a voice in his ear, "but there is something wrong in the transmitter."

"Then switch to the alternate," Craig yelled.

"That was the alternate," the voice said. "Maintenance estimates it will have the primary repaired in three point oh eight minutes."

"Shit!" Craig slumped back in his chair. This was like playing on a night when you couldn't make a saving roll for love or money. Well, three minutes wouldn't make that much difference in that part of the battle and there were plenty of other places he could put his time.

Meanwhile, was it his imagination or did he hear a high-pitched sound coming from his display console—a sound like a very small giggle?

"My palm's sore," Danny complained.

"Well, don't drag it along the wall," Jerry told him. "I didn't mean that literally anyway."

Even investigating only the likely looking doors it seemed that it was taking forever to check out the rooms. Even this high up the castle was much bigger than Wiz had imagined.

The next set of doors didn't look like anything Wiz remembered, but they were big and probably important. He was just about to punch the button when they slid open and he found himself face to face with a dirty, unshaven man in a tattered flight suit waving a pistol. Over the man's shoulder Wiz could see an equally dirty and disheveled woman and a large dragon.

"Who the hell are you?" he demanded.

"Major Michael Gilligan, United States Air Force. Who the hell are you?"

"This is the Sparrow," Karin put in, stepping forward. "He is the mighty wizard I told you of." She sketched a curtsey. "Well met, my Lord."

"What are you doing here?"

"Raising hell," Gilligan told him.

"My Lords, the League is attacking the castle," Karin said breathlessly.

"I know. Look, can you get a message back to the Capital? They need to know we're alive."

361

Karin's face fell. "Alas, my Lord, the enemy is jamming our communications."

"Damn," Wiz said, entirely without heat. "All right. We're searching this floor for a computer these guys are using to cook up something really nasty. Can you help us?"

"Of course, my Lord." Karin bobbed another curtsey.

"Okay by me," Gilligan said. "You really from the USA?"

"Cupertino," Wiz shrugged. "It's pretty much the same thing."

"Hot damn!" Danny said, looking up at Stigi. "Firepower!"

"You might say that," Gilligan said, thinking of the pile of charred bodies by the gate.

"Come on then, and keep your eyes peeled. We've run into all sorts of things."

A couple of hundred more yards and two more uninteresting rooms and they came to a broad cross corridor that was carpeted in a different color and more richly finished than any they had seen so far.

"I recognize this!" Wiz said. "This is the way to the computer room."

"Great!" said Danny as he stepped in front of Wiz and out into the center of the corridor. "Let's go . . ."

A bolt of green radiance lashed down the corridor and caught Danny square in the back. He pitched forward and dropped like a sack of sand. June screamed and rushed toward him, heedless of the bolts of energy crackling around her.

Down the corridor came a packed mass of goblin troops, the ones in front firing ray guns.

Gilligan stepped forward, dropped to one knee and braced the pistol in both hands, elbow resting on knee. Three well-placed shots dropped the leaders and the rest hesitated for a moment.

Then Wiz started throwing fireballs.

"Stigi," Karin's voice rose over the noise. "Forward."

Stepping past June kneeling over Danny, the dragon shouldered Gilligan and Wiz out of the way and advanced down the corridor. The guards reformed and came on, energy bolts scoring the walls ahead. If any of them hit Stigi he didn't show it. Instead he breathed deeply and sent a gout of flame washing down the corridor.

That was the final straw. The attacking guards broke and ran.

Wiz bent over Danny, but June bared her teeth and hissed at him. The young programmer's shirt was burned away and the flesh beneath was charred and smoking. Wiz could see the white of bone from his ribs and spine. He was still breathing, but his breath was coming in great harsh gasps.

"He's dying," Jerry said quietly. His eyes were big and his face pale.

"Lord, unless you have powerful healing spells I am afraid this one is done for," Karin said quietly to Wiz.

"No," Wiz said without taking his eyes off Danny. "Nothing like that."

"Then I am truly sorry, my Lord."

"Goddamn!" Wiz breathed. If skilled healers could reach him in the next few minutes he still had a chance. But there were no healers among them and no way to get Danny to a healer in time. They could not walk the Wizard's Way from inside the castle. The opposing magic was too strong. There just wasn't time.

*Time!*

Quickly Wiz knelt again and reached for his friend's arm. June bared her teeth again and fumbled in her skirt for her knife.

"I'm trying to save him, dammit!" June looked hard at him, but she relaxed slightly.

363

Wiz reached out and touched the ring of protection Danny still wore on his right hand. Before June could object he twisted the stone and Danny froze in stasis as the protection spell took hold.

"He's all right," Wiz said to June. "Don't you see? The spell will keep him safe until we can get him back to a healer." June looked down at her husband and bit her lip, but she made no move to touch the ring.

"Help me carry him further down the corridor." He turned to Karin. "I don't think there are any more branches off this corridor until we get to the computer room. Once we move Danny, can you back your dragon up past the intersection and hold them off here?"

Karin nodded.

"Great. Jerry, help me move him. We don't have to be too gentle. Stasis is better than a backboard."

"Then what?" asked Gilligan, looking down the corridor in the direction their attackers had fled.

"Then," Wiz said in a hard cold voice, "we're gonna find that goddamn computer and stomp a couple of people flat."

Craig sat glued to his workstation and played as he had never played in his life. Slowly it dawned on him that this wasn't just a couple of early setbacks. He was losing.

It wasn't all one-sided. He was hurting them plenty, but it wasn't enough. His carefully constructed defenses were washing away like sand. His warbots were powerful but the attackers were hitting him in ways they weren't programmed to handle. If he took direct command of a unit he could do pretty well, but he couldn't be everywhere at once and besides, his damn communications kept failing.

A motion at the corner of his screen caught his eye. There, superimposed on the glowing battle display was a little manlike being perhaps six inches high.

Unlike the rest of the screen image it was in full color and high resolution.

The thing turned toward him and pressed its face and palms against the inside of the tube, as if it was looking out. It wasn't an image, Craig realized, there really was something inside his monitor!

The tiny being turned and gestured across the screen. Another manlike little thing stuck its head around the edge of the screen and peered at the world outside. Behind and around it the battle display scrolled on, unnoticed by the gremlins or by Craig.

The first creature tossed the glowing ball into the air and batted it with his free hand. The ball flew across the screen leaving a glowing trail behind it. The second thing leaped up and deflected it before it could touch the far side of the screen. The ball bounced off the bottom and ricocheted toward the upper right corner, smearing a goodly portion of the display. The first creature made a mighty jump and deflected it back toward the bottom left. His opponent dived for it, but the ball bounced over his head and off the side of the screen. The first gremlin chortled and held up a single finger.

Craig watched helplessly as his screen filled up with the lines of the ball tracks.

"Maintenance!" he yelled.

"He's off this way," Glandurg called back to his companions. "Down this side shaft, now."

*No more climbing for a bit*, Glandurg thought. *That's a piece of good news.* Although he never would have admitted it, he was just about done for. His arms and shoulders ached from clinging to fingerholds in the ventilation shaft and his calves and thighs were cramping from pressing his body flat against the wall. It would be a relief to just walk for a while.

He didn't know how far they had climbed; a league

or more, perhaps. But at last the arrow in the talisman had stopped pointing upward and was pointing off to the side.

As he started down the horizontal shaft, Glandurg reached back to touch the hilt of Blind Fury. Soon enough they'd be done with this climbing and sneaking into honest battle.

He wondered if battle was as exciting as the skald's tales made it out to be.

It took nearly fifteen precious minutes for the maintenance robots to fix the display on Craig's workstation. By the time he was back in control the situation had deteriorated even more. The last of his air force had been swept from the skies, and with it all of his recon drones. Now he was reduced to viewing the battle through the cameras and sensors mounted on the castle itself. Two critical outposts had fallen and even as he attempted to assert control a third one went.

In the southern quadrant the attackers were almost up to the last line of defenses at the base of the castle walls. Craig turned his attention there. Quickly he switched to one of the cameras on a forward emplacement to try to find a weak spot. He still had a couple of squadrons of warbots he could throw into the battle here, but he would have to command them directly if they were going to be any good.

As he scanned the line of approaching men, a shadow fell over the camera. He swiveled up in time to see a dragon diving straight at him. He flinched and tried to bring a weapon to bear but it was too late. The last view Craig had was of gaping jaws and an enormous golden eye as the dragon crashed head-on into the emplacement.

Cursing, he switched to an alternate view only to get a jerky low-resolution picture that barely resolved itself into blobs of light and dark. Two more switches and he found a camera high up on the walls that was working.

What he saw wasn't good. Lines of dotlike figures, rendered tiny by the distance, were converging on the gates of the castle. Many of them were too close for the artillery, and the machine guns were strangely ineffective.

Some of the figures went down to energy beams or mines, but many more did not. They swarmed over the smoking ruins of his defenses and began to disappear down the tunnels.

Frantically, Craig ordered all his remaining robots to the lower levels to try to stem the attackers.

And then it was all too much. Craig turned and bolted from his war room, leaving the defenses entirely on automatic. He just couldn't face any more fighting and losing.

Mikey! Mikey was working on something. Maybe Panda, the master hacker, could pull this out of the fire for them yet.

Mikey was sitting on a bench cradling something in his lap. As Craig came closer he saw it looked a lot like the figure that had been growing on the computer screen.

"We've got trouble, man."

"No we don't," Mikey said softly. "We've won."

"Goddamn it, they're all over the fucking castle!"

Mikey looked up at him and smiled. For the first time Craig saw the mad, red glint in his eyes. "It doesn't matter," he said almost gently. "It's all working according to plan.

"I was wrong about you, Craig," he went on in the same gentle, hair-raising tone. "You and your robots were important. You were a wonderful diversion. The robots got them to grab the computer. All we had to do was bring them here. Now we'll crush them. We'll just fucking annihilate them."

He caressed the black sphere in his lap. "We own the world. We own both worlds. And we're going to prove it."

Craig drew back in horror.

"You're fucking crazy!"

"No man, I'm sane. Crazy is letting these fucking maggots walk all over you."

He reached out and patted Craig's forearm in a way that made Craig's flesh creep.

"You did good, you know. You kept them so god-damn busy chasing around after your toys they never had a chance to focus on the serious stuff." He caressed the thing in his lap.

"They couldn't get at it. Did you know that? For all their power they couldn't make what they needed without us. They needed the computer. And they needed us."

Craig stared in horrified fascination.

"You see what that means, don't you?" Mikey was talking to himself now, looking down at the black thing in his lap, crooning to it. "It means they're not all-powerful. We can do things they can't and that means we're more powerful than they are.

"When I get done I'm gonna be master of all I survey." He chuckled and his eyes glinted even redder, like live coals. "I'm gonna rule the whole goddamn world."

Craig backed away from his former friend and then turned and ran.

There were problems, Glandurg admitted, even with an infallible magic direction finder.

It was undoubtedly pointing at the Sparrow, but it didn't show the way to go to get to him. That was a problem when you were in a maze of ductwork that ran only in straight lines and right angles. A half-dozen times now they had followed the arrow directly only to be balked by a dead end. Glandurg suspected the Sparrow was moving around also. But so far they hadn't gotten close enough to be sure.

They didn't want to leave the vents. The roars, screams, explosions and gunfire echoing through the vents—not to mention the smell of burnt flesh—made it clear there was a battle going on out there.

"He is over this way," Glandurg told his weary followers. "Forward."

"We can't go that way," Thorfin protested.

"And why not?"

"Because it's a blind tunnel, that's why."

"He's right you know," Snorri put in. "We've been there twice already."

"I'm the leader and I say we bloody go this way!"

"You may be the leader, but you've got the sense of direction of a blind pig," Thorfin said without heat.

"S'truth," young Gimli added. "Remember the sewage tunnel back home."

Glandurg reddened and puffed up like a toad. Then he got control of himself and exhaled slowly.

"Very well," he bit out. "For this job I will appoint a scout. Snorri, you go first to find the way. But I'm still the leader, mind!"

Without a word, Snorri moved past Glandurg and led the party off.

*What now?* Craig tried desperately to think. The lower levels were already overrun, the control center was out of commission and he didn't even want to think about what Mikey was up to. It couldn't end like this. Not after so much. But now what?

It took him a minute to separate the shrill tone in his ear from the background noise of the battle and a minute longer to realize what it meant. The computer room! Someone had reached the computer room already. He touched a stud on his bracelet and the tiny screen lit up with a view of the computer room. He gaped at what he saw.

Zumwalt and the others were with the computer! Craig slapped his palm against his forehead and swore. A trojan horse! He'd brought them into the castle himself and they'd turned out to be a trojan horse. No wonder half his equipment wasn't working. They must have been sabotaging it for days.

Craig looked at the tiny image and felt his gorge rise. Somehow those sonsofbitches were responsible for everything that had gone wrong since he got here. They were behind his defeat, his every loss.

Well, maybe he'd lose, but they sure as hell weren't going to profit by it!

He turned on his heel and ran down the corridor, away from the War Room and toward his private workshop.

Craig met nothing in the halls. The robots and goblins were all fighting elsewhere. Half the lights were out and the elevators didn't work. Now and again the sound of battle or a muffled explosion would reach him by some trick of acoustics, but otherwise the castle was deathly silent. Even the air tasted stale and he realized the air conditioning system had quit.

The automatic door opener wasn't working either, so Craig had to use a spell to burn his way into his own workshop. Once inside, he pulled the door shut behind him and looked around.

There in the middle of the room, surrounded by scaffolding and equipment, was his latest creation: A full suit of Legion battle armor with some special improvements that no game master would ever have allowed.

The bottle-green armor glinted dully in the bright lights of the shop. It was almost twelve feet tall and so broad it looked squat by comparison. There was no neck, only a low rounded dome for a head. The arms were enormous, with oversized forearms to accommodate the blasters and heavy machine guns mounted in them. The hands were six-taloned metal claws, sharp as razors and hard enough to tear through armor steel. The legs were elephantine in proportion with all the actuators hidden behind layers of super-strong flexible armor.

It was hunched forward until its metal claws almost touched the ground and the upper back was opened up like a clam shell. In spite of his anger and haste, Craig stopped to pat the massive knee joint and look up approvingly.

Everything he knew, everything he had learned, was incorporated in this one lethal package. It wasn't as big as his warbots, but thanks to the power of magic it was nearly as heavily armed. It could run at over a hundred miles an hour and slam through walls and buildings as if they were not there. Instead of jump jets it had anti-gravity plates that would let it fly from the surface of the planet out into space if the wearer wished. It could withstand a nuclear explosion and its own firepower was measured in kilotons per second. It was the ultimate warbot, the culmination of his dreams of power.

And now it existed for just one purpose. To destroy the people who had caused his ruin.

Craig mounted the scaffold and chinned himself on the grab bar to ease his legs into the suit. He wiggled the rest of his body in, fitting arms and legs into the sensor harnesses. Finally he touched a switch and the back sections slid noiselessly shut behind him.

He watched the screen displays for a moment as the power gauges rose levels and the view out the front port came alive with a network of glowing lines and cryptic inscriptions. A breath of cool air washed over him as the climate control system activated. This was one design that could stand up to dragon fire and not even feel it.

Once he was sure everything was operational, he

stood erect and stepped away from the scaffolding, brushing it aside with a casual gesture that sent pieces ricocheting off the workshop walls. He turned and stepped lithely toward the door. As he passed the workbench he reached down and scooped up the thermonuclear hand grenades laying there. Maybe they would be good for something after all, he thought as he dropped them into a pouch on the armor.

Stigi couldn't use his tail, but that didn't matter much. He very nearly blocked the passage physically. The attackers' only approach was through a mass of fire and straight into the dragon's fangs and claws.

Even if the castle guards had been equipped with dragon-slaying arrows it would have been hard to take Stigi out. As it happened that wasn't part of their equipment and so the problem was very nearly impossible. Warbots might have been able to handle Stigi, but they had all been sent to the lower levels to confront the League forces battling their way up through the castle.

Not that the guards stopped trying. They came on until their charred bodies reached nearly to the ceiling and then they climbed over the smoking corpses to keep coming. By the sheer mass of their onslaught they managed to force Stigi back a pace or two with every attack. But it was a long, straight corridor and Stigi had lots of room to back up.

The door at the end of the corridor was locked, but that didn't stop Wiz. He wasn't fancy about it, he just used a fireball to blow the lock off. Almost without breaking stride he kicked the door open and stepped through. Jerry and Mick were hard on his heels.

The computer was sitting in the middle of the floor, almost exactly where Wiz's double had been standing when Mikey hit him with the fireball. It was up and running quietly away with the image of the key rotating slowly on the screen.

"Is it my imagination," Jerry asked, "or is that thing a lot more detailed than the last time we saw it?"

"Your imagination's not that good. Let's smash the computer and go get Craig and Mikey." Wiz raised his arms to throw another fireball, but Jerry put his hand on his shoulder.

"You're not thinking. Without the key how are we going to close the gate?"

Wiz turned his head and looked at him. "What's your plan?"

"Make a copy of the file first. Binary representation should be as good as any other for the purposes of spell casting."

Wiz dropped his arms and nodded. From down the corridor came roars and yells as Stigi held the entrance. "We've got the time. Let's do it."

Craig heard the fight in the corridor as soon as he stepped off the stairs. The din echoed and re-echoed through the entire level of the castle. His sensors reported combustion byproducts in the air, including some that came from burning flesh. Finally he saw the carpet of bodies in the corridor leading to the computer room. Cautiously he stuck his massively armored head around the corner.

The smoke was so thick he had to resort to his sensors to see what was happening. Up ahead was a packed mass of warriors, some living, some dead and some wounded and down. Every one who could move was pressing ahead. As he watched the scene was backlit by an enormous gout of flame that turned the figures to black silhouettes against a fiery background.

With his battle armor he could undoubtedly charge through the mass and handle whatever was blocking his guards. But that would take time. What he wanted was to get his hands on Zumwalt as fast as possible.

He turned and ran back the way he came. Plenty of time to finish this bunch later.

Several hundred yards and a number of turnings later he was in the corridor leading to the side entrance to the computer room. He had only gone a few yards when he heard a rhythmic banging coming from an alcove ahead of him.

In the alcove two light warbots were beating their heads against the wall, literally. They would step forward, run into the wall, bounce back and then step forward again. From the looks of the wall they had been doing it for some time.

"Halt!" Craig ordered and the robots froze in mid-step. Quickly he ran diagnostics and found the robots had a bug screwing up their obstacle-avoidance routines. Fortunately they were light warbots or they would have long since walked through the wall.

A couple of quick commands and the warbots were functional again.

"Follow me," Craig ordered and set off down the corridor with the two killing machines at his heels.

"Come on, damn you," Wiz muttered, but the tape cartridge spun on unheeding. He only wanted one file, but the file was enormous. The tape backup was designed for reliability over speed; its designers had never imagined someone would have to transfer information to tape in the middle of a battle.

"They're in there," Snorri reported breathlessly. "I can hear them."

"At last." Glandurg thrust his scout out of the way. He turned to the others. "I will go first. Remember, give me room in battle to wield Blind Fury."

His followers nodded. Glandurg motioned the others to follow him and trotted forward, Blind Fury slapping against his back at every step.

Craig paused outside the door to the computer room. *One more thing.* He took a thermonuclear grenade from his belt pouch and pulled the pin. Now the only thing preventing a multi-megaton explosion was his clawed grip around the grenade. If anything happened and he loosened his hand, everyone in the tower would die in a flash of nuclear fire.

Then he kicked down the door.

The side door to the computer room fell in with a crash and Craig and his robots stormed in. Gilligan was at the main door watching the fight in the corridor and Wiz and Jerry were at the console waiting for the download to finish. All of them jerked up at the sight of the three armored apparitions bearing down on them.

"Kill!" Craig screamed. The robot to his left took one step forward, caught one foot behind the other and tripped headlong with a metallic crash. The second robot raised both its arms to sweep its built-in lasers across the group.

"Drop," Gilligan yelled and all of them pressed themselves to the floor as the beams of ruby incandescence swept toward them.

Wiz felt something gently warm across his back, unsquinched his eyes and looked up. The robot's head swiveled back and forth as it looked from one gently glowing arm to another. It nodded twice, executed an about-face and marched headlong into the wall.

"*Oh shit!*" Craig screamed. Then he went for Wiz.

He could have used his blasters. He could have used his machine guns. He could have let go of the thermonuclear grenade. Instead he lumbered forward with one taloned hand outstretched. He didn't just want to kill Zumwalt, he wanted to tear him apart, to trample him beneath the battle armor's steel feet until there was nothing left but a thin red smear on the computer room floor.

Wiz dodged the first swipe of the hand by ducking under the massive arm. He got a desk between himself and Craig, but Craig picked the desk up one handed and threw it across the room. There was a terrific *crash* as the flying desk hit the window wall and the sheets of glass collapsed.

Mick Gilligan dropped to one knee and emptied his pistol at Craig. He ejected the empty magazine, slammed another home and kept on firing. Bullets bounced off Craig's armor and ricocheted wildly around the laboratory, knocking up puffs of rock dust when they hit the wall and leaving neat holes in what was left of the big window.

Craig swiveled and pointed the arm holding the grenade at the pilot. A beam of roiling green fire lanced out. Mick dove for cover, but the very edge of the blaster bolt caught his left arm and side. He went down moaning.

Then Craig turned back to Wiz. Inexorably he closed in with one arm outstretched and his claws gaping. Wiz backed away, trying to dodge behind furniture. Craig kicked one piece after another out of his path as he herded Wiz back into a corner.

*"Die, Wizard!"*

In a single motion Glandurg kicked the grille free and sprang from the vent, screaming his war cry and brandishing Blind Fury. The enchanted sword hummed through the air in a mighty blow aimed straight at Wiz's neck. At the last minute the blade twisted and struck Craig's battle armor, slicing through the armor plate just above the knee joint.

Craig stopped and looked down in wonder at the oil and fluids gushing out of the cut. Slowly and almost gently the leg collapsed under him and he sank to one knee. Wiz just stared open-mouthed.

Undaunted, Glandurg drew back and struck at Wiz two-handed. Again the sword twisted, this time upward to catch Craig in his massively armored chest.

Again the sword bit deep, cleaving through magically enhanced armor and what lay beneath it.

The suit's speakers amplified Craig's scream to a deafening level. Sparks and fluids poured out of the gaping wound in his chest. He rose on his good leg and tried to stagger back. The suit's gyros moaned as they worked to hold him upright, then screeched as the bearings failed for lack of lubricant. Craig rocked backward, caught himself, overcorrected and fell forward just as Glandurg brought Blind Fury down in a mighty overhead chop to cleave Wiz in half.

Instead the enchanted sword connected with the back of battle armor's domed head. Blind Fury went deep and came out with the tip stained with a wash of crimson. The battle armor jerked convulsively and then lay still.

Glandurg looked down at the fallen metal giant, over at Wiz and up at his bloodstained blade.

"Shit," he said.

Then he looked down at his feet. A gray egg-shaped object had rolled clear of the armor's lax hand. Now it lay on the floor between the dwarf and his quarry hissing quietly.

The dwarves didn't know what the thing was, but their magic told them it was dangerous. Very dangerous.

"Run away!" Glandurg yelled to his men. It was wasted breath. The dwarves had turned as one and jumped for the air vent. There was a mad scramble as dwarves bounced off each other in mid-air, pushed one another out of the way and tried to squeeze three dwarves through an opening that wasn't big enough for two. Glandurg wasn't the first through the vent, but he wasn't the last either.

Wiz and the others pressed themselves flat behind the console as the grenade hissed evilly. Then the hissing stopped. Wiz jammed his fingers in his ears and squinched his eyes tightly shut waiting for the explosion.

At last he opened his eyes, took his fingers out of his ears and cautiously peered around the corner of the console.

The deadly gray egg still lay in the middle of the room, rocking gently. As Wiz watched, the fuse protruding from one end slowly unscrewed itself and fell to the floor. A tiny head poked out of the fuse hole and peered about, enormous ears flapping.

The gremlin pulled itself out of the grenade and grinned widely at Wiz.

"Wheee," it squeaked.

## Forty-six
# MIKEY

Wiz leaned against the wall, one hand on his chest, and enjoyed the luxury of breathing deeply.

Jerry came over and knelt by the battle armor.

"Is he . . . ?" Wiz asked.

Jerry stood up. "Yeah," he said flatly. "He is."

He turned to Mick Gilligan. "Are you all right?"

"Just burns," Gilligan panted. "Not too bad, but it hurts." He looked down at his flight suit. "Good old Nomex."

"We'll get a healer to you as fast as we can," Wiz said. "Meanwhile, we've got one other thing to do."

Jerry raised an eyebrow.

"Mikey," Wiz said grimly.

"Someone call me?"

Mikey strolled through the broken door as casually as if it was still his castle. He was cradling a dark, misshapen thing in both hands. Wiz recognized it and sucked in his breath.

Mikey smiled and shook his head. "You poor dumb shits. You never did figure it out, did you?"

He stepped around the fallen robots and moved to the shattered window wall, shards of glass crunching under his feet.

"Now it's too late." He looked down at Craig's corpse. "While that little shit kept you running around in circles, I finished this."

Mikey held his prize high. A trick of reflection from the broken window made it appear that there were two of him, one floating in air and both holding the key.

Gilligan growled and scrabbled for his gun. Mikey looked over at him and he froze. Wiz wanted to scream, he wanted to run, he wanted to go for Mikey's throat. But he couldn't do any of it. Like Mick and Jerry he was rooted where he stood.

Mikey looked up and Wiz saw his eyes were red and glowing like an animal caught in the headlights.

"Always one step ahead. That's the difference between a real master hacker and people like you, Zumwalt. We're always one step ahead.

"Anyway, I just wanted you to know before . . ."

Out of the corner of his eye, Wiz caught a movement in the shattered window wall. Now there were two reflections in the glass. He shifted his eyes back to the room, but Mikey was alone with the key.

Then he looked in the window again. There was someone standing in front of Mikey's reflection.

Duke Aelric.

The elf's silvery armor was marred and stained. There were nicks in the blade of his curved sword and what looked like a burn mark along his helmet. Wiz had no idea where he had been, but he'd obviously been in a hell of a fight.

The elf stepped forward and laid both his hands on the key.

"Mine," he said.

There was still no one in the room but Mikey took the black convoluted thing in a double death grip.

"I made it," he yelled. "I can use it. It's mine!"

The muscles in his arms quivered and the veins in his neck bulged as though he was trying to hold the key against a tremendous pull.

In the window Aelric's teeth were set and splotches of high color stood out on his pale cheeks. His muscles swelled and rippled under his mail as he strove to wrest the key from Mikey's grasp.

Aelric and Mikey both seemed to flicker. Behind them Wiz thought he saw other things, some of them manlike. The sky darkened and began to run like wax—or perhaps it was his vision closing in. Faster and faster the images flickered until it was like watching an old silent movie. Then they flickered faster yet and there were two images superimposed on each other in the glass.

Mikey alternated with something large and vaguely manlike with fur and the pointed ears of an elf. The thing with Aelric was manlike too, but it shone so brightly it hurt Wiz's eyes.

Mikey's breath was coming in harsh gasps and his arms were shaking from the strain. Aelric was straining too, but he wasn't shaking. A fraction of an inch at a time the key moved toward the elf.

With a cry the Mikey in the window broke away. As soon as he released the key it was as if he had been sucked down a tunnel. With a despairing wail he dwindled and vanished in the distance.

The real Mikey whimpered, slumped to the floor and lay still. The black thing he had held was gone.

There was still no sign of Aelric in the room, but in the glass he stood with the key resting in the crook of his arm.

"Well done, Sparrow," the image said.

Wiz found he could move again.

"Are you really there?"

"I am here," the reflection said. "As for reality . . ." He shrugged in the old Aelric manner.

"Now," he said, turning serious, "I think you will find that resistance has collapsed. You will have perhaps another day before this World starts to decay. I would suggest that you and all your people be gone by then."

"And the key?"

"With it we can close the gate forever on these others." He seemed to sway a little and then caught himself.

"Lord, are you all right?"

Aelric smiled tightly. "I am as you see me, Sparrow. Now if you will excuse me, it would be best to get this to safekeeping."

And with that he was gone.

Moira was with the first group of wizards and healers to come to Caermort. She and Wiz had time for a brief tearful reunion before the demands of their work pulled them apart. That night they ate a dinner of cold field rations on a terrace at Caermort and stood on the parapet looking up at the strange night sky with only a few odd stars.

"A fell place," Moira said with a shiver. "I will be glad to be gone."

"You and me both," Wiz said, leaning over to kiss her.

"Ah, I hate to disturb you folks," Jerry's voice came out of the darkness. "But there are some people here who want to talk to you."

Wiz and Moira turned. There was Jerry with twelve dwarves clustered around him.

"Oh, wizard," Glandurg called. "We would have speech with you."

Wiz stepped forward. Moira started to come with him but he stopped her.

"Stay back here. It's all right."

"What about you?"

"Whatever happens I'll be perfectly safe," he said with more confidence than he felt. "But I don't want you close to me if he starts swinging that sword."

Surreptitiously Wiz readied a fireball spell, but he stepped up to the group as if he hadn't a fear in the world. "Glandurg, isn't it?"

"Aye," said the dwarf leader. "We have come to bid you farewell."

"Very nice—but not to bring up a sore subject—what about your debt of honor?"

"Oh that," Glandurg said. "We were hired to slay an alien wizard whose magic was wreaking havoc upon the World. The wizard is dead so our contract is fulfilled." He looked slyly at Wiz and Moira. "After all, the trolls did not say *which* alien wizard they wanted killed."

Wiz could only nod.

"We go now," said Glandurg. "The evil wizard is slain, the balance is restored to the World and our debt is paid. Perhaps our paths shall cross again should you need doughty warriors to stand at your back on some great quest."

With that Glandurg and his followers turned and filed through the door. Then they began to sing, jauntily but very off key.

" 'Debts must be paid,' " Jerry quoted as the dwarf song died out in the distance. "Those guys are the kind who would pay off a debt in subordinated debentures—if they knew what subordinated debentures were."

"Don't tell them," Wiz said. "The last thing this world needs is gnomes of Zurich."

"But those are not gnomes, they are dwarves," Moira said. Wiz and Jerry broke up laughing and she jammed her elbow into Wiz's ribs, making him splutter. "Oh all right! You and your silly name jokes."

"I wonder how they expect to get off this island?" Wiz said, massaging the suddenly sore spot on his short ribs.

"Burrow for all I care," Moira said. "I do not understand how they got here in the first place."

" . . . and you should have seen the wizards' faces when that dragon rider and her dragon popped up in the chantry next to Major Gilligan," Judith said laughing. The others laughed too and she helped herself to more bread and cheese.

They looked like a halloween party. There was Wiz in his usual tight pants, open-necked shirt and sleeveless tunic. Mick Gilligan was sitting next to him in his

Air Force green flight suit. Then came Moira in a long gown of russet velveteen with forest green lining showing in the insides of the flowing dagged sleeves. Jerry was beside her in a medieval-looking tunic with a most un-medieval patch pocket full of felt-tip pens. Finally there was Judith wearing the open-backed hospital gown she had arrived in, now artfully dirtied and torn.

It had been barely twenty-four hours since Caermort had fallen and none of them had gotten much sleep. But everyone agreed that the sooner they got Mick and Judith back to their own World the better.

Pots of blackmoss tea and pitchers of chilled fruit juice shared the table with platters that had held small cakes and other delicacies. There was a sun dial very conspicuously planted in the middle and everyone made small talk while they waited for the shadow to shorten.

"How is Danny?" Judith asked.

"Bronwyn says he will recover well enough," Moira told her. "There is sickness in his blood and the burns were of a dangerous kind. Still, she can pull him through. " She bit her lip. "But the energies released did something to him she cannot repair. He will have no more children."

"Damn," Wiz said softly.

"I'm so sorry," Judith said.

Moira shrugged. "Such things happen. Considering the carnage all about them they got off lightly."

"And June?" Judith asked.

Moira smiled. "With him night and day, of course. They have brought the cradle into the sick room so she may tend both of her men at once."

"What about Duke Aelric?"

Wiz shrugged. "He took the key and vanished. I imagine we won't see him for a while."

Judith poured herself another cup of fruit juice,

drained it and sighed. "My one chance to meet an elf. Gone."

They all fell silent for a moment.

"Well, anyway, I'm glad I got a chance to see you again," Judith said as she put her cup back on the table.

"And we are glad to see you, my Lady," Moira said. "I only wish it could have been a more pleasant visit."

Judith nodded and looked again at the creeping shadow of the sun dial.

"What are you going to tell them?" Wiz asked.

She looked down at the carefully soiled hospital gown. "That when I woke up I was wandering around downtown San Jose in this."

"That doesn't explain anything."

Judith's eyes twinkled. "I know. That's the best kind of explanation."

"They'll probably think you halfway came out of the coma, wandered out of the hospital and you've just been roaming around ever since," Jerry said.

Judith smiled. "How would I know? I was in a coma."

Wiz turned to Major Gilligan. "I wish I could reward you for your help, but I think anything we gave you would just complicate your life."

"I've been rewarded already," Gilligan told him. "And yeah, it would be a little hard to explain showing up with a bag of gold or something." *As if this isn't going to be hard enough to explain,* he thought.

"Okay, we understand you want to go back to the Air Force as if you'd crashed in the ocean."

"I've pretty much got to."

"You know we would put you down just about anywhere in the world."

Gilligan shook his head. "I've got a duty to go back and it will be easier if it looks like I just crashed."

"We'll put you and your gear down on an uninhabited island not too far from where you disappeared. From there you can use your radio to get help."

"How far is that island from where I went down?"

"About 200 miles."

Gilligan frowned. "That's thin."

"We could put you and your raft in the water about where you crashed."

Gilligan thought about the freezing, fogbound Bering Sea and how long it would take to get rescued.

"I'll take my chances on the island."

"Okay, one other thing. We could heal your burns completely, but you'd be left with marks you didn't have when you took off." He looked Gilligan over. "Or, we can partially heal you, so it will look as if you were burned when your plane went down."

"I've already been over this with your medics. I want to look like I was injured when I bailed out."

"You understand that once you're on the other side the pain spells won't work. Those burns will hurt."

*Not half as much as some other things will hurt,* Gilligan thought. But he just nodded.

Wiz nodded in return. "Very well, then. Your equipment's in the next room. You might want to check it over and make sure you've got everything you need while you've still got time. Bronwyn will meet you there for the healing."

Just about all his gear was there in a neat pile, even the things he had discarded when he came ashore on the island. It was all restored by magic. Somehow they had even managed to refill the magazines of his pistol.

"Mick."

He turned around and saw Karin in the door. His equipment forgotten, he took her in his arms and kissed her. The burns made him clumsy but neither of them noticed. "Where have you been? Why didn't you come with me?"

"Looking after Stigi and telling my superiors what

had happened," she said in a small voice. "I could not come until my squadron leader released me."

He held her in his good arm close to his unburned side.

"Listen to me. I've got two more years left on this tour." *If they don't courtmartial me over this*, he thought. "I'll serve out my time and resign my commission. Then somehow, *somehow*, I'll find a way to come back."

Karin looked deep into his eyes. "I will be waiting."

There was a discreet cough behind them.

"Time, my Lord," Arianne said. "Trooper, if you wish to accompany him to the chantry you may."

The wizards and others were already assembled when Gilligan and Karin came into the chantry.

As they came in, Wiz handed Gilligan a small wooden tablet. "Before you go, you might want to memorize this."

Gilligan looked down at it. "Is this what I think it is?"

"Yep, it's an 800 number. Direct line to the Wizard's Keep from any phone in the USA. Just don't use it unless you really need to."

Gilligan looked up at Wiz. "I'm not going to ask how you did this."

Wiz shrugged. "It wouldn't do any good. It was one of Danny's projects. We figured we might need to contact people over there again and Danny set this up."

Gilligan stared intently at the scrap of wood and his lips moved as he burned the number into his memory. After a minute he handed the tablet back to Wiz.

"Is this legal?"

Wiz hesitated. "Like I said, it was one of Danny's projects."

This time there were two circles of blue-robed wizards in the chantry. Bal-Simba stood at the head of one of them and Arianne led the other.

Mick and Karin embraced for one final time, then

Arianne waved him to the center of her circle, next to his gear. Judith took her position in the other and the chants began.

*I hope to God I can pull this off*, Major Michael Francis Xavier Gilligan thought fervently as he faced the three men across the table. He had managed to get his blues on over his bandages and the meeting was in an office rather than his hospital room, but he still felt lousy from the burns and spacey from the pain killers.

This wasn't a formal inquiry. Gilligan had only been back at the base for twelve hours. It was more of a preliminary attempt to find out what had happened over the Bering Sea.

"Now Major Gilligan," the debriefing officer began, "you say you can't remember anything from the time you bailed out until you found yourself on the island?"

"Nossir. I think I cracked my head on the way out, but the first thing I really remember is being on that island with the radio." He paused. "Ah, I was delirious most of the time, sir."

The debriefing officer didn't respond, but the black man behind him, the one wearing the flight suit with no insignia, half-nodded. Obviously he had already seen a report of Gilligan's description of his "hallucinations."

It was thin and he knew it. Especially in light of what must be on Smitty's tape. But it was the best story he could come up with and he'd stick to it for as long as he could.

"The cold salt water apparently restricted the damage from those burns. You're extremely lucky, do you know that?"

A flash memory of blue eyes and a little dusting of freckles over a straight nose. "I figure I'm about the luckiest man in the Air Force," Gilligan said sincerely.

The debriefing officer nodded and the man sitting next to him in the flight suit with no insignia remained impassive.

Step by step they went over Gilligan's story—what there was of it.

"And you say you don't remember anything after you sent your wingman back?"

"Nossir, not a thing."

"Perhaps this will refresh your memory," the man in the flight suit said. He leaned forward and handled Gilligan a folder.

*Here it comes,* Gilligan thought as he opened the folder. Then he looked at the photograph.

"Nossir," he said, fighting to keep his composure. "I'm sorry. This doesn't look familiar to me at all."

The picture was obviously the result of a lot of work with an image processor. The image had long, thin wings and a small tail set at the end of a tapering, torpedo-shaped fuselage. Just forward of the wings was a central turret with what was obviously intended to be a sensor array. The wings and body were marked with what were clearly intended to be phase-array antennas. On top of the wings were heavily baffled intakes for jet engines buried in the body. The tail showed additional inlets for cooling air to dilute the jet exhaust coming from the shielded tailpipe.

The man with no insignia frowned. "Pity. Some of the details are conjectural and we were hoping you'd be able to fill them in for us."

"I'm sorry, sir. I don't remember anything like this."

"Well, it doesn't matter much. *Aviation Week* ran that picture in last week's issue." His face showed he didn't care for that at all. "We know now the thing isn't Soviet, so in the next week or two the Japanese or the South Koreans or the Israelis or whoever the hell else really did build it will let the information leak out." He shook his head. "It's a small world, Major, and you can't keep secrets long."

"Yes sir," said Major Mick Gilligan, thinking of another World entirely. "It is a very small world."

## Forty-eight
# WINNERS AND LOSERS

The now-useless computer sat in a cellar at the Wizard's Keep. The pieces had been unpacked and set together in a pale imitation of a working system. It looked strangely out of place in the low room with the beamed ceiling and the rough masonry walls.

Wiz was sitting at the console with his back to the door, idly tapping on the keyboard with one hand.

"What are you doing, love?" Moira asked as she came up behind him.

Wiz shook himself out of his reverie and stood to kiss her.

"Just thinking," Wiz said after the kiss. "When I was back in Cupertino I dreamed of having one of these things all to myself. Now I've got one and it won't work here."

"I wonder if it is worth keeping?" Moira said with a housewife's practicality.

"I wouldn't feel right throwing it away. Maybe we can find a use for it."

"As a haven for gremlins, no doubt."

"I don't guess the gremlins are interested in machinery that doesn't work."

"Just as well," Moira said. "Else there would not be a moment's peace."

They stood arm in arm looking at the computer for a while.

"Well," Wiz said heavily. "At least that's over."

"Not quite, mortal."

Wiz and Moira whirled. There stood the elf Lisella.

Lisella smiled, cold and beautiful as the full moon at midwinter. "I mean you no harm, mortal. I come with a message. Duke Aelric bids you to him."

390

Moira moved in front of Wiz like a terrier protecting her master.

"Why does not the duke deliver his invitation himself?"

Ice blue eyes locked onto flashing green. "Because he is dying, Lady."

Duke Aelric lay on snowy linen in a cavern with softly glowing walls. He was so still and composed that at first Wiz thought they were too late. But as they approached he turned his head toward them.

"So Sparrow, we meet again." His voice was as firm as ever but he sounded weary, as if tired out by a great exertion.

"Yes, Lord," Wiz said numbly. Even this close he could not see a mark on the elf duke, but his normally pale skin was now almost chalk white.

"I wanted to see you once more to thank you. You have performed a great service for the whole World, including the ever-living."

"We almost screwed it up, Lord."

"You did very well indeed." His eyes flicked to Lisella. "Much better than some expected."

He stopped speaking and he seemed to drift for a moment. Then his eyes focused and he turned his attention back to Wiz. "You have my personal thanks as well." He sounded even wearier. "Ennui is part of the price the ever living must pay." He smiled slightly. "Our association has been many things, perhaps, but it has never been boring."

"No, Lord." Wiz smiled through his tears. "It was not boring."

"No," Duke Aelric muttered almost beyond hearing. "Not boring."

Then he was still.

Silently Lisella placed a hand on Wiz's shoulder

391

and guided him away from the bier. Behind him he saw other elves drape the linen over the body.

"It was the key, wasn't it?" Wiz said at last. "That was what those others wanted all along."

"Of course," Lisella said. "You did not realize that it could be used to destroy a World as easily as to close it off?"

"Well, why the Hell didn't he tell me the thing was that dangerous?" Wiz blazed. "We came within an ace of losing it to Craig and Mikey and losing the entire World with it."

She looked at him with amusement. "Would you have dared to use your Mousehole to construct it if you had known?"

"Then why . . . Oh! You can't build one, can you? You can't make a key on your own."

"Not so precisely as to be that powerful, no. Neither could the others. To attempt to make it by magic is to warp the very fabric of the World."

"So you used us," Wiz said dully. "Just like those others were using Craig and Mikey."

"You disapprove, Sparrow?" the elf said coldly. "You find the price high?" She tossed her head in the direction of the still form under the linen draping. "Consider the price *he* knew he would pay."

Wiz gaped. "He knew?"

Lisella cocked a raven eyebrow. "Why do you think he took such an interest in you?"

"But why? I mean if he knew it was going to kill him . . ."

"Because he knew there was a better chance of success with you and your alien magics than working only with the ways of his people. He chose a road of certain destruction because it gave a better chance— not a certainty, only a better chance—that the World, would live."

She looked at Wiz oddly. "It must be a strange and

wonderful thing to be so attached to a place you would willingly go down to non-existence for it."

Lisella raised her hand and made a gesture in the air. "Go in peace, mortal. Our business is at an end."

And suddenly they were back in the computer room.

For a long time neither of them said anything.

"Well," Wiz said at last, "the prophecy was true. The mightiest among us died and all of us lost."

"Craig lost his life. Danny and June lost the chance for more kids. Mick and Karin lost each other. Glandurg lost his quest. Judith lost months out of her life and we lost . . ." He stopped and swallowed hard, unable to go on.

Moira wiped her eyes. "Not everyone lost, I think. Mikey can be said to have gotten his heart's desire. So the prophecy was truly fulfilled."

Wiz thought about that. "Yeah," he said flatly. "You're right. He did get what he wanted."

Sunlight streamed through the mullioned windows of the Wizard's Keep in golden shafts and painted warm bright patches on the floor. Dust motes danced in the beams.

Mikey looked at the dust, fascinated. He stretched out his hand and tried to catch the dancing specks in his fist. But they would not be caught and he had more important things to do.

Very deliberately he plumped down on the floor and returned to the job of arraying his army. With exaggerated care he added a new tin soldier to the end of the first line of men. Then he took brightly painted wooden blocks from the pile beside him and added a new building to the town behind his men. He rearranged the cutout trees next to the town and leaned back to survey his work.

Looking out at the kingdom of block villages and tiny metal soldiers spread over the floor of his playroom cum prison cell, Mikey the Great beamed and gurgled with joy.

At last he was truly the master of all he surveyed.

## THE END